"I'd like you to me⟍ ⎯⎯⎯⎯ ⎯ptain of the
***Starhawke.*"**

She held her hands out as Admiral Schreiber had, silently daring Sly'Kull to touch her.

He must have gotten the non-verbal message, because he hesitated, the blue of his eyes darkening.

As his cool, smooth skin touched hers, a crawling revulsion rolled over her like a swarm of cockroaches. She held still, tamping down the instinctive push of her energy shield.

He had no power over her, and if she wanted a shot at taking down the Sovereign, she needed him to believe she was excited about the proposed mission. "It's a pleasure to meet you Delegate Sly'Kull."

"Indeed." His accented Galish made the word come out in a heavy drawl, his grip tightening. "You have been a difficult female to track down."

THE SIEGE OF ALLIANCE

Starhawke Rising Book Five

AUDREY SHARPE

Ocean Dance Press

Want more interstellar adventures? Check out
these other titles in the Starhawke Universe.

Starhawke Rising

The Dark of Light

The Chains of Freedom

The Honor of Deceit

The Legacy of Tomorrow

The Siege of Alliance

Starhawke Rogue

Arch Allies

Marked Mercenaries

Resurgent Renegades

Starhawke Romance

Guardian Mate

I always write to music, and I select a different piece of music for each story, one that feeds the mood I need to get the words flowing. If you'd like to experience this story the way I did, listen to the soundtrack for *The Avengers* while you read.

One

"Ready to break Admiral Payne's grandson out of the ICU?" Aurora Hawke asked Dr. Lelindia "Mya" Forrest, seated in the back of the ambulance beside her.

Her friend's skin looked a little sallow, especially with the blonde wig concealing her dark hair, but her eyes behind the blue-tinted contacts — part of her disguise — didn't show a hint of hesitation. "Absolutely."

Aurora tapped her comband, activating her earpiece. "Cade? What's the team's status?"

Cade Ellis' rich voice came over the connection. "All players are in place. We're a go."

"Acknowledged. We're pulling up in front of the emergency room entrance now." The flash of red and white signs out the front windshield confirmed they'd reached their destination.

Two days earlier Celia Cardiff and Tracy Reynolds had scouted out the location in preparation for the breakout, gathering intel on the security offices, ambulance bay, laundry room, and locations of cameras, especially around the ICU. Today they were part of the extraction team, stationed at key points inside the hospital, ready to intervene if things went sideways.

Christoph Gonzalez parked the ambulance in the bay near the wide double doors. "All clear," he said, turning toward the back where Aurora and Lelindia sat beside the empty gurney.

Aurora smoothed a hand over the bangs of her brunette bob wig and down the front of her EMT shirt. "How do we look?"

Gonzo ran an assessing gaze over her and Lelindia. A grin spread across his lean face. "Your own mothers wouldn't recognize you."

Considering the time Gonzo had spent with both their mothers over the past few days, that meant something. The wig and brown contacts had startled her the first time she'd caught sight of herself in a mirror. "We'll see you in twenty minutes."

"I'll be here."

Opening the back doors, Aurora hopped out, surveying their surroundings. The morning sun had almost burned off the Pacific marine layer, but the late December chill put a bite in the air.

Lelindia stepped down beside her, pulling the gurney out of the back of the ambulance.

Aurora took charge of it while Lelindia gathered the other items they would need to stabilize Payne's grandson and make a convincing show of their stated purpose here.

Lelindia closed the ambulance doors with a metallic thunk. "Follow me."

Aurora strode beside her, the gurney hovering across the concrete at waist height as they passed through the emergency room's front entrance. Red and green wreaths with silver and gold ornaments decorated the walls and a Christmas tree stood in a corner of the waiting room, remnants of the holiday just passed.

Hard to believe five days ago she'd been on a Hawaiian beach with her dad and brother, celebrating Christmas with them for the first time since she was two.

Life had hit the fast-forward button after that day. Her childhood home had burned to the ground following a Setarip attack, Lelindia's parents had almost died at the hands of Aurora's grandmother, Aurora's mother and father had reunited after twenty-seven years apart, and her brother Micah had become a permanent fixture on the *Starhawke* for the foreseeable future.

His presence was the main reason she'd stopped calling Mya by her nickname, and started calling her by her given name, Lelindia, or the nickname Micah used, Lee-Lee. My-a had been her brother's childhood nickname, and now that he was back in her life, calling Lelindia "Mya" created uncomfortable emotional dissonance. Since Aurora's parents, Lelindia's parents, and

Jonarel were all calling Lelindia by her given name, she'd started doing the same, and the rest of the crew were following suit.

A member of the ER staff wearing a bright red badge that said *Charge Nurse* moved to intercept them as they walked toward the doors leading to the ICU. "Where're you headed? We weren't notified of an incoming."

Lelindia paused. "We have a BLS transfer from the med/surg floor to hospice." Not a hint of nervousness tinged her voice. Her demeanor projected relaxed competence, giving no indication they were about to wreak havoc in the ICU.

Her calm might be a result of the command experience she'd gained recently. Facing down Siginal Clarek in order to escape Drakar, the Kraed homeworld, seemed to have made her stronger and more confident, especially in tense situations. Or maybe that was a result of her blossoming relationship with Jonarel Clarek.

The charge nurse nodded, stepping aside.

"First hurdle down," Aurora murmured over the comm line as they passed through the doorway into the corridor beyond.

"I'll be with you every step of the way," Cade replied.

That was the other big change. She and Cade had healed the rift she'd caused when she'd booted him off the *Starhawke*. The past four nights she'd slept better than she had in weeks. When they'd slept, that is.

She glanced at Lelindia. "You good?"

"Yep. See you upstairs."

Grabbing a small bag off the gurney, Aurora peeled off, heading to the nearest bathroom. She was in luck – it was empty. Closing herself into one of the stalls she removed a set of disinfected scrubs, booties, and the surgical cap Tam Williams had taken from the hospital laundry area the day before. She also pulled a white lab coat and stethoscope from the bag, borrowed from Lelindia, putting the scrubs and then the coat on over her EMT uniform. The added weight and bulk didn't help with maneuverability, but it increased the effectiveness of her disguise.

She collapsed the bag and stuffed it into the pocket of her pants under the scrubs. "Wardrobe change complete. Ready for phase two."

"Justin and Kire are set," Cade confirmed.

"Acknowledged." Slipping out of the bathroom, she headed for the same oversized elevator Lelindia had used to reach the floor for the ICU, passing a redheaded woman in a voluminous blue sweatshirt and baggy jeans sitting on a bench reading on a tablet.

Aurora smiled to herself. If she didn't know the woman was Reynolds, stationed to monitor the elevator and their progress, she never would have recognized her.

Male laughter drifted toward her as she exited the elevator and strode down the curving corridor, the exterior windows brightening the hallway with morning sunshine. She passed Lelindia on the way, standing near the gurney with her back to the corridor and her shoulders hunched, talking in an irritated voice to someone on the other end of the line about a screw-up regarding her transport orders. None of the hospital staff gave her presence a second look, just as she'd assured Aurora they wouldn't, allowing her to be near the ICU entrance without drawing attention.

Rounding the curve to the ICU she spotted Kire Emoto and Justin Byrnes standing next to an empty food cart, talking with a female food service worker who looked barely old enough to drive.

Thanks to their disguises, both men looked college age rather than late twenties and early thirties. Kire had a subtle goth vibe to his outfit, with spiky black hair, dark eyeliner and lipliner, and contacts that made his hazel eyes almost black. His clothes matched, a combination of black, grey, and white that transformed him from a Fleet Commander to a hip vampire wannabe.

Justin had opted for a grunge look. A mane of long brown hair trailed over the shoulders of his black T-shirt, which was mostly covered by an oversized black and white patterned button-up shirt that hung open in front. His faded and ripped grey jeans were slung low on his hips, paired with scuffed grey work boots.

The girl was clearly enthralled by both of them, her eyes bright and lips parted. Their conversation was low enough Aurora couldn't pick up the words, but it was easy to see the kid was clueless that she was interacting with two of the smoothest talkers ever to graduate the Academy. Unfortunately for the girl, despite her obvious eagerness, she wouldn't be getting a date with either one.

None of the trio so much as glanced at Aurora as she brushed past, making it easy to snag the badge Justin had pilfered from the young woman and held in his hand behind his back. She and Justin had practiced the handoff so many times the day before she could do it with her eyes shut.

Moving steadily toward the ICU doors, she caught a glimpse of Micah seated in one of the waiting room chairs to her right, his attention on the tablet in his hands.

She'd argued against his presence here, not wanting to put him in harm's way. He'd insisted on being on site in case she needed his help to get Payne's grandson – and the rest of the team – safely out of the building. She'd lost the battle when he'd pointed out he was the one person who didn't need a disguise. The Sovereign had no idea who he was.

She used the badge to key herself into the ICU, the doors opening onto a corridor that formed one side of the square

ICU outline, with all rooms on the exterior and staff and admin areas at the center. "I'm in," she informed Cade.

"Justin's already on the move. Cardiff's exiting the waiting room elevator now."

Aurora continued down the corridor with purpose in her stride, a doctor here to check on a patient.

"Cardiff's a go. Micah's engaged Justin."

The harsh bark of raised voices — Justin's and Micah's —reached her over the low background music playing through the ICU speakers. The angry yells were at complete odds with the flare of amusement she sensed from Micah.

"Lelindia's notifying security of the Code Grey."

Code Grey. Combative individual or patient in the ICU.

The music cut off abruptly. "Code Grey, Code Grey, Code Grey. ICU waiting room," a male voice said in clipped tones over the speaker.

As the announcement was repeated a second time, the ICU nurses left their stations, hurrying past her as they proceeded to the front desk for the Code Grey response team.

Conveniently leaving the ICU rooms unmonitored by personnel. That left the video cameras.

Tam Williams' voice came over the comm channel. "Drew has the dummy feeds running for all the room vids. You're clear. The patients you want are in A3, A5, and A10. Keenan Payne is in A7."

"Got it."

Williams and Bella Drew were stationed in a surveillance vehicle outside the hospital. Yesterday they'd tag-teamed with Justin and Kire to gain access to the ICU's computers. Drew was running technical interference during the mission while Williams was on hand to monitor any medical complications that might arise with the other patients. That freed Lelindia and Aurora to focus on Keenan.

Room A3 was on Aurora's left. Moving through the open doorway, she pulled one of three syringes from her pocket, injecting the contents into the patient's IV.

She, Williams, and Lelindia had discussed this step at length. Williams had come up with the idea to inject three patients with a medication that would cause heart stoppage within a few minutes, but which was easily counteracted with a shot of adrenaline. The resulting chaos in the ICU from three simultaneous Code Blues would provide them with the diversion they needed to get Keenan out of his room without drawing attention.

However, the decision put the patients at some risk, even with Williams in the wings to back them up, which is why Aurora had insisted on being the one to administer the drug. Lelindia was a healer to her core, sworn to do no harm. Saving Keenan couldn't come at the cost of her principles.

But there was no way Aurora was leaving the ICU without knowing all three patients wouldn't suffer any long-term effects.

The first dose down, she moved to A5, then quickly to A10, passing Keenan's room on the way. A peek inside confirmed he was alone. The Sovereign clearly believed Admiral Payne was too intimidated by the threats to her grandson's life to attempt a rescue, which meant no guard had been posted to monitor the room.

That would make Aurora's task easier.

She reached A10 without incident, the confused chatter from the front desk providing background noise. She inserted the final needle into the IV. "All injections complete."

"I've got them from here," Williams replied. "Dr. Forrest is approaching the ICU doors."

Screech!

The first alarms screamed from A3, followed seconds later by the alarms in A5. Aurora hurried toward the ICU entrance.

"Code Blue, Code Blue, Code Blue. Room A3 and Room A5." The front desk clerk's call went out over the ICU speakers a second time as the staff rushed like a wave in the direction of the two rooms.

Aurora hit the button to open the ICU doors. Lelindia pushed the gurney through, following Aurora as they hurried the opposite direction past A10 to reach Keenan's room.

Screech!

"Code Blue, Code Blue, Code Blue. Room A10!" The front desk clerk had lost his emotional detachment, panic edging his voice. The pounding of running feet and barked orders joined the shrieks of the alarms.

Lelindia's jaw flexed, her neck muscles tensing as she guided the gurney into Keenan's room and attached it to the side of his bed.

Aurora rested a hand on her arm. "They'll be okay."

"I know." Lelindia's emerald-green energy field engaged as she placed her hands on the sides of Keenan's swollen and bandaged face.

His copper-brown skin and dark hair disguised some of the cuts and bruising, but the damage still looked severe. The white ventilator protruding from his mouth resembled a giant earthworm emerging from an underground cavern.

"How bad is it?"

Lelindia's lips flattened, her eyes narrowing as she focused all her attention on her patient. "The trauma isn't the main problem. There's a toxin in his system that's preventing his body from healing."

"Can you clear it?"

"Yes. But not here. Let's move." The glow of her field intensified around Keenan's body.

Aurora added her energy field as well. Keenan would need the additional support while they worked.

They'd practiced the steps for the transfer in the *Starhawke's* med bay until they had it down to under ten minutes. Muscle memory kicked in as the thrum of disconnection alarms joined the general cacophony when Mya switched off the machines. But no one came running, thanks in large part to the false status and video data Bella was transmitting to the front desk.

Lifting Keenan to the gurney ended up being the biggest challenge. He was tall for sixteen, taller than her and Lelindia, with the lean muscle of a runner. "Could have used Jonarel's help for this," she muttered as she hefted from her side. Her heavily muscled Kraed engineer could have lifted Keenan one-handed.

"Help for what?" Cade asked.

She'd forgotten he was listening. "Nothing. We're almost done here."

While Lelindia switched Keenan to the machines attached to the gurney, she disengaged her energy field and checked in with Williams. "What's the status on the patients?"

"Proceeding as planned. No complications. Go now."

She glanced at Lelindia. "Ready?"

"Yes."

"Cade, we're on our way out."

"Acknowledged. Kire and Micah are waiting for you."

She blocked out the tense activity in A5 and A3, following Lelindia as she guided the gurney to the ICU entrance and out into the corridor beyond. No sign of Justin or the food service worker whose badge they'd taken, but Kire sauntered toward them on his way to the waiting room, his expression bored.

She palmed the stolen badge the way they'd practiced, the seemingly normal swing of her arm bringing her hand in contact with his. He plucked the badge from her hand with a feather touch and continued on to dump the stolen badge into one of the biohazard trash cans.

She caught up with Lelindia at the service elevator they'd taken earlier, which opened as they approached. Micah stood inside, his gaze still on his tablet, which would be feeding him information from the rest of the team.

He looked up with a nonchalance that would have fooled a casual observer, but she sensed his relief as they stepped onto the elevator with him.

His presence decreased her stress level by a thousand percent.

Lelindia punched in the floor number as Aurora moved to the corner of the elevator out of sight of the doors. Yanking off the stethoscope and white coat, she grabbed the hem of her scrubs, stripping them off in record time and balling them up with the booties and surgical cap. When the elevator reached the ground floor, her EMT disguise was in place and the lab coat and stethoscope were back in the collapsible bag.

She dumped the scrubs into the laundry chute on their way to the emergency room entrance. As planned, Micah lagged behind, keeping an eye out for any potential complications while playing the role of a visitor headed to the parking lot.

"We're almost to the ambulance bay doors," she murmured into the comm line. "What's the status?"

"ICU is still blind. No one's realized Keenan's missing. Gonzo's waiting at the bay entrance."

Lengthening her stride, she activated the bay doors. Sunshine and cool moist air greeted her as they stepped out of the building.

Loading the gurney into the back of the ambulance took seconds, but she didn't breathe easy until she'd pulled the back doors closed, sealing them inside.

Gonzo had the ambulance in motion before she sank beside Lelindia, whose green energy field had already wrapped around Keenan like a cocoon.

Engaging her pearlescent field, she rested one hand on Lelindia's, twining their fields together around the teenager's still form. "We did it."

Lelindia's gaze met hers, the tension draining away as their energy fields danced in the enclosed space of the ambulance. "Yes, we did."

Two

The woman lay in the grey light, a discarded toy left out overnight.

A frown carved lines in her smooth skin. She lifted a hand to her face, rubbing her eyes. They felt gritty, like she'd been sleeping too long or staring without blinking.

Had she been sleeping? Her mind struggled to make connections. Groggy. Unfocused.

Where was she?

Grey walls. Grey ceiling. Grey floor. Even her clothes were grey.

She sat up slowly.

The room tilted. Nausea swept over her.

She pressed a hand to her gut. The sensation leached away into the greyness.

Tangled strands of brown hair fell in front of her eyes.

The only warmth in the colorblind room.

What was this place?

The hard platform pressed against her bones, unkind and unforgiving.

Why was she here?

She shook her head to clear it. The nausea flared again.

Pulling her knees to her chest, she rested her back against the wall, taking slow, deep breaths.

Grey walls. Grey ceiling. Grey floor. No doors.

A vibration through the wall. A motor, or engine, or...

Engine. Interstellar engine.

Her hand flew out, smacking the bulkhead.

A starship.

Fractured memories tumbled like shards of broken glass, sharp and painful. Grey skin. White hair. A cool touch.

Her heart pounded. This was wrong. Very wrong. She shouldn't be here.

A soft click in the far corner.

An invisible hatch swinging open.

Two forms, silent as snakes. Towering. Menacing.

She recoiled, pressing into the unyielding bulkhead.

A third figure. A metallic voice beneath a dark hood. A black-gloved hand touching her skin with the gentleness of an iron claw.

Her blood ran cold. She remembered.

No. Please, no. Not again.

But it was pointless. She had nowhere to go.

Three

Lelindia Forrest fought to contain the rage building inside her as she assessed Keenan Payne's condition. He might have the body of an adult, but he was only sixteen, and completely innocent in the deadly machinations of the Sovereign, the person responsible for his injuries.

At the Academy, she'd had concerns about Reanne Beck's behavior, particularly towards Aurora and Jonarel. But she'd held her tongue, allowing Aurora to handle her in her own way. When the friendship had ended, she'd breathed a sigh of relief.

She didn't feel relief now.

"Lee-Lee?"

She lifted her gaze, a bittersweet pang twinging her chest at Aurora's use of her childhood nickname rather than calling her Mya.

It was a sign of the changing dynamics in their lives. Ever since their families had come onboard the *Starhawke*, Aurora — and everyone else on the crew — had switched to calling her Lelindia, or Lee-Lee.

It felt right, returning to her true self, but it also meant letting go of a part of her identity she'd held onto most of her life. That loss caused a touch of grief — for the relationship she and Aurora had forged under the name Mya, and what they'd been through together since then.

Aurora was watching her, frown lines grooving her forehead under the bangs of her brown wig. "You okay?"

"No." Their energy fields continued to twine, the familiar sensation of love and support a counterpoint to the grief and her deep sense of injustice. "He's just a kid." Heat bloomed in her chest and climbed her throat. "How could Reanne—"

Aurora squeezed her hand. "She's unbalanced. And power-hungry. She doesn't care who she hurts to get what she wants." Her gaze drifted to Keenan's face. "She enjoys causing pain."

The steel in Aurora's voice cut through Lelindia's anger, reminding her she wasn't the only one dealing with outrage. "She won't hurt him anymore."

A soft smile smoothed the lines from Aurora's face. "No, she won't."

That counted for a lot.

"Let's—" Aurora paused, cocking her head, listening to her earpiece. "What is it Cade?" She shot Lelindia a look and grinned. "Someone wants to talk to you."

A millisecond after Aurora tapped her comband, a deep voice reached out from the device's speaker. "Lelindia? Are you safe?"

Ribbons of warmth and happiness flowed through her body, pushing back her anger. "I'm fine, Jonarel." The timbre of his voice had the power to heal her from the inside out. "We're on our way to the rendezvous point."

His voice dropped to an intimate purr. "I will see you soon."

A choked wheeze made her look at Aurora, who had a hand clamped over her mouth. She was muffling a laugh, judging by the sparkle in her eyes visible even through the dark contacts.

Lelindia grinned back. It meant more than she could say that Aurora was delighted by Jonarel's change of heart.

Having his overprotective behavior focused on her was still taking a little getting used to. It had certainly made planning this mission trickier. He'd wanted to stay with her, which had never been an option. No one on the team had the skill to disguise an oversized Kraed with deep green skin, the face of a god, and a body to match. His presence at the hospital would have torpedoed the mission from the moment he stepped inside.

That fact was the only reason he'd eventually conceded, agreeing to wait at the rendezvous point with Brendan Scott.

"See you soon," she promised.

A small click preceded Cade's voice over the connection. "You'll be happy to hear all three patients are stable, and the rest of the team has exited the site and will be on route to the airfield shortly. Micah has already joined Williams and Drew, and Justin and Kire are on their way to pick up Reynolds and Cardiff. We're clear."

"Where are you?" Aurora asked.

"Look out your back window."

They both turned. A nondescript black sedan coasted behind the ambulance. The muscular blond man behind the wheel gave a wave.

"Well, hello stranger." Aurora waved back, even though Cade wouldn't be able to see them through the tinted glass. "Come here often?"

Lelindia didn't bother smothering her laugh.

"Only when you're in town," Cade replied smoothly.

"Good to know." She turned to face front, her voice switching to captain mode. "How close are we, Gonzo?"

"Should be there in thirty-five minutes," he called back.

She glanced at Lelindia. "Do you want to get Keenan off the machines before we get there?"

She returned her attention to his still form. The toxin tainted his bloodstream like an oil slick in the ocean. Based on the levels she was seeing, he'd been on a steady drip of the stuff ever since he'd sustained his injuries. She didn't recognize the compound, which indicated it could be Teelian in origin.

Her anger returned, suffusing her chest, but she shoved it aside. Keenan needed her healing abilities way more than he needed her indignation. "I need to clear the toxin first."

"Let's do it."

Working with the smooth harmony born of their Suulh bond as energy sisters, she and Aurora surrounded Keenan with the interwoven energy of their fields. Lelindia dove beneath the surface, isolating the toxin, scrubbing it from the surrounding tissues and neutralizing it with her field, the waste materials flowing out through the catheter.

His body responded to her energy and the clearing of the toxin with the vibrancy of youth, his internal systems kicking in to smooth out his heartrate, breathing, and circulation.

Now she could focus on removing the ventilator and healing his injuries. She glanced at Aurora. "I'm going to keep him in an induced coma until we reach the *Starhawke*."

"Good idea. We don't want to freak him out."

Aurora helped her unhook Keenan from the support machines and catheter, their energy fields keeping him stabilized. With the artificial constructs out of her way, Lelindia concentrated on steadily healing the physical damage caused by the initial trauma and the extended ICU stay.

She kept the flow of energy moving through his body, repairing internal damage to nerves, tissue, and bone, starting with his autonomic functions.

Aurora's pearlescent glow gave added strength to the healing, but even so, she gritted her teeth in frustration. If she'd treated him when the injury had occurred, she would have been able to repair the damage in moments. But the passage of time and the toxin's malevolent influence made the task more challenging.

The steady drone of the highway faded as Gonzo guided the ambulance onto an offramp. A quick glance out the back window confirmed Cade was still right behind them.

"We'll be at the airfield in a couple minutes. Is he stable enough for us to take a break?" Aurora asked her.

She balked. Stopping a healing session in progress went against her instincts, but working while transferring him from the ambulance to the *Starhawke*'s shuttle wasn't a good idea, either. "For now. He'll be okay until I get him on the shuttle."

Aurora's lips set in a thin line as her energy field winked out. Sitting back, she reached up and pulled her wig off, shaking her long blonde hair out and popping the brunette wig into a bag. She ran her fingers through her hair and sighed. "Free at last."

Lelindia doubted she was referring to the wig, but it was a good idea anyway. She pulled off her own wig, the color a few shades darker than Aurora's golden blonde, and dropped it into the bag Aurora held out. "You look much better as a blonde than I do."

Aurora grinned, already working her hair into its customary braid. "And you look better as a brunette."

Strands of Lelindia's shoulder-length brown hair fell forward, and she brushed them back behind her ears. She hadn't planned ahead for taking the wig off, which Aurora obviously had, and didn't have a hair tie with her.

Her mom had offered to cut her hair for her before they'd left the *Starhawke*, a task she'd been wanting to check off for months, but she'd hesitated. Jonarel had developed a fondness for running his fingers through her hair, something he wouldn't be able to do as easily if she went back to her shorter pixie cut. She was loathe to give up that particular delight for the sake of practicality. Besides, Celia had given her an assortment of ponytail holders and hair clips that worked with her current length. She'd just neglected to bring any with her.

Her colored contacts joined Aurora's in the bag as well. Changing out of her EMT uniform, however, would have to wait until they returned to the ship.

"Approaching the airfield now," Gonzo informed them as he pulled onto a side road, tapping a command on his comband to open the closed gate.

An aircraft hangar lay at the end of the road like a giant lizard sunning itself on a rock, the beige exterior blending in with the muted colors of the surrounding hillside. Gonzo drove the ambulance inside the shadowed interior, Cade's vehicle following right behind.

A heartbeat after the ambulance came to a halt, the back door swung open before she or Aurora could reach for the handle. Jonarel's large form appeared in silhouette, backlit by the sunshine flooding in through the open hangar doors.

"Lelindia." He reached for her hand, clasping it in his sure grip.

A tingle raced up her arm. "Hi."

With impressive strength and unerring grace, he plucked her from the back of the ambulance and pulled her into his arms, surrounding her with the firm and deliciously warm muscled wall of his body. His hand stroked over her hair and down her back, his lips nuzzling the top of her head. "You are safe."

"I'm fine." But having a little trouble breathing normally.

As much as she'd studied and observed Kraed culture over the years, she was still adjusting to Jonarel acting like a true Kraed around her, rather than the watered-down version of himself he'd always shown her and Aurora. His desire for full-body contact on a regular basis, especially after they'd been apart, was one of many traits that caught her off guard.

Not that she was complaining. She'd spent years of her life fantasizing about being with him. Reality blew her daydreams away like space dust in a solar wind.

She pressed her cheek against his chest and slipped her arms around his waist, soaking up the feeling of safety and belonging that filled her.

"You're getting quite adept at undercover work."

She opened her eyes at Cade's words, but he was looking at Aurora, not her. They had their arms around each other's waists, and Aurora was watching her and Jonarel with a soft smile.

"I don't plan to make a habit of it," Aurora replied, turning to Cade. "But I can see the appeal when you're outwitting people like Weezel and Reanne."

So could Lelindia. Aurora had filled her in on their adventures dealing with the slimy shipyard owner she and Cade's team had stolen Cade's ship *Gladiator* from. Judging by Aurora's description of Weezel's misogynistic and predatory behavior, liberating the ship from under the man's nose had been almost as satisfying as getting Keenan out of Reanne's grip.

Which reminded her — she still had a lot of work to do. She tilted her head back, meeting Jonarel's beautiful golden gaze. "Keenan."

His grip loosened immediately, but his fingers trailed down her arm as he stepped back, making her entire body tingle.

"Where's my dad?" Aurora asked Jonarel as she moved to join Lelindia.

"In the shuttle, talking with your mother on the comm."

"Do they have Payne's family?"

"Yes. They are returning to the *Starhawke* now. Your father wanted to inform them that Keenan had arrived here safely."

Lelindia's dad had flown one of the *Starhawke*'s shuttles, with her mother, Libra, and Admiral Schreiber onboard, to the meeting location to pick up Admiral Payne, her son and daughter-in-law, and Keenan's sister.

"I'm sure they'll be relieved to hear that. They'll want to see him as soon as possible." Aurora glanced at Cade. "How long until the rest of the team arrives?"

He checked his comband. "About fifteen minutes."

"Then let's get Keenan moved to the shuttle and start stripping the ambulance."

Aurora's dad met them at the top of the ramp as they entered the *Starhawke*'s shuttle, which sat at the far end of the hangar beside an antique four-person passenger plane painted red and white. Brendan's company, Far Horizons, owned the airfield they were using as their base of operations for the hospital heist.

Brendan hugged Aurora. "How'd it go?" His gaze shifted to Keenan's still form as Jonarel lifted him off the gurney and laid him on the shuttle's portable med platform.

"Pretty smooth, considering. And thanks for the loan of the ambulance. Now we need to get it back to its original condition."

The ambulance they'd used for their mission was part of Far Horizon's emergency response unit that serviced this airfield. Since the one runway airfield was shut down for the holidays, they'd been able to arrive unnoticed in the *Starhawke*'s shuttle the previous night and retrofit the ambulance's exterior to match the local company that serviced the hospital Keenan had been in.

"Glad to help. I was feeling a little useless in all this."

"Hardly." Aurora gave her dad another hug before turning to Lelindia. "Do you need me to stay?" Her gaze flicked to Keenan.

"No. I can take it from here." She shooed her toward the ramp.

As Brendan and Cade followed Aurora off the shuttle, Jonarel moved beside her, his arm settling over her shoulders, drawing her against his side. "You are extraordinary."

The look in his eyes warmed her like sunshine. "What do you mean?"

"You have always been an exceptional healer, but now, you are an exceptional leader."

A flush crept up her neck. Praise from him was another item she was learning to handle gracefully. "Thank you."

He cupped her cheek in his large hand. "You saved Keenan's life. And you are the star at the center of mine."

Her body went liquid, the interplay of sensual awareness and intense emotion in his gaze stealing her breath.

He bent down, brushing his velvety lips over hers in a tender kiss. She whimpered softly when he pulled away.

Amusement danced in his eyes. "Later," he promised.

Later. Yes, definitely later, because right now she had a patient who needed her attention.

Tearing her gaze from his, she focused on Keenan.

Her Nedale senses allowed her to see the microfractures in his facial bones under his bruised skin, likely the result of his head striking the ground after the fall. If he hadn't been so young and in such good shape, the drop over the cliff onto the rocky ground below probably would have killed him.

Her anger rekindled in her chest, glowing like coals, but she kept it in check. Better to focus on rewriting his story and erasing all the physical damage he'd endured.

Engaging her energy field, she set to work.

Four

"You make a very convincing hostile visitor," Celia Cardiff commented to Justin Byrnes as she climbed into the backseat of the unmarked white van a couple blocks from the hospital. She settled in beside Tracy Reynolds, her security counterpart in Admiral Schreiber's Elite Unit.

Byrnes shot a grin over his shoulder from the driver's seat, his short blond hair slightly mussed now that he'd taken off his wig. "Thanks. I promise I don't normally smack into pregnant women, knock them down, and then tell them to watch where they're going."

When she'd exited the elevator in the waiting room, he'd knocked into her hard enough to look convincing to anyone watching. She'd stumbled into the wall and gone down on one knee. Micah had played the indignant observer, jumping to his feet and confronting Byrnes, demanding he apologize while Lelindia, who'd been nearby in her EMT disguise, helped her to her feet.

Given an option, she wouldn't have chosen Micah as her defender, but he'd been the logical one to fill that role. "That look you gave Micah deserved an acting award. I thought for a moment you were really going to take a swing at him." Which she would have enjoyed seeing. That man bugged the heck out of her.

"Glad it looked authentic. If I had, Aurora would have killed me, even if it would have been in character. Besides, I wanted to get thrown out, not arrested."

"Mission accomplished," Kire Emoto commented from the passenger seat. The smile he gave Celia as he turned didn't match the vampire look he was sporting. "You were equally convincing as a pregnant woman. First time I've ever seen you act meek."

But far from the first time she'd used that particular trick to lull her enemies into complacency. She pulled off her dirt brown wig and dropping it into the bag Emoto held out before sliding her hands under the hem of her long tunic to unstrap the rounded belly pad. "I don't know how any woman puts up with this for nine months."

"Neither do I," Reynolds agreed, adding her red-haired wig to the bag and running her hand through her short blonde hair. "I'd feel like a toad."

Emoto chuckled. "And this is why I'm grateful men don't have to make that choice."

"Me, too." Byrnes pulled the van into traffic. "But I'd bet it would be different if you were carrying your kid, an actual little person inside you, rather than a bunch of padding. Besides, it's not like you're that big for the whole nine months."

Celia reached forward, casually dropping the belly pad in Byrnes' lap. His startled *oof* made her smile. "When the woman you love is carrying your kid, you be sure to tell her that."

Byrnes had the grace to look sheepish. And judging by the slight tinge of red on his neck, he was thinking about a specific woman in that context — Bella Drew.

She'd never caught them in an embrace, or slipping out of each other's cabins, but she'd trained too long at detecting subtle cues not to have figured out they were into each other. They just hadn't chosen to do anything about it.

She got that. They worked together in an intense job that required focus and objective detachment during a mission. Sex was one thing. Romance, and all the emotional entanglements that came with it, was a distraction that could cost lives.

Not that she was against romance as a rule. Seeing Lelindia and Aurora lit up now that they'd settled into their respective relationships made her happy. They'd each found a partner who made them stronger, more focused, not less.

Unfortunately, most relationships didn't turn out that way.

"Are Williams and Drew on their way?" Reynolds asked.

"Yep," Emoto replied. "They picked up Micah a few minutes ago."

Micah. The name poked her like a needle, making her grit her teeth. His presence had put her on edge since the moment they'd met, her senses switching to high alert whenever he walked into the room, indicating a serious threat. She didn't trust him as far as she could throw him. Less, actually. She could probably toss him a fair distance, even with his muscle mass.

Her scrutiny had become a sore point with Aurora. That bugged her too, but she couldn't back down, not when her friend's objectivity was compromised. She'd only reconnected with her brother a few weeks ago, after twenty-seven years apart. How well could she actually know him?

And then there was the matter of their weird Suulh-related connection. She'd peppered Lelindia with questions after Micah was brought onboard the *Starhawke*, trying to get a handle on exactly what type of influence he could exert on Aurora. Lelindia had assured her that their connection was positive, enhancing Aurora's Suulh abilities, but the way the two behaved around each other made her twitchy. Like they were in each other's heads.

Unfortunately, she seemed to be the only one concerned, which was another irritant. Even Jonarel Clarek, Mr. Overprotective himself, had accepted Micah without question.

So she'd keep watch on her own. And maybe drag Micah into a dark corner so she could make it clear how much damage she could do if he endangered Aurora or the crew.

Reaching under her tunic again, she tightened the drawstring on her pants, then untied the sash she'd hidden beneath the padded belly and re-tied it around the outside of her tunic, cinching in the bulky fabric. The disguise had been effective, but she wasn't volunteering to put on maternity clothes again anytime soon.

Byrnes and Emoto kept up a lively dialogue as the highway led them into the hills. The private runway and small hangar Brendan Scott's company owned was tucked into a valley. Most of the time it was used as a test flight location, due to its relative isolation from the nearby metropolis, but it was conveniently closed down for the holidays, making it an ideal location for their rendezvous.

The dried scrub brush and bare trees on the hillsides provided the only visual interest as they wound their way along the road. So different from the towering trees and flowing rivers of the Clarek compound on Drakar.

She sighed, propping her chin on her hand as she gazed out the window. She might not see Drakar for a long time. The faceoff with Siginal Clarek had burned a lot of bridges.

She didn't regret their actions, but it put Aurora in a tough spot with the Kraed. And the Suulh on Azaana. The Kraed had been their allies, helping them to protect the Suulh and gather intel on Teeli activities. Now Siginal had banished his son and daughter from their homeworld.

The *Starhawke* was on her own.

Aurora and Lelindia had been focused on rescuing Keenan ever since Aurora's return, so the subject of the Suulh on Azaana hadn't been brought up, but they had to be thinking about it.

After what Signal had said about Aurora's lack of choice regarding her own future, she couldn't imagine Aurora reaching out to him. But she couldn't imagine Aurora abandoning the Suulh either, even if they were relatively safe on their island paradise. The Kraed would honor their commitment to watch over them, no matter what happened. Protectiveness was in their genes.

Ironically, it was that tendency toward overprotective behavior that had driven Signal into trying to control Aurora. In his mind, any action he took to defend his clan was justified, including forcing Aurora to mate with his son.

Well, that wasn't going to happen. Celia had known that long before Aurora or Jonarel had figured it out. They were too similar to be a good match for each other. Aurora needed Cade's playful daredevil streak to lift her out of her responsibility rut, and Jonarel needed Lelindia's gentleness and nurturing influence to balance his warrior instincts. The alterations in his behavior over the past few days had proven that beyond a shadow of a doubt.

Now that Cade and Jonarel weren't trying to kill each other, the four of them made a solid team. Hopefully together they'd come up with a solution to the Signal problem.

By the time Byrnes pulled the van into the airfield's hangar, three other vehicles sat inside the shadowy confines – a black sedan, an unmarked white van identical to theirs, and an ambulance on a lift in the process of being overhauled back to its original condition.

Tam Williams stood – beefy arms folded like a bouncer at a club – directing the rest of the crew as they stripped off temporary adhesive on the van's exterior to reveal the old paint job underneath.

Hopping out of the van, Celia strode to where Aurora was crouched, removing one of the tires, the replacement on the ground beside her. "Need any help?"

Aurora's gaze swept over her and she grinned. "Decided to forgo the baby?"

"Decided to go blonde?"

Aurora ran a hand along her braid. "Brunette's not my style."

"Pregnancy isn't mine."

Aurora held up the power tool in her hand. "How about changing a tire?"

"I'm good with that."

Working together, they had the tires switched out in a couple minutes and the ambulance lowered off the lift. As they passed behind the open back doors, she spotted Micah climbing inside. She shouldn't have been able to identify him since he was dressed in a hazmat suit, ready to spray a sanitizing agent that would break down any forensic evidence left in the ambulance.

But she did. His form and movements were instantly recognizable. She'd be able to pick him out of a crowd of a hundred. Maybe a thousand.

A nudge against her shoulder made her turn.

"You're staring," Aurora informed her.

"Observing."

"Glaring."

"Assessing." She turned her back on Micah with a casual shrug, even though it took every drop of willpower she possessed. "Are the Suulh on Gaia expecting us?"

Aurora allowed the redirection, although her look made it clear she wasn't buying what Celia was selling. "No. We didn't have time to send a message by courier and couldn't risk contacting them through the ICS, not until we know the scope of the Teeli infiltration in the Fleet and Galactic Council."

"But you're sure they'll be fine with watching over Payne's family?"

"My mom and Marina are sure. And after seeing the way the Suulh on Azaana acted toward me and Lelindia, I don't think we'll have any issues. The Suulh have generous hearts, especially when the Sahzade or Nedale are the ones asking for help."

"And this time all four of you are asking."

"Exactly. They'll have to keep their abilities a secret from the Admiral's family, but after decades of living amongst humans on Gaia, I don't expect that will be a problem." Aurora's expression grew more animated. "I'm eager to meet them. Without their help, Marina and Gryphon wouldn't have been able to smuggle my mom off Feylahn and keep her safe from the Teeli. That took guts. And they were only teenagers at the time."

"Reminds me of Raaveen and Paaw. And the rest of the teens we found on the Setarip ship." That group had shown amazing courage and determination, refusing to leave their Necri parents behind when offered the chance to escape their prison.

"Which is why I have no doubt Payne's family will be safe with them. As soon as we get them settled, we can focus on tracking down the Yruf and setting our trap for Reanne."

Five

Cade Ellis sank into a seat in the shuttle's main cabin with a satisfied sigh. The hospital heist had reached a successful conclusion, all evidence had been cleared away or destroyed, and Keenan's family was waiting for them on the *Starhawke*. Everything had gone according to plan – a rare occurrence.

He clasped Aurora's hand in his. "Ready to go home?"

Her green eyes glowed with happiness. "You bet."

He wasn't sure at what point the *Starhawke* had become home for him – for them – but it felt right. No matter how far his missions with his team might take him, returning to the *Starhawke* would always mean coming home.

Cardiff slid into the seat on Aurora's other side, the angle of her arms and stiffness of her spine conveying a tenseness and hostility he wasn't used to seeing from her.

A glance over his shoulder gave him a clue. Aurora's brother Micah sat down in the seat directly behind Aurora, his gaze moving between her and Cardiff, his normally sunny expression clouded.

Cade hadn't been able to figure out what was triggering the animosity between those two, but it was palpable. Or maybe he was picking it up with his empathic senses. He still hadn't quite accepted that the term applied to him. Brendan had assured him it did, and had promised to work with him while they were on the *Starhawke* together.

He couldn't decide if the idea thrilled him or terrified him. Aurora's ability to sense the emotions of others, especially his, had always fascinated him. He'd known on some level she was different — special — which was one of the reasons he'd been drawn to her.

Thinking of himself in those terms took some getting used to.

He wasn't the only one making unexpected adjustments. Jonarel Clarek had turned the piloting of the shuttle over to Brendan, choosing to remain in the main cabin with Mya — no, everyone was calling her Lelindia now — who was watching over Keenan. Jonarel had barely glanced their way when he and Aurora had boarded the shuttle. His focus had remained on Lelindia.

What a change from the open aggression and posturing that had been a mainstay of their relationship since the Academy. In fact, if what he was getting from his empathic senses was accurate, Jonarel *liked* seeing him with Aurora. Hades had to be whipping up quite a snowstorm right now.

Aurora's comband pinged. "It's Kelly. The other shuttle just docked."

The *Starhawke*'s pilot had remained with the ship, which was in full camouflage mode. She and Star were maintaining a search pattern and monitoring all traffic in and out of the system, keeping watch for Bare'Kold's yacht, although the Teeli delegate didn't appear to be in a rush to leave Earth. Bare'Kold would have a lot to answer for when he next saw the Sovereign. Not only had he and the Ecilam Setarips failed to capture Aurora's and Lelindia's mothers, they'd suffered losses of their own during the battle at Stoneycroft.

Libra Hawke hadn't been able to confirm how many of the Ecilam had died during the attack, but enough that they'd abandoned the field before the *Starhawke* crew and his team had arrived to provide backup.

Reanne wouldn't take the defeat well. Bare'Kold was probably buying as many days as he could before he faced what would likely be his execution.

Cade wouldn't weep for him. Bare'Kold was responsible for abducting Lt. Isabeau Magee, Admiral Schreiber's PA and good friend, and turning her over to Reanne for interrogation. Or worse. Bare'Kold deserved whatever was coming to him.

Turning back to Aurora, he gave her hand a squeeze. "What's our first order of business after we land?"

She glanced behind her to where the portable med platform attached to the bulkhead was partially obscured by Jonarel's large form and Lelindia's smaller one. "Lelindia and

Jonarel can handle getting Keenan to the med bay, and Marina and Gryphon can take care of getting his family settled in. I'll want to debrief Admiral Payne and talk to Admiral Schreiber about his next steps. I'm not sure if he'll be going with us to Gaia or not. What about your team? Has he given you any orders?"

"No. For now he seems to be putting us at your disposal."

"That's good to know. Kire could use Justin's help with the Teeli translations, and I'll need to coordinate with you for our Yruf plan after we deliver Payne's family to Gaia."

"*Plan* might be an ambitious word for what we have so far. Contacting them won't be easy." The mysterious faction of Setarips who'd kept his team prisoner for several days and then dropped them off practically at Earth's front door were elusive in the extreme. For all he knew their massive modular ship was parked right beside the *Starhawke*, watching them.

Then again, the Yruf might not be able to see through the Kraed hull camouflage the same way they saw through the sensor shield Clarek and Drew had designed for *Gladiator*, his team's ship. Like the Yruf ship, the *Starhawke* could make herself invisible, not just deflect sensor sweeps.

That's why he'd asked Star to work up a few recommendations for how they might be able to detect the Yruf ship. If anyone could solve that puzzle, it was the non-biological Nirunoc who inhabited every millimeter of the *Starhawke*.

"At this point, any recommendations you have will be helpful since I know exactly zip about the Yruf," Aurora replied. "We'll meet in the conference room as soon as Admiral Payne's had a chance to see Keenan settled into the med bay."

His gaze moved to the cockpit and the starfield visible beyond. The co-pilot's seat next to Brendan was conveniently vacant. "Hey, do you mind if I join your dad for the docking procedure?" He'd piloted the *Starhawke*, but he'd never flown one of the shuttles into the bay when the ship was cloaked. He was more than a little curious to see how it was done.

Aurora smiled and waved him forward. "Go for it."

Unfastening his harness, he crossed the short distance to the cockpit and dropped into the co-pilot's chair. "Mind if I join you?"

Brendan grinned at him, his smile almost identical to Aurora's. A couple days ago he'd shaved his beard, the smooth line of his strong jaw making him look more like Micah's older brother than his father. Only the sprinkling of white in his blond hair and the laugh lines around his eyes gave away his age, though even those didn't seem as pronounced as they had been. "I was wondering if I'd be seeing you up here."

"Oh, really?"

"You're a pilot. You wouldn't want to miss the show."

"No, I wouldn't." And he wasn't going to miss the opportunity to spend time with Aurora's dad, either. Brendan had accepted him as family from the moment he'd arrived at Stoneycroft during the fire that had claimed Aurora's childhood home.

Actually, even before then. The first time he met Brendan, during a pilot training program, Aurora's dad had treated him more like a son than a trainee. He'd even told him that he reminded him of his son, Micah. Now that he'd met Aurora's brother, he understood the comparison.

He also felt a kinship with Brendan that he'd never felt with his own father. Then again, his dad had done everything in his power to bend Cade to his will and destroy his dreams. The resulting fallout from their heated arguments had created a cold war that had lasted fifteen years. He'd talked to his mother on a few occasions, but he'd had zero communication with his dad.

Watching Brendan interact with Aurora and Micah had been a revelation. The deep love, understanding, and respect he showed them was such a sharp contrast to what Cade had experienced with his parents. He'd never expected to be part of a family dynamic that nurtured him, but Aurora's dad and brother had accepted him as one of their own. Even Libra had warmed to him during the last few days.

"How many times did Jonarel have you and Gryphon practice this maneuver yesterday?" Lelindia's dad, Gryphon Forrest, had experience flying starships — had in fact been the pilot of the Teeli ship that he and Marina had stolen to smuggle

Libra off Feylahn, the Suulh homeworld. Gryphon had jumped at the chance to pilot one of the *Starhawke* shuttles, freeing up Cade to oversee the hospital mission.

"Three times." Brendan's gaze darted into the main cabin and he lowered his voice to a conspiratorial whisper. "We would have kept at it, but I think Jonarel was eager to return to other tasks."

Cade grinned. "No doubt." He'd thought he'd known how a Kraed in love acted after watching Jonarel around Aurora, but that was a pale imitation compared to how devoted he was to Lelindia. If she asked him to carpet the deck with rose petals when she walked, he'd probably ask her which color she preferred.

A soft chime pinged in the cockpit. Brendan's gaze returned to the viewport. "That's our signal. We're in range."

Cade focused on the shadowy expanse of the moon visible on the starboard side through the viewport. No sign of the *Starhawke*, but the chimes grew closer together as Brendan guided the shuttle forward.

"How much margin for error is there?"

Brendan made a slight course correction. "Not much for the actual docking, but Star's integration extends partially to the shuttles. She can perceive potential errors long before they're a problem and adjust the beacon signal to keep the flight path on target. Once the shuttle's in range, she handles all the heavy lifting." He pointed to one of the readings in the heads-up display. "Jonarel installed a tracking display in both shuttles when he designed them, anticipating the preference by human pilots who are used to relying on visual instrument readings, but the Kraed method is much more intuitive and elegant."

And more of a fun challenge for someone like Brendan — or himself — who enjoyed tackling flight experiences they'd never tried before.

Like being the first human to pilot the *Starhawke*. Or any Kraed ship, for that matter. That might have a little something to do with his sense of belonging, too. He'd been an integral part of the crew's first flight.

But he'd been happy to turn the task over to Bronwyn Kelly so he could focus on putting his other talents to work helping Aurora on Gaia. And everywhere they'd traveled together since.

The chime became a steady tone as Brendan fired the braking thrusters. Cade watched every move he made until the shuttle's forward motion ceased and the starfield was replaced by the interior bulkheads of the *Starhawke* as the shuttle was drawn up into the shuttle bay.

"Amazing."

Brendan smiled as he powered down the shuttle. "I know you don't have much down time, but one of these days you should get Jonarel to take you out for a spin in one of the shuttles so you can get a shot at docking."

Until recently, that suggestion would have been a good way to get himself launched into the vacuum of space. But change was in the air. "I just might do that."

Six

As soon as the shuttle landed, Lelindia disengaged the portable med platform, which also functioned as a hover stretcher. Keenan's family would be eager to see him, and she didn't want to keep them waiting.

Jonarel took charge of maneuvering the stretcher. Aurora and Tam Williams flanked Lelindia as they walked behind him down the shuttle's ramp into the bay. The second shuttle sat to their right, its sleek lines making it look like a tinted ice sculpture.

Before Lelindia's boots touched the deck, the hatch leading to the central corridor and lifts opened and Admiral Schreiber entered, followed by Admiral Payne, her son, his wife, their ten-year-old daughter, Lelindia's parents, and Libra.

Keenan's mother broke away from the group, running to meet the stretcher, her gaze locked on Keenan's face. "Keenan?" Her voice shook, a visible tremor in her limbs as she touched her son's shoulder.

Lelindia rested a hand on the woman's arm, sending a subtle flow of energy over her in a soothing motion, like a cool calming breeze. "He's sedated for now. But he's going to be fine. I can bring him out of it as soon as we reach the med bay."

The woman's brown eyes widened, her mouth hanging open in disbelieving shock. The next moment she threw her arms around Lelindia and hugged her like her life depending on it. "Thank you." The words came out strangled. "Thank you for saving my boy."

She hugged her back, but much more gingerly, allowing her energy field to continue its soothing caress. Tears pricked her eyes. She wasn't a mother, but it didn't take much imagination to understand how scared Keenan's mom had been for the safety of her son. "You're very welcome."

Keenan's dad and little sister stood at the foot of the stretcher as his mother released her, but his grandmother moved to the opposite side, looking Keenan over with the battle-tested gaze of a Fleet Admiral.

Her lips compressed as she trailed her fingers over the edge of the bandages covering the right side of Keenan's cheek and brow. "You've assessed his overall condition?"

Lelindia nodded. And told a version of the truth. "He'll recover quickly now that he's here. The damage wasn't as severe as his doctors believed. He was being given a drug that was preventing his body from healing properly. I've counteracted it."

Payne's fingers gripped the edge of the sheet as banked fury shadowed her dark eyes.

Admiral Schreiber appeared beside Payne. He rested a hand on her shoulder, his lined face filled with compassion. "I told you I knew an exceptional doctor."

Payne swallowed visibly, her body language conveying the internal clash between the detachment of a Fleet Admiral and the emotional agony of a grandmother terrified of losing her grandson. "I know you did, but I didn't believe—" She shook her head. "The nightmare is over." Taking a slow breath, she pulled back her shoulders, meeting Lelindia's gaze squarely. "My family is in your debt."

She deflected the comment with a soft smile. "I'm a doctor. Saving lives is what I do."

Payne's gaze didn't waver. "You are much more than a doctor. You took a great risk saving my grandson. All of you." Payne's gaze swept the group loosely gathered around them. "Your courage and generosity will not be forgotten."

Silence descended in a thick curtain of emotion.

Aurora was the one who broke through it, clearing her throat. "Let's get Keenan settled in the med bay."

Lelindia and Williams led the way to the spacious cargo lift on the starboard side, Jonarel guiding the stretcher behind them. Her parents and Payne's family stayed with them, as did Aurora, her family, and Admiral Schreiber, while Cade led the rest of the crew in the opposite direction to the portside personnel lift.

After the doors closed, Keenan's dad rested a hand on his son's arm, a telltale sheen in his eyes, although he still held himself with the bearing of a career Fleet officer. She'd looked up his service record, and learned he was the commander on a frigate based out of Sol Station but had been on leave ever since Keenan had been hospitalized.

Keenan's sister wasn't looking at her brother. Her dark-eyed gaze kept darting to Jonarel, a mixture of awe and trepidation playing across her features.

Lelindia followed her gaze. What did the adolescent see when she looked at him? Jonarel's coloring was distinctly Kraed – deep green with threads of brown twining across the surface like the veins on a leaf. The golden hue of his eyes was arresting, too. But his most distinctive trait wasn't visible unless he chose to reveal it – the potentially lethal claws buried beneath the skin of his hands and feet.

Not that the girl had anything to fear from him, or any Kraed. As a race of warriors, they were incredibly protective of the innocent and the weak, especially children. That protective behavior made them powerful allies.

Too bad she'd been forced to break that alliance to defend Aurora and free the crew from Siginal's grip.

Aurora and the two admirals hung back, their voices low, as the lift doors parted, revealing the corridor to the observation lounge to the left and the med bay to the right. Her parents took the lead, looking completely at ease aboard the starship as they walked down the corridor to the med bay.

Funny how quickly they'd adapted to their changing circumstances. A few days ago she'd been treating her dad in the med bay after Aurora's grandmother — now a Necri soldier — had attacked and nearly killed him. Yet here her parents were, acting like they'd been living on the *Starhawke* as long as she had.

Admiral Payne and her family followed the stretcher into the med bay while Aurora and her family peeled off with Admiral Schreiber to the portside lift.

Williams worked on setting up the bio monitors while Jonarel handled transferring Keenan to one of the stationary med platforms. His movements were relaxed and tender, as if he were holding a newborn baby not a teenage boy. He helped her adjust the sheet over Keenan and slipped a pillow under his head, then gave her a long, significant look. "I will be nearby if you need me."

Translation — he didn't want Keenan waking up with an oversized Kraed looming over him. But he didn't want to be far from her, either.

"Thank you."

Her mom gestured to the door to the greenhouse. "We'll be next door."

As her parents followed Jonarel out of the med bay, Williams prepped a new IV and she snagged a syringe, filling it with an inert compound. Her healing abilities could repair the cellular damage, but Keenan's body still needed supportive therapy to restore his immune system's normal functions. And now that his family was watching him – and her – closely, she'd have to tone down her energy healing and allow his immune system to take over.

After she'd switched the IV Williams handed her, she turned to Keenan's parents. "Are you ready for me to wake him?"

Fear flitted across his mother's face. "What... what will it be like for him? Will he... know us?"

She gave her a reassuring smile. "The trauma from his injury didn't affect any of the memory centers of his brain. He'll be disoriented, may not even remember the accident. That's common with head injuries. For him, it might feel like he went to sleep in his bed and woke up here."

His dad spoke up. "What about motor functions? Speech?"

She didn't need Aurora's empathic senses to know he was fighting to keep his emotions in check, to discuss the matter as though he was talking to his ship's doctor about an injured crewmember. But he was failing, which showed he was a good parent.

"He'll be weak after his prolonged hospitalization, but there won't be any loss of functionality."

"How can you be so sure?" Admiral Payne asked. Her tone didn't reflect doubt, just a need to understand.

"I have access to Kraed technology, for one thing." Which would go a long way toward explaining any breaks in logic her energy healing might cause. The Kraed kept most of their technological innovations secret, and serving on a Kraed-built ship, she wouldn't be compelled to share any details. "I've also worked with similar situations before. I know what to expect."

Williams stepped up beside her. "I've seen her work with head trauma patients before. Your grandson couldn't be in better hands."

He was telling the truth. He'd been right beside her as she'd healed Justin Byrnes following the run-in with the Meer. They'd forged a friendship during that experience. Tam Williams was the best human doctor she'd ever met.

The lines of tension in Admiral Payne's shoulders eased. "Then please wake him."

Williams adjusted the upper half of the med platform, angling it to a thirty-degree incline.

Her abilities allowed her to see the swollen, bruised, and lacerated skin underneath the bandages on Keenan's face. Thankfully his family would never know the extent of the trauma. She'd clear them out of the room when she and Williams changed the bandages later, allowing her to minimize the damage and prevent scarring. His "miraculous" healing could be attributed to Kraed technology and the removal of the toxin.

The ambulance ride and shuttle flight had given her the time she'd needed to heal the major internal trauma. Admiral Schreiber had confirmed that none of Keenan's family had more than a basic medical knowledge — another point in her favor when it came to using her talents to maximize the boy's recovery.

"Are you ready?" She glanced up, giving his family a moment to voice any objections.

They didn't.

His parents and Admiral Payne drifted closer, his mom's fingers curling around Keenan's forearm, but his sister hung back. A quick peek confirmed she was staring at Keenan's still form with a trepidation similar to what she'd shown toward Jonarel. After all the family had been through, the weeks of fear and anxiety, the girl probably couldn't figure out which way was up.

Lifting the syringe that she'd prepped, she inserted it in the IV and depressed the plunger. But it was all for show. The real reaction came when she slid her fingers around Keenan's wrist — as if she were checking his pulse — while pushing her energy field into his system and releasing the blocks she'd put in place to keep him sedated.

Within moments his eyelids fluttered.

She and Williams stepped out of his field of vision. He blinked, his brow furrowing as his gaze focused on his surroundings.

"Keenan?"

His head turned in the direction of his mother's voice. His frown deepened as he stared at where she clutched his arm.

"Hey, big guy." His dad gave him a closed-mouth smile. "Welcome back."

Keenan ran his tongue over his dry lips. "Back?" he croaked, his gaze sweeping the room. His eyes rounded when he spotted the IV sticking out of his arm.

"It's okay." Admiral Payne rested a hand on his shoulder. "You're going to be fine."

His gaze darted to her, his chest rising and falling rapidly. "What? Grammy?"

"You're going to be fine," she repeated, shooting a look at Lelindia.

That was her cue. She stepped back into Keenan's line of sight. "Keenan, I'm Dr. Forrest. Would you like some water?"

He stared at her, uncomprehending for a two count. Then he licked his lips again and nodded.

She smiled and motioned to Williams.

He snagged a small stainless-steel cup of water from the dispenser built into the med station and handed it to Keenan.

Keenan grasped it with relative ease. Good. The energy work she'd done on his arms and legs during the shuttle flight had improved his muscle conditioning.

A million questions shone in his dark brown eyes as he sipped from the cup, his gaze sweeping the room. He lowered the cup to rest on his chest. "What happened?" He directed the question at her, rather than his family.

"You had a bad fall while running and spent time in the ICU before we brought you here."

"A fall?" He pressed back into the pillow like a crab trying to tuck into its shell. A heartbeat later, he lunged forward, the cup tumbling onto the sheet, spilling droplets of water as his palms smacked onto his thighs and calves, testing, feeling. "Am I—"

Tam snapped up the cup while she gripped Keenan's shoulder and engaged her energy field, gently but firmly pushing him back into a reclined position. "Your body is still healing, but you'll be fine. No permanent damage." Not anymore.

His breath blew in and out in a labored pant, the sudden exertion and adrenaline from his moment of panic draining what little strength he had. "I won't?"

"I promise." She kept the energy field wrapped around him, providing a steady, comforting touch, clearing out the adrenaline and normalizing his system. "I guarantee you'll be running again before you know it."

His sigh held more relief than any sixteen-year-old should ever have to feel. "Thank you."

She squeezed his shoulder. They'd just met, but she could already tell they were going to get along well. "You're welcome. You need to rest, but as long as you promise you won't try any more unauthorized calisthenics, we'll give you a chance to talk to your family in private. Okay?"

The hint of a smile crossed his lips. "I promise."

"Good." She released the energy field and turned to his family, gesturing to the door to her office. "We'll check back in a little while, but holler if you need anything."

Seven

Williams rested his hip on the edge of her desk as Lelindia sank into the chair behind it. "You handled that well."

She smiled. "I've had years of experience disguising my abilities while treating patients."

"You're good at it. If I hadn't known what you were doing, I wouldn't have suspected a thing. From what I saw in Keenan's medical files from the hospital, you were downplaying the scope of his injuries. That boy would be in a world of hurt without you."

"I know." She folded her hands over her stomach as her gut tightened. "How anyone could do that to a kid…" She shook her head. "But this is Reanne we're talking about. She doesn't have a moral compass."

"Or a heart. Hard to believe she and Captain Hawke were friends."

"Aurora sees the good in everyone. She's always believed people will be their best selves, given a chance."

"And if their best self is still rotten?"

She grimaced. "That's the rub." Reanne had proven that with big exclamation marks. Just thinking about it made her twitchy. "Would you mind if I slipped out to check in with my folks and Jonarel?" She could use their soothing presence after the intense morning.

Tam smiled. "Go right ahead. I'll hold down the fort. I need to check in with Cade anyway."

She gestured to the chair after she rose. "Make yourself at home."

The low murmur of voices from Keenan's bedside drifted toward her as she exited the office and stepped through the doors connecting the med bay to the *Starhawke*'s lush greenhouse. The energy of the plants reached out to her in a welcoming embrace.

The sensation distracted her enough that she almost bumped into Jonarel, who was standing less than a meter from the entrance. He hadn't been kidding when he'd told her he'd be nearby.

His arm snaked around her waist, drawing her to his side. "Keenan is awake?"

A giddy joy fluttered through her. This is what she needed. "Yes. Talking to his family right now. Williams and I wanted to give them some privacy."

Her mom turned away from the twining vine she'd been coaxing onto the trellis, her emerald energy field dissipating. "You must have done a lot of work during the journey to the ship. I barely saw any trace of internal injury."

She relaxed against Jonarel as he pulled her back against his chest, allowing him to cradle her. "It was a challenge. For weeks he'd had a toxin suppressing his immune system. His cells had trouble remembering what they were supposed to do."

Her mom's mouth tightened, anger flashing in her eyes. As a Nedale, such abuse of the injured would offend her to her core, just as it did Lelindia. "But he's here, now. That's what matters."

"Yeah." They were all here. And she was treasuring every moment. She scanned the greenhouse. "Where's Dad?"

"In the galley making you a sandwich."

Of course he was. As mate to and father of the Nedale, he knew better than anyone how much effort deep healing took and how tired and hungry she'd be afterward. "That sounds wonderful."

Jonarel's grip tightened for a moment, the warmth of his body enveloping her like a cozy blanket. Then he released her. "I will fetch you a drink as well."

She didn't try to stop him. Being pampered felt nice. "Thank you."

She watched him wind his way along the path that threaded through the greenhouse, his lithe movements triggering a different kind of hunger. Her mom's chuckle made her turn. "What's so funny?"

"You." Her mom's grin lit up the room. "Is there something you want to tell me?"

"Huh?" It took a moment to refocus her attention. "Oh. You mean about Jonarel and me?"

"Uh-huh."

Events had been moving so rapidly for the past few days, keeping her jumping, that she hadn't shared a critical piece of news with her parents. "He wants me to be his mate."

"Oh, Lelindia!" Her mom grabbed her in an enthusiastic hug. "I'm so happy for you."

She hugged her back. "Thanks, Mom. It's still new. I was going to tell you—"

Her mom drew back, waving away the explanation. "The past few days haven't exactly been normal. And your attention has been needed elsewhere."

She'd also been a little reluctant to talk to her mother about the thorny issue that could have far-reaching repercussions – whether mating with Jonarel would eliminate the possibility of bearing a child, a little Nedale to carry on their family line.

Her mom didn't show any signs of concern as her gaze swept the greenhouse. "This ship, what you and Aurora are doing... it's extraordinary. More than I ever imagined, and I've always imagined big things for both of you." Her brown eyes glowed softly in the warm light. "And now my precious daughter, after years of waiting for Jonarel to see what was right in front of him, will finally mate with the male she loves."

Her mom's words stunned her. "You knew? You knew all along that I've been in love with him?"

Her mother's lilting laugh danced among the greenery surrounding them. "Of course I knew. I'm your *mother*. I suspected while you were still at the Academy. The way you'd talk about him in your messages and calls home was suspicious, but I knew for certain the first time I saw you with him. You glowed, and I'm not talking about your energy field." Her gaze sharpened, the laughter fading. "Which brings up an important point we need to discuss. I assume you two have had sex?"

Memories of their recent encounters made her skin tingle. "Yes, we have."

"Did your energy field engage?"

Strange question. She didn't recall her mom ever mentioning anything about energy fields as part of their prior discussions about her sexual history. "How did you know?"

"Yes!" Her mom gave a little hop and clapped her hands. "I *knew* it!"

"Knew what?" She let out a startled yelp as her mom threw her arms around her and hugged her until she couldn't breathe. "Mom. Air."

Her mom eased up, swiping at the tears rolling down her cheeks.

"Are those happy tears?"

"Yes. Very happy."

"Want to clue me in? What are you so happy about?"

Her mom captured her hands in hers. "Because my precious Nedale has found her true mate."

Still not getting it. "We established that. But what does that have to do with energy fields?"

Her mom drew in a slow breath. "I never said anything to you before for the same reason I didn't tell Libra thirty years ago. I believed the Suulh had been wiped out, that we were the last handful in the galaxy. The odds that either of you were ever going to find a mate who could trigger your field was astronomical."

She frowned. "It means something, doesn't it? The energy field engaging during sex."

"It means *everything*. Like Libra, you've found a mate who is biologically compatible with your energy, even though he's not Suulh. Your energy field engaging means the two of you have the capacity to carry on the Nedale line."

The room expanded and contracted around her, the deck shifting under her feet. "You're saying Jonarel and I can have a child? A daughter with my abilities?"

Her mom's hands squeezed hers, steadying her. "A daughter, or possibly a son. The details aren't certain. With Libra and Brendan, Micah came first, which was a huge shock to us all. No Sahzade or Nedale had ever given birth to a son. When Micah didn't show any Suulh abilities, I thought maybe Libra's energy field engaging didn't mean the same thing as it would for two Suulh."

"But then Aurora came along."

"The most powerful Sahzade ever, despite being half-human. Or perhaps because of it."

An image of Jonarel as he'd looked when they'd first met rose into her mind, his skin fern-green and his head barely reaching her shoulder. He'd been the size of a boy of eight at the time, although he'd been eighteen. The Kraed physically matured rapidly around the age of twenty.

And now her mother was telling her that she might conceive such a child... with Jonarel. "A half-Kraed, half-Suulh Nedale."

"That's right. I can't give you any guarantees, but all the signs are there, especially since your abilities are all about nurturing and growing new life."

She splayed her fingers over her abdomen. "I could be a mother." Saying it out loud sent a tremor along her body, her pulse skipping in response. "I never imagined..."

"I did. I just wasn't certain Jonarel would figure it out in time."

"In time?"

"Before your years of fertility ended." Her mom rested a hand over hers, her energy field engaging to surround them both. "Most Suulh children are conceived before their parents reach their thirty-sixth birthdays."

Her pulse fluttered. She'd be celebrating that particular birthday in a few months. "Oh." She bit the inside of her cheek as tension coiled in her belly. "I don't know if I'm ready—"

"Of course you're not." Her mother's energy field continued to swirl around her in a loving, soothing caress. "Your situation with Jonarel deserves time and space to develop naturally. I'm not suggesting you rush into anything. But I thought you should know it was a possibility. You should have another three or four years to make a decision."

The tension eased up.

Three or four years. That was a timeframe she could handle.

Eight

Celia arrived at the conference room before anyone else, just as she'd planned. She'd been on security alert regarding Admiral Payne ever since Aurora told them about the Admiral's duplicitous behavior when she'd assigned them the supposed science mission in Teeli space.

Now that Celia had seen the Admiral's family, and the pain and suffering Reanne's minions had inflicted on Keenan, she had more empathy for why the Admiral had betrayed her oath as a Fleet officer. But that didn't mean she was ready to believe every word the Admiral said or trust her with the safety of the crew and the secrets of the Suulh.

No one had broached the possibility of taking the Admiral's family to the Suulh settlement on Azaana because Aurora's standoff with Siginal Clarek made it hazardous for the *Starhawke* to enter Kraed space. But if the idea had been put forward as the logical place where the Admiral's family would be safe from Reanne's minions, Celia would have argued against it. Vehemently.

Taking the Admiral's family to live with a small group of Suulh who were used to blending in with humans was one thing. They knew what to expect and could hide their alien nature from the Admiral's family. The Suulh who'd been living as Necri soldiers and captive children could not. They were incapable of concealing their otherness and would implicitly trust anyone Aurora and Lelindia brought to the settlement.

The Admiral hadn't proven she could be trusted.

Moving to the far side of the room, she faced the doors, attuning her senses to her surroundings and taking slow, measured breaths. She'd spent years honing her ability to identify the people around her by the patter and weight of their footsteps, the tone and inflection of their voice, and the subtle scents of their skin, hair, and clothing. Visual identification was easy to deceive, but very few people considered their unconscious movements, the pattern to their speech, or the smells that marked them as unique individuals.

She noticed all those things, cataloguing them for future reference whenever the need arose. A situation like this one was a perfect way to practice those skills.

The first steps to approach the door were light but steady and coming from across the hall. Commander Emoto, whose quarters were on this deck next to Aurora's.

The doors parted to admit him. His hazel gaze — now minus the dark eyeliner from his hospital disguise — flicked to her, a small smile teasing his mouth. "Cardiff."

"Commander." He was one of Aurora's closest friends, but Celia hadn't socialized with him except in group gatherings, preferring to maintain a professional attitude toward him rather than the more relaxed and familiar behavior he shared with the rest of the crew. If she'd been anyone else from the crew, his smile would have been bigger.

As Emoto claimed his usual seat to the left of where Aurora always sat, a pair of footsteps exited the lift, one heavier and the other stealthy. She identified the male voice as Byrnes and the whispered footsteps as Reynolds.

Before the doors opened, another male voice called out from the direction of Aurora's cabin – Cade – followed by Aurora's greeting.

That left the two Admirals still to arrive.

Aurora met Celia's gaze as she led the group of four into the room. The corners of her eyes crinkled slightly and she gave an almost imperceptible exhalation – a choked off snort. They'd been friends for too long for Aurora not to know exactly what she was up to stationed away from the table.

Aurora claimed her chair at the round table with her back to Celia. Cade sat to her immediate right, while Byrnes and Reynolds took the seats to his right.

Two more sets of footsteps from the direction of the lift signaled the Admirals had arrived.

Celia slid into the chair next to Emoto without the wood making so much as a creak.

Cade's smile of greeting was warmer than she'd ever seen it. Spending time together with Aurora's family on Hawai'i had thawed the remaining ice between them. He'd proven his loyalty to Aurora, and his willingness to do whatever was in her best interests, even when he disagreed with her reasoning. Recent events had cemented that assessment.

The doors glided open and Admiral Schreiber and Admiral Payne entered. Celia rose with everyone else, waiting until the Admirals had settled into the two chairs to her left before resuming her seat.

Admiral Schreiber folded his hands on the table, the overhead lighting creating a warm yellow glow on his bald head. "Before we begin, I want to commend you all on the success of your recent mission. I set very high expectations for this team, but you always manage to exceed them."

"Thank you, Admiral," Aurora replied.

"I would like to say something, too." Admiral Payne's dark-eyed gaze moved around the table before settling on Aurora. "Today, your crew pulled off a miracle. The fact that you did it, knowing that I had betrayed your trust with regards to the Teeli, makes it all the more remarkable. I am in your debt."

The Admiral scored a few points with Celia for directness and taking full responsibility for her actions.

Aurora's chin lifted, her green eyes clear and calm. "This is what we were trained to do, Admiral. Provide help in troubled times. It's what we will always do."

The comment could have been a rebuke, but it wasn't. No hint of condemnation or judgement tainted the purity of Aurora's words. Only empathy and understanding.

Admiral Payne's throat moved in a convulsive swallow. "Thank you, Captain."

"You're welcome." Aurora's face softened in a closed-mouth smile. "Now we need your help. Can you confirm my assumption that the mission you had planned to send us on was a trap?"

To her credit, the Admiral didn't flinch. "Correct. They planned to ambush and capture your ship."

A similar plan hadn't worked well for the Teeli at Burrow, but apparently they thought the outcome would be different in Teeli space. Admiral Payne wasn't aware of that part of the crew's history, and it was important to keep it that way, considering how many Fleet laws they'd broken by going to the forbidden planet.

"Were you given any details of the plan?" Cade asked.

"No. The first time Delegate Bare'Kold approached me, he presented the opportunity the same way I did to Captain Hawke. It was to be a joint science venture. The only part that struck me as strange was his insistence on keeping the mission confidential until Captain Hawke agreed to the terms. Admiral Schreiber was on medical leave at the time, so I had the authority to do as he asked, but no way to get in touch with the *Starhawke* until you returned to Earth."

"When did that first meeting take place?" Cade asked.

"Mid-October."

Before the attack at Burrow, then. Celia smiled to herself. The Sovereign had worked multiple plans simultaneously to ensure their capture and had still failed.

Aurora sat forward. "But when we met to discuss the mission a few weeks later, you already knew it was a trap."

Payne's forehead crinkled. "How could you have known that?"

Aurora's lips pressed into a flat smile, but she didn't answer.

Payne's eyes narrowed. "You're correct. About a week before I met with you, Bare'Kold called me to the Embassy again. This time, his manner was completely different. Cold. Harsh. Menacing. I'd never seen a Teeli act that way before. They were supposed to be pacifists."

Payne's tongue slid over her lips in an unconscious nervous gesture before she continued. "He gave me the exact coordinates for the rendezvous and informed me that if I told anyone about the mission, or failed to deliver your ship, my family would pay the price."

"And you took him at his word?" Celia asked. She had a hard time believing a Fleet Admiral could be so easily coerced. They were trained to handle ultimatums.

Payne's gaze met hers. "Not at first. I asked him why the Teeli were interested in the *Starhawke*. He didn't answer. Instead, he pulled up a live video feed." A tremor entered her voice with the suddenness of an earthquake. "It showed my granddaughter at her school, playing with the other children."

Anger rose in Celia's chest and spread through her limbs.

"He didn't look at me, didn't say a word. He just watched her. The expression on his face... I'll never forget it." Payne shuddered, her gaze dropping to the carved wood table. "I didn't ask any more questions. When I got back to my office, I sat at my desk for hours, trying to figure a way out. I considered grabbing my family and fleeing. But if they were watching my granddaughter that closely, I had to assume they were watching me, too. Any change in my routine would have caused—"

Her voice choked off.

They all knew exactly what it would have caused. Keenan was proof of that.

Aurora cleared her throat, her voice husky. "So you went along with their plan, contacting me as soon as our ship was in orbit."

"Yes." The word fell like a hammer. "I'm sorry, Captain."

"Don't be." Aurora cleared her throat again. She had to be struggling to process Payne's emotional reaction. "We're not here to judge you. My decision to not follow through on the mission after we accepted it landed Keenan in the hospital. I didn't stop to consider the repercussions for you, for your family, when I made that choice."

"And I was willing to sacrifice you – all of you – to save my family."

Yes, she had. Admitting it didn't mean she wouldn't do it again. In Celia's mind, there was still a large gap in the trust bridge between her and the Admiral.

Admiral Schreiber spoke up for the first time. "We make those choices every day, Alfre. Oh, we like to cloak it in logical arguments and Fleet protocols, but when it comes to a no-win scenario, we choose to protect those we love most because we're human. It's why the Fleet doesn't allow parents and children to serve on the same ship."

Celia might agree with his argument except the Admiral continually gave orders to his own son, her former captain on the Fleet's flagship the *Argo*. Those orders often put him at risk. During her years onboard the *Argo*, they'd patrolled the most dangerous quadrant of Fleet space. They'd had their fair share of armed conflicts and Admiral Schreiber had been the one to give them those assignments.

Then again, Payne's grandchildren were civilians. They hadn't signed up for this.

Payne drew in a shuddering breath and squared her shoulders before focusing on Aurora again. "What other questions do you have for me?"

"Did Bare'Kold give you any other information about the rendezvous other than the coordinates? Any indication of how many ships they were sending, or who would be on them?"

Payne frowned. "No. All he said was the *Starhawke* would be welcomed when it arrived. Based on his previous threat, I took *welcomed* to mean *ambushed*. But I still don't understand why your ship is so important to them." Her gaze drifted around the room. "It's beautiful, certainly, but it's just a research vessel."

Only her years of training held back the indignant snort that raced up Celia's nasal passage. *There are none so blind as those who do not see.* A research vessel? Hardly. And Payne was completely missing the possibility that the ship wasn't the target. Her captain was.

Admiral Schreiber responded before Aurora could. "They're probably after the Kraed technology. They may view the *Starhawke* as an easier target than a ship crewed by the Kraed. Besides, they could never hope to lure a Kraed crew into Teeli space."

Payne's gaze swung to him. "You make them sound like the Setarips."

"Oh, no. They're much more dangerous than the Setarips."

Payne stilled, a few heartbeats passing in silence. "You were always suspicious of the Teeli, even before they joined the Council, as I recall."

"Very true. And in this instance, I'm sad to be proven right."

"So you think they're after more than this ship?"

"Yes, much more."

Payne's spine stiffened and her neck moved like a rusty hinge as she turned to face the rest of them. "And you all agree with him?"

They nodded in chorus line unison.

"I see." She processed that, tension growing around her eyes and jaw. "But you still believe you can keep my family safe?"

You have no idea what we can do. And Celia had no intention of enlightening her. That trust bridge was still looking mighty shaky.

Aurora didn't hesitate. "We wouldn't have brought you onboard if we didn't. No one knows you're with us, and no one can track where we're going. From the perspective of the Teeli, you and your family will simply vanish."

Nine

After the debriefing ended and Admiral Payne left to check on Keenan, Cade turned to Admiral Schreiber. "Will you be staying with us for the trip to Gaia?"

He shook his head. "I'll be needed at HQ to give credence to our subterfuge regarding Admiral Payne's absence. Drew and Williams were able to successfully plant the hospice discharge information into Keenan's medical files, signed by his parents, which explain his disappearance from the ICU. Officially, Admiral Payne has taken a leave of absence to spend time with her family. If their stay on Gaia is not as temporary as we hope, I also have signed letters of resignation from her and Commander Payne, post-dated six months from now."

Cade flinched. "Six months." An eternity for the Suulh living as abused slaves of the Teeli on Feylahn or as Necri soldiers under Reanne's thumb. But considering the rocky situation with the Clarek clan, and the wild card of the Yruf, defeating the Teeli armada and freeing the Suulh wasn't likely to be an easy mountain to climb.

Aurora stepped beside Cade. "Kelly can take you to your house in one of the shuttles as soon as you're ready, Admiral."

"Thank you. Inform her I'll meet her in the shuttle bay in twenty minutes. The sooner you get on your way the better."

"What about Reynolds?" Cade motioned to his security specialist, who'd moved to the back of the room and was deep in conversation with Cardiff. "I'd like her to go with you."

The Admiral's brows lifted. "Still concerned for my safety, Commander?"

"You know I am. Reanne just suffered two major defeats, first at Stoneycroft, then with Keenan. I expect her to double down on any front she has left."

"Excellent point. Very well. Please ask Ms. Reynolds to meet me in the shuttle bay."

"Will do."

After he'd given Reynolds her new orders — which she accepted with a glint of anticipation in her eyes — he joined Aurora in the corridor.

Aurora tilted her face up to his and brushed a soft kiss on his lips. "I hope you don't mind, but I volunteered us for bridge duty. Gonzo's going to take a break from monitoring for Bare'Kold's yacht and I need you to fill in for Kelly at the helm."

A chance to fly the *Starhawke* and be alone on the bridge with her? She didn't have to ask twice. "Lead the way."

A few minutes later he was seated at the navigation console, checking their flight path for any approaching vessels. Star could maintain a set trajectory on her own, but with the ship's hull camouflage engaged, any ships moving in the system wouldn't be able to see or detect them. He needed to make any necessary adjustments to avoid them.

Aurora sat at the tactical console to his left, her focus on the data in front of her. "Still no sign of Bare'Kold's yacht," she said. "Do you suppose he plans to hide out on Earth indefinitely?"

"Indefinitely isn't an option. If he's at the Teeli Embassy, Reanne could send someone to snag him. If he leaves the building, he'll be spotted in no time. Teeli sightings on Earth always cause a stir since they're known for keeping to themselves. And he'd have to stay in populated areas. He doesn't strike me as the type with wilderness skills."

"A pampered diplomat?"

"Definitely. Doesn't like to get his hands dirty. You should have heard the disdain in his voice when he complained about having to work with the Ecilam."

Aurora made a face. "Sounds charming. You must have enjoyed your time with him at the Embassy."

"Oh, yeah. Lots of fun. But at least it gave me the chance to confirm the Admiral's theory that I'm immune to Teeli influence."

"Immune?"

They'd been so focused on the mission for the past few days, he hadn't gotten around to telling her about his discussion with the Admiral. "A result of the negative association I have with Teeli manipulation from my interactions with Reanne. Bare'Kold tried to use his influence on me. It didn't work."

"So Reanne won't be able to influence you anymore, either?"

"Nope. She tried when we were on Gaia. And failed. I just didn't realize it at the time."

Aurora's smile matched the gleam in her eyes. "That's good news."

"Definitely." His console pinged. He checked the readout. "Fleet freighter leaving Sol Station." The freighter's projected flight path would intercept their course as the ship heading out of the system. He nudged the *Starhawke*'s engines back to give the freighter plenty of room.

Aurora stared at the image of Earth floating on the bridgescreen, a line grooving steadily between her brows.

"Something wrong?"

"Hm?" She angled her face toward him but her gaze remained locked on the planet.

"What's on your mind?"

"Your comment about the Ecilam and Bare'Kold got me thinking. If they're still on Earth, so is my grandmother."

Aurora sure knew how to drop a bomb. He heard the whistling wail as it fell.

"According to what my mom said, the Ecilam took my grandmother when they fled. Back to Bare'Kold, I assume. If he hasn't left Earth, then they must still be there, too."

Yet another thread he'd lost track of while they'd focused on Keenan and the Yruf. A chill passed over his skin. "Can you sense her?" He'd witnessed Aurora's reaction to the Necri firsthand on Gaia, their unsettling ability to weaken her. He'd also watched her in a pitched battle with her aunt. Not something he wanted to see repeated with her grandmother.

Her brows drew together, her breathing more measured. After a few moments, she shook her head. "If I'd known she was nearby when we arrived at Stoneycroft, I could have tracked her. Or if she was on a ship leaving the system, I'd sense her, too. But trying to pick up her warped Necri-Suulh resonance among all the feedback coming from Earth is like seeing a flashlight beam shining out from the middle of the sun. Even my mom couldn't identify her when she first sensed her at Stoneycroft, and they were in the same room."

He could sense the duality in her emotions, which might also be getting in her way. The pull towards a grandmother she'd never known, and the repulsion from a Necri who'd almost killed her mother and Lelindia's parents. "Do you want to consider adjusting our plan? We could stake out the Teeli Embassy rather than heading to Gaia. See if we can pick up the signal from the device I planted on Bare'Kold." He didn't know how long the device would remain attached and transmitting, but it might still be viable.

Seconds ticked by before she replied. "No. We need to get Payne's family settled. Much as I would like to free my grandmother from Reanne's grip, that would be playing into her hands." Anger radiated from her like flickering flame. "I've been falling into Reanne's traps, fighting on her terms, again and again."

"And now?"

She turned her head, her green eyes glowing like a white-hot brand. "Now, I'm going to force her to bring the fight to me."

Ten

"How bad is it?"

Lelindia gave Keenan a reassuring smile as she peeled back the bandage partially covering the side of his face.

She'd activated the privacy screen around the med platform, which blocked his family's view of the proceedings while she and Williams changed out the bandage. "Not bad at all." Or it wouldn't be in a few moments.

She picked up a sterile swab. "I'm going to use a numbing agent so you won't feel any pain while I clean the wound."

Keenan's brow furrowed, but the trust in his brown eyes made her heart melt. "Okay. Thanks."

She rested her fingers near his hairline. "Try to relax. Most people find this process soothing."

His answering smile was as weak as his body, but his eyes drifted closed as he sank back against the pillow.

Perfect.

Engaging her energy field, she numbed the nerve impulses around the damaged tissue, then started the healing process.

Williams stood on Keenan's other side, his calm, steady presence allowing her to focus on her patient. Tam could watch the vid monitor that gave him a view of Keenan's family waiting outside the perimeter of the privacy screen.

Keenan sighed as her energy field coaxed the ragged edges of the laceration near his brow to knit together. The cool comfort of her field should feel wonderful compared to the throbbing burn of the injury. She couldn't get away with healing the skin completely — that would generate questions she wasn't prepared to answer — but by the time she dissipated her field, all the damage underneath his skin had been corrected. Only the visible redness around the area and the thin line where the skin had reconnected showed where the injury had occurred.

She glanced at Williams as she reached for the replacement gauze.

His gaze shifted briefly to the cut, a delighted smile curving his lips. "Looking good."

Keenan's eyes slid open. "Yeah?"

"Yep." He held Keenan's gaze while she worked on affixing the strip of gauze. "We'll leave the bandage on for the rest of the trip, but we should be able to remove it when we reach Gaia."

Keenan's chest rose and fell in a relieved sigh. "That's good." His legs moved restlessly under the sheet. "When can I walk?"

She checked the monitor. Admiral Payne was taking a turn around the med bay with Keenan's sister while his parents waited outside the screen, their arms around each other in a hug that telegraphed anxiety and concern.

If they could see Keenan on his feet, that would go a long way toward easing their anxiety. She could make it happen, but she had to come up with a plausible path to get there.

"Your muscles are weak from all the bed rest. If you tried to stand now, you'd fall. But I have access to some advanced supportive therapies we could try."

Williams turned his head, no doubt hiding a smile.

"If you're okay with it, I'll switch out your IV and we'll see if that gives your body a boost so you can try standing and walking."

Keenan nodded vigorously, then flinched as the movement upset his body's inner balance.

She could help with that, too.

"That would be great."

"Okay. Hang on a sec." Fetching a much smaller IV bag, she injected it with a colored agent that turned it yellow. Looked impressive. Did absolutely nothing. But Keenan didn't know that.

After she switched out the bags, she rested her hand on his arm right next to the IV injection site, a bio scanner in her other hand that she positioned so she could see his body over the top edge. "This will feel cool as it begins to flow into your system. If it's working, you'll start to feel stronger, and moving your head shouldn't make you dizzy anymore."

He nodded again, much slower this time. "How long will it take?"

"Not long." She started the flow of energy into his system, directing it from the IV site through his bloodstream as though the energy were coming from the IV drip. His cells responded to the nurturing flow, shaking off the unnatural slumber that had kept them sluggish for weeks. "How is that feeling?"

"Good. Energizing."

She smiled, watching as his body's systems blossomed before her eyes. She kept the bio scanner up to maintain the illusion that it was giving her the readings she needed.

He bent his knees, digging his heels into the mattress as he pumped his legs, making the sheets rustle. "Wow, that feels amazing. Like the ultimate endorphin rush."

He wasn't wrong. She'd released endorphins into his system, too.

His athletic build and age made treating him easier. His body knew what optimal health felt like and moved eagerly in that direction now that she was providing the roadmap.

"Everything okay in there?" Keenan's father called through the privacy screen.

"Just fine," she replied. "We'll be done in another minute or so." She tapered off the energy flow. Keenan's body had gotten the jumpstart it needed. She could see the beat of his heart pushing the healthy cells through his bloodstream, his body regaining much of the ground it had lost after the fall.

Removing her hand from his arm, she lowered the bio scanner and clamped the IV line before disconnecting it from the plug in his arm. "You ready to try standing?"

He popped into a seated position, looking like he was ready to start dancing. "Yeah."

Williams moved beside her, each of them providing a supporting arm as they guided Keenan off the bed. He wobbled a bit as his feet touched the floor. Tam wrapped a muscled arm around Keenan's rib cage. Good thing. Standing, the boy was taller than she was and probably outweighed her, too. He could have knocked them both down.

Keenan took a slow breath and set his feet wider apart, then straightened his shoulders. The pressure on her arm lessened as he took more of his own weight. "That's better."

She motioned to the privacy screen. "You ready?"

"Yeah."

"Screen down."

Star obeyed the order immediately, the visual projection of the temporary wall vanishing.

"Keenan!" His sister's shout almost drowned out the sharp inhale from his mother, whose eyes had widened to twin moons as her hand went to her throat.

His sister darted forward, sliding to a stop in front of him. "You're standing!"

He grinned down at her. "So are you!" he echoed in the same tone of excited amazement.

His sister giggled, the happy titter filling Lelindia's heart with joy. "Can you walk?" She bounced a little on her toes, like she could will her brother into motion.

"I'm gonna try." His attention swung to his parents as they stepped closer.

His mother didn't look like speech was an option at the moment. Her gaze was locked on Keenan like she didn't dare believe what she was seeing.

His dad's voice wasn't exactly steady, either. "You can walk?"

"A little," Lelindia answered for him. "We wanted to test his balance and see how his muscles are responding to therapy." She eased away from Keenan as his dad took her place at his side to steady his son. "Go ahead and give it a shot."

As Keenan took slow, shuffling steps forward, Admiral Payne moved to Lelindia's side. "Kraed technology did this?"

She kept her focus on Keenan. "It helped a lot." Which was true. Without the *Starhawke*, this rescue wouldn't have been possible. It just wasn't the reason Keenan was healing so rapidly.

"I had no idea their medical knowledge was so superior."

It's not. Or at least the Clarek clan's wasn't. Jonarel had told her that each clan had its own specialties, skills, or knowledge they were known for. Maybe there was a clan of Kraed who excelled at medical treatments. "Keenan gets a lot of the credit, too. He's young, and his body was in peak shape before the injury. Once I removed all the roadblocks that were keeping him from healing, his body responded incredibly well to healing therapy."

"So I see."

Keenan had almost made it to the med bay door. He turned in a wide hairpin and started back toward them, Williams and Keenan's father on either side while his sister hop-skipped backwards in front of him, urging him on. His mother had stayed rooted where they'd left her, watching the scene with rapt attention, tears tracking silently down her cheeks.

Lelindia could see the first glimmers of fatigue setting into Keenan's body, but the energy work she'd done would continue to fast-track his progress. By the time the ship arrived at Gaia, Keenan might be able to make the trek to the shuttle bay without needing the stretcher.

He bent closer to Williams and murmured something she couldn't hear.

Tam nodded, changing their trajectory to lead Keenan toward the compact bathroom hidden behind a panel in the corner of the room. Tam glanced over at her. "The guys are going to need a minute."

"You bet."

Keenan's mother clued into the discreet message and corralled her daughter as Williams gave the order for the privacy screen to appear around the bathroom. The projection shielded the three of them from view.

Keenan's sister continued to bounce up and down like a pogo stick. "He walked, Mama! He *walked*!"

His mother nodded. "I saw, baby." A single tear trickled down her cheek from the corner of her eye, followed by another, and another.

Admiral Payne moved beside her daughter-in-law, wrapping an arm around her shoulders. The tears continued to rain down in a silent stream as the two women stared at the privacy screen.

Lelindia crouched so she was eye level with Keenan's sister. "Do you and your brother like to play games together?"

The girl stopped bouncing, shyness overtaking her enthusiasm. "Yeah."

"He still needs to stay in bed and rest, but I'm guessing he's going to get bored. It would be a big help if you'd be willing to keep him entertained while he's resting — play card games with him, tell him stories, stuff like that."

Her dark eyes regained their sparkle, the shyness fading. "I could bring his sketchbook. It's in our cabin. He can sit for *hours* when he's drawing."

"He likes to draw?" She hadn't gotten that particular piece of intel.

"Oh, yeah. He's always sketching. He's drawn me lots of times. Mama and Papa, too."

"Well that sounds perfect."

Keenan's sister gave another hop. "I'll go get it!"

Admiral Payne moved to intercept her, clasping her hand to keep her from darting toward the door. "I'll go with you. We'll be back shortly."

Keenan's mom gazed at Lelindia as the pair left the room. She swiped away the tears that had slowed to a trickle. "I don't know how to thank you."

She smiled. "Seeing Keenan back on his feet is all the thanks I need. He's a strong kid with a positive attitude. He's making my job easy."

"I was so afraid—" She cut off as Tam's voice reached them.

"Screen down."

The privacy screen dropped, the trio coming back into view as they shuffled toward the med platform. Keenan looked tired but happy. Being back under his own power and restoring a piece of normal behavior he'd probably taken for granted until today had lifted his spirits even more.

She adjusted the sheet so he could slide under it easily. "Your grandmother and sister are fetching your sketch pad."

His face lit up. "Yeah?" He pulled the sheet up to his chest and settled against the pillow with a sigh. "That would be awesome."

She chuckled. "Just remember to take it easy. I get the impression you know your body's limits, so as long as you listen to what it's telling you, you can have some fun, too."

"Thanks, Dr. Forrest. You too, Dr. Williams."

"You're welcome," they said in unison.

She checked the chronometer on the wall. "My dad, Brendan, and Micah are in the galley preparing dinner for your family. It should be ready in half an hour or so. They'll bring it to you." She turned to Keenan's parents. "I have a meeting with the captain right now, but Dr. Williams will be in my office if you need him. Any questions before I go?"

Keenan's father rested a hand on his son's shoulder, the tension that had been making him move like the Tin Man now conspicuously absent. "I think we can handle things from here. Thank you for all you've done for us."

"Our pleasure."

Eleven

Aurora's mom and Marina had requested a meeting to discuss how they'd handle the arrival at Gaia. Aurora also wanted them to fill in the gaps in hers and Lelindia's knowledge about the Suulh living there. She'd volunteered her cabin for the occasion while Cade was across the corridor in the conference room with his unit, discussing the Yruf issue.

Marina stood as the cabin door chimed. "There she is." As soon as the door opened and Lelindia stepped inside, Marina pulled her into a hug.

She'd been doing that a lot since the fire at Stoneycroft. The horror of that night continued to cast a shadow, making them all cherish the important things. Like hugs. And spending time together.

"Would you like some tea?" Marina asked. "I made a blend from the herbs in your greenhouse."

"I'd love some." Lelindia accepted the mug Marina handed her and settled onto the couch beside Aurora while Aurora's mom and Marina took the chairs opposite them.

"How's Keenan?" Aurora asked, picking up her own mug.

"Really good. He's taking this all in stride better than I'd expected."

Aurora sipped her tea, the delicate, earthy flavors drawing a happy sigh from her lips. "I can only imagine what this is like for him. One moment he's running on a path and gets knocked off a cliff, then he wakes up on a starship and learns he can't go back to Earth. The emotions I've sensed from him are remarkably mellow. It's a wonder he's not freaking out."

"He's an optimist at heart. That helps. His sister's bringing him his sketch pad. He was excited about that."

Marina smiled. "Admiral Payne mentioned that he likes to draw. How is he physically?"

"Still weak, but he was able to walk around the med bay and use the facilities. I snuck in another healing session after I changed his bandage, so I'm hoping he'll be able to walk on his own by the time we take him to the Suulh."

Aurora gave her a one-armed hug. "With you as his doctor, I have no doubt he will." She turned to her mom. "Speaking of which, it's time for you to tell us about this group of Suulh we're going to be meeting."

Her mom wrapped her hands around her mug and settled into the cushions of her chair with a sigh. "There were six originally. Their names — or rather the names they chose after we arrived on Gaia — are Skye, Oracle, Amethyst, Wolf, Leo, and River, and they're Marina's and my aailee."

"Aailee?" Lelindia glanced at Aurora.

She shook her head and shrugged. "I'm not familiar with that word."

"And for good reason," her mom responded. "It never applied to you and Lelindia. There's no direct translation for it. In Suulh tradition, the Sahzade and Nedale go through three distinct cycles as they move from childhood to adulthood. The first is the discovery cycle, which begins at birth and ends on the eighth birthday. During those years, they are in training with the other Sahzade and Nedale, as well as the current aailee."

"And the aailee are...?" Aurora asked, taking another drink. She had a feeling she'd need the calming influence of the tea for this discussion.

"The aailee are the critical part of the second phase, the gathering. After the Sahzade or Nedale's eighth birthday, focus shifts to meeting and interacting with girls and boys close to their own age who may end up becoming part of their aailee. Think of the aailee as familial crewmembers. When a girl or boy commits to becoming part of the aailee, it's for life. Most make that decision on their fifteenth birthday, although it can be any time before they reach twenty-two. Once the commitment is made, their family moves permanently into the sonea laanaa. From that day on, they work with the Sahzade and Nedale to serve the common good."

"Sonea laanaa?" Lelindia frowned in confusion. "I know laanaa means home, but I'm not familiar with the term sonea."

"Sonea laanaa is what our people call the expansive dome where our families lived, the center of wisdom for our society. Laanaa means home, but also refers to the physical structure of the Suulh dome. The sonea laanaa is ten times bigger than the standard laanaa, which are closer to the size of Stoneycroft."

It sounded like a larger version of the setup the Kraed had built on Azaana. Jonarel had done a better job of mimicking Suulh cultural norms than Aurora had realized. "Are there always six aailee?"

Marina answered that question. "There are no set rules, but usually a minimum of four and potentially as many as twenty after both the Nedale and Sahzade have gone through their gatherings."

"Huh." She'd always believed the binary pair she and Lelindia represented was the extent of the Suulh leadership system. Clearly not.

Marina nudged Aurora's mom with her foot. "The aailee also provide support to the Nedale when she's dealing with a precocious Sahzade."

Her mom made a face. "I wasn't *that* bad."

Marina grinned. "I remember things differently."

Aurora chuckled. "Are you saying my mom was a handful?"

"She had her moments. But then again, so did you. Micah served many of the same functions as an aailee after you were born. When he and your dad left, Lelindia had to handle you on her own."

Those had been rough times. Thank goodness the years of separation and deception were over. "And the aailee is always a mix of boys and girls?"

Marina nodded. "But the girls are selected first, when the Nedale or Sahzade is between eight and eleven. Between twelve and fifteen, the boys are selected, with an emphasis on candidates who would also make good potential mates during the third cycle, the awakening, which lasts through age twenty-one."

Aurora's brows lifted at that. "Arranged mating pairs?"

Marina shook her head. "Not at all. When I was in my gathering cycle, the choice as to which boys would participate was mine alone. My mother and Sooree would offer opinions if I asked, but ultimately, I chose my companions. And we kept inviting candidates and expanding our search until the day I met Gryphon. He and his sister were the last two to join my gathering group."

Lelindia's tea mug banged against the coffee table as she set it down with a thunk. "Dad had a sister?"

Marina winced before meeting her gaze. "Actually, your dad *has* a sister. Amethyst."

Lelindia blinked, her dark eyes rounding. "One of the Suulh on Gaia is Dad's sister?"

"Yes, your aunt. Her mate River is your uncle, and their daughters Crystal and Brook are your cousins."

Lelindia's gaze snapped to Aurora's. Her expression probably mirrored the one on Aurora's face. Apparently their parents weren't out of secrets after all.

Aurora's mom cleared her throat, drawing Aurora's attention. "That's not all. You have family on Gaia, too. Skye's mother was my father's sister, which makes Skye my cousin. Her children — Luna and Sirius — are your second cousins."

Her heart stuttered. *Stellar light.* She'd just picked up more relatives she hadn't known existed.

She stared at her mom for several beats. "You buried the lead when you said there were Suulh living on Gaia."

Her mom stared back calmly. "I know. It was intentional. You had a challenging mission to focus on. Marina and I didn't want the complications of additional family to distract either of you." Her gaze included Lelindia, an apology in her eyes.

Lelindia folded her arms, her eyes narrowing. "Did they all come to your mating ceremony? I remember other people were there, but I couldn't recall who they were."

"All six were there."

"Did you tell me at the time I was related to them?"

Her mom exchanged a look with Marina. "We didn't make a point of it. You knew they were Suulh, but since that was the only time you saw them, and you were so excited about Aurora's impending arrival — which ended up being Micah first — you soon forgot about them."

Frustration swirled around Lelindia like a slow-moving cyclone. "Why didn't you remind me? Talk about them? It would have been nice to know they existed."

Her mom met the gale head-on. "Because I was afraid. You didn't have any Suulh in your life other than me and your parents. I didn't want you pining for contact with the Suulh on Gaia when I wasn't ready to take the step of traveling to see them. Revealing our family connections would have made it worse."

"Although that almost changed," Marina said. "Libra and I had been talking about it a lot after your eighth birthday, when you traditionally would have started your gathering. Luna, Tyger, and Crystal had all been born at that point. Tyger is Oracle and Leo's oldest son. He's the same age as Aurora, and his brother Kyt is four years younger. All of them would have been potential future members for yours and Aurora's aailee. Brendan was ready and willing to facilitate transportation so we could go see them and discuss the possibility of reintegrating our families."

"So why didn't we hear about them?" Aurora asked, her frustration matching Lelindia's. "Or meet them when my dad offered?"

"The Teeli." Her mom gazed into the depths of her mug, the haunted look Aurora knew so well settling over her like a shroud. "They made contact with Earth a month after Lelindia's eighth birthday. A couple months later, I sent your father and Micah away."

Aurora sighed as she sank against the couch cushions. "And we went on lockdown. No hope for an aailee."

"I don't know about that," Marina said. "From what I've seen, yours and Lelindia's relationships with Celia, Kire, Jonarel, and Cade are similar to a Suulh aailee. Whether by instinct or fate, you built what we couldn't supply."

Aurora's gaze swept the room, taking in the contours of the ship she loved, the home Jonarel had provided for their chosen family. "I guess we did." She turned to her mom. "So what can you tell me about my cousins?"

"Skye is Marina's age and holds the position of ilkeen aailee. It's kind of like Kire's position on this ship. In my and Marina's absence, she leads, makes decisions for the group. She's mated to Wolf, whose father was part of our mothers' aailee. Wolf and Skye both grew up in the sonea laanaa, rather than being brought in during the gathering."

"And she's a hugger," Marina added.

A smile crept around Aurora's mouth. "Really?"

"Big time. She's the one who got me in the habit when we were kids."

"What about Aunt Amethyst?" Lelindia asked. "Is she anything like Dad?"

Marina smiled. "They have the same sense of humor. And she's feisty. She always kept him on his toes."

"Is she younger or older?"

"Four years younger. She was the youngest member of my gathering."

"And she and Uncle River have two daughters?"

"Yes. They're both younger than you and Aurora. Crystal's twenty-eight and Brook's twenty-four."

"What about Skye and Wolf's kids?" Aurora asked her mom. "How old are they?"

"Luna's a year older than you and Sirius is three years younger."

"Do you have any pictures of them?"

Her mom glanced at Marina.

Tension stretched across the planes of Marina's face. "Gryphon and I did. At Stoneycroft."

Which ended that particular line of questioning full stop. Silence settled over them as the specter of the house in flames ghosted through the room.

"But you won't have any trouble figuring out who you're related to," Marina added. "The physical resemblances are strong. You'll want to talk to Oracle, too. Her mother was part of our mothers' aailee, and a gifted communicator. Oracle taught herself the Teeli language in a couple months. We couldn't have made our escape without her help."

That was an unexpected bonus. "Kire and Justin are going to want to meet her."

"I'm sure she'll be happy to offer any assistance she can. Kyt share's his mom's passion for language. They both might be able to help with the translations Kire has been working on."

"What about the others? Would they have any skills or knowledge that might help us combat the Teeli?"

Marina ran her finger around the rim of her mug as she considered the question. "Leo and Wolf studied the Teeli weaponry and ship defenses that were onboard the ship we stole. But that information would be forty years out of date now. So would the details Skye and Amethyst learned about Teeli engineering."

"Might still be helpful, though." Aurora glanced at Lelindia. "Think Jonarel and Celia would want to talk to them?"

"I would imagine so. Although—" She shot Marina a look. "The Suulh have never met a Kraed before, have they?"

"No. His presence will be a... surprise. Although they do know you have a Kraed friend."

Jonarel was much more than a friend to Lelindia now. How would the Suulh react to that? "Do they know about the *Starhawke*?"

"No. The last time Skye and Wolf visited Stoneycroft you and Lelindia were still on the *Argo*."

"And you don't communicate with them except when they visit Earth?"

Marina gave an awkward shrug, her gaze darting to Aurora's mom.

Her mom lifted her chin, taking the hit. "That's my fault. As the Teeli presence in Fleet space kept growing, I forbid Marina and Gryphon from sending or receiving written messages from the Suulh except in an emergency."

Oh, the irony. Her mom had finally encountered an emergency related to the Teeli, and the Suulh were still in the dark. "So this entire visit will be a huge surprise?" She knew a thing or two about how that would feel.

"To say the least." Her mom's closed-lip smile was self-mocking. "But they'll adapt. It's what we do best."

Twelve

Aurora searched the night sky through the viewport in her bedroom, the curve of Gaia's nightside visible below.

A shiver passed over her skin despite the relative warmth in her cabin. Reanne was out there, somewhere, her hatred growing day by day.

She couldn't feel it — even her empathic senses had limits — but she knew it was true. However, knowing and understanding were completely different constructs. Intellectually she accepted her childhood friend was the monster who called herself the Sovereign, the one who'd almost killed Keenan, who'd tortured and imprisoned the Suulh, who'd tried to capture her.

But believing that the laughing girl of her memories was the cold-hearted architect of this nightmare was a leap her mind, and heart, didn't want to make.

Cade's arms slid around her from behind, pulling her back against the firm wall of his chest. "Hey."

She rested her hands on his forearms and let her head fall back onto his shoulder, soaking up the soothing comfort he offered. "Hey."

"You know, this empathic thing is still freaky, but I'm beginning to understand why you always knew when I needed you."

She sighed, snuggling deeper into the circle of his arms. "You're right. This is exactly what I needed."

He bent his head, brushing a kiss against her temple. "What's on your mind, Sahzade?"

She gave a little start. "You've never called me that before."

"It seemed appropriate. You look like you're carrying the weight of the entire Suulh race on your shoulders."

Her gaze dropped to Gaia. "I suppose I am." Today she'd meet her relatives and the other members of her mom's aailee who'd helped her mom escape the Teeli. But she wasn't only thinking about them. Or Feylahn, the Suulh homeworld.

Earth was out there among the stars, too. And Azaana.

Each planet had provided a home for her people. A chance at a future.

But Reanne and the Teeli wanted to rule them all, to subjugate the Suulh, use their abilities to amass power and dominance, now and forever. The future their vision created chilled her to her core.

And to think six months ago when she'd become captain of her own starship, she'd believed it was the biggest leap in responsibility she'd ever make. If only she'd known. "I was thinking about Reanne."

"Hmm." His grip tightened, drawing her closer. "You still determined to turn her trap against her?"

"Yes. But that wasn't what I was thinking about." She ran her fingers along his forearm, enjoying the tactile sensation of touching his bare skin. On the *Starhawke* they were both usually dressed in long sleeves except when they were in the gym. Or the bedroom. Skin-to-skin contact with him always grounded her.

"She and I were so close once. Good friends, almost like sisters. We had fun together, laughed together, worked together. Now she's out to enslave or murder my family, capture me, and destroy anyone who gets in her way of galactic domination. How did that happen? How could all the good and light that was inside her get swept away?"

She hadn't meant it as a rhetorical question, but he didn't answer her. She finally craned her neck so she could see his face. His expression matched the sad ache she sensed in his emotional field.

"You see the potential in other people, Aurora. It's one of your gifts." His fingers stroked her hair, making her nerves tingle. "Most of the time you draw out the light and goodness within others, make them better people for having known you.

But Reanne isn't like you. She never was. What you saw in her wasn't real. It was a reflection of what you saw in yourself."

"You're saying I made it up?"

"I'm saying that if you're a magnet, Reanne is a mirror. A warped one. With you, it created an image of goodness that wasn't there. With me, it reflected all my insecurities about myself, about you, about us, convincing me to believe things that weren't true. With Jonarel, it reflected his anger, overprotectiveness, and sense of injustice."

"But we were friends."

"I know. That's how generous your heart is. Reanne's a black hole, but your light still managed to escape being swallowed up."

The ache in her chest had been sitting like a troll. Now it stood and stretched, expanding through her body. "So there's no getting through to her." She didn't phrase it as a question.

Up until that moment she hadn't acknowledged that a part of her still wanted to believe Reanne could be saved, that their previous connection could overcome the hatred that festered like an open wound.

Cade brushed a kiss on her forehead, then rested his chin on top of her hair. "She was lost long before she met you."

Thirteen

The *Starhawke* glided through the clouds overhanging the western coastline of Gaia's second largest continent. The similarity to Earth tempted Aurora to believe they were back home.

For the Suulh who lived here, this was home. And for the foreseeable future, it would be home to the Payne family as well.

"Kelly, do we have a clear landing approach?"

Kelly nodded, her curly red hair bobbing in her thick ponytail. "A few boats in the water, but they're close to the shoreline. I'll bring us down well out to sea."

The hull camouflage would prevent anyone in the area from getting a visual of the ship, but there was only so much Star could do to compensate for the water displacement as the ship touched down on the waves.

They'd broken orbit after sunrise local time, although the cloud layer kept their surroundings in shadowed light. The boats Kelly had mentioned moved slowly but steadily away from the harbor. Magnifying the image revealed they were local fishing boats.

"Will we have any issue avoiding marine traffic?" They'd never put the *Starhawke* down in a populated area before.

Kelly shot an amused look over her shoulder. "I can handle it."

"Does that mean you'll be stuck on perpetual bridge duty while we're here?"

"Not unless you want me to be. Commander Ellis offered to fill in. Your dad volunteered to take a couple shifts, too."

"Ah." She should have known Cade and her dad would be looking out for the needs of a fellow pilot. And that her dad would be itching to get his hands on the *Starhawke*'s controls, even when the ship wasn't flying. "Then I'll have Kire work out a rotation schedule."

After the ship touched down, the lift door opened and her mom and Marina stepped onto the bridge. The magnified view on the bridgescreen of the distant shoreline drew their attention, almost identical ripples of joy and longing flowing off them.

Her mom turned away first. "Do we have a way to contact Skye from the ship?"

Kire answered from the comm station. "I've already tapped into the local comm system. I just need their number to patch you through."

"Oh."

Aurora suppressed a smile at her mom's startled expression. By choice, her mom's interaction with technology had always been severely limited. She'd viewed it with suspicion, possibly because of a negative association with the Teeli. She'd gotten away with it because Gryphon and Marina had handled any needs for the family. Her dad probably had, too, during the years he and her mom were together.

But since coming onboard the *Starhawke*, her mom's attitudes had been shifting. The technological wonders of a Kraed starship could have that effect.

Her mom strode to the comm station. Marina followed close behind.

"Do you want a private channel?" Kire asked, holding up a headset.

Her mom shook her head. "Not necessary. Gryphon said they only have one number for the household."

Marina gave Kire the number. Seconds later the ringing filled the bridge, followed by a woman's voice. "Hello?"

Aurora's heart thumped.

"Skye?" Her mom asked.

"No, this is her daughter."

Her cousin, Luna. What a bizarre experience to hear the voice of a relative she'd never seen or met. Unnerving, but exciting, too.

"Can I tell her who's calling?"

Her mom swallowed audibly, the sense of longing Aurora had detected earlier growing stronger. "Luna, it's Libra."

Silence followed for two beats, three, four. "Libra? Libra Hawke?" Luna's shock and disbelief came through loud and clear over the line.

"Yes. It's good to hear your voice."

"It's... um... you too, Sahzade." She'd lost the casual tone she'd answered with, now sounding like she was having trouble gathering her thoughts. "You're here? On Gaia?"

"Yes. I need to speak with your mother."

"Of course. Right away." A muffled stage whisper was followed by rapid thumps that could have been running footsteps. "Tyger's fetching her from the garden."

Tyger. That would be Oracle and Leo's oldest son, the one who was Aurora's age.

"Thank you." Her mom's gaze shifted to her, the wellspring of emotion in her energy field mirrored in her blue-grey eyes. This was the first time her mother had been on Gaia since she was an adolescent. Memories had to be popping up like wildflowers in spring. "How is everyone, Luna?"

"Um, we're fine. Is... is everything... okay?"

Aurora recognized the hesitancy in her tone. She'd encountered it a lot when first interacting with the Suulh after they were freed from their Necri existence. Luna was clearly struggling with the fact that she was talking to their race's leader, a woman she was related to but probably never expected to meet. Only her parents had visited Earth after the Teeli had made their presence known.

"We're—"

"Libra! What's wrong?" a panicked female voice called out in the background, accompanied by a herd of running footsteps. "Is it the Tee—"

"We're fine, Skye. I didn't mean to scare you."

A deep inhalation on the other end. "But... but you're here? On Gaia? Why? How?"

"It's a long story, but I'm with Marina and Gryphon on Aurora's ship. Brendan and Micah are with us, too."

In the quiet that followed, Aurora could easily picture the stunned and confused looks passing back and forth among the Suulh. Her mom had vowed never to leave Earth, had done everything in her power to keep Aurora from leaving as well. She'd also lied about Aurora's dad and brother for nearly three decades and hidden the existence of the Gaian Suulh. Their abrupt arrival here, now, was a Grand Canyon sized gap in logic for anyone who knew those facts.

Skye's next words confirmed it, as did the disbelief in her voice. "Brendan and Micah are with you?"

"Yes. I'll explain when we see you."

Another pause. "Of course. How soon will you arrive?"

Her mom glanced at her.

She turned to Kelly.

"It's about five minutes by shuttle," Kelly replied.

"We'll be there in fifteen minutes," her mom replied.

"We'll be awaiting you."

Kire closed the channel and turned to Aurora. "I assume you're going with them?"

"You assume correctly. If you and Kelly take first watch, Cade and I will take the next shift."

"Works for me."

Aurora opened a shipwide channel. "All members of the landing party meet in the shuttle bay in five minutes."

Fourteen

Cade watched from the co-pilot's seat as Jonarel guided the *Starhawke* shuttle over the treetops that spread out from the shoreline of the coastal village. He'd been startled but pleasantly surprised when Jonarel had asked if he wanted to observe the shuttle landing procedures for a compact space.

The Suulh homestead was located in a densely forested area of tropical trees. The nearest clearing was a kilometer away, so they were headed for a site where they could make an unconventional landing that would use the shuttle's adaptable design.

Jonarel had never offered to show him anything before, but their path to friendship kept widening now that the guy was head over heels for Lelindia.

That was fun to watch. Their interactions were giving him some ideas of his own, but he'd sensed Aurora wasn't ready to have those conversations yet.

That was fine. They both had a lot to deal with right now. As long as they were together, he was a very happy man.

He studied the tree line. "How tight a space can the shuttle fit into?"

Jonarel glanced at him. "That depends on the number of passengers. The interior is capable of converting into a slender profile but not when all the seating is in use."

"So you have to set it up that way in advance?"

The muscles around Jonarel's mouth softened. Not a smile. More of a cat with a canary look. "The shuttle can adapt at any time during flight."

"During flight?" He shot a look over his shoulder to the main cabin. It looked solid. Then again, he'd seen apparently solid sections of the *Starhawke* shift, too. "How long does it take to convert?"

"A minor change takes a few seconds. To shift from maximum to minimum capacity takes three times longer."

"Ten seconds?" That hardly seemed possible, but he didn't doubt it was true. "That's impressive."

"That is Clarek technology."

He picked up on the flicker of pain mixed in with family pride. Strange to be sensing emotions from Jonarel other than rage. And to be acknowledging that they were coming from an empathic connection rather than observation. Brendan had told him his sensitivity would increase as he began using his abilities intentionally. He was right.

"Our landing coordinates are ahead."

Cade focused on the view outside. The landscape reminded him of southeast Asia, the aquamarine water of the coastline giving way to dense vegetation interspersed with towering rock formations that rose from the greenery like mythical denizens of the deep.

The area Jonarel was guiding the shuttle toward sat on a slope near the base of one of the formations, with the rock at its back and the shoreline spread below. The curve of a beige dome peeked through the treetops. Not unlike the settlement on Azaana, come to think of it, although this homestead was located on a stretch of the mainland rather than an island.

Were all Suulh drawn to tropical latitudes? Had their abilities to grow plants and heal injury developed because they'd been surrounded by an environment filled with an abundance of life? Aurora had thrived on Azaana, and Hawai'i too, apparently. Her mother seemed to have regained her vibrancy in that environment as well. Something to keep in mind as he and Aurora looked toward their future.

Jonarel throttled back the shuttle, bringing it into a silent hover over the swaying branches and fluttering leaves surrounding a tiny clearing. He tapped the console, projecting a 3D lined schematic of the area outlined in green. "The imaging system gathers the necessary information. Tehar adapts the exterior hull configuration to fit like an interlocking groove."

A yellow schematic of the shuttle appeared next, the yellow lines adapting until the two images merged and changed to brown.

"Conversion complete."

Cade blinked as Jonarel lowered the shuttle toward the ground. "You mean that just happened in real time?"

"Of course."

Wow. He'd noticed a slight vibration, but had attributed it to the hover. "You said Star adapts the hull. How does she do that from the ship?"

Jonarel settled the shuttle onto the ground with the lightness of a bird touching down on a branch. "Her non-biological nature allows her to be a part of both the ship and the shuttles. But her integration with the shuttle's systems is much more limited, as is her ability to communicate with the crew."

"Is that why you use the homing beacon system for docking?"

"Yes."

Fascinating.

The bustle of movement from the main cabin drew his attention. Aurora and Lelindia had already started toward the gangway with their parents and Micah.

He turned to Jonarel. "Guess we're bringing up the rear."

Jonarel stood. "Lelindia believed it would be best if I was not the first person the Suulh saw."

Huh. It hadn't even occurred to him. He was so used to Jonarel's presence that he didn't think of him as different anymore. But his striking appearance would be a bit of a shock to the Suulh. "Good call."

He followed Jonarel off the shuttle, their pace keeping them back a bit from the rest of the group. A warm breeze blew through the trees, carrying the scent of fresh loam and rain. He breathed it in, catching floral notes mixed in as their path led them past broad-leaved plants with bright flowers. The presence of the Suulh became obvious as he studied the plants. They had the same vibrant lushness he'd observed from the edible plants the Suulh refugees had grown in the greenhouse they'd constructed on Burrow.

Too bad the rest of his unit were missing out on this. They'd stayed on the *Starhawke* with Kire, Kelly, Cardiff, and Admiral Payne's family. Justin had wanted to work on his Teeli translations with Kire, and Bella had asked Kelly to give her a lesson on the *Starhawke*'s navigation systems. Williams was monitoring Keenan in the med bay, and Gonzo was collaborating with Cardiff on their strategy for the mission into Teeli space.

"Sahzade! Nedale!" A woman's happy shout from up ahead pulled his attention in that direction. Marina and Libra broke away from the group, running to meet the three women racing down the path toward them — one blonde, one redhead, and one brunette. The laughter, group hug, and flaring of all five energy fields that followed created a joyful rainbow under the canopy of the tree branches.

"I can't believe you're here!" the blonde woman said, pulling back so she could take a good look at Libra.

He sensed, rather than saw, Jonarel melt into the greenery, temporarily concealing himself from view.

Cade did the same.

The woman turned as Lelindia and Aurora moved next to their mothers.

"Oh my goodness. Can this be little Lelindia? And Aurora!" The woman reached out to pull Aurora into an enthusiastic hug, her energy field expanding to include them both.

Aurora's startled laugh reached him as her pearlescent energy field blended with those of the other Suulh. "You must be Skye."

"I warned her you were a hugger," Libra said as Skye released Aurora and wrapped her arms around Lelindia.

"Of course I'm a hugger," Skye said, her gaze sweeping over Brendan and Micah. "If ever there was a time for hugs, this is it."

Gryphon seemed to agree with her. He had his arms wrapped around the brunette, who must be his sister, Amethyst. Cade had gotten the family rundowns the night before during his dinner with Aurora's parents and Micah.

Gryphon didn't seem inclined to let go of Amethyst anytime soon, so Skye opened her arms to Brendan next.

"It's good to see you again, Skye," Brendan said, his smile warm.

"It's good to see you and Sahzade together again," she replied, a slight hitch in her voice. "And Micah. How you've grown. You were only two the last time I saw you." She reached out to Aurora's brother.

Micah allowed Skye to pull him into a hug. "You knew me as a kid?"

"Briefly. Wolf and I came to Earth after Aurora was born. Oracle was very pregnant with Tyger at the time," she gestured to the woman with wavy pumpkin-orange hair, "so she and Leo couldn't make the trip and we couldn't stay long. Amethyst and River stayed with them, but I had to see you and Aurora."

Amethyst had extracted herself from Gryphon's bear hug and was clasping Lelindia's hands in hers, their murmured words too low to hear.

Lelindia's gaze swung around, a frown on her face. "Wait. Then why don't I remember you? I was six by then."

"And off on a camping trip with your scouting group and your dad," Marina said, slipping an arm around her daughter's shoulders. "At the time we didn't think it would be a big deal that they'd miss seeing you."

The words carried a wealth of meaning, the looks that passed among the women echoing the emotions Cade sensed.

Skye pointed in the direction she, Oracle, and Amethyst had come. "Let's all head up to the house. We have much to discuss."

"Hang on." Aurora held up a hand. "There are two more members of our group you need to meet first." She pivoted, staring right at him even though he was fairly certain she couldn't see him. Her internal GPS at work.

He stepped away from the shadow of the greenery, with Jonarel following.

Skye, Oracle, and Amethyst all sucked in breaths as they caught sight of Jonarel, but Cade didn't sense any fear, only surprise.

Aurora and Lelindia met them as they approached. Aurora laced her fingers through his while Lelindia slipped her arm around Jonarel's waist. "This is Cade Ellis," Aurora said, lifting their joined hands slightly, "and Jonarel Clarek."

The three women shot Libra and Marina questioning looks, their gazes darting back to him before lingering on Jonarel.

He could imagine why. Aurora and Lelindia had just made the nature of their relationships very clear. He wasn't the first human to join their midst — Brendan held that distinction — but the Suulh had probably never expected to meet a Kraed, let alone learn that their Nedale was involved with one.

Fifteen

Lelindia tightened her grip around Jonarel's waist as a slight quiver passed through him. A month ago she might not have known how nervous he was, but now his reaction shone like a spotlight.

He cared what the Suulh thought of him. He wanted their approval. And he feared he wouldn't get it.

Considering how his father had treated him, his concern was easy to understand. He was a Kraed without a clan, unheard of in her experience. She was his clan now — she and the crew. Rejection by her people would cut almost as deep as banishment from his homeworld.

She didn't expect that to happen. Her parents and Aurora's were Jonarel's biggest fans, had welcomed him with open arms. Her aunt and the rest of the Suulh would take their cues from them. Probably.

She licked her dry lips. Maybe Jonarel wasn't the only one with nerves. After all, she was the one who'd suggested he remain hidden when they first arrived. She might be just as afraid of their reaction as he was.

Skye stepped forward, facing Aurora and Cade, her arms open in the Suulh gesture of greeting. "It is an honor to welcome you Cade Ellis." Her tone had become more formal, but it came across as a sign of respect, not censure.

Lelindia's Aunt Amethyst stepped forward next, facing Lelindia and Jonarel. "It is an honor to welcome you Jonarel Clarek," her aunt repeated with the same respectful tone and gesture of welcome. Then she gave Lelindia a wink.

The tension melted away.

"Thank you." Jonarel inclined his head.

"It's a pleasure to be here," Cade added.

Skye's smile included all four of them. "Please, come." She motioned them forward again, leading the way to the house as Oracle and Aunt Amethyst fell into step beside Lelindia's mother and Libra.

Lelindia clasped Jonarel's hand in hers and followed behind Aurora and Cade. First hurdle crossed.

The structure that took shape through the dappled sunshine of the trees was familiar and foreign at the same time. The high domed roofline at the center was reminiscent of Stoneycroft, but the materials used to construct it, and the overall impression of the building reminded her more of the sonea laanaa she'd seen on Feylahn rather than her childhood home or the structures the Kraed had crafted on Azaana.

Her dad had mentioned that the Suulh had built this home themselves after he, her mom, and Libra had left for Earth. Climbing the front steps reinforced the feeling of an alternate reality, with a light wood door in a natural finish replacing the heavy, ornately carved dark wood of Stoneycroft's entrance.

Or what had been Stoneycroft's entrance — now a pile of charred beams and ash. She hadn't seen the front entrance after the fire, but her time in the inferno of the main room and gallery made it easy to envision the destruction to the rest of the house.

The interior of this home was different, too. Rather than two half-moons on each side, this structure had a third at the back of the house, opening past the staircase that led to the upper gallery. Maybe that was the typical design for a standard laanaa. Or maybe it was an adaptation for the three couples who'd made their home here. She hadn't seen any standard laanaa intact on Feylahn, so she had no way to compare. Only the sonea laanaa had stood strong against the Teeli's glass and metal overhaul of the city.

Three men her parents' age stood in a semi-circle in the central room along with six Suulh younger than her, three female and three male. One of the women stepped forward to join Skye — Aurora's cousin Luna, based on the family resemblance. The brown-haired, broad-shouldered man behind them had to be Skye's mate, Wolf and the muscular blond man who looked a little like Micah had to be Luna's brother, Sirius.

Her gaze moved to her aunt, who'd moved beside a man with dark brown hair and electric blue eyes — her Uncle River —

which made the two women beside him her cousins, Crystal and Brook. They looked almost like twins but born several years apart, with the same rich brown hair as their mother and the arresting eyes of their father.

Oracle stood with her redheaded mate Leo, and their two redheaded sons, Tyger and Kyt. Tyger's beard, ponytail and muscled physique was a contrast to his younger brother Kyt's short hair and slender profile.

Luna looked a little starstruck as she gazed at Libra. "I'm delighted to finally meet you, Sahzade."

Libra smiled as they clasped hands. "The honor is mine, Luna." Her gaze shifted over Luna's shoulder. "Hello, Wolf."

Wolf's welcoming smile made him look less imposing than his bodyguard physique suggested. "Hello, Libra." He came forward and gave her a hug before gesturing to Aurora, Brendan, and Micah. "I see you finally brought your family to see us."

"Yes. This visit is long overdue."

As the introductions continued, Luna, Crystal, and Brook made their way toward Lelindia and Aurora. "I have long wished to meet you both," Luna said. "My parents have told us much about you."

Aurora laughed, the sound carrying in the domed room. "Don't believe everything you hear."

Her laughter coaxed an answering smile from Luna, the subtle tension easing from her stance. "So you were not the youngest commander in the Galactic Fleet?"

Cade slipped his arm around Aurora's shoulders. "Oh yes, she certainly was. Don't let your cousin's nonchalance fool you. She's a force to be reckoned with."

Luna's smile widened. "That I believe. She's the Sahzade."

Crystal held her hands out to Lelindia. "I'm glad we finally meet, cousin."

She clasped them, the familiar flow of connection making her giddy. "Me, too. I'm afraid we don't know much about you, though. We didn't learn about your existence until a few days ago."

Crystal nodded. "We understood the Sahzade's desire for secrecy, for anonymity. We would do anything to protect the last of our race."

Soooo, she'd forgotten that the Gaian Suulh hadn't been clued in regarding the existence of the Suulh on Azaana and Feylahn. They still believed that the group gathered here were the only survivors.

This was going to be a very long day.

Sixteen

Aurora caught the brush of unease from Lelindia, which matched her own. She'd known the Gaian Suulh would be walking into this situation blind, but Crystal had just put a fine point on it.

"Actually, that's part of the reason we're here." She'd been debating how to broach the subject. She raised her voice so the rest of the group would hear her. "We have a lot of information to share with you. But it might take a while to get through it."

Skye picked up on the subtle cue. "If Gryphon and Brendan will help Amethyst and Crystal with refreshments, the rest of us can arrange the seating for our gathering."

"Sounds perfect."

The two groups took on their respective tasks like they'd been working together all their lives. The fact that everyone in the room except Aurora's dad, Cade, and Jonarel had Suulh blood flowing through their veins helped. Their instinctive connection made such group efforts easy.

Then again, her dad and Cade had the advantage of their empathic abilities, and Jonarel had been raised in a clan-focused society that fostered cooperation. No wonder they blended with the Suulh seamlessly.

After everyone had helped carry out platters of finger foods and mugs of tea, they gathered around the conversation circle with the Suulh facing Aurora's group.

Cade had settled on her left, with Micah on her right. Their solid presence steadied her as she took a deep breath, her gaze sweeping over the Suulh. She was about to blow up their world. She wanted to do it as gently as possible.

"Several months ago my crew and I were given a mission here on Gaia, to investigate the mysterious plant destruction that was devastating crops."

Luna's eyes widened. "You knew about that? You were here?"

"Yes. But we didn't know about you yet." She felt a tremor of sadness and regret from her mother. Reaching across Micah, she clasped her mom's hand and gave it a squeeze before continuing. "A ship run by Setarips had brought beings of unknown origin here. Those beings were the ones causing the destruction."

The Suulh exchanged alarmed looks. "The news stated it was Setarips," Wolf said. "That they used the destruction as a cover to steal food and supplies. They never mentioned other beings."

Which is exactly how Admiral Schreiber had spun the story.

"They also said the Setarip ship self-destructed while attempting to escape," Luna said. "Everyone onboard was killed."

"That was the official story. The truth is much more complicated. When Lelindia and I encountered the beings the first time, we had a very strong reaction to them. We were drawn to them, but we had no idea why."

She felt the shift in emotion from the Suulh, a rising tension. "They were misshapen. Unrecognizable. But when we infiltrated the ship, we discovered children. Children who looked human but weren't."

Another shift, more dramatic, as understanding rose like a wave.

"Who were they?" Skye's voice was breathy, her emotions indicating she already suspected the answer.

"They were Suulh."

The collective gasp sucked all the air out of the room. Bewilderment, shock, hope, fear, and shame pummeled her like twelve beating drums.

"How can that be?" Skye looked to Aurora's mom and Marina, a plea in her green eyes.

"We aren't the last Suulh," her mother responded, her voice remarkably even. "Aurora and Lelindia rescued three hundred Suulh from the Setarips during that mission. And Lelindia recently returned from infiltrating Feylahn. Our people are still there, but under Teeli control."

Skye's hand covered her mouth, her eyes wide. "No. All this time…" She shook her head, an unconscious denial. "They've been prisoners?"

"Yes. The Teeli didn't exterminate them as we'd thought. They enslaved them." Anger fueled her mother's words, as well as a healthy dose of self-recrimination. "It's my fault. I failed our people. I was too afraid to even consider the possibility of returning. Of confirming what had happened to them." She dropped her chin, the look she leveled at the group strong as iron. "But fear won't hold us back any longer."

Aurora wanted to cheer. She settled for squeezing her mom's hand again. On some level, she'd always known there was more to her mother than the frightened, overprotective parent she'd clashed with while she was growing up. Now, she understood the person her dad had fallen in love with, the one he'd loved every day since.

"Where are the Suulh now?" Luna asked Aurora. "The ones you rescued?"

"Safe on a planet in Kraed territory. Jonarel's clan helped us build a permanent home for them. It's a lot like this, actually." She swept a hand to encompass the room.

"And..." Luna's words grew hesitant. "And the ones on Feylahn? What's... how..." She struggled to formulate her question.

Lelindia dove in with both feet. "For the most part, they're unaware that they're captive. At least that was true for the younger and weaker ones we met. The Teeli have convinced them that they're in danger from the Setarips. In exchange for the Teeli's supposed protection, the Suulh produce food and goods that the Teeli take as payment. The setup allows the Teeli to live in the lap of luxury while the Suulh do all the work."

"And the ones who do know they're captive?"

Lelindia winced. "The older Suulh are treated as servants or slaves, abused and neglected. Which is a picnic compared to what they do to the stronger Suulh, the ones with abilities like ours."

Skye made the leap, her gaze snapping to Aurora's. "The misshapen beings you described. That's what happened to the Suulh, isn't it?"

"Yes." The pain of their Necri existence still haunted her. "The Teeli have figured out a way to reverse the effect of our energy fields to destroy rather than create. That's how they wiped out the crops. But in doing so, the Suulh hurt themselves, twisting and crippling their bodies."

Sympathy pain flowed from the Suulh.

"How do the Setarips fit in?" Skye asked, her voice rough.

"They're working with the Teeli, or for them. We're not sure of the exact arrangement. But the Setarips used the children as leverage, and also to help heal the cellular damage to the parents so they could continue the attack."

Chairs creaked as the Suulh unconsciously drew closer together, avoiding eye contact as they processed the news.

Might as well hit them with the last arrow. "A few nights ago, Stoneycroft was attacked by a group of Ecilam Setarips sent by the Teeli."

Another collective gasp, and a flare of panic as all focus went to her mother and Marina.

"They found you?" Skye asked in a harsh whisper. "Is that why you're here? To hide from them?"

Her mother's smile was grim. "Actually, no. We're not the ones hiding. But that confrontation is the reason I have my family back. And why I know my mother is still alive."

Skye's face went slack. "Sooree lives?"

"If you can call it living. She's a Necri." At Skye's blank look, Aurora's mother waved a hand. "The term Aurora and Lelindia gave to Suulh who've been forced to destroy. I saw my mother's body, but her mind was locked away. She didn't recognize me. Or Marina."

A shard of pain lanced out from Marina and Aurora's mom.

Her mom's blue-grey eyes darkened. "She attacked them, nearly killed Gryphon. But when she tried to attack me, it didn't work. She ended up in some kind of stasis, unresponsive to the Setarips' commands. She wasn't conscious of her surroundings, either."

"And you defeated them?" Wolf asked, his emotions, particularly a sense of protectiveness, running strong and deep.

"Yes. But it was Aurora, Micah, Lelindia, and Jonarel who rescued us from the fire."

"Fire?" Oracle spoke up for the first time. "What fire?"

"They burned Stoneycroft to the ground."

Empathy wafted out from the Suulh like a summer breeze.

"Oh, Sahzade." Skye's green eyes glistened.

But Aurora's mom smiled and shook her head. "It's just a building." Her gaze swept over the group, coming to rest on Aurora's dad. "I have everything that matters to me right here."

Her dad wrapped his arm around her mom's shoulders, pulling her close. "So do I."

A flicker of hope and joy overlaid the anguish and pain coming from the Suulh.

"We bless the day our Sahzade met you, Brendan," Wolf said, his arm circling Skye's shoulders.

Skye curled into him, giving and receiving the comfort they offered each other.

The gesture reminded Aurora of a fact her dad had mentioned to her last night at dinner. Until the day her dad crash landed his plane and woke up in her mother's bedroom, her mom had been set to mate with Wolf. But it hadn't been a love match, more of a practical choice to ensure the continuation of the race and the power of the Sahzade. Her dad's arrival had freed Wolf to mate with Skye instead, which had worked out better for everyone.

Oracle leaned forward, her red curls brushing her knees as she pinned Aurora's mother with a frank look. "If you didn't come to us because of the attack, what motivated you to leave Earth?" The *what scared you more than a Teeli-ordered Setarip attack* was implied.

"Helping a family escape the machinations of the leader of the Teeli forces."

Skye sat up straighter. "You brought some of the Suulh here?" She glanced toward the front door as though she expected them to walk through it.

"No. A Human family. A Fleet Admiral, her son and his wife, and their two children."

The Suulh exchanged confused looks. "Why would a Human family need protection from the Teeli?" Wolf asked.

Aurora fielded that one. "Because the person who's leading the Teeli tried to force the Admiral to betray me and my crew. When she failed to deliver us as expected, the Sovereign — that's the Teeli leader — put the Admiral's grandson in the ICU and promised to kill him if the Admiral didn't toe the line."

The Suulh didn't seem nearly as shocked by her description as she'd expected.

"That's how the Teeli operate," Wolf muttered. "It's why we assumed our people had been slaughtered after our escape. The Teeli had made it clear they would kill every last Suulh if the Sahzade and Nedale failed to obey them. As the years passed with no word from Sooree or Breaa," his gaze slid to Aurora's mom and Marina, "we believed they'd died trying to save our people."

"And now the Teeli are using the Humans to get to Aurora and Lelindia." Skye pursed her lips, her gaze on Aurora. "They have never stopped hunting you. How did you figure out the Admiral was being coerced?"

"My empathic senses. Her words and actions didn't match up with her emotions. But I didn't anticipate Reanne would go after her family."

"Reanne?"

"That's the Sovereign's real name. We were roommates at the Academy."

That bomb created a shockwave.

"Roommates?" several voices echoed at once.

"Yep. We used to be friends."

Skye's mouth opened, closed, then opened again. "You had a Teeli roommate at the Academy?"

"No, Reanne's human. Well, actually, she's probably half-human and half-Teeli."

Skye blinked, like she was hearing the words but they weren't making sense. "Half-Teeli?"

"Yes. Her mother is human, but we believe her father is a Teeli, most likely a powerful military leader or part of the royal family."

"Is that biologically possible?" Oracle asked. "And if so, why would a Teeli want to bear a child with a Human? They view themselves as superior to all other beings. They hid that fact when they came to Feylahn because it suited their purposes to flatter us, but I learned the truth after I went through the logs and comm records on the ship we stole. Only the Sahzade and Nedale held any standing in their eyes."

"We don't know the answer yet." But it reminded Aurora of her other task. "I'm hoping you'll share everything you know about the Teeli with my crew, especially our language specialists. They were both taught a version of Teeli that was apparently gibberish. They've been working to relearn the real language based on recordings Kire made while the crew was on Feylahn, but your input would be invaluable."

"Of course." Oracle's mouth tightened, the light of battle burning behind her eyes. "I would do anything to help our people."

Seventeen

"What about this Human family you rescued?" Skye asked. "How can we help them?"

Lelindia had been waiting for this question. Aurora had asked her to field it when it came, since she'd spent the most time with the Admiral's family. "They need a place to stay." She drew a slow breath before making the big ask. "We were hoping they could stay with you."

Skye's brows rose slightly, but she didn't hesitate. "Of course. We have plenty of rooms." Then her mouth turned down. "But no extra beds. We didn't anticipate..." She gestured to Libra.

"I can help with that," Brendan chimed in. "Whatever we need to pick up in town, I can be in charge of fetching."

"I'll go with you," Micah offered.

"I'll go, too." Wolf flexed his muscles and grinned at Brendan.

Skye rolled her eyes, her focus returning to Lelindia. "What about the boy who was in the ICU? You have healed his injuries?"

"Yes, but his family doesn't know that — about us, about the Suulh. They think I used Kraed technology. We'll need you to maintain that belief while they're here."

"Not a problem," Wolf responded. "We've had lots of practice hiding our abilities from Humans."

"Just remember you'll be dealing with a Fleet Admiral and Commander," Aurora warned. "They're going to be a lot more observant than anyone you've encountered on Gaia."

The Suulh nodded in understanding.

"Keenan's still weak and shows physical signs of the trauma," Lelindia continued. "I had to minimize the external healing to avoid suspicion. In addition to the head injury, Reanne's minions pumped a toxin into his bloodstream that suppressed his normal immune response."

A shadow passed over Skye's face. "How old is he?"

"Sixteen. He's a great kid — a runner, and an artist. He did some wonderful drawings of the greenhouse this morning."

Skye stared at her in confusion. "The greenhouse?"

"On the *Starhawke*, Aurora's ship. Jonarel included a greenhouse in the design."

The Suulh's focus split between Aurora and Jonarel.

Jonarel's thigh brushed Lelindia's as he shifted closer.

"You have your own ship?" Luna asked Aurora.

"Uh-huh. She was a gift from Jonarel. She's offshore, concealed by her hull camouflage."

The Suulh's curious gazes darted back to Jonarel. She could imagine the questions they wanted to ask. But the answers were complicated.

"Would anyone like to see her?" Aurora asked, directing focus back to her, no doubt sensing Jonarel's discomfort.

"I would," Crystal said immediately, a speculative look on her face as she gazed at Lelindia and Jonarel.

"Me, too," Kyt said.

"So would I," Skye and Tyger said at the same time.

The rest of the Suulh murmured their agreement.

Aurora grinned. "Great. But unless Jonarel leaves the rest of us here, we'll have to take you in shifts. The shuttle only has twelve passenger seats."

Jonarel cleared his throat. All attention swung in his direction. "The shuttle can adapt to accommodate more."

Really?

"Really?" Aurora voiced Lelindia's silent question, her eyes narrowing. "How many more?"

Jonarel perched on the edge of his seat like it was growing hot, his gaze moving to Cade, of all people. "It is flexible."

Cade's grin confirmed he had inside information the rest of them didn't.

Aurora sighed with what sounded like a mixture of amusement and resignation. "Then I guess you could all come at once."

Skye shook her head. "You said you need Oracle's help. She can go with the kids. The rest of us will get rooms ready for our guests." She turned to Lelindia. "Do they need clothing?"

"No, they were able to pack bags before we broke Keenan out of the hospital. But they need shelter and food. We don't know for how long." *Please let it be a short time.* She wanted to believe Aurora's plan to capture Reanne with the help of the Yruf would work. Then they'd be back here to take Admiral Payne's family home.

"They will be welcome for as long as they need," Skye replied. "We know how it feels to be hunted."

So did Lelindia, although her experiences paled compared to what this group had gone through to escape the Teeli. She couldn't imagine the sacrifices they'd made to keep her mom and Libra out of the Teeli's grasp.

Aurora stood, everyone else rising with her. "Then we'll head back to the ship." She turned to Brendan. "You'll contact me as soon as everything's ready for us to bring Admiral Payne's family here?"

He tapped the comband on his arm, an even fancier version than the ones the crew used. One of many perks of being the owner of Far Horizons Aerospace. "As long as the stores have what we need, it shouldn't take long."

The group broke up, Aurora and Cade leading the way to the shuttle as Lelindia and Jonarel brought up the rear.

"The shuttle's seating is flexible?" Lelindia murmured to Jonarel as they entered the vibrant green foliage surrounding the house.

His hand closed around hers as his strides shortened. "All Kraed vessels are flexible."

The way he said *flexible* momentarily flipped her mind onto a very different track. She dragged it back. "And you didn't mention this feature to Aurora and me before because...?"

"It had not become relevant."

That was Kraed logic for you. "Are there any other not-yet-relevant items we should know about?" She said it with a teasing tone, but he stiffened ever so slightly. "Jonarel?"

He didn't look at her, his focus on the group walking ahead of them. "A Kraed vessel is always adapting. It is our way."

That was quite a non-answer. "There's something you're not telling me."

"Yes."

His honesty about not being completely honest confused the heck out of her. "And you aren't going to tell me?"

He glanced at her then, hesitation in his golden eyes. "It is not... ready."

"But it's a good thing?"

"Yes. It will be a... gift."

A gift? She was totally intrigued and befuddled by his answers. But she also trusted him completely. If this mysterious thing wasn't ready, then she'd just have to wait until it was.

Kyt, Oracle's younger son, glanced back at them and slowed his steps, walking along the edge of the path closest to Jonarel. "I never expected to meet a Kraed on Gaia."

Jonarel inclined his head. "We do not often visit Human settlements."

"So I gathered. There isn't a lot about your race in the news archives, or at least not much about your culture. I was lucky to find a Kraed language book in the town's library, which allowed me to learn the basics."

Jonarel cocked his head. "You speak my language?" he asked in Kraed.

"A little," Kyt replied in the same language.

Lelindia knew enough Kraed phrases to follow the exchange, although Kyt's accent sounded nothing like Jonarel's. She doubted the language book he'd found had included any recordings of Kraed speech.

Jonarel studied Kyt with interest, switching back to Galish. "Why did you choose to learn the language of a race you never expected to meet?"

"I never expected to meet a Kraed on *Gaia*." Kyt's gaze darted to his mom, who was walking a few meters ahead of them with his brother Tyger. He lowered his voice. "But I never intended to stay on Gaia forever, either. I've wanted to visit Earth since I was a kid. Drakar, too, if I ever had the chance."

Jonarel's hand squeezed hers as Kyt's words pushed on a pressure point.

"Is there a reason the Kraed don't tend to visit Human settlements?"

Jonarel hesitated before replying. "Most of my people choose to remain on our home planet. Those who do travel to other systems prefer to explore uncharted areas."

"Then how did you end up on a ship with our Sahzade and Nedale?"

"After I gifted the ship to Aurora, I chose to remain as the engineer."

Kyt's grey-green eyes widened. "Are there more Kraed onboard?"

Jonarel flinched at the frank question. "No. I am the only one."

Kyt finally caught on to Jonarel's discomfort, shooting Lelindia a confused look. Typically, Suulh were open and honest to a fault. The poor guy had no idea why his questions would be causing a problem.

She wouldn't reveal Jonarel's pain, but she could give Kyt some background. "Jonarel attended the Academy with us after his father took a teaching position there, and we served together on the *Excelsior* for five years before he left the Fleet to build the *Starhawke*."

"You were in the Fleet?"

Jonarel nodded.

"Why wouldn't you serve on a Kraed ship instead?"

His shoulders drew back in a move she'd seen thousands of times over the years, revealing the warrior keeping watch below the surface. "I was protecting Aurora and Lelindia."

The confusion cleared from Kyt's face. "You knew who they were."

"Yes."

"Is that why you built the ship and gave it to Sahzade? To protect them?"

Kyt was fitting the pieces together with a deft touch.

Jonarel hesitated. "Partly." His gaze met hers, his golden eyes like liquid honey. "Mostly it was a labor of love."

Their first night together, he'd admitted that he'd created the ship for Aurora, but while he'd worked on the greenhouse, he'd thought only of her, of what would bring her joy.

And then he'd found a million new ways to do just that.

Eighteen

The Suulh peppered Cade and Aurora with questions during the walk to the shuttle, showing the same innate curiosity and quick minds as the Suulh Cade had shepherded to Burrow, and then Azaana. Their excited chatter reminding him of Raaveen, Paaw, and Sparw while they'd been working on the greenhouse project.

Aurora's frequent laughter and the flow of her emotions made him smile. She was enjoying the interaction immensely. And why wouldn't she? These were her people, and Luna and Sirius were blood relatives. Her core instinct was to connect with them. This gave her the perfect opportunity.

Jonarel ushered him into the pilot's seat for the flight to the ship, with Luna in the co-pilot's seat and Crystal crouched behind her chair. Jonarel remained in the main cabin with Lelindia, Aurora, and the other five Suulh. The steady buzz of conversation made it clear the Q&A session was continuing.

Cade answered Luna and Crystal's numerous questions pertaining to flying as he guided the shuttle to the camouflaged *Starhawke*. Their gasps of shocked awe when the shuttle bay opening appeared apparently out of thin air, hovering over the rolling waves, preceded a new barrage of queries.

After they landed, Lelindia volunteered to take Oracle and Kyt to meet with Kire and Justin. Cade suspected she was also planning to check in on Keenan. Williams had the same inability to leave his charges for long.

Cade and Jonarel stayed with Aurora as she started the tour of the ship. The questions Luna and Crystal fired at Jonarel made it clear they had a background in engineering. That explained their fascination with the shuttle.

"That's what our moms were studying before the Teeli came to Feylahn," Luna explained. "My mom was apprenticing to be an architectural engineer, and Amethyst was focused on mechanical engineering. But after the Teeli arrived with their starships, they both focused on aerospace. That's what enabled them to keep the Teeli ship they stole functional until they made contact with their first Humans and settled here."

Jonarel paused, turning to face her. "The Teeli taught them aerospace engineering?"

"Uh-huh. Apparently they encouraged our people to gain practical skills." Luna sighed. "At first our parents believed the Teeli were helping them to advance their society, to become part of the galactic community. In reality, from what you told us about the current situation on the homeworld, my guess is the Teeli wanted a trained slave work force."

She said it calmly, but Cade sensed the ache of sadness. "So once your parents caught on to the deception, that's when the threats started?"

Luna nodded. "We've heard stories since we were kids. Our parents wanted us to know what we were up against. And why they'd sacrificed so much to keep the Sahzade and Nedale safe." She glanced at Aurora. "And now you're here."

Aurora's steady gaze held a galaxy's worth of hope and determination. "And you know we're not alone. This is only the beginning."

The collective uptick in positive emotion from the Suulh surrounded him like a fluffy cloud. He'd never met anyone who could inspire confidence the way Aurora did.

She guided them in the direction of the lift, her gaze moving to Crystal. "What about your dad? What did he study?"

"Planetary science," Crystal said. "He and Brook can talk about it for hours."

He caught a flutter of amusement from Brook in reaction to her older sister's lack of enthusiasm for the topic. "And good thing, too. He's the one who figured out how to obtain water during their trip."

"And Wolf and Leo trained themselves in the defensive arts, correct?" Aurora asked Luna.

"That's right, although building things is their passion." Luna punched Tyger lightly on the shoulder as they entered the lift. "Tyger and Sirius take after them, hence the muscles."

"Defensive arts, huh?" Cade took a second look at Tyger and Sirius as the lift doors closed. He'd already noted their toned muscle definition but had attributed it to physical labor rather than fight training. He'd never met a combat-trained Suulh before. "Any particular discipline?" he asked Tyger.

"We started with techniques our dads taught us from the Teeli combat manuals they found onboard the starship they stole. My mom translated the text for our dad and Wolf," Tyger replied. "But we've expanded into any discipline we can find instruction for."

And if Tyger and Sirius were as adept at learning new skills as the rest of the Suulh he'd met, they were probably pretty good, especially Tyger, who was close to Cade's age. "We have a very talented hand-to-hand fighter on our crew, Celia Cardiff. If you ever get the chance to spar with her, take it. You'll learn a lot."

Aurora nudged him with her shoulder as they exited the lift and entered the cargo bay. "Or you could spar with Cade. He's no slouch in that department, either. I watched the two of them go at it once and it was… exhilarating."

And led to a night of passion that had reignited the smoldering embers of their former relationship, creating a blaze that continued to burn like a star.

"I was wondering if you were a fighter." Tyger's gaze flicked to Aurora. "It would be fitting."

"He's also an empath who can see our energy fields," Aurora added. "Just like my father."

Tyger's grey-green eyes widened, his emotions indicating pleased surprise. "You are?"

"That's right." He was getting more and more comfortable accepting it as normal.

"That's good. Very good." Tyger glanced at Luna, who was walking by his side.

Her reaction mirrored Tyger's, a subtle but clear release of tension and low-grade anxiety melting away, allowing a burst of joy and eagerness to push through.

Strange reaction.

And then it hit him. Tyger was Aurora's age. And a full-blooded Suulh.

As they stepped into the training center, he pulled Tyger aside, lowering his voice as Aurora and Jonarel led the rest of the group to the hydrotank. "I may be off base here, but were you worried that Libra and Marina were here to match you up with Aurora or Lelindia?"

Tyger squared his shoulders. "I've always known it was likely, especially with the Nedale nearing the end of her fertile cycle."

That was news to him. Lelindia was mid-thirties, not fifty. Maybe the rules were different for Suulh women.

"Nedale could choose Sirius, but Sahzade only had my brother and me to choose from." He frowned. "Although I guess that isn't true now that we know about Feylahn. And the Suulh she rescued."

"Well, it won't matter." A silent roar of masculine pride vibrated through his chest. "She's chosen me."

Tyger eyed him curiously. "You're already mated?"

"Not yet. But we will be, as soon as she's ready."

Where had that pronouncement come from? Sure, he'd been thinking about it, especially now that Jonarel was no longer standing in his way, but it had been a distant thing, not imminent the moment Aurora said yes.

A quick internal check confirmed it was the truth. He wanted to be mated to Aurora more than he wanted air.

Tyger gave him a knowing smile. "I understand what you're feeling. I feel it, too, for Luna. But I haven't dared to dream it would happen, not as long as the Sahzade and Nedale were unmated." He gazed at the group, who were still gathered on the opposite side of the room. "What about Nedale? Has she chosen Jonarel for her mate?"

"Are you kidding? They haven't had a ceremony or anything, but you couldn't pry those two apart with a crowbar."

Tyger's smile grew. "I'm happy for them. And for myself. Mating with a relative stranger never held any appeal." As soon as the words left his mouth, a spike of fear shot from him. "Not that I wouldn't be honored to mate with the Sahzade or Ned—"

Cade held up a hand. "You don't have to explain. I know those two women very well, and they'd hate being mated to someone they weren't in love with." He had that on good authority.

"I suspected that when I saw the four of you together." Tyger watched Luna as the group moved back in their direction, his emotions rising in a joyful spiral. "Now that I know I'm free to follow my heart, I will ask Luna to mate with me as soon as *she's* ready."

Cade clapped his hand lightly on Tyger's shoulder, a grin spreading across his face. "Based on the look she's giving you right now, I predict it'll be a short wait."

Nineteen

"You have a really light touch." Keenan met Lelindia's gaze as she peeled back the bandage on the side of his face.

"Thank you." It helped that she'd blocked the pain receptors associated with the area, although she always tried to be gentle with her patients.

Keenan's family had left a few moments earlier to gather their belongings in preparation for departure. She was taking the opportunity to give Keenan one final healing session while removing the bandage. She wasn't using the full power of her energy field, but it didn't take much to repair the underlying damage and seal the lacerations so Keenan wouldn't need the bandage anymore.

The Kraed tool in her hand was designed to repair skin damage, but it was the physical connection of her fingers on Keenan's skin that made the real healing possible. "Hold still," she cautioned to foster the illusion.

"I will." He focused on the med bay doors, his breathing slow and even.

She turned on the device and swept it back and forth across the damaged tissue while her energy did the work from the inside out. Within moments the skin showed significant improvement. "All done." She set the tool on the side table and snagged a hand mirror. "Ready to take a look?"

Keenan's jaw tightened, but he nodded. "Better to know."

She smiled as she handed him the mirror. "I think you'll be pleasantly surprised."

He held it up, his eyes widening as he caught sight of his reflection. "Hey, that's not bad at all." He turned his head to the side, studying the faint reddish edge of the cuts that now blended in with the warm brown of his skin. "I was expecting horror show. This looks like I smacked my head on the edge of a door."

"The benefits of powerful healing modalities."

He lowered the mirror, his gaze holding hers. "And an amazing doctor. From what my gram told me, I was in big trouble until you came along. Thank you, Dr. Forrest. For everything."

She smiled. "It's been my pleasure. You're the most upbeat patient I've ever had."

He grinned. "I try." He picked up the sketchpad lying beside him on the bedsheet. "Want to see my latest sketch?"

"Absolutely!" She'd loved everything he'd drawn so far. It was easy to imagine his work ending up in a famous gallery one day — but only after she and Aurora dealt with the threat from Reanne. Until then, he'd be living in obscurity on Gaia.

"What do you think?" he held up the sketch.

A chuckle bubbled out of her throat as a beefy doctor with a shaved head stared back at her. "Oh my goodness. You captured him perfectly. Has he seen it?" Tam would be honored that Keenan had chosen him as his latest subject.

"Not yet. I wanted to make sure I got his eyes right."

"You certainly did." The twinkle in those eyes made it look like Williams was about to step off the page.

"I won't have time to colorize it, but I wanted to give it to him as a thank you."

"He'll love it."

Keenan pulled the sketch out of his book before flipping the cover closed. "I'm working on one for you, too, but it's not ready yet." His brow furrowed. "Will you be leaving as soon as you drop us off?"

"I doubt it." Aurora hadn't said anything specific, but she couldn't imagine missing the opportunity to spend at least one evening with the Suulh. Her parents and Libra would certainly be in favor of it, and she wanted a chance to talk to her aunt, uncle, and cousins. "My guess is we won't take off until tomorrow morning at the earliest."

His grin returned. "Good. That'll give me time to get it right. I want to—" His eyes rounded as he caught sight of something over her shoulder.

She turned.

Aurora, Cade, and Jonarel had entered through the door leading from the greenhouse, the group of Suulh right behind them. Keenan's focus was locked on Jonarel.

She rested a hand on his shoulder as they watched the group approach. "That's Jonarel Clarek, our engineer. He's a Kraed." Stating the obvious there, but Jonarel's appearance had stunned Keenan into wide-eyed shock.

Jonarel halted as the rest of the group continued forward. No doubt he'd heard her whispered comment and caught Keenan's reaction.

She glanced at Keenan. "Would you like to meet him?"

Her question broke the spell. He nodded, his gaze bouncing between her and Jonarel like they were the only two people in the room despite the large contingent who'd come to a stop between them.

Lelindia motioned Jonarel forward. "Keenan would like to meet you, Jonarel."

The Suulh parted to allow him through. He moved to her side. "Hello, Keenan."

"Hi." Keenan studied him with rapt fascination. "I've never met a Kraed before."

"Most Humans have not."

"Are you the reason this ship has all the cool Kraed technology?"

Jonarel's mouth twitched in a small smile. "Yes. I designed her."

"Really?"

"Yes."

"Wow." His focus slowly moved to Lelindia. She caught the exact moment he realized how *close* Jonarel was standing to her. And that Jonarel's hand had come to rest on the small of her back. He grinned. "That's awesome."

She recognized the sparkle in his eyes and the unconscious movement of his fingers on his sketch pad. He was visualizing a sketch idea.

She turned to the group waiting patiently a respectful distance from the med platform. "How's the tour going?"

Luna practically glowed with excitement as she hurried forward. "The greenhouse is amazing. What a gift to have it with you as you travel the stars." She turned to Jonarel. "Your race's engineering talents are extraordinary."

Jonarel accepted the compliment with a slight nod.

Lelindia doubted the Suulh's tour had included a meet and greet with the true engineering marvel on the ship — Star. To maintain the secrecy of the Nirunoc's existence, Star had been silent and invisible since they'd left Earth. Revealing her presence to the Suulh would have saddled them with one more secret they had to keep from Admiral Payne's family.

Luna's gaze moved to Keenan. "I understand you're going to be staying with us. I'm Luna."

Keenan laid his sketch pad on his lap and reached out a hand. "It's nice to meet you, Luna. Thank you for taking my family in."

Luna clasped his hand in hers. "We're always happy to help those in need."

Keenan grimaced. "Well, I'm not used to being needy. Dr. Forrest says I'll be back up to my usual strength within a week. At that point I can make myself useful. I'm good with tools, or I can draw anything you want — portraits, landscapes, conceptual designs, you name it."

Crystal moved beside Luna. "You'll get along great with my dad then. He's an artist, too. And Skye likes to sketch. I'm Crystal, by the way, and that's my sister Brook."

"And this is Tyger," Luna said as the tall redhead stepped to Luna's other side, "and my brother Sirius."

Keenan's white teeth flashed. "Pleased to meet you all."

As Cade stepped forward to introduce himself to Keenan, Lelindia slipped around Jonarel and motioned Aurora aside.

"That's a promising beginning," Aurora murmured as the Suulh started asking Keenan questions about his family and their life on Earth.

"Exactly what I'd hoped for."

"Me, too. By the way, I learned a bit more from the Suulh during the tour. Apparently Wolf and Leo trained Tyger and Sirius in defensive arts. We'll want to have a sit-down with them tonight to let them know what tactics we've encountered in the past from the Teeli, Setarips, and Reanne, in case Reanne finds a way to track Admiral Payne's family here."

Lelindia frowned. "Do you think that's possible?"

"Not really, but I'm through underestimating her."

Yes, they'd all been guilty of that.

Aurora watched the increasingly jubilant group gathered around Keenan. "I'm glad this time she underestimated us."

"It's nice to have a solid win for a change." When it came to Reanne, they'd usually had losses or draws. "And after the way your mom handled the Setarips, Reanne might think twice about sending them to do her dirty work."

"Although my grandmother almost killed your parents. And Kreestol tried to kill me." Aurora's lips thinned, her green eyes flattening to grey. "This has to end. Soon."

"I know." But right now they had other issues to consider. "Keenan asked when we were leaving. Have you given it any thought?"

"I have. We'll definitely stay tonight. I got an update from my dad. Typical Suulh – they've invited everyone to a feast this evening. He also mentioned our moms will be staying at the house overnight rather than returning to the ship. When Luna heard that, she invited you and me to spend the night, too, if we wanted."

Lelindia laughed. "You mean like a slumber party?"

"I guess so. We didn't get into any specifics. I did ask if we could invite Celia, since she's the equivalent of our aailee. Luna and Crystal agreed that was a great idea."

"Then let's do it." She hadn't been to a slumber party since she was eight, back when she was part of a scouting group. That had ended when the Teeli had arrived on Earth. Micah had left with Brendan, and leaving Aurora alone for the night had been unthinkable. "You'll finally get to see what a sleepover is all about."

"I'm guessing it will be more fun than the Academy team building exercise I did during leadership training. By the time we'd hiked to the remote cabin, completed all the team challenges, and fixed dinner over an open fire, we just crashed on the floor until dawn."

"I remember you telling me about that. Sounded brutal."

"It was, but didn't you do something similar during your med training? Setting up an emergency unit in a remote area?"

She made a face. "Yeah. I wouldn't use the terms *slumber* or *party* to describe that experience. And I'm guessing Celia's never attended a slumber party, either."

"That's a given." A hint of mischief lit Aurora's eyes. "It'll be a new adventure for all of us."

Twenty

By early afternoon the Suulh were ready to head back and help with preparations to welcome their new houseguests. Aurora stayed behind on the *Starhawke*, taking bridge duty with Cade. Boats crossed the waters offshore as the sun dipped toward the horizon, keeping Cade busy at the helm.

Oracle and Kyt were still working with Kire and Justin on the translations so Jonarel and Lelindia had flown the rest of the Suulh back home, picking up Skye, Wolf, Leo, River and Amethyst for the return trip. They'd given them a tour of the ship, ending in the med bay to gather Keenan and his family before shuttling the entire contingent to the mainland.

The most recent message Aurora had received from Micah indicated meal preparations for the welcome dinner were well underway.

Aurora tapped her fingers on the arms of the captain's chair. "I know my dad and Gryphon volunteered to take over bridge duty when they bring the shuttle back for us, but I hate for them to miss the dinner. Or for anyone to miss it, for that matter." Unfortunately, they couldn't leave the *Starhawke* without a bridge crew. Star's limited navigation abilities were absolutely no help in this situation.

Even if Star could manage it, they'd have a hard time explaining to Admiral Payne how the entire crew could leave the ship while it was camouflaged without it posing a hazard to boat traffic. Explaining Star's presence wasn't an option.

Cade glanced at her. "Should we consider taking the *Starhawke* into geosynchronous orbit? Star could maintain the ship's position while everyone's at dinner. There wouldn't be any cross traffic on the night side since Gaia only allows launches and landings on the day side."

"Do you think the Admiral would accept that as a plausible explanation for–"

"Plausible explanation for what?" Bronwyn Kelly asked as she exited the lift, Bella right behind her.

Cade pivoted toward her. "Taking the ship into orbit so everyone can participate in the dinner."

"Or," Kelly flicked a look at Bella, "I have a different suggestion."

"Oh?"

"How about letting me and Drew take bridge duty for the evening."

Cade looked to Aurora.

"It's not your turn in the rotation," she pointed out. "And you'll miss the dinner."

"We know," Bella answered, "but this evening is about your family and Dr. Forrest's. Your dad and Gryphon should be there."

"Wouldn't you like a chance to go ashore?"

Bella shook her head. "Not really. I'd rather take the opportunity to practice what Kelly taught me this morning."

"And I'd always rather be on the ship," Kelly added.

Aurora sent Cade a questioning look.

He spread his hands. "Fine with me."

"Okay. Far be it from me to order you off the ship. I'll let my dad know you'll be staying." She sent a short message.

He responded right away. *Tell Bronwyn and Bella thank you. I'll head to the shuttle now to pick you up.*

"My dad says thank you."

"It's our pleasure."

As Cade stood and stretched, Kelly settled behind the navigation console with a contented sigh. Bella rested her hip against the side of the chair.

Aurora smiled. Kelly might be the youngest and newest member of the crew, but she'd claimed ownership of her section of the bridge. Her offer to stay behind was generous, but it also might be a subtle reaffirmation of her position, letting Aurora know she wasn't about to acquiesce her role to Cade, Aurora's dad, or Gryphon, except on a temporary basis.

Tapping the console on the captain's chair, Aurora opened a shipwide channel. "Everyone who's going ashore, meet in the bay in ten minutes."

Fifteen minutes later she was settled into her seat in the shuttle's main cabin beside Celia, Gonzo, and Williams, with Kire, Justin, Oracle, and Kyt behind them and Cade and her dad up in the cockpit.

Aurora twisted in her seat to face Kire as the shuttle lifted off. "So, what's the verdict on the translations?"

He rested his forearms on the back of Gonzo's chair. "Well, the good news is we now have a solid translation program for the Teeli language."

"And the bad news?"

"The recordings didn't provide any information we can use."

"Nothing?"

Justin shook his head. "Apparently the Teeli chain of command is so paranoid they don't share any details on comms that aren't absolutely necessary. I'd suspected that from the work I'd already done, but Oracle confirmed it."

"It's something I learned while we were on Feylahn." Oracle scrunched up her nose like she'd smelled rotting vegetables. "At first I thought the Teeli were purposely speaking in vague terms when I was around, that maybe they'd figured out I was learning their language. But then Amethyst engineered a couple recording devices that we planted in out of the way places. The conversations we captured were just as uninformed as what I'd overheard myself."

"So we'd need to tap into a conversation between two upper echelon leaders to learn anything valuable," Kire added.

"Like when we overheard Reanne talking to Bare'Kold," Justin said. "And figured out what she had planned for Libra and Marina. We just weren't able to act on it quickly enough."

"And that's the other sticking point," Kire said. "Any plan that might have been in place when we made these recordings has likely changed as a result of Reanne's failure to capture you or your mom. Now she's lost Admiral Payne as her pawn, too. Next time she attacks, she's going to be swinging for the fences."

"We're in a whole new ballgame," Gonzo agreed.

"We certainly are," Aurora murmured. And losing was not an option.

Her dad pivoted from the co-pilot's chair to face them. "I understand all the gals are staying the night at the house after the dinner." He clapped Cade on the back. "That leaves us fellas sitting on our hands."

Cade sighed dramatically, glancing back at her. "I know. I'm feeling very unwanted." He winked, then turned to her dad. "Hey, Brendan. Do you play cards?"

"What do you think?"

"I think maybe the gentlemen should have a late-night poker game on the *Starhawke* while the ladies enjoy their slumber party."

"Great idea! You guys in?"

An enthusiastic yes from her male seatmates answered his question.

Her dad grinned, hooking a thumb at Cade, his gaze shifting to Aurora. "I knew I liked this guy."

She chuckled. "Me, too."

After Cade landed the shuttle, they made the now familiar trek through the overgrowth until the house appeared before them, the setting sun burnishing the dome in shades of yellow-gold and the shadows taking on a purplish cast. She almost expected to see miniature pixie lights dancing among the leaves of the trees as they swayed in the evening air.

The resonant tones of male laughter and the clatter of dishes greeted them as they stepped through the front door into the main room. She spied Gryphon in the center of the kitchen, wielding a wooden spoon like he was directing an orchestra as those around him picked up platters of food and carried them to the oversized dining table.

Micah was right next to him, shooting Gryphon amused looks while ladling a chunky stew into a large tureen. His gaze snapped to her, but his broad grin slowly faded as he spied Celia next to her.

A problem for another day.

The room had been set up buffet-style, with the seating from this morning expanded to almost twice the size. Several of the chairs looked new, no doubt compliments of her dad's shopping trip with Micah and Wolf. Having money at your fingertips certainly had its advantages.

Admiral Payne and her son moved through the scene like they'd been born to it — a benefit of their years with the Fleet — but Keenan's mother and sister looked a lot more uncertain of their surroundings. They hovered near Keenan, who was seated on one of the plump couches, his feet propped up on an ottoman, his sketchbook in hand. Looking at him now, no one would believe forty-eight hours ago he'd been clinging to life in the ICU.

Aurora headed in his direction. "What are you working on?"

He smiled, pivoting the sketchbook so she could see the pencil drawing of Gryphon.

"Wow." He'd captured the vibrant humor in Gryphon's eyes, his teasing grin, and the bigger than life movement of his body. "That's amazing."

Keenan's smile turned shy but he didn't look away. "Thanks. I told Marina I'd finish it tonight."

"It's a gift for her?"

"Yeah. I already finished one of her for Gryphon, and also gave them one of Dr. Forrest."

"That's generous of you."

A thin line creased his brow. "It's nothing. They saved my life. All of you did. I can't repay that."

The earnestness behind his words pulled at her heart. It reminded her of how Raaveen and Paaw had reacted after her crew had rescued them from the Setarip ship.

But she saw Keenan's situation quite differently than he did. Responsibility for his pain lay at her feet, a result of her conflict with Reanne. He owed her nothing.

Crouching, she settled her hand on his arm. "Seeing you safe and happy is all the thanks we'll ever need."

Gratitude and deep respect rolled through his emotional field. Setting aside the sketchpad, he tentatively rested his hand on top of hers. "Thank you, Captain."

She smiled, soaking up the positive, creative energy he probably wasn't even aware he was giving off. "You're welcome."

Giving his arm a squeeze, she stood and strolled into the kitchen.

"Hey, sis." Micah pulled her into a sideways hug as she came up beside him.

"Hey, yourself." She hugged him back, inhaling the wonderful aromas emanating from the pots on the stove and the platters on the dining table. "Smells heavenly."

"It should. We've had a team of extremely talented cooks working tirelessly all afternoon." He gestured to himself and Gryphon and gave her a wink.

She laughed. "And so modest, too."

Gryphon grinned as he picked up a fully loaded breadbasket. "Modesty in the kitchen is overrated."

Amethyst, her wavy brown hair piled into a topknot on her head, passed them heading for the refrigerator. "Modesty has never been one of Gryphon's strong suits," she commented as she brushed past him.

Gryphon groaned. "Are you *still* sore that I figured out the ship's navigation coordinate problem before you did?"

"Your solution was great." She snagged a pitcher of iced tea from the top shelf and closed the refrigerator door. "The interminable bragging that came with it was not." The teasing quirk of her lips made it clear this was an old and much beloved argument. "It was all we heard about for two months straight."

Gryphon shot Aurora a sheepish look. "I was eighteen and cocky."

She blinked, stunned that they were joking about an event that must have taken place after they'd fled Feylahn and the Teeli — before they'd reached Gaia, before they'd found a modicum of safety.

Amethyst gave Gryphon a friendly pat as she paused next to him. "Now he's sixty-two and—"

"Still cocky," Marina said, resting her forearms on the high counter across from them. "Just the way I like him."

The look Gryphon gave Marina matched the outpouring of emotion that flowed over Aurora like a warm spring rain. He leaned down and brushed his lips across Marina's in a tender kiss. "Thank you, my love."

Aurora's parents appeared beside Marina, her dad's arm around her mom's shoulders. "I seem to recall he accused me of being cocky the day we met."

Gryphon gave him a mock-stern glare. "You *were* cocky, boy."

"So were you, old man."

"All right, enough you two." Aurora's mom tugged her dad toward the dining table. "This is a celebration. Let's eat."

The boisterous meal that followed reminded Aurora of what she'd always imagined a large family reunion would feel like. She'd never expected to be a part of one. Until recently, her family had consisted of her mom, Lelindia, Marina, and Gryphon.

But a lot had changed since then.

The stories the Suulh shared were clearly edited for content, with no mention of the Teeli or the hardships the Suulh had endured reaching Gaia. Instead, she heard about the bonds of family and friendship that had united them, including amusing anecdotes about their time together as children and headstrong teenagers.

Wolf shared stories about Aurora's mom, too, with the humor and affection a doting older brother would show for his baby sister.

So strange to think at one point her mom had planned to mate with him. If her dad hadn't arrived on the scene, and Wolf had been her father, she wouldn't have a brother or her empathic abilities. If she was the second born child, she wouldn't be the Sahzade, either. Her older sister would be. And she probably wouldn't have joined the Fleet or had her own starship.

Not a reality she wanted to contemplate.

Cade's arm wrapped around her waist, drawing her close. "You okay?" he murmured.

Oh, yeah, one more fun fact. She wouldn't have Cade. "Yeah. Just feeling incredibly grateful for my life."

He brushed a kiss on her cheek. "Me, too."

The gathering broke up not long after. With so many helping hands, they had the kitchen and main room ship shape in no time. Admiral Payne and Keenan's parents went with Keenan and his sister up to their rooms, looking exhausted but a lot more relaxed than they'd been on the ship. Knowing they'd reached their temporary home and had a dozen new friends to back them up had lowered their collective stress level.

Which brought her to the less pleasant part of the evening.

Settling back into the seating area, she broached the topic of Reanne to the group, keeping her voice low in case anyone from Payne's family reappeared on the stairway. "We have every reason to believe Reanne won't be able to track the Admiral's family here, but she's surprised us too many times in the past not to consider the possibility."

Wolf sat forward, his gaze on Aurora's mom. "You said she sent Setarips to capture you. And tried to use Sooree's abilities against you. Do you think they would try something similar here?"

Aurora's mom glanced in her direction. "Aurora's in a better position to answer that. Or Cade. They've been Reanne's targets a lot more often than I have."

Harsh images of previous confrontations rose in Aurora's mind, but she forced them down and took a slow breath. "It's unlikely Reanne has any idea you exist. For one thing, Lelindia and I didn't know until a few days ago. There's no trail from our shared past for her to follow. Also, if she'd known you were on Gaia, she would have sent the Setarips or Necri to fetch you while she had a ship here. In fact, she could have done it before starting the plant destruction that brought us here and used you as leverage against us when we arrived."

The rest of her crew nodded in agreement.

"However," Cade said, "she's as vindictive as they come. Admiral Payne isn't likely to be her personal focus right now, but she'll have someone, or several someones, working to track her down and exact retribution for her escape."

"I understand now why you wanted them here, rather than at a Rim colony," Leo said. "The personality you describe would expect her prey to flee as far as possible, not hunker down close to home."

"And having them stay here isn't something I would have thought of," Aurora said. "My mom suggested it, which is even better. Reanne can't anticipate this action based on my established patterns. The more moves like that we make that she can't predict, the stronger our position will be when we confront her."

"So you do plan to confront her?" Skye asked.

"Yes. She'll never give up. Her hatred is laser-focused on me. The damage she causes to others is incidental, at least to her."

"But she has the strength of the Teeli fleet behind her," Wolf said. "How could you possibly hope to defeat her?"

"Because I have to." Whatever it took. "And we're not without resources." Though fewer now that she was in a cold war with Siginal Clarek. "We have the head of the Galactic Fleet on our side, and his son, my former captain. We're also hoping to recruit the Yruf to our cause."

"The Yruf?" Wolf's spine stiffened. "Why would you ally with Setarips? You said they were working with the Teeli."

"Not the Yruf faction," Cade answered. "My team encountered them during our last mission, and we had some success communicating with them. They're not like the other factions. They're seeking peace, not war."

"And you should see their ship." Gonzo stroked a hand over his goatee, a gleam in his dark eyes. "Or I should say, when it's *visible* you should see it. It has amazing cloaking ability. It's also modular, creating one massive ship from seven smaller ones. Well, six now, I guess. The Ecilam managed to blow one up."

Wolf and Leo exchanged a wary look. "And you believe you can trust the Yruf?" Leo asked.

"Yes." Cade's voice didn't hold a hint of doubt. "They had us captive, completely at their mercy. But they helped us rather than harming us, even though they had no reason to. They're our best hope for neutralizing the other Setarip factions in the fight, or possibly turning them against the Teeli."

Skye's gaze rested on Aurora. "I'm sorry this burden has fallen to you, Sahzade. We had hoped—" She gave a helpless shrug.

Aurora nudged her mouth into a semblance of a smile. "It's not all bad news. It brought my family back together. I sought out my dad's help because of my empathic connection to the Necri Suulh. When I injured one of them trying to escape, it felt like I'd injured myself. And when one died—" Her throat closed up as the memory squeezed like a vise. Raaveen's mother, eyes clear and lucid, freeing herself from the Setarip's grip, making a conscious choice to let go, and plummeting to her death.

Her body breaking apart had rendered Aurora semi-comatose, the excruciating pain and sudden void overwhelming her senses.

Skye leaned forward, her gaze intent. "Did you know the Suulh who died?"

"No. Not at the time. But now I know her mate Ren, and their daughter, Raaveen. They're leading the settlement on Azaana."

Skye's gaze moved to Aurora's mother. "She has your strength, Sahzade."

Aurora's mom shook her head. "She has so much more than I ever did. More than I can possibly imagine. They both do." She reached over and clasped Micah's hand in hers. "They saved me, freed me from a prison of my own design."

The words hung heavy in the air for a moment, an acknowledgment of decades of pain and loss that broke apart with a collective sigh.

"I bless this day, Sahzade," Skye said, her gaze returning to Aurora. "I bless you. You have returned our family to us and given us hope for the future of our people. Whatever you need from us, whatever sacrifice we can make—"

"You've already taken in—"

"That isn't a sacrifice. It's an honor." The power of Skye's emotions rolled over Aurora. "Long ago, we left our home, our families, our way of life, to ensure the strength of the Nedale and Sahzade would not become weapons in the hands of the Teeli."

The pain of memory dissipated in the glow of hope. "But you have shown us that the battle continues, that our people — our families — need us now more than ever. The pledge we made to your mother and Marina has not changed. We will stand with you for the rest of our days."

Aurora's lips parted, words tumbling through her mind, but she couldn't push them through her vocal cords.

The collective energy fields of the Suulh flared to life, sweeping around the group like a circular rainbow, triggering hers, her mother's, Marina's, Gryphon's, Lelindia's.

The touch of Lelindia's field grounded her instantly, her steadfast presence the constant that had provided a guiding light in the darkness all her life.

Now it blended with the pearlescent energy of her mother's field, her unique energetic connection to Micah, her empathic connection to her dad and Cade, the nurturing energy from Marina and Gryphon and all the Suulh, and the emotional resonance of Jonarel, Kire, Celia, Justin, Gonzo, and Williams.

This was her team. Her tribe. Her family.

And no matter the risks or challenges they faced, they would never let her down.

Twenty-One

Celia picked her way through the overlapping jumble of sleeping bags, blankets and pillows that covered the floor of Skye and Wolf's bedroom. The open windows let in the balmy night air and the pale light of the crescent moon.

Aurora sat on a navy-blue blanket, her gaze towards the window. Celia settled onto one of the sleeping bags beside her. Her friend had been subdued ever since they'd wrapped up the security debriefing downstairs. She recognized the look in Aurora's eyes. She was focusing on her next obstacle.

Lelindia walked in from the attached bath where hers and Aurora's moms and Skye were carrying on a lively conversation while washing up. Her hands settled on her hips as she frowned at Celia. "How do you do that?"

She glanced down. Plain black tank top and leggings. Simple cross-legged position. Nothing unusual. "Do what?"

"Always manage to look like you're ready for a photo shoot no matter what you're wearing or what setting you're in."

Oh, that. She shrugged. "Genetics?"

"And innate style," Aurora added, her gaze shifting from the window. "I'm convinced you could make a burlap sack look good."

Lelindia sighed as she sank down beside them. "I clearly didn't get either of those genes."

Celia smacked her on the knee. "You poor thing." She laid the sympathy on thick as peanut butter. "You have to settle for cellular-level sight and saving people's lives with your energy field."

That triggered the smile she'd wanted. "Good point."

"Great point." Aurora stretched out on her side and propped her head on her hand. "And clearly Jonarel likes you just the way you are."

Now a blush joined Lelindia's smile. "Yeah, he does."

"So what are you complaining about?" Aurora asked.

"You're right." Lelindia gave a decisive shake of her head. "No more comparisonitis. It's a bad habit that needs to go." Her smile widened. "Being me is awesome."

"Glad to hear it." Celia held her hand up for a high-five.

Lelindia smacked it with enthusiasm, making them both laugh.

Celia surveyed the haphazard collection of bedding. "So, is this how a slumber party normally works? I kinda figured we'd each have our own sleeping bag." This looked more like a camping store had been hit with an earthquake. Not that she minded the arrangement. The generous pile of bedding was cushy as a cloud.

Aurora gave a one-shoulder shrug. "No idea. Never been on a sleepover before."

Crystal strolled through the door from the hallway, Brook and Luna right behind her. "Did I hear you right? You've never done this kind of thing?"

"Nope," Aurora replied, "unless you count building a sheet tent with Micah when I was two."

"We've done that, too," Luna said, "but it's not the same."

"You missed out." Crystal dropped down next to Lelindia. "Luna, Tyger and I used to do this all the time, rotating through the three wings. I think our parents encouraged it because it gave four of them a quiet night since all the kids were contained in one area. Mostly." She grinned at Luna. "But when Sirius was old enough to join the mix, we had a tendency to... explore."

"Especially after Tyger convinced him and Kyt they should climb out the window with us and go on unauthorized night hikes," Luna said.

Crystal nodded. "Brook was too young to climb trees. One of us always stayed behind with her. That worked for a while, but one night she pitched a fit, wanting to go."

Brook grinned at her sister. "I started yelling after Tyger and Luna had already made it down. Our parents came in the room to check on me and... well, you can imagine the fallout. Nobody was happy."

"And with good reason," Amethyst said as she and Oracle walked into the room, pillows under their arms. "The Teeli had established their embassy on Earth by then, and their ships were traveling in this region of space. You and Luna were old enough to know the danger they posed. Tyger, too."

"I know, Mom." Crystal shot Aurora and Lelindia a chagrined look. "We never did it again."

Amethyst sank down next to her daughters. "But the concept had merit. River and Leo led group night hikes after that."

Aurora smiled. "Seems like an equitable solution."

"It was. And Brook turned out to be the biggest fan of those excursions. She and her dad still go out together a couple times a month."

"I can see why," Libra said as she joined the group from the bathroom archway. "It's a beautiful location."

"Skye and River found it," Amethyst said.

"Found what?" Skye asked as she and Marina followed Libra and settled onto the sleeping bags.

"This location."

"Ah. We must have checked out a hundred possibilities before choosing this one."

"It reminds me a lot of Feylahn," Marina said.

A cool breeze blew through the room that had nothing to do with the open window. Aurora flinched and sat up, no doubt picking up on the emotions Marina's comment had triggered in the group.

Skye cleared her throat, turning her attention to Lelindia. "Speaking of Feylahn, I was hoping you could give us more details about what you saw while you were there. Did you go to the city? Was the sonea laanaa still intact?"

Lelindia glanced at Celia, all traces of humor erased from her expression. "That's the huge dome we saw," she explained.

She remembered it. But she also remembered the Teeli hitting and kicking the Suulh who'd been picking up trash on the nearby walkways.

Lelindia turned back to Skye. "Yes, it's still intact, but the Teeli have put up structures of metal and glass around it that give the city a cold, harsh feeling."

"Is that where you saw the Suulh who are supplying the Teeli with food and goods?" Skye asked.

Celia grunted.

Lelindia shot her a look. "No. That's where we saw a few of the older Suulh who were working as servants or slaves."

Celia's fingers curled into the folds of the blanket draped over her lap.

Oracle's gaze moved to her, understanding in her eyes. "The Teeli were hurting them, weren't they?"

"Yes." But it wasn't her place to share what they'd seen. These were Lelindia and Aurora's people, not hers. She was only a guest.

Aurora's knee brushed hers. Warmth spread over her from the point of contact, the sensation familiar after having participated in several Suulh circles. Aurora was sensing her anger and had engaged her energy field, offering comfort and support.

Celia pressed her knee closer in acknowledgment.

Lelindia's gaze flicked between them before she continued. "The younger Suulh providing the food and supplies were living in a remote village far from the city. Isolated and alone. It was clear they didn't interact with anyone other than the Teeli."

"What about the more powerful Suulh?" Amethyst asked, tension lines bracketing her mouth. "Like the ones you rescued. Did you encounter any of them on Feylahn?"

It clearly wasn't an idle question. Every Suulh in the room came from a powerful family. They had to be wondering about the fate of their parents and other relatives.

Lelindia's voice became guttural. "Yes. They're gathered on a tropical island called Citadel, and completely unaware of the Teeli's treachery. Except for one." She stared at her fingers, which twisted and turned like snakes in a basket. "That's where I met my grandmother."

Twenty-Two

Lelindia almost couldn't get the words out, her voice faltering.

Skye, Aunt Amethyst, and Oracle inhaled in an audible rush of air. "Breaa's alive, too?" Skye's gaze swung to Lelindia's mother, then back.

"Yes. I spoke with her." One of the most heartbreaking conversations of her life. "She's not a Necri like Sooree. She knows she's captive and what the Teeli are doing. The Teeli kept her to train the powerful Suulh, to prepare them for their Necri existence. Any time she's tried to resist the Teeli coercion, they've tortured or murdered the Suulh closest to her."

Her mother gave a jolt, her eyes briefly squeezing shut.

Skye's lips pressed together. "She told you that?"

"Actually, no." She rested a hand on her mom's knee before continuing. "She told me to leave Feylahn and never return. I heard the story from Zelle, one of the Suulh we rescued from the Setarips. She was my grandmother's apprentice until the Teeli pressed her into service as a Necri soldier."

Skye, Oracle, and Lelindia's aunt exchanged haunted looks.

Oracle's ginger-red hair stood out like a hazard cone against the pallor of her skin. "When I didn't hear from my mom or sister, I had to accept their deaths. All my family's deaths." Her gaze drifted to Libra with agonizing slowness. "This is worse."

Libra nodded. "I know. Marina and I have had a month to adjust but that hasn't made it any easier. I didn't want to hear it when Aurora and Lelindia first approached us. But they made me listen." She gave Aurora a sad, crooked smile. "At least now we understand what we're up against. And what really happened to our people. It's horrifying, but there's hope, too."

"There's one other thing you should know." Aurora hugged her bent knees, but her voice was steady. "Kreestol's alive, too. I fought her. She's working with Reanne."

"*What?*" Skye's outrage was echoed by Aunt Amethyst and Oracle.

"She's alive?" her aunt asked in disbelief.

"She's working with Reanne?" Skye asked at the same time. "But she's the daughter of the Sahzade. She wouldn't turn on our people."

Aurora shook her head. "I don't think she knows what Reanne's doing. The only Suulh she sees are on Citadel. They're as blissfully unaware of the truth as she is. But Reanne has poisoned her against me. Against my mom. Convinced Kreestol that my mom betrayed and abandoned her. She believes she's the rightful Sahzade and my mom and I are traitors."

"Stellar light." Skye pressed a hand to her heart. "Then she doesn't know what's happened to Sooree?"

"I don't see how she could. When I tried to convince her that Reanne was her enemy, not me, she accused me of lying. And Reanne used her Teeli influence to wipe away any doubts."

"Teeli influence?" Skye peered at Aurora. "What do you mean?"

"It's how we believe the Teeli are able to bend others to their will," Aurora explained. "They influence behavior, particularly hostile or aggressive behavior, possibly through touch."

Rather than clarifying, Aurora's explanation seemed to confuse everyone even more.

"You don't remember anything similar happening when the Teeli arrived on your homeworld?" Celia asked.

Skye, Oracle and Lelindia's mom all shook their heads.

Lelindia exchanged a surprised look with Aurora. She'd assumed the Teeli had manipulated the Suulh from day one. "No one acted strangely?" she asked her mom. "Became uncharacteristically aggressive or did things they wouldn't normally do?" *Like attack a fellow cadet in a jealous rage?* She hadn't witnessed Jonarel and Cade's Academy fight, only the aftermath, but Aurora's description of their out-of-control behavior was etched like glass in her mind under the heading *Threat: Reanne Beck.*

"Not that I recall," her mom answered. "We were a peaceful people. Aggression wasn't in our natures. Even anger was rare. But we were naïve, overly trusting. We believed the Teeli were there to help us, to teach us how to move beyond the boundaries of our planet. We'd never had any reason to distrust or fear the unknown."

Lelindia had vague memories of what that felt like, back when she was a young child, enjoying life without being continually on guard against potential dangers. "How did you figure out the Teeli were a threat?"

"Your father." Her mom's voice was soft. "He was the first to suspect the Teeli's interest in me and Libra wasn't benign, and that the training we were all receiving wasn't what it seemed. He got into an argument with the Teeli who oversaw his flight training group when she evaded his questions. A few nights later, there was an explosion in his room at the sonea laanaa."

Her mom drew in a shaky breath, her gaze moving to Lelindia's aunt. "He was out in the gardens with me at the time, but both his parents and Amethyst were badly injured in the blast. It took out the adjoining walls between their rooms."

"It might have killed him if he'd been in his room," Aunt Amethyst said, fire burning in her eyes. "That was the beginning of the end."

Celia leaned forward. "And no one suspected the Teeli?"

Lelindia had the same question. That seemed unlikely.

"No," Lelindia's mom answered. "You have to understand that until they arrived, we'd lived a comparatively simple life. We'd never developed glass, or electricity, or weapons, because we had no need for them. The Teeli brought technological wonders and dangers we'd never imagined. It was easy for them to blame any accidents – even deaths – on our ignorance."

Celia swore under her breath and her teeth clicked together like she was grinding them.

"They claimed the explosion was the result of an electrical overload of a device in Gryphon's room, which was probably true," Lelindia's aunt said. "But he didn't cause the overload, they did. Unfortunately, it was easier for most people to believe that he had made a mistake than that the Teeli would deliberately try to kill us."

Lelindia's mom stared into the middle distance, the warm brown of her eyes flattened to stone. "None of us trusted the Teeli after that night. Well, no one in our aailee. But we didn't have any proof the Teeli were responsible."

Lelindia's nails bit into her palms. She was still reeling from the knowledge that her dad had almost died without ever making it off Feylahn. If that had happened, none of them would be here. He'd been the pilot of the ship that had carried them all to safety. "What about Breaa? And Sooree? What did they think?"

"Your dad and I tried to convince Sooree that the Teeli posed a threat, but she was a tender-hearted soul who believed the best of everyone. She couldn't conceive of the evil intentions we described. Neither could Taal, Libra's father. They thought we were suffering from mental exhaustion as a result of our intense training with the Teeli, or that our teenage imaginations were in overdrive – too many stories from the Teeli about other worlds and alien creatures."

Aurora made a strange sound, kind of a cross between a whimper and a moan, her forehead dropping against her bent knees. As driven as she was to take responsibility for any injustice or harm to others, hearing her own grandparents had dismissed the danger had to be tying her in knots.

Join the club. Lelindia's stomach had an abundance of knots, too. "What about Breaa and my grandfather? Did they believe you?" she asked her mom.

"They were concerned, but not convinced. My mother wasn't spending as much time with the Teeli as I was, but she was healing any injured personnel they brought to her and teaching them about the medicinal herbs on our planet. They always treated her graciously, never pushing like they did with us."

"So she dismissed the danger, too?" Celia asked.

"Not entirely. She promised to keep our concerns in mind."

Crystal and Brook exchanged a look with Luna that created several new knots. Clearly they'd heard this story before. Whatever came next, Lelindia was going to hate it.

"Up to that point, the Teeli had limited interaction with Libra and Sooree. Libra had been in her discovery cycle when the Teeli had arrived on Feylahn, not yet seven. Our traditions had kept her social circle limited to those living in the sonea laanaa, which excluded the Teeli. Much of Sooree and Taal's time was devoted to Libra's training and Kreestol's care since Kreestol was a year old at the time."

"But you were much older." Which had put her mom in the line of fire.

Her mom nodded. "Fifteen when the Teeli showed up, already starting my awakening cycle. That's why my parents and Libra's strongly encouraged me and the rest of the aailee to interact with the Teeli as much as possible. We were the perfect age, the Suulh developmental stage where we could absorb information and master skills with ease." Her mom held her gaze. "The awakening cycle is why you were far ahead of your classmates at the Academy when you arrived and why Aurora shot to the top of her class around the time she turned fifteen."

"Huh." That from Aurora, who was looking at Libra. "I guess that's another reason you didn't want me to go to the Academy at thirteen."

Libra grimaced. "I don't think I would have been any happier if you'd waited until fifteen."

Aurora sighed. "True." She turned to Lelindia's mom. "So since the Teeli couldn't easily get time with Sooree or my mom, they focused on you and Breaa."

"Yes. After they'd established a trade system to meet their immediate needs for food, water, and resources, and built facilities for their scout ships outside the city, they started studying our culture. That's when they began to understand the Sahzade's and Nedale's importance, though it took a long time for them to figure out why we were held in such high regard."

Celia's eyes narrowed. "Why? Wasn't it obvious?"

Her mom's tone turned ironic. "How long did it take you to confirm Lelindia and Aurora had abilities beyond what you could see?"

Celia acknowledged the point with a nod. "But they were hiding their abilities, or at least disguising them. You wouldn't have."

"No, but we also didn't use them in flamboyant ways that would draw attention. Sooree's training sessions with Libra took place in the sonea laanaa, as did most healing sessions my mother and I did. The Teeli weren't privy to either. If we needed to travel outside the city, that took us out of sight of the Teeli as well. The explosion in Gryphon's room shone a spotlight on us. Sooree and her mother Wiin used their abilities to temporarily stabilize the structure until braces were in place, and my mom and I healed Amethyst and her parents afterward. The Teeli witnessed all of that because they came running — as did most of the nearby residents — right after the explosion."

"So they had another reason for setting off the device," Celia said, her lip curling in a snarl. "They could use it as a test of your abilities."

"Exactly. I made excuses not to work with the Teeli for a while after that, buying time as the aailee discussed our options and the extent of the danger. But I couldn't put it off forever, not without making them suspicious. The next time I visited their medical facility where they were training me in Teeli physiology and their healing techniques, the Teeli doctor in charge, Sly'Cer, announced he wanted to extract blood and tissue samples from me and Libra, to figure out the genetic traits that made my healing and her shielding possible."

A chill raced down Lelindia's spine, making her shiver.

"I refused. That's when I saw their true faces." Her mom paused, her jaw working like her words were having a fistfight in her mouth. "The veneer the Teeli had hidden behind fell in an instant. Sly'Cer gave me an ultimatum. Go along with whatever he demanded, or watch Suulh die until I complied."

The chill turned into an iceberg.

"He brought in ten older Suulh from the outlying villages. They were clearly confused, unaware of why they'd been brought to me. Sly'Cer picked up what I had thought was a medical tool but turned out to be a weapon. He fired at a metal lab table, blasting a hole in the surface. The Suulh screamed, pushing into a tight cluster, trying to get to me. But the Teeli held them back. Then Sly'Cer aimed the weapon at one of them and asked me if I was going to comply."

A curse hissed from Celia's lips, her dark eyes almost black. "So you complied."

"Yes. I held out my arm and one of the doctors took the blood and tissue samples. But Sly'Cer shot two of the Suulh right afterward anyway, just to prove his point. And when I tried to go to them, to heal them, he shot a third."

Aurora swore next, her face scrunching up.

Lelindia's stomach went into freefall, dragging all her air down with it.

"That's when I realized the Teeli placed no value on our lives." Her mom's hand trembled, rubbing the ends of her thick hair between her fingers. "Whatever their end goal was, it didn't involve helping us, or even working with us. We were tools to them, disposable."

Her mom's voice grew even softer. "Sly'Cer ordered the three he'd shot to be left where they'd fallen while the other seven were taken out of the room. He wanted me to watch them die slowly, painfully, knowing they were too injured to heal themselves." Her gaze met Lelindia's, a plea for understanding in her eyes. "None of us had ever had to heal from wounds like those before. The damage I saw to their bodies — it was terrifying. He told me if I ever defied him again, the killing would never stop. That's the moment when I knew we were all as good as dead, anyway."

Lelindia scooted closer, her thigh touching her mom's as she engaged her energy field. She understood the agony her mom had endured. To have the power to heal and yet be helpless to save someone was her greatest fear, too. "I'm so sorry."

Her mom's field joined hers, the connection easing the shared pain. Her mom inhaled slowly before continuing. "What Sly'Cer didn't know is his actions had summoned Sooree and my mom. The Teeli weren't aware that we could sense when the Suulh were in danger or pain. They also didn't understand our ability to communicate with thought images. When my mom and Sooree reached out to me, I sent them the images of the dying Suulh. And of Sly'Cer holding the weapon as he fired."

"You gave them the evidence they needed to be convinced," Celia murmured.

"Yes. Sooree was trusting, not foolish. As soon as she understood the scope of the danger, she realized we needed to coordinate our response without the Teeli knowing. We were unprepared and outgunned. She made the tough call and didn't send a force to the facility to try to save the dying Suulh. Instead, she left Kreestol with Taal while she, Wiin, and Skye gathered

Libra and the rest of the aailee — theirs and ours. My mother came to fetch me from the medical facility on some innocuous pretext the Teeli would believe."

Lelindia peered at her mom. "And the Teeli didn't get suspicious when Breaa arrived at the facility?"

Her mom shook her head. "The doctors there knew her. Her presence wasn't unusual. Neither was her request that I was needed at the sonea laanaa. And since we were in communication the whole time, I was able to project Sly'Cer's reactions to her. She could prepare herself so there were no surprises. The Teeli didn't let her into the room of course — I don't remember what excuse they gave her — but Sly'Cer sent me out. He also warned me that if I told anyone what had happened, Gryphon and Amethyst would be the next to die."

"Charming," Celia drawled, her fingers twitching like she wanted a weapon in her hand.

"I knew he'd make good on his threat. I'd also figured out the intention behind Sly'Cer's demands. He wanted to duplicate our abilities, mine and Libra's. But I knew he would fail." Her mom stared at the floor, her voice becoming almost robotic. "Because of the inner sight I have as the Nedale to see how our biology interacts with our energy fields, I knew our talents weren't just about genetics. They're also about how our minds interact with our environment, something the Teeli couldn't replicate. Ultimately, the only way the Teeli could gain control of our abilities was to control *us*, to manipulate our minds. And they found a way."

Her gaze rose to meet Lelindia's. "They created the Necri."

Twenty-Three

Silence pulsed in the room like a fading heartbeat.

The emotional input from the group was pushing Aurora's newly acquired skills to the limit, but she worked to maintain an even keel. She needed to hear this story, no matter how much it shredded her heart and her control. "What happened next?" she finally prompted Marina.

"Sooree and Wiin were the only ones in the city with the power to defend against the Teeli weapons, to protect our people from being slaughtered when we fought back. Libra was still too young, not yet physically or emotionally mature enough to focus her abilities on a grand scale."

Aurora slid her gaze to her mom. The emotions coming from her were a complicated maze. She couldn't imagine how surreal and disturbing it was to relive trauma as an adult that she remembered from a child's perspective.

Marina sighed, the shuddering breath coming from the depths of her soul. "If it had only been my abilities the Teeli had coveted, I would have let them do whatever they wanted to me, let them control me. Anything to keep our people alive. But Sooree knew the real danger was from Libra's abilities."

Aurora's gaze flicked to her mom again. She was clutching one of the pillows in a death grip.

"The Teeli had figured out that our abilities grew stronger when passed from mother to first daughter. Libra was still young enough to be molded and shaped to their purposes. Sly'Cer had proven he could control my behavior by threatening the Suulh. Libra was still a child. She would have been even easier to manipulate."

Now her mom's skin looked as white as the pillowcase she was clutching.

Letting go of the tight hold she had on her bent knees, Aurora wrapped an arm around her mom's shoulders instead.

Marina gave Aurora a flicker of a smile, her chest rising and falling like a runner in the last stretch of a marathon. An emotional one.

"Sooree believed it wouldn't be long before the Teeli would take Libra and me, just as they'd taken the Suulh villagers. She and Wiin refused to let that happen. If the Teeli found a way to turn us against our own people, the combined force of the Teeli technology with our abilities would have made them unstoppable."

Marina's gaze shifted to Lelindia, a sheen of moisture coating her eyes. "We left to prevent condemning our people to a fate worse than death – to be eternally tormented by their own Sahzade and Nedale, to be pawns in the Teeli's twisted machinations. But the Teeli found a way to make that a reality anyway."

Aurora's heart wept for the impossible position they'd all been thrust into.

"Sooree understood our people were already caught in a trap they might never escape. She also knew the stakes if they failed to defeat the Teeli. Sly'Cer had made that clear. That's why she and my mother wanted to send us far from the Teeli's reach before the fighting started. They couldn't bear the thought of us becoming the Teeli's malignant puppets."

The ache in Aurora's chest expanded through her entire body, Marina's tale making breathing a real chore. She didn't want to ask her next question, but she needed to know. "What about Kreestol? Why didn't Sooree send her with you?"

Marina's eyes squeezed shut. "She wanted to, planned to." She opened her eyes, her gaze on Aurora's mom. "You have to believe that. She and Taal had her with them as we made our way to the ship in separate groups of three to keep from drawing attention. But Kreestol wasn't like Libra. She was fussy, clingy. She would cry if anyone other than her parents tried to hold her. Sooree couldn't give her to us until the last minute."

Marina's voice broke, her head drooping.

Oracle took up the story, giving Marina time to collect herself. "Marina and Wolf were in charge of Libra. Skye and Gryphon had taken Amethyst and gone ahead to sneak onboard the ship and get it ready for takeoff. Leo, River and I were supposed to take Kreestol from Sooree and Taal when we reached the ship. But the Teeli had upped their security around the shipyard. We encountered a Teeli patrol. They fired on us and hit Leo."

"Everything happened so fast," Marina murmured. "The Teeli went after Sooree and Taal, cut them off from us. I saw Leo get hit and rushed to help him while Wolf grabbed Libra and ran for the ship."

"River and I tried to find an opening to get Kreestol," Oracle said. "We could see Taal trying to reach us, too, but the Teeli were firing on us and advancing on the ship. That's when Sooree screamed in my mind, ordering us to go, to save Libra and Marina. So that's what we did."

Kreestol had been wrong. She hadn't been abandoned or betrayed, except by the Teeli. Aurora's gaze swept over Marina, Skye, Oracle, and Amethyst. "So the nine members of your aailee are the only ones who escaped?"

Oracle blanched, her hand drifting to her throat. "Actually, there were twelve in our aailee."

The sharp pain from Oracle made Aurora shudder, giving her a clue as to the fate of the other three even before she asked the question. "What happened to the others?"

Oracle drew in a shaky breath. "I had an older sister, Siih. She was a powerful communicator already much stronger than my mother. She could talk telepathically with any of the Suulh, but our bond was especially intense. She insisted on staying behind so that when they defeated the Teeli, she could reach out to me wherever we were and tell me it was time to come home."

Her voice had grown softer with each word, so that *home* was barely a puff of air.

"And you never heard from her?"

Oracle lifted her head with agonizing slowness. "Once, shortly after the fighting started. I lost contact as we were heading to our jump window. Then nothing for days and weeks that turned into months. That's why we knew they'd failed."

"We held out hope for a while," Skye said, resting a hand over Oracle's. "We didn't know for sure what kind of range Siih's abilities had. She knew which direction we'd traveled and had shared that information with Sooree. The two remaining members of our aailee were Wolf and Leo's brothers. They stayed behind to join the fight. They'd promised us that if something happened to Siih, or she didn't get a response from Oracle, they'd gather a crew after the battle and come find us."

"But they never did." Marina sighed, turning her gaze to the ceiling, where stars glittered through the skylights. "Oracle never heard from Siih again. I felt the pull of our people's pain for a while. So did Libra. But eventually even that faded. So we ran, as we'd promised Sooree and my mother we would, and never looked back."

The choices they'd made didn't surprise Aurora in the least. She'd seen more courage and self-sacrifice from her people – whether children or adults – to know it was their default setting. She seriously doubted there were words in the Suulh language for concepts like *coward, selfish,* or *greedy.*

The same could not be said for the Teeli. Or Reanne. They had a growing mountain of crimes to atone for.

Now that Keenan was safe, her nemesis would feel the force of her full attention.

Nothing was going to stop her from defeating Reanne Beck and freeing the Suulh once and for all from the tyranny of their Teeli enslavement.

Twenty-Four

"I see your two and raise you four." Cade placed the stack of six chips beside Brendan's two at the center of the table, his gaze shifting to Justin on his left.

Justin eyed him, his forefinger tapping the edge of the cards in his hand. "You know, it just occurred to me that we're playing with a couple of empaths." One brow rose toward his hairline as his gaze moved to the large stacks of chips in front of them. "You two wouldn't be using those abilities to your advantage during the game, now would you?"

Cade placed his cards face down on the table. "Are you asking me that question to trigger a tell?"

The corners of Justin's mouth tilted up. "Maybe. I can beat you at pool, but I've never had much success with poker."

"That's because you're too busy chatting up the table," Gonzo said, taking a sip of his margarita. "You in or not?"

"Not." Justin set his cards down and stood. "Anyone else need a refill?"

Kire and Tam both raised their hands.

While Justin fetched the margarita pitcher from the cold storage unit, Gonzo tossed six chips into the pile. "I call."

Tam and Kire folded, bringing the bet to Kelly.

She'd accepted their invitation to join the game after they'd returned from dinner. Jonarel had taken her place on the bridge, watching for any late-night boating traffic with Bella, who'd jumped at the chance to be in the navigator's chair.

Jonarel hadn't shown any interest in playing. Apparently the Kraed culture didn't include gambling or games of chance. Jonarel had reacted to the words *poker game* like Cade had suggested he try breathing underwater.

Kelly had proven to be a wily competitor. Her stack of chips was the third largest, behind Brendan and Cade's but ahead of Micah's.

"I call." She set six chips in the center.

Micah's gaze had been fixed on Brendan since his dad had made the initial bet, but now his attention swung to Kelly.

She gazed back at him with the placid, unreadable expression of a marble statue.

He lowered his head and tossed his cards in with the other discards. "I'm out."

Brendan added four chips to the pile. "I call."

They'd invited Gryphon to join the game, too, but he'd declined, heading to his cabin to rest. After the long day of lively social interaction, he'd been dragging his feet, his angular face a little haggard. Considering he'd almost died during the Setarip-Necri attack less than a week ago, it was amazing he'd managed to keep up as much as he had. His strong Suulh constitution and the devoted healing efforts of his mate and daughter probably had a lot to do with it.

Picking up the dealer's stack, Micah dealt the last card in the seven-card hand face down to the remaining four players.

Rather than looking at his own card, Cade focused on the reactions of the other three as they looked at theirs. Justin's question about whether he was using his empathic abilities to win had been a calculated prod to get under his skin, a tactic that often worked to his advantage at the pool table.

But in truth, even if Cade consciously tried to cheat that way — which he never would — it wouldn't have done him any good with this crowd. Brendan and Micah were professionals when it came to controlling their emotions, Kire, Justin, and Gonzo were all Fleet trained to suppress their emotional reactions to unwanted stimuli, and Kelly barely seemed to *have* emotions. Only Tam gave any emotional flickers, but they were minor compared to his physical tells. Despite his ability to remain calm when faced with emergency trauma that would send most people screaming from the room, the man had never developed a poker face. Hence the pathetic state of his chips.

Cade lifted the edge of his seventh card, then set it back down and met Brendan's intense, clear-eyed gaze.

Brendan wasn't using his abilities, either. He'd spent enough time around the man during the past few days to recognize the subtle shift in his eyes when he was tuning into the emotions of those around him. He hadn't seen it happen once since they'd sat down at the table.

But a hint of amusement sparkled in his eyes in reaction to Cade's scrutiny. "Ten." He picked up the pale blue chip and set it in the center without looking down.

Cade reran the calculations in his head. Brendan had two kings, a seven and a four showing, three of them in the same suit —hearts. He could have three of a kind, but more likely a flush or full house. Neither would stand up against Cade's four queens, two of which were showing, along with an eight of spades and the ace of diamonds. The only threat Brendan posed was if he had pocket kings. His kings would beat Cade's queens.

One way to find out. "In ten, and raise ten." He placed the chips in the center, noting the subtle quirk of Brendan's lip without being able to gauge if it meant he was about to win or go down swinging.

Gonzo placed his cards on the table. "Too rich for me. I'm out."

Kelly gazed at Cade's cards in silent contemplation, then at the two chips he'd added to the pile. She had two aces showing, and the seven and ten of diamonds. Since he had one of the other aces, she couldn't have four of a kind, but she could still have an ace high full house. Based on the cards he and Brendan were showing, she might assume they had king or queen high full houses, which would put her on top. What she couldn't know is if either of them had four of a kind.

Plucking three pale blue chips from her stack, she placed them in the pile. "Your twenty and raise ten."

Gutsy. Not that he expected anything less from a pilot, which is why he wasn't that surprised when Brendan raised the bar higher, adding three chips to the pile. "Up another ten."

Did he have the cards? Or was he bluffing?

Cade wasn't about to fold, but bumping it up again wasn't likely to push either of them out, either. They clearly believed they had cards worth playing. This was already the biggest pot of the night.

He dropped two chips in. "Call."

Kelly tossed another chip in as well. "Call."

Brendan flipped over his cards. "Full house, kings over fours."

Respectable, but not the winning hand. Cade grinned as he flipped over his pocket queens. "Four of a kind."

Brendan growled good-naturedly but Cade paused with his hand hovering over the chips when he saw Kelly's smug smile.

She flipped over her cards while holding his gaze. "Straight flush."

He stared at the cards. "Damn." He'd been so focused on the aces that he'd discounted the diamonds. In addition to the seven and ten, she had the eight, nine, and jack. Her straight flush beat his four of a kind. "Nicely played."

She shrugged as she raked the chips forward and started stacking them in neat piles. "Could have gone either way. I caught the jack on the river."

"And took us to school," Brendan said with a grin.

She grinned back. "Glad to help."

As Brendan started shuffling the cards for the next hand, Micah rested his forearms on the table, his gaze on Kire. "Can I ask you a question?"

"Sure." Kire lifted his drink and took a sip.

"How long have you known Cardiff?"

Kire's thin brows lifted. "Not long. We met right before we first came onboard the *Starhawke*. Why?"

"But you were good friends with Aurora since the Academy, right? And you've worked closely with her on the ship?"

"Yes."

"Did Cardiff grill you about your history with Aurora when you met? Keep track of your movements when you arrived on the ship?"

"No." Kire squinted at Micah in confusion. "What's this about?"

Cade threw him a bone. "You and Kelly have been spending most of your time on the bridge the past few days, so you may not have picked up on Cardiff's antipathy toward Micah."

"Antipathy? Really?" His relaxed demeanor changed into Fleet officer mode, zeroing in on Micah. "Why would she act that way toward you? You're Roe's brother."

Micah shrugged. "That's what I've been trying to figure out. She watches me like she thinks I'm about to stage a coup and take over the ship."

"If it makes you feel any better," Cade offered, "she wasn't too keen on me at first, either. In fact, when we sparred during the trip to Azaana, she told me she'd stop my heart if I ever hurt Aurora."

Kire's gaze swung to him. "She *said* that?"

"Yep. And meant it. Not that I blamed her after what I'd put Aurora through."

"Maybe, but still…" Kire's eyes narrowed. "I'm going to have a talk with her."

Micah waved him off. "Please don't. I don't want to get her in trouble. It would give her another reason to hate me."

Kire's fingers drummed on the table as his lips pressed together. "I don't get it. Why would she hate you? Roe's thrilled that you're here. I haven't seen her this happy since… well, ever."

Cade had to agree. She wasn't living under the cloud of her mother's disapproval anymore, and reuniting with her father and brother had put a definite spring in her step.

"And from what I understand, you make Roe stronger. From a security perspective, that should be a bonus."

"Cardiff doesn't agree," Micah muttered before taking a long pull from his margarita. He turned to Cade. "How did you get her off your back?"

"It wasn't any one thing. At first, I made it clear I wasn't going anywhere unless Aurora told me to get lost." His lips curled in a wry grin. "And then she did. Threw me off the ship in an attempt to protect me. I tried to convince Cardiff to let me back onboard, but she wouldn't budge. I think she respected my point of view, though, may have even agreed with me."

"And now she's fine with you being with Aurora?"

He considered his answer. "I think so. She hasn't threatened my life recently, so that's a win."

Micah glanced at his father, who was shuffling the cards in an offhand manner. "Care to weigh in on this? She hasn't been treating you like a threat."

"Because I'm not a threat. My influence on Aurora is minimal compared to yours. Or Cade's."

"How so?"

Cade wanted to hear this, too.

Brendan met Cade's gaze first. "Celia perceived you as a threat — rightly so — because of your past history with Aurora. Not because of the pain that had resulted, but the potential for future pain. I doubt Aurora was indifferent to you when you appeared on the *Starhawke*."

"No, she wasn't." And Cardiff had been there to witness their initial interaction. That had set the tone.

"As a security chief, it was her job to protect her captain from harm. Aurora being her friend made her even more determined to minimize potential threats. You had to prove yourself before she could lower her guard."

"And she had backup," Gonzo interjected. "Clarek was watching you even more closely than she was."

"True." So much had changed in the past week that those days felt like a lifetime ago.

"But I've never hurt Aurora." Exasperation roughened Micah's voice. "And I never would. Hell, the first time Cardiff saw me, I'd just helped Aurora save our mom and Lelindia's parents from the house fire. That should have bought me bonus points, not put me under a microscope."

"I know." Brendan's voice held the measured calm of a trained psychologist. "I'm not saying her reaction is logical. Emotions rarely are. But seeing Aurora relying so heavily on someone, especially after being gone from the crew for a couple weeks, could have made her wary."

"Wary I could handle. But this." Micah gestured around the room. "That woman stalks me like a tiger everywhere I go, especially here or the greenhouse. I can't walk into this galley without wondering if I'm on the menu."

"Are you sure you don't want me to talk to her?" Kire asked. "I could give her extra duties to keep her occupied."

Micah shook his head. "She's too smart for that. She'd know I said something, and probably use that as evidence that I can't be trusted." He sighed. "I'll give it time." His gaze met Cade's. "How long did it take for you?"

"Months."

Micah groaned.

He felt for the guy. "You want my advice?"

"Absolutely."

"Ask her to train you to fight."

Micah's skin paled under his tan, his fingers unconsciously curling into fists. "Wouldn't that give her carte blanche to beat me bloody?"

"She's a fighter, not a bully. And she respects anyone who will meet her on the mat. Besides, you have an ace up your sleeve."

"What's that?"

"Thanks to your Suulh blood and your connection to Aurora, Cardiff can't hurt you without hurting Aurora, too. And that's something she would never do."

Twenty-Five

When Jonarel arrived with the shuttle in the morning, Lelindia was swept off her feet.

Literally.

He reached her in four long strides. Her startled squeak turned into a sigh as his warm breath caressed her neck and face when he snuggled her close.

"I missed you," he murmured in her ear, making her pulse thrum and her skin warm.

"I missed you, too." Being in his arms felt like coming home, but she was acutely aware of Admiral Payne's curious stare and the amused looks from the Suulh.

Jonarel set her back on her feet, but kept their bodies hip to hip, his fingers wrapped protectively around her shoulder.

Her dad, Brendan, Micah, and Cade had come with him. Her dad had his arm around her mom, though with significantly more air between them than Jonarel was allowing. She doubted even a drop of water could work its way between their bodies.

She and Aurora had already said their goodbyes to the Suulh after breakfast. While her parents and Aurora's bid their adieus, Aurora turned to Admiral Payne. "You have the comband my dad gave you?"

Payne nodded. "If there's any trouble, I'll alert you."

"And we'll do the same. The combands link to Far Horizons' private comm system, which will route any message from your comband directly to my dad and the *Starhawke*."

The door behind the Admiral opened and Keenan stepped onto the front porch with his family. The morning sun burnished his bronze skin and dark hair, chasing away the last visible remnants of his recent trauma. The sight warmed Lelindia's heart, fulfilling the vision she'd had when she first saw him lying frail and broken in the ICU bed.

His gaze swept the gathering until he spotted her with Jonarel. He descended the steps with an ease that made her smile. She'd checked on him this morning before breakfast, and his healing was progressing nicely. He'd probably be back to running in less than a week.

As he approached he held out a thin covered portfolio. "What's this?"

"It's a thank you gift. I just finished it."

She'd been wondering if he was going to create a sketch for her after she'd seen the one of Tam and the ones he'd done for her parents. She accepted the portfolio, flipped open the cover, and went completely still.

"I hope you like it."

His voice reached her from the far end of a tunnel, all the sounds around her muted as she stared at the paper in her hands.

Jonarel's fingers tightened on her shoulder, pulling her even more firmly against his body.

"Do you... like it?"

Like it? When her head started to spin she sucked air into her lungs like a vacuum.

"It is beautiful," Jonarel answered for her, the rumble of his voice sending shockwaves through her body.

She looked up at him. The emotions shimmering in his golden eyes matched the ones that held her captive. She also saw a yearning that seriously threatened her ability to keep taking in oxygen.

Tearing her gaze away from his took a monumental effort, but she forced herself to focus on Keenan. "It's perfect." Getting the words out took even more effort considering her throat had shrunk to the size of a pinhole.

Keenan's worried frown indicated he didn't believe her. "You're sure? You like it?"

Her gaze dropped to the sketch. "I love it."

The image depicted her and Jonarel, their arms around each other in a loving embrace. Unlike Keenan's other sketches, which had been pencil drawings without color, this one displayed the interwoven rich color of Jonarel's deep green skin contrasting with the paler tan coloring of hers. In the pose, she was gazing up at him with anticipation as he bent his head toward hers.

But it was the look Keenan had captured in their eyes that held her transfixed. She'd seen that look in Jonarel's eyes, knew the emotions that drove it, but she'd never imagined what it looked like on her own face. Seeing them together, the wonder and joy the image evoked, made her heart alternate between squeezing tight and pounding furiously.

A single tear threatened to roll down her cheek onto the paper. She hastily swiped it away, unwilling to loosen her grip on the portfolio. "Thank you, Keenan. I will treasure this, always."

His smile finally broke through on a relieved exhale. "I'm glad you like it. It was the least I could do after you... well, saved my life."

Another surge of emotion jammed more tears against the backs of her eyes. She fought them down. What was wrong with her? She wasn't usually prone to emotional outbursts. Aurora was the one who struggled with emotion. She was the calm and practical doctor.

But she couldn't get a handle on calm and practical right now, not with the image in her hand and Jonarel's arm steadily reeling her in until her back was pressed securely to the wall of his chest.

As the heat from his body surrounded her, her emotions smoothed out, allowing her to steady her breathing. "Saving people is what doctors do."

Keenan's look showed a wisdom far beyond his years. "Yes, you do."

He was a smart young man, and incredibly perceptive. The sketch made that clear. He may have figured out, or at least suspected, she'd done far more than any other doctor could have given the same tools. That her abilities went beyond the norm and it wasn't technology that had facilitated his miraculous recovery.

But he accepted her without the need to question, to have all the answers. It was enough that she'd given him back his life, and helped provide his family with a safe haven.

On impulse, she pulled free from Jonarel's grip and wrapped her arms around Keenan, carefully holding the sketch so it pressed against his back. "Take care of yourself."

He didn't react for a moment, clearly startled, but then his long arms came around her and he hugged her back. "You, too."

She soaked up the joy of the moment, but when the tears threatened again, she pulled away and patted him lightly on the chest. "We'll see you soon."

His crooked smile didn't quite match the solemn look in his eyes. "I hope so."

Jonarel ushered her into the co-pilot's seat for the shuttle ride back to the ship, while everyone else settled into the main cabin. She alternated between staring at the sketch in her hands and staring at the real-life version guiding the shuttle out over the water.

His gaze met hers every time, sending a zing through her system like an electric shock. The yearning look hadn't left his golden eyes. In fact, he seemed to have transmitted it to her, the sensation growing in her belly to the point that she had to physically stop herself from leaving her seat and crawling into his lap.

What was going on? She'd never felt so discombobulated in her life.

Her parents were waiting for her in the main cabin after Jonarel settled the shuttle into the *Starhawke*'s bay, but the rest of the group had already headed into the ship.

"What did Keenan give you?" her dad asked.

As Jonarel stepped up behind her, she flipped open the cover and turned the sketch so they could see it.

Her dad's eyes widened. "Wow."

Her mom's gaze moved from the sketch to Jonarel and back. "He's a talented young man."

"Yes, he is," Lelindia agreed. The emotional wave started gaining momentum again, so she switched gears, motioning them toward the shuttle's ramp. "What are you and dad going to do when we get back to Earth?" she asked as the four of them stepped into the shuttle bay.

Her parents exchanged a glance as the group headed toward the lift. "You mean, will we be going back to work?" her mom asked.

"Yeah. You haven't talked much about what you plan to do now that Libra's back with Brendan."

"Oh, we've discussed it plenty. Brendan's wrangled some time off. He's having his TA's fill in for his first week or two of classes. He's already rented a cabin for us where we can stay while we figure out our next steps regarding Stoneycroft, our clinic, and Hawke's Nest."

Tension coiled in her chest. "What about the Setarips? And Sooree?" Her parents had barely survived the last attack. "If Reanne tries again..."

The comforting weight of Jonarel's arm settled over her shoulders.

Her mom shook her head. "After the way things turned out the first time, I don't think we have to worry. Even if they tried again, Brendan will be with us. His empathic talents would enable him to alert us long before they showed up. From what Aurora's said, Setarips aren't particularly good at concealing their emotions from empaths."

"And Libra's not afraid to use her power anymore," her dad added as the lift doors parted on the guest quarters deck.

"The Setarips would be fools to attack her when she's defending Brendan."

"Good point." Libra was every bit as protective as Aurora. Or Jonarel.

Her parents stepped off the lift. "Can you meet us for lunch later?" her dad asked.

She glanced at Jonarel. "Do we have anything scheduled?"

"I do not believe so."

"Great!" Her dad clapped his hands together. "I'll be in the galley or the greenhouse whenever you're ready."

"Sounds good."

But as the lift doors slid closed the emotional wave she'd battled during the shuttle ride rippled under the surface.

Jonarel turned her to face him, cupping her cheek in his palm. "Lelindia, what is wrong?"

She struggled to put the sensation into words. "I feel... I want..." But words wouldn't come. She blew out a breath in frustration.

He sighed and pulled her into his arms. "May I make a request?"

"Anything." If he could give her something else to focus on, maybe this weird feeling would go away.

"It is customary in my culture to welcome the parents of one's checana with a feast. It's called the tamlenac."

Tamlenac. She knew the term. When two Kraed clans or families were to be joined by a mating of their members, they shared a ceremonial meal together.

But his clan couldn't participate, except for Star. She'd expected their mating plans to be on indefinite hold until after Aurora had reopened communication with Siginal and cleared the banishment ruling he'd imposed on Jonarel and Star.

Apparently Jonarel saw things differently.

"I was not able to hold the tamlenac when your parents boarded the ship – our mission took priority – but if you are willing, I would like to do so tonight."

His words acted like a rock tossed onto the surface of her emotional well, creating ripples that rapidly morphed into waves. "No."

His body jerked. "No?" He pulled back to stare at her, a flash of hurt in his eyes. "You do not wish for me to welcome them?"

"Yes. I mean no. I mean—" She waved her free hand, the one not holding the sketch, as if she could push the wave of emotion out into words. "I want more than that. Yes, we can have the tamlenac, but before we do that, I want to have our mating ceremony."

Twenty-Six

She'd stunned him. Jonarel's eyes widened and his lips parted in shock.

Not an easy feat to accomplish with a Kraed. Their heightened senses made them difficult to surprise.

His tongue moistened his lips. "You... you wish to have a mating ceremony? Today?"

She nodded, then gave into the urge to put her mouth where his tongue had been. The velvet glide of his lips against hers made the emotional wave crest, but now she felt like she was riding it rather than being dragged under.

"I know it sounds crazy," she breathed as she broke the delicious contact. "Sudden. Impulsive. Not like me at all. But after what I heard last night from the Suulh..." She shuddered, pushing the disturbing images aside. "My parents and Aurora's are here. Now. We don't know when we'll be together again. If you're willing to hold the tamlenac without your clan, then why wait—"

He cut her off with a kiss of his own, his arms circling her torso and snugging her in flush with his body. His very warm and aroused body.

He backed her against the wall of the lift, which had stopped moving although the doors remained closed. When she was completely caged in, a rumble rose from his chest, not quite a growl or a purr, the vibration urging her to press closer and slacken her jaw.

His tongue swept across hers, worshiping rather than dominating, the glide of his hands on her back making her whole body tingle.

He broke the kiss with a groan that she echoed. "My lovely Lelindia." His lips touched down on her cheeks, her forehead, her hair. "Your generosity knows no bounds."

That made her chuckle. "Generosity? I want to claim you as mine for all time. And I don't want to wait another day. That sounds selfish."

The liquid gold of his eyes stoked her like a furnace. "Not to me."

She lost track of what exactly happened after that, although she did remember setting the sketch down on a table in Jonarel's cabin. But she ended up naked and panting in his bed, sweat slicking her skin as her cries of pleasure joined with his. When their breathing finally settled back to a normal level, she turned her head, gazing at the relaxed beauty of his face. "Was that a yes?"

His eyelids fluttered up. Keenan's talents had captured that look perfectly. "Yes."

A giddy joy expanded in her chest, making her wriggle in anticipation. "So we're really going to do this? Have a Suulh mating ceremony and a Kraed tamlenac feast tonight?"

He rose onto his elbow and brushed the back of his fingers along her cheek. "Tonight, you will make me your mate." The fire that leapt in his eyes made it clear he wasn't talking about the public ceremony. His lips curved and parted in a smile that stole her breath.

She captured his hand in hers and kissed his fingers. "And you will make me yours."

His large body shivered at her caress.

What a heady experience, to have all that raw, masculine power reacting to her touch, ready and willing to give her anything she needed, anything she wanted.

She wanted him. Had always wanted him. From the first time they'd met, more than a year before he'd become the rippling mountain of muscle and lethal grace before her, he'd fascinated her. At first she'd thought it was because her Nedale senses were picking up on their physiological differences, like the hidden claws in his hands and feet. It made him intriguing.

But that never explained why she'd find excuses to stay at the library with him and Aurora when they were studying together. Or why she spent her free time researching everything she could find about Kraed culture, even though it had never caught her interest before.

AUDREY SHARPE

She'd resonated with him on an instinctual level. Now she understood why.

The happy sigh that spilled from her lips made his smile widen.

He laced his fingers with hers. "But we have much to do before that time comes."

"You're right." She rolled to her side, wrapping the sheet around her torso as she stood, leaving him partially covered by the dark brown blanket. Yowza. Too bad she couldn't get Keenan to capture *that* pose. Then again, if she had that image to gaze at whenever she wanted, she'd never get anything done. "I need a shower."

He gestured to his bathroom. "I will bring you fresh clothing."

"That's silly," she protested. "I'll get dressed and go to my—"

She squealed as he moved with the speed of a panther, sweeping her off her feet and depositing her next to the shower enclosure.

"I would prefer for you to remain here."

When he said it in that sexy low rumble, how could she possibly say no? "Um, okay."

He bent his head and nuzzled her neck before drawing back. "I will return shortly." Then he was gone.

An excited shiver started at the top of her head and worked its way down to her toes. She was going to be mated to Jonarel. Today!

Her little hop disengaged the sheet as it slid to the floor. She'd already wet her hair when Jonarel's shadow fell over her. He held her rose-scented shampoo in one hand and her lavender soap in the other. His gaze followed the stream of water down her body and his fingers curled around the soap.

"Do you want to join me?" She barely recognized her seductive purr.

His gaze snapped to hers, turning the shower into a sauna. "Yes. But now is not the time."

She didn't miss the silent promise in his statement. She claimed the two items from his hands with trembling fingers. "I'll be out soon."

While she dried her hair — it took a lot longer now that it had grown to her shoulders — he showered and dressed. The dark brown tunic he pulled over his head sculpted to his muscles like a second skin, distracting her from her task. How had she managed to hide her reaction to him for so many years?

Well, that was an easy question. He'd been in love with Aurora. Or convinced himself he should be. If Cade Ellis hadn't set foot on the *Starhawke* and reminded Aurora what passionate love felt like, their lives would have had all the makings of a Greek tragedy. She'd have to remember to thank Cade later.

As they headed out of the cabin, Jonarel clasped her hand in his. "Your parents or Aurora?"

"Aurora." In his culture, he normally would have consulted his parents before arranging a mating ceremony with the person he'd chosen. The consultation was a formality rather than a requirement, but as clan leader, his father had the right to object to the pair bonding of members of his clan. That's why Signal had been so assured that Jonarel would follow the course he'd laid out.

In Suulh society, individuals were free to choose their mates without consulting their parents or their leaders. But as the Nedale, she needed Aurora's support for the mating ceremony to continue, not only because she was the Sahzade, but also because she was the captain.

They found Aurora on the bridge talking with Kire and Brendan. Brendan sat at the helm, but his chair was swiveled to face Aurora in the captain's chair, while Kire reclined in the chair to her left where Lelindia often sat.

They all turned as she and Jonarel stepped off the lift. But it was the trio of matching smiles on their faces that tipped her off that something was up, even before Aurora spoke. "You have something you want to ask me, don't you?"

And here she'd thought their announcement would be a surprise. She'd neglected to anticipate Aurora and Brendan's empathic abilities. Aurora must have been tuned into her emotional state ever since Keenan had given her the drawing, which explained why she'd hustled everyone off the shuttle when they'd returned to the ship. She'd wanted to give them some time alone.

Lelindia glanced at Jonarel, whose bemused expression confirmed he'd reached the same conclusion. "Yes, we do. We want to hold a mating ceremony and tamlenac feast today."

Aurora's whoop and accompanying punch in the air pulled her right out of the captain's chair. Her steps closed the distance as she engulfed Lelindia in a hug, her energy field engaging in a burst of joy. "I knew it!" she crowed, pulling back with a wide grin. "We've been waiting here for half an hour."

Brendan pulled her into a hug next. "This is what I've always wished for you," he whispered in her ear, his voice a little husky.

She hugged him back just as tightly. "Thank you."

Kire stepped beside Jonarel and smacked him on the back. "I'm happy for you, big guy. For both of you. So does this mean I get to be best man? Is that a thing for the Kraed? Or the Suulh?"

Jonarel's jaw flexed, a shadow of pain crossing his face. "We stand with our family." He bowed his head. "I would be honored if you would stand with me."

Kire diffused the descending grey cloud with a high-intensity smile. "Always. Though I guess we won't have time for a bachelor party."

Jonarel frowned. "Bachelor party?"

"Never mind." Kire flicked his fingers. "It's a human tradition."

"Speaking of which," Brendan said, turning to Lelindia. "What type of ceremony are you planning to have?"

"I'm not exactly sure." Her thoughts hadn't traveled much farther than the announcement. "I know I was part of your ceremony, but I don't remember much except I think it was outdoors."

"Yep. Near an ancient redwood Libra and I... liked." His lips compressed into a self-conscious smile. "It was a beautiful ceremony, but designed for a circle of Suulh. I was the only human. Here, the humans outnumber the Suulh. It might not have the same effect."

"And it wouldn't include any of Jonarel's traditions."

Jonarel clasped her hand. "I do not mind. We will have the tamlenac afterward. If your father will make the meal preparations with me beforehand, that is enough."

She blinked in surprise. "You cook?"

He gave her a mock-affronted glare. "All Kraed young learn to prepare food."

"Oh." She'd never seen him do it, but that didn't mean anything. At the Academy everyone ate in the mess hall, and the same was true on the starships they'd served on together in the Fleet. On the *Starhawke*, Celia ruled the galley. "Good to know."

His voice dropped to a low rumble only she could hear. "There is much we will learn about each other." The flare of heat in his eyes that accompanied that statement made her melt.

But she still shook her head. "I want the ceremony to represent *both* of us."

Brendan cleared his throat. "If you're holding it on the *Starhawke*, won't it automatically do that? Libra and I mated on Earth, my home, but had a Suulh ceremony to honor her traditions. This ship," he gestured around them, "was designed and built by Jonarel, for you and Aurora. Any ceremony you have here will honor both of your cultures. Maybe you just need to stand together and say what's in your hearts."

The wave of emotion rose again as she met Jonarel's gaze. "What do you think?"

His fingers caressed hers with a lover's tender touch. "I think we have everything we need."

Twenty-Seven

Aurora followed Lelindia and Jonarel to the greenhouse, where Aurora's mom, Marina, and Gryphon were helping to turn the space into a more verdant jungle than it already was, their energy fields twining and dancing over the branches and leaves of the plants.

"Hey guys!" Gryphon called out from his spot near the babbling creek. "Ready for lunch?"

Lelindia's steps had a lot more bounce in them than usual, almost as if she were skipping as she and Jonarel led the way along the winding path. "Actually, we want to talk to you about something first."

Gryphon rubbed his chin in puzzlement, but Aurora caught the knowing glance Marina and her mother shared. Apparently she and her dad weren't the only ones about to have their suspicions confirmed.

"What's up?" Gryphon asked.

Lelindia took a deep breath. "Jonarel and I want to have our mating ceremony today."

Marina's squeal wasn't quite as loud as Aurora's whoop had been, but still impressive. She launched into Lelindia's arms, almost taking her down. "Oh, my sweet girl, I'm so happy!" She hugged her hard, her dark eyes luminous. "What can we do to help?"

Lelindia laughed. "Wow, that was easy."

Gryphon moved to Lelindia's other side, gathering his family into a group hug. "What were you expecting, an argument?" He waved Jonarel over, who'd hung back near Aurora and her mom.

Jonarel moved forward hesitantly, which Gryphon didn't allow. Reaching out one long arm, he pulled Jonarel in close. "In case my daughter hasn't made it clear, we're huggers in this family."

Jonarel gave a whimpering sigh as he bent his head close to Lelindia, cocooning her in between him and her parents. The emotions came off him in fits and starts, bursts of joy and stabs of pain.

Aurora ached for him. He'd found a wellspring of happiness with Lelindia, something he never would have had with her, but he'd paid a heavy price by defying his father's wishes. The unconditional acceptance from Marina and Gryphon was an incredible gift, but also a harsh mirror when compared to Siginal's unrelenting demands for absolute obedience. It might take Jonarel a while to find his new normal.

In the meantime, he'd have the love and support of everyone on this ship to back him up, including Star, who'd materialized in his line of sight. She looked as delighted by the announcement as everyone else. "Shall I begin a conversion of the observation lounge for the ceremony?"

Jonarel took a step back and gazed at Lelindia. "Checana?"

"Whatever you and Star set up is fine with me. I trust you."

Another flare of the joy-pain. He rested his hand lightly on Lelindia's hair. "I will endeavor to please you."

She almost didn't catch Lelindia's whispered reply. "You always do."

The flash of desire from both of them wasn't nearly as subtle. Aurora turned to hide her reaction to the emotional influx, and found her mother watching her.

"You ready for this?" her mom asked in an undertone.

It wasn't a casual question. By mating with Jonarel, Lelindia was setting in motion the turning of the wheel that bound the Sahzade and Nedale together. If they successfully produced a daughter from their union — which was by no means certain — the clock would be ticking for Aurora.

Her stomach did a backflip. Romance was all well and good, maybe even a mating ceremony at some point, but she wasn't remotely close to considering motherhood. She was just getting the hang of being captain of her own ship.

"It's fine." The words came to her lips automatically, as they had for most of her life whenever she didn't want to say what was really on her mind or in her heart.

"Mm-hmm." Her mom correctly parsed that two-word response, her eyes narrowing. "Nothing wrong with taking things slow, Sahzade."

Aurora's jaw hinged open. Her mother had never, *ever*, called her that. Saying it now wasn't an accident.

Her mom slipped an arm around her waist and squeezed. "Trust your instincts, and your heart. They'll never lead you astray."

"Th-thanks." She barely got the word out with her jaw still on the floor.

Gryphon's voice called her attention back to the group huddle. "To repeat my beautiful wife's question, what can we do to help?"

"How about cooking?" Lelindia asked. "After the ceremony, Jonarel would like to hold a traditional Kraed welcome feast."

If Gryphon had had buttons on his shirt, they would have popped. "I'd be delighted. Just tell me what you need and I'll get to work." He turned to Aurora and her mom. "Can I rope in Micah and Brendan, too?"

Aurora chuckled. "I'm happy to volunteer them. Cade or Drew can take over at the helm for the rest of this shift. But I guess we'll need to draw lots to see who will be on bridge duty during the ceremony."

Star's image vanished and reappeared by her side. "Not necessarily."

"Oh?"

"The bridge controls are designed with Humans in mind, but that setup is not essential to the ship's function. I can convert any part of the ship to act as a navigation interface, including a section of the observation lounge. No one from the crew will need to be absent for the ceremony and feast."

Aurora took a step forward and opened her arms before reality kicked in and she grinned. "Star, I'd hug you right now if I could."

Star's eyes glowed like miniature lanterns. "Not an option, Captain, but I appreciate the sentiment."

Aurora turned to Lelindia and Jonarel. "Should I alert the rest of the crew? Or do you want to do it?"

Lelindia stepped back into the circle of Jonarel's arms. "You're the captain."

"Alighty then. Star, please open a shipwide channel."

"Open."

Aurora cleared her throat. "All crewmembers. It has been brought to my attention that later today we're going to be celebrating the pair bonding mating ceremony of Lelindia and Jonarel."

She paused for a moment as emotional fireworks exploded all over the ship – the crew reacting to the news.

"All those with cooking skills, report to Gryphon and Jonarel in the galley for assignment. Everyone else head for the observation lounge to help Star decorate. Cade, I need you to take over my dad's shift at the helm for a few hours. Mom, Marina, you're with me and Lelindia for food and greenery gathering."

And when that task was done, she and Celia would be whisking Lelindia up to her cabin. The next time Jonarel saw his beloved, Aurora wanted his heart on his sleeve and his tongue on the floor. Lelindia deserved no less.

Twenty-Eight

The cool spongy surface of the sparring mat in the training center warmed under the pads of Celia's fingers. Her weight balanced perfectly through her wrists, arms, and torso up to the tips of her toes suspended in the air.

Breathe in, breathe out. Release tension. Stay centered.

A subtle background click preceded Aurora's voice coming through the ship's speaker system.

"All crewmembers. It has been brought to my attention that later today we're going to be celebrating the pair bonding mating ceremony of Lelindia and Jonarel."

Celia's body swayed a fraction. She'd anticipated this turn of events, but the timing was even quicker than she'd expected. She tipped her legs forward into a front walkover, her bare feet touching down on the mat as she rose to standing.

"All those with cooking skills, report to Gryphon and Jonarel in the galley for assignment."

That was her. She snagged a towel, draped it around her neck, and listened to the rest of Aurora's message before heading out of the training center and into the lift to her cabin to make a quick clothing change.

The galley was already bustling with activity when she arrived. Gryphon had claimed the role of head chef, directing Brendan and Micah, who were both busily washing and sorting vegetables as Aurora and her mom delivered them from the greenhouse.

Gryphon grinned when he spotted her. "Just the woman I was looking for. I understand you've had some experience making Kraed dishes."

"I've dabbled." She'd worked to learn the favorite dishes of all the crewmembers, including their engineer.

"Then I'm turning you and Micah over to Jonarel so Brendan and I can focus on the items on Lelindia's wish list."

A sour taste coated her tongue as her gaze drifted to Aurora's brother. This assignment had taken an abrupt turn for the worse.

He didn't look any happier than she was, although his expression wasn't quite as guarded as it had been the past few days. Still wary, but not quite antagonistic.

She couldn't say the same. But this wasn't about her and Micah. It was about Lelindia and Jonarel, who'd finally broken through all the barriers to their happiness. If supporting them meant spending time with Micah for a little while, she'd just have to muddle through.

Jonarel's gaze flicked between them as they joined him on the opposite end of the galley. As perceptive as the Kraed was, he had to know she wasn't one of Micah's fans. But he didn't suggest a change in arrangement.

He pointed to the display panel above the counter. "You have made this dish before."

She checked the description and list of ingredients. "Yeah, I remember this. No problem." So far she'd enjoyed all the Kraed dishes she'd tried. They weren't subtle when it came to flavorings, especially spices with a kick.

"The second dish is traditional, but more complicated. It is typically prepared during celebrations."

Micah leaned in, crowding her a bit, his gaze running over the display. "The prep work I understand, but I don't recognize any of the ingredients. Do you?"

"Yes." She didn't quite keep the smugness out of her voice. "Lelindia and I took cuttings and seeds for these plants the first time we visited Drakar."

His nostrils flared and his jaw tightened. "Then I guess you're in charge."

How right he was.

Jonarel stepped back. "Lelindia and I will fetch what you need from the greenhouse."

"Sounds good," she replied, already pulling pans out of the cupboards.

Micah propped his hip against the counter and folded his arms. "What would you like me to do?"

Get off this ship.

His fingers curled and his biceps flexed like he'd heard her. In reality, he'd probably just guessed her answer to his open-ended question as soon as he'd asked it.

Or maybe he'd lied about the scope of his abilities. The jury was still out on that one. She knew he could communicate with animals in a mental dialogue. Why not humans, too?

"You can grab one of the cutting boards and a knife."

One blond brow lifted, like he was surprised she'd suggested he fetch a weapon. But he did as she asked.

While he washed and cut the items Jonarel and Lelindia brought in from the greenhouse, she focused on the sauce for the more elaborate dish. She and Micah worked in silence, but the galley was filled with sounds. Gryphon and Brendan kept up a lively banter interspersed with singing and occasional drumming on the counters or pans. She recognized some of the tunes, but most were unfamiliar.

Brendan had a great voice, something she'd learned while staying at his house on Hawai'i. He loved to sing or hum while he cooked.

Gryphon joined in, and so did Libra whenever she passed through the galley on her way to the observation lounge with greenery.

Micah did not.

Curiosity got the better of her. "You don't sing?"

He looked at her out of the corner of his eye as he peeled an onion-like vegetable. "I sing."

"But not now?"

He turned his head a few centimeters and looked her right in the eye. "No, not now."

Her gut tightened and a strange flutter in her pulse almost pushed her into a fighting stance. She forced her hand to loosen the defensive grip on the wooden stirring spoon in her hand. "Because I'm here."

"Singing's something I do with family and friends. We're not friends."

"No, we're not." At least they agreed on that point.

"I do have a question for you, though." He focused his attention on the round vegetable in his hand and resumed peeling.

She waited, stirring the sauce in a rhythmic motion.

"Would you teach me how to fight?"

Teach him to fight? Her muscles locked up, preventing any air from entering her chest and freezing her in place. Her brain wasn't processing any new input, suspended in a shocked stasis.

He turned his head, his green eyes assessing her reaction. "I'll take that as a no."

She inhaled through her nose, shaking off the paralysis as quickly as it had taken hold. "I didn't say no."

"No?" The muscles around his mouth relaxed a fraction. "Then you'll consider it?"

Oh, she was considering it plenty now that the initial shock had worn off. What better way to break through his façade than putting him through grueling training sessions on the mat? He was gift-wrapping himself for her. She couldn't have asked for a better opportunity. "Yeah, I'll do it."

"You will?" His voice rose on the last syllable, and not just because it was a question. She picked up a note of trepidation, too. Her eagerness had made him nervous.

Even better. "Absolutely. It's my job." And she was soooo looking forward to doing it. "We'll start tomorrow."

He backed up a half-step — an unconscious move — his tanned skin a little paler than it had been a second before. "Uh, okay. Good."

"Uh-huh." She hid her smile as she turned her back on him and walked to the pantry. Micah Scott was going down.

Twenty-Nine

"Breathe, Lee-Lee."

Lelindia dutifully followed Aurora's quiet order, her chest rising and falling rapidly as she stared past Aurora's shoulder at the ornate doors of the observation lounge.

Jonarel was through those doors, waiting to become her mate.

The reality of the moment had caught up with her as she'd followed Aurora off the lift, their mothers and Celia behind her. Her feet had rooted to the deck as her pulse leapt, throwing off her balance.

The familiar warmth of Aurora's energy field surrounded her, joined a moment later by the echo of Libra's field and the soothing coolness of her mother's.

Aurora's concerned gaze filled her vision as she moved to block the view of the doors. "What's bothering you?"

"It's just... I've wanted this... daydreamed about this for so long..." She took another slow breath, allowing Aurora's energy field to ground her. "It's irrational, but I'm afraid if I walk through those doors, I'll wake up and lose it all."

Aurora's understanding smile eased the fear. "I get that. It's how I felt when Jonarel brought me to the *Starhawke* for the first time. And then with Cade..." She trailed off and waved the rest away before clasping Lelindia's hands in hers. "But this is *real*. What you have with Jonarel is real." She dropped her voice to a conspiratorial whisper. "I can't wait to see you two get hitched."

That sparked a laugh, releasing the tension and the deck's grip on her feet. "Then let's do this."

Aurora took up her position in front of her, her blue dress and golden hair shimmering amidst the pearlescent glow of her energy field. The dress had been a gift from Daymar, Jonarel's mother, during their first trip to Drakar, as were the ones she and Celia wore.

The Suulh mating gown that her mother and Libra had each worn during their ceremonies – the one they'd saved for her and Aurora – had been destroyed in the Stoneycroft fire. Wearing the dress Daymar had given her allowed her to honor the Kraed connection and further integrate Jonarel's culture into the festivities.

Besides, it was the most beautiful garment she'd ever owned. The first time she'd worn it she'd ended the night with an uncomfortable discussion with Jonarel about his first kiss with Aurora. How far they'd come.

She smoothed her hand over the silky ice blue fabric, her finger moving from the flared skirt to the bodice, tracing the rich brown accents that perfectly matched her hair.

A pang of longing rolled through her. She wanted Daymar here. Siginal may have behaved disrespectfully, but Jonarel's mother had always been gracious and kind. Whether Daymar disagree with hers and Jonarel's decision to mate or not, missing their ceremony would cause her pain and regret.

At least Tehar was making a holographic recording of the ceremony, which gave her some consolation. Hopefully one day soon she'd be able to welcome Daymar to the *Starhawke* and replay this moment for her.

She glanced over her shoulder at her mother. Her yellow-gold dress borrowed from Celia perfectly complimented her emerald-green energy field swirling around her. "I'm so glad you're here."

Her mom's smile trembled. "I wouldn't miss it."

Lelindia's gaze moved to Celia, who looked stunning in the burgundy dress Daymar had made for her that showed off her toned physique and bronze skin. Celia winked at her, a hint of *I told you so* in her brown eyes.

Yes, she had. Thank the stars she'd been right.

Libra, in an aquamarine dress — also Celia's — looked vibrant surrounded by her pearlescent energy field. Libra gave her a saucy smile. "Go get him, firefly."

The use of her childhood nickname popped the top on an internal champagne bottle. Bubbles of excitement poured through her, her body growing lighter and bouncier by the second, her energy field expanding.

Aurora took that as her cue, stepping forward.

She followed suit. How many times had she walked this corridor since her first day on the *Starhawke*? How often had Jonarel been by her side? Yet she felt like she was seeing it all for the first time.

The wooden doors of the observation lounge, with their kaleidoscope of inlaid color, parted soundlessly.

Starlight glimmered beyond the wide windows that circled half the open space, but it was the thousands of twinkling lights dancing around the trunks of massive denglar trees along the perimeter of the room that made her steps slow. She'd swear she'd entered the Clarek compound.

Her gaze swept the space. Tehar had outdone herself. The trees were an illusion, of course. But whether a projection, like Tehar herself, or an elegantly crafted replica, the result was breathtaking, especially when combined with the live plants temporarily transported from the greenhouse. She couldn't tell where reality ended and fantasy began.

And speaking of fantasy...

Aurora stepped to one side, revealing the god standing at the center of the room.

She stared, the rest of her surroundings fading out of existence.

"Lelindia?"

Jonarel's voice caressed her as she feasted on the sight of him. His thick dark hair gleamed in the light, flowing in waves to his shoulders. His tunic looked like spun gold and fit like a second skin, outlining the muscles of his arms and chest. A dark brown vested garment gave his outfit a more formal look, with elaborate braiding in tones of gold and brown. His muscular legs were clad in form-fitting brown pants of a material similar to the vest, the colors bringing out the tendrils of brown that decorated the deep green of his skin.

Forget the ceremony. She wanted him in her bedroom. Now.

Her fingers made contact with his chest before she realized she'd taken a step. His sharp inhale brought her gaze to his.

Tightly leashed fire burned in his golden eyes, but beneath it glowed something even stronger. It called to her, pulling her forward as his arms circled her like she was made of glass.

"Lelindia."

This time her name was a plea, a prayer, and a promise all rolled into one.

She spread her fingers over his rapidly beating heart. "Jonarel." Her tone matched his, her heart pounding just as fast. She could stay locked in this moment forever.

His fingers touched down on the small of her back with the lightness of a hummingbird. Her entire body vibrated in response.

"My lovely Lelindia."

She couldn't stand it. Rising on tiptoe, she brushed her lips across his.

A growl rumbled from his chest and his fingers flexed a millimeter, but he didn't try to take the kiss further. Instead, he held perfectly still as she paid homage to the beauty of his mouth.

Her dad cleared his throat, but she caught the muffled chuckle underneath.

Calling a halt to the kiss took a supreme act of will. Jonarel was so... delicious. "Tonight," she murmured as she drew back.

His guttural response was barely discernable as words. "Yes, checana." His chest heaved as he released her, his hand enveloping hers, the warmth of his skin making her shudder.

Together, they faced Aurora, who was waiting patiently, a soft smile curving her lips. Lelindia's mom, Libra, and Celia formed a semi-circle behind them.

"I am Aurora, daughter of Libra, Sahzade of the Suulh." The words flowed over her, adapted from the traditional Suulh ceremony. "The Nedale Lelindia, my energy sister, has chosen her mate, the Kraed Jonarel."

Lelindia's fingers squeezed Jonarel's.

Aurora's gaze shifted. "Do you accept this gift given freely by the Nedale?"

Jonarel turned his head, the emotion in his eyes making Lelindia tremble. "With all that I am and will be."

Her knees wobbled, and Jonarel's grip tightened.

Breathe.

The word floated into her mind from Aurora, a gentle reminder. Meeting Aurora's gaze, she drew in air, and her knees started working again.

Aurora's smile grew a bit as she continued. "Lelindia, Nedale of the Suulh and my energy sister, you have chosen your mate, and he has accepted your gift."

Lelindia expanded her energy field, wrapping it around Jonarel, enclosing them together in its emerald glow. His finger pads pressed into her palm, the tip of his claws resting against her skin like a cat kneading with its paws.

"This bonding is a gift to all." Aurora's voice carried the authority and strength of the leader of the Suulh. "Nedale and Sahzade, throughout the ages, have nurtured and protected our people. With this pairing, Lelindia and Jonarel will nurture and protect each other, and all those who are blessed to know them, all the days of their lives."

Aurora stepped back as a circle formed, but all Lelindia saw was Jonarel. Thankfully he was able to hold her gaze while also guiding them into their place in the circle at the same time. Otherwise they would have stayed like statues at its center.

But she needed to get her brain in gear so she could complete her part of the ceremony. Focusing her thoughts, she said the words that would bind her to Jonarel now and always.

"I am Lelindia, daughter of Marina, granddaughter of Breaa, Nedale of the Suulh. In the name of my mother and grandmother, I pledge myself to Jonarel, my mate, and to all the Suulh, past, present, and future."

Jonarel's jaw flexed as he gazed at her as if enchanted. It took a moment before he seemed capable of saying his part of the Suulh mating pledge. "I am Jonarel, son of Daymar, mate of the Nedale." He paused, as though savoring the words on his tongue. "I pledge myself to Lelindia, my mate, and to all the Suulh, past, present, and future."

Her breath caught.

They'd done it. Jonarel was her mate!

Well, almost. Now they moved to the Kraed half of the ceremony.

Jonarel squeezed her hand before releasing it and stepping into the center of the circle. Tehar moved beside him and Kire stepped forward to flank his other side.

Jonarel's gaze lingered on her for a long moment. Her heart fluttered with each beat.

His attention locked on her parents, who'd moved to either side of her. "Most honored guests, the givers of life to my checana. My sister Tehar and I welcome you on behalf of clan Clarek. As this moment comes at a time when the rest of my clan cannot be with us," his voice gave a subtle hitch, "the brother of my heart, Kire, and my *Starhawke* family have consented to serve as representatives of my clan."

At his words, the crew broke ranks from the circle and formed a cluster behind him.

That's when she noticed Kire and Kelly were dressed in the formal attire Jonarel's mother had given them on Drakar while Cade and his team were dressed in all black.

Aurora had moved to stand beside Cade.

Lelindia hadn't received any intel on this part of the ceremony. She shot Aurora a look but got a secret smile and a wink in return.

"Your presence here is an honor and blessing." Jonarel's gaze rested on her again, silence stretching out as the look in his eyes told her everything that was in his heart. "The path we have walked has been challenging and fraught with danger, yet through it all, my checana has been a light in the darkness for me, even when I did not realize it."

Every time she thought she couldn't possibly love him more, he proved her wrong.

He finally broke eye contact, taking a deep breath, and addressed her parents again, his next words coming out constricted, like he was struggling to get enough air. "I have never received a gift equal to the one you have bestowed upon me, the life blood that flows in Lelindia's veins."

He spread his arms, palms up, and sank to his knees, drawing a collective inhale from those around her. Her pulse thrummed, her throat tightening.

"In return for this precious gift, I offer you the blood of my veins. And my pledge. On the honor of my forebears, the future of my descendants, and the forfeit of my own life, I pledge my blood shall spill or burn to insure that no harm shall ever come to her for as long as I draw breath."

Her chest constricted. She'd seen Jonarel bleed and burn, more than once. Sometimes for her. His pain shredded her more than if she'd suffered the wounds herself.

His gaze returned to her.

She forgot to breathe.

His voice dropped to a whisper. "She is my checana. She is my life."

Moisture spilled onto her cheeks and pattered onto her clenched hands.

You are mine she mouthed, unable to push air past her vocal cords. Her vision contracted to the Kraed warrior on his knees before her, pledging his life to protect her. And love her.

Her dad cleared his throat, much more solemnly this time, but it was her mother who spoke.

"Jonarel, your words honor us and our beloved daughter. As do your actions. Last week you demonstrated the truth of your words when you risked your life to pull us out of the burning wreck of our home. Not only did you carry us to safety, but you returned for Lelindia, suffering painful injury to guarantee she would not."

The image of Jonarel dropping onto the remains of the burning gallery like a panther, sweeping her onto his back and carrying her through the flames, would stay with her forever.

Her mother's and father's energy fields enveloped her, wrapping her in love and joy.

"We could not ask for a better indication of your commitment to Lelindia," her mother continued, "or the depth of your love for her. It is with full hearts that we accept your pledge of blood to protect our daughter as your mate. May joy walk with you both all the days of your lives."

Thirty

The raw emotions pouring off Lelindia, Jonarel, Marina, and Gryphon buffeted Aurora, but she welcomed the gale force, using the techniques her father had taught her to handle it with relative ease.

Such unfettered joy deserved to be treasured.

Two of the people dearest to her in the universe had found love with each other. She couldn't have asked for a better outcome for a situation that had once been cloaked in misery.

As Jonarel rose to his feet and drew Lelindia into his arms for a tender kiss, Cade's hand slipped into hers. His emotions washed over her, too, but with a very different focus. It was easy to figure out he was thinking about their future, perhaps whether a ceremony like this awaited them.

They hadn't talked about it in specific terms. Agreeing that they wanted to be together was as far as they'd gone. Did he want an official mating ceremony? Did she?

Her parents had told her about their Suulh ceremony. The idea appealed to her, but it wasn't a step she was ready to take. A traditional Suulh ceremony would push her into a decision about the future of the Sahzade line.

Lelindia and Jonarel hadn't included that element in their ceremony because there were no guarantees they'd be able to produce children. But her parents had proven Suulh and humans were perfectly compatible from a genetic standpoint.

Becoming a Fleet captain had been her goal for as long as she could remember, which made having a family more complicated. Now she had her own ship. And her entire race to save. Continuing the Sahzade line wasn't a priority, especially if there was a chance the Nedale line would end with Lelindia.

She'd need to be clear on where she stood on the matter before bringing it up with Cade.

Clarity seemed a long way off.

As Lelindia and Jonarel came up for air, Star and Kire motioned everyone away from the center of the room. A banquet table and chairs rose to fill the space, the curving lines creating a vaguely crescent shape.

Jonarel led Lelindia and her parents to the chairs at the top curve of the crescent while Kire directed Aurora's parents and Micah to the seats on the opposite side of Lelindia.

Aurora sidled closer to the table, watching for Lelindia's reaction. She caught the flutter of confusion when Lelindia realized Jonarel hadn't left a chair open for himself.

"You're not sitting with me?" she asked.

"It will be my privilege to serve you and your family."

The tenderness in his eyes apparently turned Lelindia's knees to rubber, because she sank onto the chair, her gaze still locked with Jonarel's.

Aurora captured the moment in her heart, cherishing her energy sister's emotional response to her new mate. All the challenges they'd overcome to get to this point made this scene all the sweeter.

After bending to give Lelindia another soft kiss, Jonarel turned and nodded to Aurora and Cade.

They sprang into action. Star summoned the serving tables from the subterranean delivery system that connected to the galley. Aurora snagged a carved wood pitcher of tenrebac while Cade fetched one of water. The rest of the crew picked up the serving dishes of food.

Aurora carried the pitcher around the table to where Lelindia sat, still looking befuddled. "Tenrebac?" she offered.

Lelindia held out her goblet and Aurora filled it. "I can't believe the entire crew was in on this and I didn't know."

"You've been a little preoccupied." She tilted her head toward Jonarel, who'd passed behind her to serve Marina and Gryphon from the large platter in his hands.

"Yeah, but... everyone?" She motioned to Cade, who was pouring water into Micah's glass, and lowered her voice. "I'm surprised Cade and his team agreed to go along with it."

Aurora pinned her with a look. "They love and respect you both. And he and Jonarel have come a long way."

She sensed a wave of gratitude from Lelindia, but also a ripple of emotion from Jonarel, who'd obviously overheard her comment. With his superior hearing, it was almost impossible for him *not* to eavesdrop.

She rested a hand on Lelindia's shoulder. "As Jonarel said, we're a family. This is a wonderful day for all of us."

Lelindia gripped Aurora's forearm, a tremulous smile on her lips. "Thank you, Sahzade."

A laugh bubbled up from her chest. "I should be thanking you. I've never had such a happy crew."

The rest of the evening passed in a blur. The steady flow of tenrebac might have had something to do with it. After the guests of honor were served, Jonarel took his seat facing Lelindia and the rest of the crew followed suit, filling out the large table. Star circulated during the meal, acting as hostess for the event, while Kire and Jonarel made sure everyone had plenty of food and drink.

After the meal, Jonarel serenaded Lelindia with the lyrical music of a traditional Kraed love song, the resonant tones of his baritone filling the room and bringing an adorable blush to Lelindia's cheeks. No one suggested the happy couple should stay longer when they rose to leave, even though it was their party. Their heightened emotional state was tangible even to those without empathic abilities.

The rest of the group continued the celebration late into the night, with Gryphon and Aurora's dad sharing stories from Lelindia and Aurora's youth. Star provided a few fascinating stories about Jonarel's childhood as well.

By the time Aurora walked with Cade to the lift, she was feeling more relaxed than she had at any time in recent memory. And more than a little tipsy.

As the lift doors closed, she turned into Cade's arms and brushed her lips against his. "Thank you."

"For what?"

"For being you."

"No one else I'd rather be." His lips captured hers in a firmer grip, sending warmth flowing through her. He released her when the lift doors parted on the command deck but kept her close as they strolled down the corridor to her cabin.

Correction. *Their* cabin. She never wanted him sleeping in one of the guest cabins again.

The door swung open, the soft lighting within welcoming them. She sighed as they stepped over the threshold. "I love having you here."

He drew her back into his arms, his lips hovering a hair's breadth over hers. "I love being here. And I love you."

The tenderness in his kiss emphasized his words.

She tunneled her fingers into his hair, sinking into the delightful bliss of his touch. "And I love you," she murmured as his lips moved along her jaw and down the column of her neck.

"Glad to hear it." He continued his lazy exploration as he backed her into the bedroom. "Care to show me how much?"

The heat in his gaze sparked an answering flare in her body. "Absolutely."

"Glad to hear that, too." Nudging her back to the bed, he guided her to sit on the edge as he crouched in front of her.

His hands moved to her feet, then stopped. "Uh, these look complicated."

She chuckled, pivoting her calf to expose the laces of the dress shoes. "They are." Daymar had taught her how to lace them when she'd delivered the dress. She'd never worn them when she was with Cade before. "Want me to remove them?"

"Yes, please." He rested his hands on her knees, his fingers slowly inch-worming the hem of her dress up to expose her bare thighs.

He wasn't helping her concentration. Releasing the laces she captured his face in her hands and covered his mouth with hers. "Then you'd better stop before you reach your destination," she warned.

His throaty laugh made her tremble. "Yes, ma'am." Sitting back on his heels, he watched as she worked the first shoe off. When she had one leg free, he took her foot in his hands and massaged her arch.

She moaned, her fingers stilling on the second set of laces.

"Good?"

"Um-hmm." But her feet weren't where she wanted his hands. She got the second shoe off in record time. As it hit the deck she latched onto the front of his black tunic with both hands, pulling him against her. "Now where were we?"

Thirty-One

"Can I talk to you for a moment?"

Micah stepped away from the bulkhead to intercept Celia as she left the observation lounge headed for the lift. She flinched but covered it with a casual shrug. "Sure." He'd obviously assumed that she'd follow him out of the room when he left the celebration and had been lying in wait for her.

He'd assumed correctly. She had not.

Micah watched her like she was a beautiful but venomous snake he didn't want to turn his back on. "I've been thinking about our discussion today, and I'd like to have our first lesson now."

"Now?" He'd surprised her again. Not a good thing.

"No time like the present. The tenrebac has loosened me up enough that I might not mind the pain so much."

She hadn't partaken in more than a few mouthfuls of the Kraed wine, not with Micah in the room. Maybe on some level she'd anticipated this turn of events. But her professional pride still prompted a response. "I'm not going to injure you."

He barked a humorless laugh. "Sure you aren't." He moved past her toward the lift. "Meet you in the gym in five minutes."

She stared at the lift doors for several seconds after they'd closed. She'd expected hesitancy from him, reluctance, after the way they'd ended the discussion this afternoon. Instead, he was showing the courage to face his fears head-on. That was the first point he'd scored in his favor.

He was waiting for her in the training center when she arrived, but only because she'd taken time to tame her thick hair into a tight braid.

He'd changed into navy sweatpants and a snug T-shirt that outlined his muscle definition, courtesy of his surfing and snorkeling habits. She'd dug up quite a few news clippings with action shots of him on his board, taken during his competitive years. He'd made a striking picture of athletic prowess and grace, two things she valued highly. Retiring from competition didn't seem to have softened him one bit.

Too bad the sight of him set off alarm klaxons. If he viewed her as a venomous snake, she viewed him as a skulking shark.

His gaze swept over her, taking in her skin-tight black leggings and tank top. An appreciative light burned for a moment but guttered and died when his gaze met hers. The flatness of his mouth matched the wary look in his eyes. "How do we start?"

She gestured to the rectangular mat, slipping off her shoes and stepping onto the cool surface. He did the same, maintaining several meters of space between them. Now that the moment had come, she could see the lines of tension in his body, the anticipation of future pain, as well as the grim determination to fight through it.

"What kind of sparring experience do you have?"

"Want to know all my weaknesses?"

"No, I—"

"The only person I've sparred with as an adult is Aurora, and she can't hurt me without hurting herself, so it made for interesting sessions."

She went still. "Hurting you hurts her?"

He looked at her like she was several arrows short of a full quiver. "I'm half-Suulh, remember? That's why she came to Hawai'i — to learn how to handle her physical reaction to Suulh pain."

Right. She hadn't factored that into this scenario.

He didn't miss the slip-up. "If you had visions of turning me into pulp, she's going to feel it. Although right now I'm guessing she's distracted and might not notice unless you do serious damage."

She reiterated her previous statement. "I'm not here to hurt you." Well, maybe a little. Learning how to fall and take a punch wasn't a painless process.

"Oh, really?" He folded his arms. "What about hurting Aurora? Whether you hurt me physically or not, your vitriol toward me is hurting her emotionally. She hates seeing us at odds."

"I know. That's why we're here."

"I very much doubt that's why you're here."

"You don't know me."

He laughed, the sound more than a little ironic. "And you don't know me. At least we're even on that score."

But she *did* know him. Something about this, about him, felt so... familiar. "Then show me what you can do."

"You want me to strike first?"

"Uh-huh."

"Okay."

He moved quicker than she'd anticipated for his size. She still dodged his punch with ease, her fist making contact with his chest before he could block. But she pulled the power of the punch, hitting him as hard as she'd hit Aurora, rather than with the anger-fueled force her subconscious craved.

He staggered, his hand rubbing his sternum as he regained his balance. His green eyes narrowed but his mouth curved up a fraction. "Try that again."

She did. This time he got an arm up to deflect the blow, but she still connected with his shoulder, following up with an elbow to his abdomen before spinning to the floor and sweeping his legs.

He hit the ground with a grunt but without the heaviness his muscle mass would indicate. And he was back on his feet with an easy flip.

His surfing training was serving him well. He was more nimble than she'd expected. He also knew how to fall without getting injured. Teaching Aurora that lesson had taken a long time. Celia had figured out later that suppressing her natural shielding ability had divided her focus. Micah didn't have that problem.

"You're quick," he said with grudging respect.

"So are you." She came at him again, changing her approach to a kick sequence that knocked him back but not down. "You planning to do anything besides stand there?"

The taunt had the desired effect. He'd been on defense, but his jaw tightened as he darted forward. His punch was expected. The kick that followed it was not, or the grace and strength with which he delivered it. She still handled both, but she started reassessing. "Have you had fight training before?"

"Just with Aurora. But I'm a quick learner."

Obviously. All the time he spent in the water probably helped, too. He was used to working his muscles against physical resistance. Moving in air would feel like floating by comparison.

He balanced his weight on the balls of his feet as they circled each other. "You're toying with me, aren't you?"

"What makes you say that?"

"No blood yet."

Her molars scraped together. "I told you, I'm not going to hurt you." If she did, she'd hurt Aurora — physically, mentally, and emotionally. Her goal was to prevent Micah from doing that, not do it for him.

He shook his head, a short lock of blond hair falling over his forehead. "I don't get you. You treat me like public enemy number one for a week, but now that you have your shot at me, you're holding back. Why?"

"I'm not holding back." She moved in for another strike. He blocked her, and she neatly flipped him onto the mat. The thump gave her some satisfaction, but he rolled with it, popping back onto his feet.

"You're lying about your experience," she growled. No beginner moved the way he did.

"I'm not a liar," he growled back, fire flashing in his eyes. "I know my body and I'm good with balance and agility." His closed-lip smile held more than a hint of smugness. "And I really enjoy irritating you."

His comment grated like nails on a chalkboard. She came at him quicker this time and with more force, driving him to the edge of the mat. He dodged to the side and she pivoted with him, landing more blows than he blocked. "You are a major irritant."

"So are you." His punch caught her shoulder.

She moved with it, spinning around and nailing him with a kick to the solar plexus that drove him to the ground. This time he didn't spring back up and she pounced, flipping him to his stomach and pinning him. "Are we having fun yet?" she whispered in his ear as she tightened the pressure on his arm to a painful level.

"Oh, yeah." His words came out as a groan against the mat, but defiance still radiated from his body. "Big fun."

Now that she had his undivided attention, she pushed for the answers she wanted. "Why did you really decide to stay on the *Starhawke?*"

He stared at her out of the side of his eye, his cheek squished into the mat. "What?"

"You told Aurora you were staying to help her. But you're a marine biologist, not a pilot or tactician or engineer." She increased the pressure a notch. "There's no logical reason for you to be on this ship."

His lip twisted and the muscles around his eye tightened in what was probably a glare. Hard to tell with half his face mashed into the deck. "She's my sister."

"What do you want from her?"

His chest moved in hitches as he struggled against the pain she was inflicting. "Nothing. I want to help her."

An arrow of anger shot through her chest. "No, you don't."

He cringed, a soft whimper escaping his lips.

She eased up. If Aurora felt his pain and came looking for them, providing an explanation for this scene wouldn't be easy. But she could blast him with the force of her words. "What do you want? Why are you here?"

Abruptly all resistance melted away, his muscles going slack. He rotated his head the fraction his position would allow so he could see her with both eyes. "Why do you hate me so much?"

The question threw her. But it was a trick. Had to be. If the confusion and misery in his eyes and every line of his body were real, she was in serious trouble.

She loosened her hold.

He didn't try to move, just stared at her.

Her heart pounded like a drum as she stared back. "I don't know." She'd never felt this kind of aggression before. Even during pitched hand-to-hand combat, her mind and emotions remained focused, calm. But being around Micah made her feel untethered, out of control, threatened in a way that left her vulnerable. Weak.

He moistened his lips with his tongue, a nervous tell. "Would you... feel better if you hit me? Really hit me?"

Would she? From the moment she'd stepped into the room, that's all she'd wanted to do. Her training, her professionalism, and her concern for Aurora had prevented it.

But seeing the resignation on his face, the draining away of his will to stop her, to resist her, released the pressure valve on her anger. "No."

"Are you sure? You look like you want to." He rolled his shoulder a few centimeters, probably to relieve a crick in his neck from the awkward angle. "If it would help, I'll let you. No sparring. Just take whatever shots you need to."

She opened her mouth, but no words came out. Instead, her throat tightened. Was he seriously offering himself as a human punching bag? Willingly?

"I heal quickly," he added, his gaze searching hers. "And if Aurora asks, we'll tell her it was my idea. Star can corroborate so you won't get blamed. Right, Star?"

The Nirunoc's image appeared beside the mat, her expression as troubled as Micah's. "If you wish it."

The klaxon that had been driving Celia since the moment she'd laid eyes on Micah abruptly cut off, leaving her in deafening silence. "Why would you do that?"

"Because you're hurting." The focus in his eyes intensified. "I can't feel it like Aurora can, but I can see it, plain as day. And I seem to be the trigger. If letting some of that pain out would help, then..." His shoulder moved in a constrained shrug.

She released him like he was on fire, shoving to her feet and backing away. "No."

He rose onto his elbows. "What—"

"No!" The air heated around her, suffocating her. She stumbled as her foot slid off the edge of the mat, but instinct kept her upright. "This is wrong. This is all wrong."

A girl's scream and choking sob echoed in her ears, the bitter taste of bile sliding across her tongue. A metal clang and harsh laughter followed her as she backed to the door.

Clapping her hands over her ears, she turned and fled.

Thirty-Two

Aurora woke with a stiff left shoulder and strange aches in her chest and arms. At first she attributed it to the fun she and Cade had enjoyed the previous night, but when her energy field failed to banish the discomfort, she went in search of Micah.

She found him in the hydrotank. An image of an aquamarine ocean and tropical fish played against the interior walls, while Micah swam against the surge of rolling waves.

Using a technique her former captain Knox Schreiber had taught her to cut through background noise – which he referred to as *command voice* – she made herself heard over the splashing water. "What happened to you?"

Micah stopped mid-stroke, the strong current momentarily pushing him toward the back of the tank.

She turned off the wave function with a touch of her finger as she crouched by the tank's edge.

He treaded water, droplets dripping from his hair and down his face. He smiled, but it wasn't convincing. "Good morning."

She didn't return his smile. "What happened to you?"

He coughed self-consciously, shook the water from his hair and swam over to her. "If I tell you, you have to promise you won't get mad."

She propped her chin on her palm. "I love conversations that start out that way."

"I mean it, sis."

"I know you do. And all I can say is, I'll do my best."

"Fair enough." Placing his palms flat on the deck he glided out of the water with the grace of a seal.

She handed him the towel he'd left on the deck.

He ran it briskly over his chest, arms, and hair before draping it around his neck. "It's about Cardiff."

"Uh-huh." She'd figured out that much already. "Were you sparring?" The aches she was sensing had that familiar feel. If so, Celia had been tough on him. Now that he was out of the water, she could see the faint hints of healing bruises on his arms and chest.

"It started out that way."

"Hmm." Stepping forward, she placed her hands on his chest. "Hold still."

He did as she asked, her pearlescent energy field engaging and surrounding him in its glow. Healing Micah was almost as easy as healing herself. In a few seconds the echo of discomfort she'd been sensing vanished and the coloration on his skin returned to normal. "That's better." She pointed to one of the deck lounges. "Have a seat."

She settled next to him, hip-to-hip, the physical contact soothing. "Start from the beginning."

He gave her a rundown of his proposal for the sparring match, and the antagonistic battle that had followed. He didn't spare any details, painting a clear picture until he reached the point where he was pinned to the mat. The pain he described explained the sore shoulder.

She studied him for a moment, letting the information process through her subconscious. "Do you have any idea why she thinks you want something from me?"

"No."

"But she believes it?"

"She did. Now, I'm not sure."

"What changed?"

"I offered to let her beat me up."

She sucked in air. "You did *what*?"

He shrugged. "It seemed like the only way to break through her anger. For her to release whatever's bottled up inside."

Ice and fire burned through her chest. "Micah, she's lethal." She didn't often think of her friend in those terms, but imagining her brother on the receiving end of whatever emotional issue Celia was grappling with scared the stuffing out of her.

"Not to me. She can't hurt me without hurting you." He gave her a weak smile. "I pointed that out to her, and I could tell she was thinking about it while we fought."

Enclosing his hand in hers, she wrapped her energy field around them, needing the reassurance. "But her reaction to you is irrational. Why would you offer yourself up as her punching bag?"

He stared at their joined hands. "You didn't see the look in her eyes. I've helped with enough of Dad's students to know a look like that reflects deep trauma. Someone abused her, badly. Someone who probably has a passing resemblance to me."

Her brother's empathy humbled her. As soon as he'd figured out the underlying cause of Celia's aggression, he'd opened up his heart and offered himself as a sacrifice.

A sacrifice she would never in a billion years let him make. "She is not going to take her anger out on you anymore." She started to rise, but he pulled her back down.

"You don't need to worry about that."

"Why not?" He'd given Celia carte blanche to use him as a target. She needed to countermand that order.

"Because she ran away."

"She ran away?" Her brain stalled. She'd never seen Celia run from anything.

"Once she realized I was serious, she... broke. Raced out of the gym like it was on fire."

Nope. She couldn't visualize it. Which meant Celia might need her a lot more than Micah right now.

She reached out with her senses, pinpointing her friend's unique energetic resonance above them. "Star, is Celia in her cabin?"

Star's image appeared near the water's edge. "Yes. She has been there since last evening."

Another bad sign. Celia spent less time in her cabin than any member of the crew. When not on duty, she preferred to hang out in the greenhouse or med bay if she wasn't cooking in the galley or working out in the gym.

Micah didn't try to stop her when she stood this time, but he didn't let go of her hand, either. "Do you want me to come with you?"

"Not now." Micah's nearness was enhancing her empathic abilities, allowing her to tune into the subtleties of Celia's emotional field. Her friend's agitated state wouldn't be improved by more exposure to her trigger. "But I have a feeling we'll both need you in the near future."

His steady gaze held hers. "I'll be here."

"I know." Giving his hand a squeeze, she headed out of the training center to the lift. A few deep breaths on the way to the crew deck helped focus her mind and ease the tension lifting her shoulders toward her ears.

She should have anticipated something like this, but she'd counted on Celia's discipline to keep things from getting out of hand. In a way, it probably had. When confronted with a situation where she couldn't possibly win, she'd fled the field of battle. And saved Micah from his own good intentions.

She touched the chime outside Celia's door. The musical tones drifted over her.

Seconds ticked by without a response.

She tapped the chime again.

Still no response, although she sensed Celia's agitation increasing.

"Star, what's going on in there?" The door chime was one of the many human-based elements Jonarel had incorporated into the ship's design. The Kraed didn't use them. On Drakar, the Nirunoc announced a visitor's presence, negating the need for a chime.

"She is aware of your presence, but reluctant to open the door."

Another phrase she'd never expected to hear regarding Celia. "Then you'll need to do it for her."

With a soft click the door swung open.

Thirty-Three

So this is how a cornered animal feels.

Celia stared at the door to her cabin as the chime trilled a second time. She should answer it. Needed to answer it. But she couldn't get her body to move.

The door swung open with the soft click of a hand grenade exploding.

She braced, every muscle taut, as Aurora stepped inside.

She'd known she'd come. The inevitability of this moment shone like a spotlight in her eyes. She'd seen no way out, no move that would free her from the trap she'd created for herself.

"Hey." Aurora's voice reached her across the distance, her steps slow and measured as she approached. "You look like hell."

The unexpected comment startled a puff of air from her chest, easing the pressure.

Aurora perched on one of the chairs across from the couch, forearms on her knees in a pose designed to look casual. But there was nothing casual about this visit.

"What happened?"

Her friend asked the question, but her captain watched her closely.

She licked dry lips. "I screwed up."

"Okay."

"I thought I could handle sparring with Micah. I was wrong." Her fingers tightened in her lap. "He said he wanted to learn to fight. I should have said no when he suggested it, but I didn't. I wanted to fight him."

Aurora was silent for a few moments. "But you did say no later."

She flinched. "He told you about that?"

"That he offered himself as a punching bag? Yeah. I'm very glad you didn't take him up on it."

"Never." But that moment seared like a brand in her memory. The look of empathy in his eyes, the feel of his muscled body completely at her mercy. His willingness to sacrifice himself to help her. Something deep inside had cracked, like a calving glacier, leaving her raw and exposed.

"That's good to know." Aurora settled back into her chair. "I understand you've been hiding out here ever since. Any particular reason?"

She'd come up with a hundred reasons over the past few hours, but only one mattered. "I'm ashamed."

Aurora took that in with a slow nod. "That's not an emotion I've ever sensed from you before."

"It's not an emotion I've felt in—" A memory knocked at the back of her mind, an image of herself as a child shortly after she'd arrived at the prison camp. Before she'd learned that shame was pointless, an irritant to be conquered. "A long time."

Aurora had never asked for details about her experiences before being rescued by the Fleet, and she'd never offered them. Her training had given her the tools to deal with her past in a way that kept it from intruding on her present.

Until now.

"You want to talk about it?"

She'd never *wanted* to talk about it. After her rescue, she'd tried to convince her mentor that she didn't need counseling, that she'd put her experiences behind her. That hadn't cut it when she'd decided to join Fleet Security. Psychological profiles were standard procedure, and she'd sunk like a stone.

She'd had her first counseling session the day her mentor told her she'd never work in the Fleet unless she faced her demons. So she had. For two years she'd rooted out the tortured pain of her past, slaying the monsters that had controlled her fate for far too long.

But if the situation with Micah was any indication, one had hidden in the shadows, biding its time, sinking its teeth into her neck when her back was turned. "Can I take a raincheck until after we've gotten our plan for contacting the Yruf settled?"

It was an excuse. They both knew it.

Aurora countered. "You don't have to talk to me, but you do have to talk to my dad."

A knot formed in her stomach. "You want me to talk to your dad about why I don't trust his son? That'll go well."

Aurora gave her a look. "He already knows you don't trust Micah. He's an empath, remember? But he's also trained in helping people work through their emotional blocks. If anyone can uncover what's behind your negative reaction to Micah, it's him."

The knot was joined by a few of its closest friends. She could try to wriggle out of it, but Aurora wouldn't let this go. "When do you want me to talk to him?"

"Star, is my dad awake?"

"Yes, Captain," Star said over the cabin speakers. "He is having breakfast with your mother in their cabin."

"Let him know Celia will be heading down in a little while for a chat." Aurora's gaze rested on her. "No time like the present."

She bit back a groan. Like it or not, she was going back into therapy.

Thirty-Four

Lelindia's body hummed from her night with Jonarel. She'd never been so loved, so *worshipped*, in her life. He'd drawn pleasure from her like an elixir, taking delight in bringing her to the heights of ecstasy again and again before finally joining her in the nova of sensation.

She'd awoken with his arms and legs curled protectively around her, the heat from his skin warming her from the inside out.

Her mate. Jonarel was her *mate*!

Her happy squeal had woken him, leading to a lusty morning that ended in a shared shower. He'd made good on his promise from the previous day. She'd stepped out very clean and extremely relaxed.

Now he was down in the greenhouse and galley, preparing breakfast for her. She'd offered to join him, but he'd requested that she remain in his cabin and allow him to serve her this first morning of their mating. He'd practically glowed like a Suulh at the prospect, so she'd relented.

But that left her with nothing to do but wait. She'd dried her hair and put on the clothes he'd brought from her cabin. The dress she'd worn for their mating ceremony still hung in a place of honor beside the archway to his bedroom. Or was it their bedroom now? They'd never discussed how their change in status would affect their cabin arrangements.

Her fingers brushed over the silken folds of the dress.

"My mother crafted that garment with much love."

She turned to find Tehar's image beside her, her thick dark hair swept back from her face in an elaborate braid and her lithe form covered in a Kraed outfit of rich brown. The illusion looked so real she had to remind herself that Tehar's clothes were made of light, not cloth.

"She would be very pleased that you wore it for your mating ceremony with my brother."

"She would?" Her gaze swept over the gown. "She wouldn't feel betrayed?" Siginal certainly would.

"My mother and father saw the path of Jonarel's future quite differently." Tehar stepped closer. "My mother is devoted to our clan, to nurturing and protecting Drakar, but she does not have my father's — what is the phrase you use? — tunnel vision."

An apt description of Siginal's world view.

"Since the day Jonarel was born, my father focused on my brother's importance to the clan. My mother focused on his happiness. She realized early on that he didn't share my father's dream of becoming the leader of our clan, though he went along with my father's plans. But when we came to Earth to seek out you and Aurora, everything changed."

"We?" She blinked. "You were at the Fleet Academy with the rest of the family?"

"Yes."

"I had no idea."

Tehar's expression softened. "Of course not. I kept my visible form hidden. But I was able to observe all Jonarel's interactions with you and Aurora in our home. Jonarel confided in me as well. We talked about the pain he endured when Aurora chose to be with Cade. But I also saw how much your presence calmed and centered him, how he would gravitate to you without even realizing it."

"He did?" She didn't remember that. He'd always been laser-focused on Aurora, much to her dismay.

"Oh, yes. He sought you out when he was hurting because yours was the connection he subconsciously craved. My mother saw it, too. We both knew you had strong feelings for him, that you cared deeply for him. He just couldn't see it. He was too blinded by the expectations of my father, of the clan."

Rejecting those expectations had cost Jonarel and Tehar a future with their clan.

"My mother and I discussed your relationship with Jonarel many times, including shortly after he asked me to bond with the ship. My father wanted him to mate with Aurora, but my mother and I wished for him to mate with you."

Her jaw dropped. "You did? Why?"

"We knew you would bring him joy."

She blinked as moisture coated her eyes. She'd had a cheering section and hadn't even known it.

"Part of the reason I accepted this path so readily was with the hope that I could help him see the truth of his feelings."

Her chest tightened. "That was selfless."

"Not really. Jonarel was not the only one who dreamed of exploring the galaxy."

"Huh." She'd never considered Tehar's dreams. Very short-sighted of her.

"Very few Kraed or Nirunoc feel the way we do. Even those who wish to explore beyond our region of space do so in clan ships, maintaining their family bonds even when they are away from Drakar. Jonarel's likelihood of finding a mate amongst our people who understood and accepted him for who he is, who shared his vision of the future, was infinitesimal. But he found you."

And changed her life forever. "Thank you for telling me this."

"My mother would want you to know. To see him as happy as he has been these past days would bring her much joy. I wish I could have shared this information with you sooner. Eased the burden you bore for so long."

"But you couldn't." Not when Jonarel was still committed to following his father's plan and mating with Aurora.

"No. The path was Jonarel's to walk. He had to figure out the answers on his own." Tehar's golden eyes glowed like sunlight through amber. She raised her hand, palm out, in the Kraed gesture of greeting. "I am honored to be the first of my family to welcome you into our clan."

Her heart fluttered as she raised her palm to align with Tehar's. "I'm honored to be part of your clan. I just wish that you… that Jonarel…" She couldn't figure out how to finish the sentence.

"Do not feel sorrow, dear sister. This journey is different from what my brother and I envisioned, but our hopes for the future are entwined with yours. We would not change the events that brought us to this moment, no matter the price."

Much more of this and she'd start crying fat, sloppy tears. "Jonarel is blessed to have you by his side."

"And you."

The cabin door chimed its lyrical melody.

Who would be coming to Jonarel's cabin this morning? Aurora had made it pretty clear yesterday that she didn't expect to see them until later in the day. It wasn't her parents, either. She wasn't sensing Suulh energy. "Who is it?" she asked Tehar, taking a step toward the door.

"Jonarel."

She paused, looked back at Tehar. "Why is he using the door chime for his own cabin? Why aren't you opening the door?"

"Our traditions prohibit my brother from entering with the first shared meal until you welcome him as your mate. You must go to him."

"Oh." Clearly she still had a lot to learn about the nuances of Kraed culture. "Do I have to do anything special?"

Amusement flickered across Tehar's face. "Your instincts will guide you well." Then she vanished.

O-*kay*.

Taking a deep breath, she strode to the door. It parted as she approached. Her tummy did an excited backflip as she beheld the sight beyond.

Jonarel stood with a tray of covered food dishes balanced in his large hands. Two fragrant roses in a bud vase stood in the center of the tray.

But it was the look in his eyes that pulled her forward like a magnet.

His gaze swept over her and his words came out in a deep rumbling purr. "May I have the pleasure of feeding you this morning, checana?"

Oh, yeah. And she wasn't thinking about food. She reached out, her palm making contact with the hard muscles of his chest. Her fingers curled into the fabric of his tunic, pulling him toward her. "This morning and any morning you feel the urge, my love."

He inhaled sharply, the tray rattling as the tenderness in his eyes flared into something hotter.

She kept up the steady tug on his shirt as she backed into the cabin. He followed, his gaze locked on her.

The tray kept a barrier between them, giving her a few moments to enjoy the view. Her grip stretched the tunic taut over every delicious plane and curve. His damp hair curled around his jaw and neck, the dark locks brushing his shoulders. His lips were parted, his breathing uneven.

"You are intoxicating," he murmured.

Her thoughts exactly. But she couldn't act on them, couldn't give in to the heat building between them, at least not yet.

Tehar had told her to trust her instincts. The care with which Jonarel had prepared the tray and the tradition of welcoming him into the cabin to share this meal with her meant this moment was significant. She didn't want to blow past the opportunity. In fact, if she handled it right, it could be delightful foreplay.

Guiding him toward the seating area rather than the table, she sank onto the couch. He followed her, deftly setting the tray on the coffee table without a glance as he sat beside her. Spatial orientation was another enhanced Kraed skill.

He leaned in, his gaze focused on her mouth, but she flattened her palm against his chest, holding him back. He stilled instantly, a question in his golden eyes.

"I want to kiss you. Desperately. But I want to share this meal with you even more."

Right answer. His eyes widened a fraction and then his chest swelled beneath her hand. He sunk his fingers into her hair and drew her forward, but not into a kiss. Instead, he touched his forehead to hers. "My checana," he breathed. "How did I ever live without you?"

She chuckled. "Well technically, you didn't. I've been right there." She pointed at the bulkhead that separated their cabins.

"And I have been blind."

Tehar would agree with him. But after years of watching Aurora struggle to chart her own course against Libra's expectations, and all the pain and heartache it had cost her, Lelindia understood Jonarel's dilemma. She would never fault him for choosing to follow the path Signal had laid before him, especially when he believed doing so would help Aurora, too. "You have been honorable. And compassionate. And a dear friend."

His hand slid to her cheek, cradling her jaw. "And now I am yours."

This time when he bent his head to kiss her, she didn't stop him. His lips touched down with exquisite tenderness, coaxing a happy sigh. "I love you, Jonarel."

"And I love you, my lovely Lelindia."

She would never grow tired of hearing those words from his lips. Brushing her mouth over his in a feather kiss, she pulled back and gestured to the tray. "What did you bring me?"

His eyes sparkled with mischief. "Lift the coverings and find out."

She shot him a mock-glare at the double entendre, determined to make it through everything on the tray before satisfying her other cravings.

He didn't disappoint. The meal delighted her senses almost as much as the tempting male feeding it to her. He'd undersold his cooking talents, too. The items he'd prepared could all be eaten without utensils, which gave her ample excuse to lick his fingers as he placed bite-sized pieces in her mouth.

The fire built in his eyes with each passing moment, fueling her body's response. He gave her the same treatment as she fed him in return. By the time the last morsels were gone, she was a powder keg with a millimeter fuse.

So was he apparently. One open-mouthed kiss launched them into a maelstrom that ended with her in a naked boneless heap, draped on top of him as he lay on the couch, her head tucked into the crook of his neck.

She traced the pattern of brown tendrils on his chest with her finger, eliciting the rumbling purr she loved so much. She smiled. "I guess my instincts were spot on."

"Instincts?" He tilted her chin up so he could see her face.

"About how to handle our first meal. Tehar told me to trust my instincts."

A glow that had nothing to do with sex flared in his golden eyes. "Yes, checana. Your instincts are perfect."

That glow turned her insides all soft and gushy. "Then I have a question for you."

"Anything."

Such a common word, yet so filled with meaning. His ability to trust her completely, to be open and vulnerable, especially after what he'd been through with his father, humbled her. "How are we going to handle our living arrangements going forward? I know you like having me here, but I can't have you fetching my clothes every morning. That would feel weird."

"Weird?" The spark of amusement in his eyes made it clear he was teasing her.

"You know what I mean. I'm used to having my things at hand, to taking care of my own needs. Your willingness to wait on me is sweet, but—"

"Sweet?" he growled, his arms tightening around her as he bared his teeth in a soft snarl.

"Sexy," she amended, fighting to hold back a grin. "A major turn-on. Makes me weak in the knees."

The snarl morphed into a snort. "Better."

"So what are we going to do about our two cabin dilemma?"

He stroked his hand over her hair, sending tingles down her spine. "The solution is simple. Our two cabins will become one." He gestured to the bulkhead.

She blinked. Not what she'd expected. "You mean literally become one cabin?"

"Yes."

"You can do that?"

The smile that lit his face transformed him from a mortal to a god. "Did I not tell you that all Kraed vessels are flexible?"

"Well, sure, but..." She scrutinized the bulkhead that separated their cabins. The very solid, very permanent-looking bulkhead. "Are you going to add a doorway?"

He laughed. Actually *laughed*. "That is not my plan."

The full-throated sound was so foreign it startled her into sitting up. She'd heard him chuckle, but never *laugh*. It did funny things to her equilibrium. "You laughed."

All amusement vanished in an instant. "Did I offend you?"

"No, not at all. I just... I didn't know the Kraed could laugh."

The worry lines smoothed out. "On my planet, intense sounds that carry, such as laughter or shouting, are a potential hazard, especially when we are young and untrained in the dangers of our world. We learn to protect ourselves from predators by being vigilant and silent, which carries over into adulthood. But that does not mean we are incapable of such things."

She'd certainly heard him shout before, both in the midst of battle and the throes of passion. Nothing quiet about either. "Does your laughter mean you feel safe here with me?"

His mouth curved as he trailed the backs of his fingers along her cheek. "I have never felt such peace. When I am with you, I can be exactly who I am. You are my home."

Wow. He certainly knew how to make her heart flutter.

Since leaving Stoneycroft for the Academy, she hadn't given the concept of home much thought. Aurora's choices had governed both their paths, leading them to two Fleet ships before landing them on the *Starhawke*. She loved this ship, but it was the beautiful male who'd crafted it, and who now wanted to adapt it for their future, who made it feel like home.

What was that old Earth saying about home? *Home is where the heart is.* Now she understood what it meant.

Settling her hand over his she pressed a kiss to his palm. "You're my home, too."

Thirty-Five

Celia stood outside the door to Brendan and Libra Hawke's guest quarters, contemplated the carved wood design of a winged trebolk, an animal native to Drakar. They'd seen a pack of them during their first trip to the Kraed homeworld. Their thick bodies, refined heads, and elongated tails were distinctive, but their sheer size and flocking behavior had kept her hand near the weapons controls until Aurora had assured her they didn't bother ships.

The carving on the door was exquisite, perfectly capturing the grace and power of the creatures. This one was seen in partial profile, its foreground wing tipped up to show the trebolk's body and the curved talons of its feet.

Beautiful work. She'd never taken the time to appreciate the skill the artist had displayed. A shame, really. Now that she was here, she should peruse the other doors along the corridor, find out what—

The door swung inward.

Aurora's dad stood on the other side. "Hello, Celia."

"Hello, Brendan."

The spark of laughter in his eyes and his complete lack of surprise at finding her outside his door reminded her who she was dealing with. As an empath, he probably knew exactly how long she'd been playing statue in the corridor, unwilling to take the last step.

He must have gotten tired of waiting.

"Come on in." He stepped back and waved her into the room.

She held in the sigh that pressed against her ribcage, determined to maintain her professional dignity if it killed her.

Libra appeared behind Brendan, dressed in a bathing suit partially covered by a thin robe loosely knotted at her waist. "Celia. Nice to see you. I'm off to join Micah at the hydro tank."

Celia flinched.

If Libra saw it, she ignored it. After giving Brendan a kiss on the cheek, she sailed out the open door, which closed softly behind her.

Trapped.

"This isn't an execution."

She really didn't like having her emotions read like a book. "I take it you know why I'm here."

"I have a good idea. Let's sit." He walked to the couches and upholstered chairs that formed a seating circle in the main room.

She chose the couch facing the door.

Brendan picked up a tablet from the compact dining table and settled into the chair across from her. His body language projected calm and relaxation.

Her body disagreed.

"I gather you don't want to be here."

The couch she was sitting on wasn't nearly as comfortable as it looked. "I'm surprised you want me here. I have a problem with your son."

"And you're one of my daughter's closest friends. This situation with Micah is creating an unpleasant working environment for all of you. I want to help you clear the air."

His words eased a little of the tension from her spine. "What if you can't?"

"What if I can?"

She respected the confidence he exuded, the faith in his abilities. He reminded her of Aurora in so many ways. "How do you propose to do that?"

He crossed his ankle over his knee and rested his tablet on his calf. "Why don't you start by telling me your first impressions of Micah? What you saw and felt the night you met."

The memory rose like the smoke and fire that had consumed Stoneycroft. The scents of the forest mingled with the pungent odor of destruction. Dark shadows moved through the moonlit evergreens. "He and Aurora appeared in the clearing where Lelindia, Marina and Libra were working to heal Gryphon." The moonlight had revealed the sweat-streaked ash and soot on his face. He'd frozen as soon as he'd seen her, like a thief caught in a searchlight.

"Aurora was holding his hand. She pulled him to Gryphon's side, asked him to help with the healing. He hesitated." She kept a tight grip on her emotions, delivering the information like a Fleet security report.

"Why did he hesitate?"

"He wanted to know if he'd end up like Gryphon. Aurora told him he wouldn't. That's when he agreed to help." She didn't quite hold back the note of derision in her voice.

Brendan didn't comment on it. "Did Micah notice you?"

Oh, yeah. He'd looked right at her when he'd said *I'm in*. "Yes."

"How did he react to you?"

She shifted on the seat cushion. Aurora needed to get more comfortable couches for this room. "He stared."

"Is that an unusual reaction when people meet you?"

"No." Her physical attributes had been a curse most of her life. Only hard experience and the guidance of her mentor had taught her how to use them as an effective misdirection.

"What was different about Micah's response?"

"What makes you think it was different?"

"Wasn't it?"

"Not really. With seven other people in that clearing, including his sister and mother, his focus was on me."

"And that bothered you?"

"Shouldn't it?"

"You tell me."

An emotion flickered, but she couldn't define it, couldn't put it into words.

"Celia? What bothered you about the way he looked at you?"

"I don't know. It just did."

Brendan made a note on the tablet. "Can you describe how you felt in that moment?"

Pressure built in her gut. "Cautious. Alert. Battle-ready."

"Because of the situation with the Setarips and the fire?"

"Because of him."

Brendan's brows lifted. Whether at her words or her tone, she couldn't say.

"How soon after you saw him did you feel this way?"

"Almost immediately."

Another note on the tablet. "Does Micah remind you of anyone you know? Maybe someone from your past?"

"No." Her quick response shot out like a bullet.

Brendan's gaze didn't waver. "Are you sure?"

"Yes." Although she didn't sound sure, even to her own ears.

He didn't pursue it. "Let's talk about your role as head of security for the *Starhawke*."

Much better topic.

"What are your responsibilities regarding anyone who is brought onboard?"

"To assess any threat they may pose to the ship or the crew. To monitor all activity while they are onboard and report any concerns to Aurora."

"And how do you make your assessments?"

"Background checks. Research into Fleet and public records. Personal observation."

"Have you followed all those protocols with Micah?"

Irritation bubbled up. "Yes."

"What did you learn?"

"He lives alone. Never married, no children. Spent many years as a leading surfing competitor. Currently working as a university professor in marine biology. Rated highly by his students. No criminal record." She'd been hoping she'd dig up some skeletons during her checks, but the man was squeaky-clean. After reading the rave reviews on the university website, she'd wanted to punch the bulkhead.

"What about your personal observations?"

"He expects people to like him. He talks a lot." Or at least he had until he'd caught on to her scrutiny of his behavior. "He's always watching Aurora and stays close to her when he can. They have an unusual connection, most likely a result of their shared Suulh-Human heritage, which ramps up Aurora's abilities."

"Have you witnessed it in action?"

"No." And she wasn't sure she wanted to. Which didn't make any sense. Gathering as much information as possible was her default setting. And her job. "Oh, and he can communicate telepathically with animals."

"And hopefully the Yruf."

She sat up straighter. "I hadn't heard about that."

"It's something I'll be bringing up at the meeting today. From what Cade's told me, it's possible the way Micah communicates with animals might be similar to the way the Yruf communicate with each other."

Which put Micah in a position of power. Her jaw tightened.

Brendan sighed. "I can feel your fear."

"I'm not afraid," she snapped.

He gazed at her.

"I'm concerned."

"Concerned that Micah's a threat."

"He's dangerous."

Setting the tablet on the side table, he rested his elbows on his knees. "Do you believe I'm dangerous?"

The question blew across her anger like a cool wind. "No."

"Why not?"

"You're Aurora's father." That wouldn't cut it. Micah was Aurora's brother, and that wasn't buying him a pass.

"I'm also an empath who can sense the emotions of others and project my emotions to them. Yet you don't react to me negatively. Why?"

She held her body still but squirmed on the inside. "You don't trigger my threat response." Lame, but the best she could do.

"And Micah does?"

She nodded.

To her surprise, he smiled. "A subconscious reaction. That's helpful."

"Why is that helpful?"

"Because unpacking trauma buried in the subconscious is one of my specialties. The signs indicate there's something embedded from the past that's triggering your reaction to Micah. By working to uncover it, we can clear it, and hopefully clear your negative reaction to him along with it."

"You're saying it's not Micah, but something from my past?"

"Yes."

He was confirming her suspicions. She didn't want them confirmed. "Wouldn't I know that? Have come across it during previous counseling sessions?"

He didn't seem surprised to hear she'd been in counseling before. "Not necessarily. We process or block trauma in a myriad of ways. It could be a memory from a very young age, or something you suppressed."

"A memory I don't know I have?" That concept triggered a spike of fear she couldn't contain.

His blue eyes softened with empathy. "It's more common than you might think. It might be why you were drawn to security and law enforcement. The work can become a coping mechanism."

Her mentor had said something similar, that those who'd suffered early trauma were often drawn to security professions.

But she'd never contemplated the possibility of suppressed memories before. She already had plenty of front and center memories from her time in the prison camp that played in full 3D color. Uncovering new ones that she'd locked away without even realizing it sounded as appealing as swallowing razor blades. "Maybe this isn't such a good idea."

"On the contrary. It could open up entirely new horizons for you." He stood, crossing to the couch and settling beside her. "You're a fan of botany, right?"

"Yes."

"Then think of it this way. Clearing your past trauma would be as beneficial to you as pruning damaged or diseased branches from a tree. By doing the work, you allow yourself to grow and flourish. Without it, you're dragging dead weight." He rested his hand over hers, his touch warm and comforting. "And you won't face it alone. I'll be there for you whenever you need me."

What a foreign concept. Memories of her own father were hazy at best. He'd died during the attack that had resulted in her imprisonment when she was six. The sudden loss of a parent at a young age was something she and Aurora had in common.

Or used to have in common.

Aurora's father had come back. But the look of determination in his eyes made it clear he intended to adopt her as part of his family.

Rejecting his offer would be foolish and self-destructive, two adjectives that had never applied to her. "All right. What do I have to do?"

He smiled. "I'd like to start with hypnotherapy. We don't have enough time for a session before the crew meeting, but we can get started this afternoon if you're available."

She had a feeling Aurora would make her available no matter what. "Okay."

"I also want you to spend as much time as you can with Micah."

Yep, saw that coming.

"While you're together, use your analytical training to note every detail you can – which emotions come up, what you're thinking, what physical reactions you have when you're with him. That information will help us when we work our way into the past."

"I sparred with him last night." Might as well get the ugliness out in the open.

He didn't seem surprised. "How did it go?"

"Not well."

"Did you lose control?"

"No." As bad as her reaction had been, that would have been far worse.

"That's good to hear. Still, if you choose to spar again, might I suggest you have either Aurora or Cade in the room. They can track your emotions and intervene before you fall into an emotional landslide."

Her pride took the hit, but she couldn't deny he had a point. When it came to Micah, she wasn't herself. "You say that like it's inevitable."

"It probably is. Suppressed memories mean suppressed emotions. Neither tend to come out in neat, orderly packages. That's why it's important to have support, people to catch you when you melt down."

Her hands curled into fists. "Lovely."

"Hey." He cupped her tight fists in his hands. "You'll get through this. Your strength, your discipline, your training will be an asset. And remember, everyone on this ship has your back."

"Except Micah."

His fingers tightened around hers. "*Even* Micah. Despite what you may think, he wants to be your friend. He just doesn't believe you'll let him."

He was right. The idea of becoming friends with Micah Scott made her blood boil.

And she had no idea why.

Thirty-Six

"What's our game plan for contacting the Yruf?" Aurora's gaze swept the group gathered around the expansive carved wood table in the observation lounge. Micah, her mom, and her dad sat to her right, Cade on her left, with Kire, Justin, Drew, and Gonzo beside him. On the opposite side of the table Lelindia sat with Jonarel, her parents, Celia, and Williams, with Star's projected image behind Jonarel and Lelindia's chairs.

Only Kelly was absent, currently on the bridge taking the ship through the necessary jump window maneuvers to bring them into the Sol system. Since the ship was making a visible entrance this time, they had to change their trajectory so it would appear they were arriving from Kraed space rather than Gaia, which was in the opposite direction.

Drew spoke first. "When the Yruf used their non-lethal torpedoes against *Gladiator* and took over the ship's systems to bring our team onboard their ship, I had a front row seat to watch their tech at work. Their nanotech essentially made *Gladiator* function as part of their modular collective."

"Is there a chance they could still control *Gladiator*?" That wasn't a potential liability she'd considered when they'd left

Cade's ship docked at Sol Station, orbiting Earth, before taking off for Gaia.

Drew's lips pursed. "I don't know. The systems looked clean, but after talking to Star and Jonarel, it's clear there could be hidden elements I wouldn't have been able to spot. Jonarel's offered to take a look at *Gladiator*'s systems when we arrive at the station."

"Kire and I think there's a chance *Gladiator* is still tied into the collective communication framework," Justin said, "which could allow the Yruf to track the ship's movements. Regardless, *Gladiator*'s the only ship they know. We'll need to take *Glad* when we make contact."

"Agreed. But this time you won't be going alone." Her gaze flicked to Cade, who smiled.

"What about their modular separation and camouflage ability? Do you have any theories on how that works?"

Drew gestured across the table. "Star had some thoughts on that."

All focus turned to the Nirunoc.

Star folded her hands. "From what Justin and Bella have told me, it's possible the Yruf have developed a non-biological entity that works symbiotically with them in much the same way the Kraed developed my race on Drakar."

A subtle flicker of her image indicated either the pain of loss from mentioning her homeworld or potential excitement at the concept of another race similar to her own.

Cade nodded. "That would explain the ease with which the ships worked together and how the flowing interior spaces were controlled. It could also indicate why the Yruf took time to reclaim every piece of the ship that was destroyed by the Ecilam."

Aurora's gut clenched. Star had told her once that the Kraed never left a downed ship behind because it would mean abandoning the Nirunoc who inhabited it. Only one ship had ever suffered that fate, plummeting to the surface of a highly radioactive world where the Kraed couldn't follow. She'd sensed the Kraed and Nirunoc still mourned that loss, even though the event had occurred long ago.

If the Yruf had a similar bond with a non-biological entity, the loss of a ship would cut deeply.

"Do you think you would be able to communicate with this other entity?" she asked Star.

Star lifted her shoulders in a graceful shrug. "Perhaps. If nothing else, I might be able to detect the presence of such a ship. I have had... practice lately, detecting and hiding from my own kind."

Aurora felt Jonarel's reaction, caught his subtle flinch. His and Star's wounds were fresh, the pain just below the surface. She was humbled by their sacrifice on her behalf. She was also determined to find a way to clear the air with Signal and reunite them with their clan. How she would accomplish that was a huge question mark, but there was zero chance she'd allow things to continue as they were.

Her gaze moved to Gonzo. "Could the Yruf be monitoring *Gladiator* now?"

He grunted. "I'd be surprised if they weren't. Gathering intel seems to be their specialty. I'd give a sixty to seventy percent chance that they followed us to Earth, but we don't know for certain that they hung around afterward."

"So we may not need to track them down, just let them track us?"

"Possibly."

She looked at Kire and Justin. "And if they did leave?"

Justin leaned his forearms on the table. "I'd suggest we take *Gladiator* back to the location where they dropped us off. If they're not there, we could transmit a transponder signal similar to the one we originally designed for sending a message to the Admiral. If the Yruf are paying any attention to us at all, they'll figure out we're trying to make contact."

"And when they respond?"

Justin motioned to her dad. "Brendan had some ideas about that."

Pivoting to her right, she met her dad's calm gaze. Hard to believe a few weeks ago she hadn't known he and Micah existed. Now their presence in her life seemed as vital as oxygen.

He looked comfortable and relaxed in jeans and a long-sleeved mint green shirt. "From what Cade's told me about his experiences with the Yruf, they're empathically sensitive to projections of anger or anything that signals potential aggression." He glanced at Cade. "Agreed?"

"Definitely. I was the only member of the team they were threatened by. I didn't realize I was projecting my emotions and mental images they could see."

"But you were also the only one capable of establishing a telepathic connection, of seeing the images they projected as part of their communication."

"Correct."

Her dad turned to Micah. "How close do you think their method of communication is to how you talk to animals?"

Micah considered the question, his gaze on Cade. "I'm not sure. But I may have a way to test it. That is, if Cade's willing to try an experiment."

"An experiment?" Cade shifted in his chair. She sensed a tendril of unease mixed in with his curiosity. "What kind of experiment?"

"I want to try talking to you the way I talk to animals."

Cade's brows rose. "Can you do that?"

"If we're right that my ability is similar to the Yruf's, then it should feel a lot like your interaction with them."

Cade's gaze slid to Aurora's dad. "Has he ever tried this with you?"

"No. It never occurred to me to try. But I'm happy to be the test case."

Her dad had picked up on Cade's unease, too.

Cade waved the offer away. "I'm the one who communicated with the Yruf. I'm the best test subject."

She rested her hand over his on the table. "Was it unpleasant? Sharing images with them?" All her image sharing experiences had been positive, but she was half-Suulh, as was Micah. It might be a totally different sensation for Cade.

He met her gaze, shadows in his green eyes. "Not unpleasant, exactly, but disconcerting. And a little disturbing."

Micah leaned in. "Was that because of the experience? Or what they were showing you?"

"Both. Can't say I enjoyed it." He took a slow breath. "But I'm game to give it a shot."

"I promise I won't show you anything disturbing. In fact…" Micah glanced at her, a smile curving his lips. "I know *exactly* what I'll show you."

She held up both hands like a traffic cop. "Hang on, hang on. Don't I get a say in this?" Micah's mischievous smile told her he'd be sharing images of her. "What are you going to show him?"

Instead of answering her, he focused on Cade. "Ever seen pictures of Ror as a little kid?"

Cade's grin mirrored Micah's. "Can't say I have."

"Want to?"

Cade's unease vanished in an instant. "You bet."

She latched onto both their arms. "I don't think—"

"Sorry, sis. You're outvoted."

She turned to her dad for help, but he seemed as amused by the possibility as Cade and Micah. In fact, the only person in the room who didn't seem tickled was Celia.

Releasing her hold on their arms, she sat back in her chair with as much dignity as she could summon. "Fine. Go ahead."

Micah's green eyes took on the slightly unfocused look she'd seen when he was talking with the dolphins and sea turtles during their snorkeling trip.

Cade had a similar look, though his smile remained. Sporadic chuckles and the vibration of amusement in his emotional field confirmed he was receiving the images Micah was sharing.

Heat climbed up her neck, but she kept quiet, not wanting to interrupt the experiment since it was clearly working.

A shared burst of laughter between Cade and Micah signaled the end. Cade's gaze dropped to her, his arm snaking around her shoulders as he gave her a hug. "You were quite a little troublemaker."

She stiffened. "I was not. I—"

"She was precocious," her dad clarified. "Determined to explore the unknown with gusto." The warmth in his eyes and voice soothed her ruffled feathers.

Her gaze met Cade's. "So what's the consensus on the experiment?"

He cleared his throat. "The experience wasn't identical to communicating with the Yruf leader, but I wouldn't expect it to be. For one thing, Micah and I share a common language and frame of reference. Understanding what he was showing me was easy. But it felt remarkably similar." He gave Micah a conspiratorial grin. "And not at all disturbing."

"Glad to hear it." Micah grinned back. "It also helps that you were receptive to the experience. Most people have mental or emotional baggage that gets in the way of open communication, especially the kind used by other animals."

"I'll bet you'd have success communicating with Raaveen, Paaw, and Sparw this way," Justin said.

Micah frowned. "Raaveen? Where have I heard that name before?"

"They're three of the Suulh teens we rescued from the Etah Setarip ship on Gaia. From the Sovereign, actually. Raaveen and Paaw are in charge of the Azaana settlement in Kraed space."

Micah glanced at Aurora. "I guess I still have some catching up to do."

So did she. She needed to talk to Justin about how they'd communicate with Raaveen and Paaw now that Siginal had drawn a line in the sand. "Do you feel comfortable reaching out to the Yruf when we locate their ship?" she asked Micah.

His gaze flicked in Celia's direction before he answered. "Yes, I do. I'll just need to know what to say."

"We'll work out the details after Admiral Schreiber and I visit the Teeli Embassy and set a timetable for our *scientific mission*," she used air quotes, "to Teeli space. As fast as the Yruf ship is, they should be able to get to Teeli space well ahead of us, assuming they agree to help with our plan."

"And if they don't?" Cade asked. "Is there a plan B?"

"We'll jump out that airlock if we come to it."

As the meeting broke up, she caught her dad's arm. "Can I talk to you for a moment?"

He glanced at her mom, who shooed them away. "Go right ahead." She hooked one arm around Micah's waist and caught Cade's hand with hers. "I'm taking these two strapping young men to the galley and greenhouse with me. I think we could all use some sustenance before we arrive at Sol Station."

Cade's startled grin and her mom's answering smile warmed her heart. The avalanche of mutual distrust that had kept them locked in a cold war had finally thawed.

"We'll join you shortly." Aurora led her dad toward the wide windows, noting that Celia had already slipped out the door ahead of everyone else. She'd switched from dogging Micah's every step to actively avoiding him. "How did things go with Celia?"

He folded his arms. "She's an interesting case. Most of the time the emotions I pick up from her are straightforward, focused, balanced. But whenever she's around Micah or talking about him, they turn chaotic. My instincts tell me he reminds her of someone from her past, someone she doesn't consciously remember. Do you know much about her history?"

"Not any details. She doesn't talk about it. Her Fleet records list her as a survivor of a prison camp. I don't know what kind. A Fleet security force freed her when she was a teenager. She enlisted in the Fleet eight months later."

"And chose the profession of her rescuers. That gives me a little more to go on."

"What I don't understand is how Micah can be reminding her of a villain from her past. He's a bright spirit, not the least bit threatening. She's met plenty of rough-and-tumble characters during our time in the Fleet together, and never gave any indication of this type of reaction. Why now? Why him?"

"That's what I'll help her figure out."

Thirty-Seven

Earth sat in the inky darkness of space like a child's polished marble on black velvet.

As Kelly guided the *Starhawke* toward Sol Station, Cade watched Aurora. The line of her jaw and the slight tilt of her torso in the captain's chair revealed a battle-ready stance he knew well. After they docked, the rest of his team and Jonarel would be heading to *Gladiator* but he, Aurora, and Kire would be catching a Fleet shuttle down to Earth to meet Admiral Schreiber at Fleet HQ.

Kire had already sent an official message through Fleet channels, announcing their arrival. Admiral Schreiber had responded in kind, requesting they meet with him to discuss their next assignment.

Last time Aurora had been given this mission, Admiral Payne had done everything in her power to keep it quiet and not draw attention – another red flag that the scientific expedition wasn't what it seemed. This time, it was Aurora who was doing everything possible to make their actions appear routine and unremarkable. If they wanted to entice Reanne into taking another shot at capturing Aurora and the *Starhawke* during this mission, they couldn't very well point a spotlight on the scene.

But the real communications had been on the secure direct line between Reynolds' comband and the *Starhawke*. While she'd been acting as bodyguard for the Admiral, she'd been able to reestablish a brief connection to Bare'Kold's transmitter. The transmission had ceased shortly after showing a glimpse of an Ecilam Setarip followed by a startled shriek of pain from Bare'Kold. All indications pointed to a quick demise for the Teeli delegate, which had cut off the transmitter's ability to draw power from the electromagnetic field generated by Bare'Kold's body.

Apparently the Sovereign had grown tired of waiting for Bare'Kold to complete his mission and had instructed the Ecilam to carry out the punishment for his failure.

The delegate's yacht had departed Sol system a few hours later. The official word that had been given to the GC was that Bare'Kold was returning home because of a family crisis, and had assigned a new delegate to take his place.

The critical question Cade wanted answered was whether the Ecilam Setarips and Aurora's grandmother were onboard the yacht when it left. "If your grandmother is still at the Teeli Embassy, will you be able to sense her?"

Aurora glanced at him, but she looked distracted, her gaze sliding away quickly. "Yes. The Necri have a distinct energetic resonance. And I'm sure she'd seem... familiar, too."

He couldn't imagine the complexity of her mental and emotional state regarding her grandmother, a woman she'd never met, had assumed was dead. Knowing she was alive should have inspired hope, but instead, the wraith her grandmother had become had almost killed Gryphon and Marina and had attacked Libra. Anger would have been a natural emotional response, but Aurora couldn't even lean into that because her grandmother was a victim of Teeli manipulation and not responsible for her own actions.

For Aurora's sake, and the sake of their mission, he prayed her grandmother was on the yacht heading far, far away.

Aurora's and Lelindia's parents were staying on the *Starhawke* until Aurora, Cade, and Kire returned to the ship. Brendan's presence on the station ensured a Far Horizons shuttle was at their disposal whenever they were ready to leave.

As Kelly navigated toward their docking berth, Celia turned from the tactical console. "Are you sure you don't want me to come with you to this meeting?" Concern drew faint lines on her face, but he also detected an underlying agitation that didn't seem connected to her question.

Aurora pinned her with a look. "I'll be fine. You have things to do here while I'm gone."

Celia's lips pressed together like a kid staring at a plate of food she hated and being told to eat up. "And if the Teeli try something?"

Aurora didn't blink. "I'll see it coming and handle it. Empath, remember? Besides, risking a public confrontation isn't Reanne's style. The Teeli Embassy is the last place she'd try to make a move. Too much potential for drawing attention. Doing so would risk exposing the Teeli for who they really are. I'm not in any danger."

The look in Celia's eyes showed agreement, but her agitation didn't change.

Aurora gave a small sigh. "It'll be fine. I promise."

He suspected they weren't talking about the meeting anymore. But whatever was bothering Celia, Aurora's reassurance did the trick. Her shoulders dropped several centimeters. "Okay."

After the ship docked, Cade joined Aurora and Kire in the lift. They exited on the cargo deck, where his team and Jonarel were gathered in the densely packed space of the bay. The airbridge to the station was already connected and open on the starboard side.

Jonarel's gaze swept over Aurora, taking in her Fleet uniform. The epaulette indicated her rank of captain, while Cade's uniform and rank of commander matched Kire's. "Making a statement?" Jonarel inquired.

"Keeping things official," she replied, "while reminding the Teeli who they're dealing with."

Gonzo grinned. "I was kinda hoping you'd be in the outfit you wore to take down Weezel. Justin said it was very effective."

Cade sent Gonzo and Justin a withering look, but Aurora snorted.

"I didn't think of that. I gave it back to Celia, but I'm sure she'd loan it to me again if I asked."

"No." The word tumbled from his mouth without conscious thought. He also discovered he'd caught Aurora's elbow in his palm, his fingers closed tightly against the fabric of her uniform.

He dropped his hand immediately, but his possessive actions didn't go unnoticed. His team, Kire, and even Jonarel all tried various methods to disguise their amusement.

Rather than getting irritated, Aurora fluttered her eyelashes at him. "Is there a problem with that outfit?"

And he was sunk. Gazing into the beautiful green of her eyes, all he could think about was how much fun it would be to work her out of that particular eye-popping number. "No problem at all."

A spark of heat flared for a split second. "Good to know," she murmured before facing Jonarel. "Do you need anything from me before you head over to *Gladiator*?"

He shook his head. "I will return after Bella and I have finished our diagnostic assessment."

Aurora checked her chronometer. "And we should be able to catch the early evening transport back to the station. Kire and Justin will be maintaining an open channel, so you'll know if we run into any issues."

Jonarel didn't give off so much as a whiff of anxiety as the groups parted. What a change from the intense overprotective behavior he'd displayed ever since Cade had met him. Now that the Kraed was mated to Lelindia, calm and contented had become his new normal.

It took some getting used to.

The flight down to the surface on the crowded Fleet transport made him yearn for the grace and speed of the *Starhawke*'s shuttles. Aurora had settled into Fleet mode, her body language conveying an air of confident command that had the other Fleet personnel onboard glancing in her direction and nudging each other.

Many of them had probably recognized her — the youngest officer ever promoted to commander — especially with her hair pulled back in the braided style she'd worn in her official Fleet personnel photo. For the past few days while they'd been with the Suulh and onboard the ship, she'd allowed the blonde locks to flow loose, an external expression of her internal relaxation.

That had changed the minute she'd left the *Starhawke*. Her mental and emotional armor had slid into place, something he'd sensed with his empathic abilities in addition to seeing her physical tells. He understood the necessity for protecting herself, but it made his chest hurt a little, too.

Kire leaned in from her other side. "They probably didn't expect to see the former commander of the Fleet's flagship onboard today," he said in an undertone.

So Kire had caught the curious glances and whispered comments, too.

"And word's gotten around that you're captain of a Kraed vessel now," Kire added.

Cade had learned early on that Kire kept his finger on the pulse of Fleet communications, particularly those pertaining to Aurora. It didn't surprise him that the news of Aurora's move to the *Starhawke* had made the rounds quickly. He'd seen the awed looks on the faces of the people they'd passed in the corridors of Sol Station who had stopped to stare at the ship through the viewports.

Aurora had been notable long before she'd become the first human to take command of a Kraed ship. Now, she was pushing towards legendary.

Unfortunately, that perception would fuel Reanne's hatred. The woman had a serious grudge against Aurora's success and the respect she'd received for her accomplishments. She'd made that clear during the face-to-face confrontation at the river shortly before Aurora had uncovered her identity.

Reanne's words had chilled him to the bone. *You, Aurora, are a worthless mongrel, one I will take great pleasure in bringing to heel.*

Her twisted perception of reality made her incredibly dangerous, with or without the support of the Teeli and Setarips. Even as a teenager she'd pitted Aurora's allies against each other and turned their anger into a destructive force, attempting to isolate and hurt Aurora. Time had focused the intensity of her hatred and desire to make Aurora suffer.

After the transport touched down in the hangar the other Fleet personnel hung back, allowing Aurora to lead the way to the exit. It was typical behavior in deference to her rank as a senior officer, but he suspected it had more to do with her star power as the *Starhawke*'s captain.

He and Kire flanked her as they made their way to Fleet HQ. The winter breeze blowing in from the coast ruffled his hair, carrying moisture and a faint tang of salt. This early in the afternoon the temperature was pleasant if not exactly warm.

Holiday decorations still festooned the streetlamps and most of the storefronts they passed. The new year had come and gone while they were on Gaia, but a feeling of renewal and optimism still permeated the atmosphere.

Aurora tilted her face up to the sun, the rays making her hair shimmer like gold and her skin glow. Tension melted from her shoulders as she surveyed their surroundings. The sparkle that had been ever-present in her eyes during the trip to Gaia reasserted itself. "I guess we missed ringing in the New Year, huh?"

He smiled. "Oh, I don't know. I think we had a fitting celebration of new beginnings yesterday." And the private celebration afterward had been stellar, too.

She met his gaze, her smile matching his. "Yes, I suppose we did."

They entered the Galactic Council admin building and took the elevator to the floor for Fleet HQ, passing through security before reaching Admiral Schreiber's office. Lt. Valenzuela, the Admiral's new PA, sat behind the reception desk. She smiled and rose when she saw him. "Commander Ellis. Wonderful to see you again."

He returned the easy smile. "You as well, Lieutenant. I'd like you to meet Captain Hawke and Commander Emoto."

"It's an honor." She shook hands with both of them, her gaze lingering on Aurora. "The Admiral speaks very highly of you."

He recognized the slightly unfocused look in Aurora's eyes as she clasped Valenzuela's hand. Whatever she sensed must have passed muster because she visibly relaxed. "I served under his son, Knox, on the *Argo*."

Valenzuela nodded. "He told me. He also told me to send you right in." She motioned to the closed door of the Admiral's office. "He's expecting you."

The Admiral stood as they entered. So did Reynolds, who'd been camped out in a reading chair beside one of the corner office's wide windows. She slid the tablet in her hand onto a side table, her gaze meeting his. "This room is secure. I just finished another security sweep."

The Admiral came around the desk. "Is everything settled?"

Aurora nodded. "We can fill you in on the details later, but it worked out even better than we'd hoped. Oh, and Lelindia and Jonarel had a mating ceremony on our way here."

The Admiral's forehead wrinkled. "That will make the situation with Siginal more complicated." He ran a hand over his head, smoothing invisible hair. "Or perhaps simpler. The Kraed pair bond for life. There's no way Siginal can coerce Jonarel now, even as head of the clan."

"Is it possible he wouldn't officially recognize the pair bond?" Kire asked. "Or claim it wasn't binding since he didn't give his approval?"

The Admiral shook his head. "There is nothing more sacred to a Kraed than a pair bond blood pledge. Did Jonarel make that pledge to Lelindia during the ceremony?"

Cade flashed on the image of Jonarel on his knees before Lelindia's parents, offering the blood of his veins to protect her. "Definitely."

"Then it's done. Signal will have to accept that pair bonding Jonarel with Aurora is no longer an option."

A weight slid off Cade's shoulders, but a nagging thorn remained. "What about another member of his clan? Would he try to push a different Kraed pair bond on her?"

Aurora's eyes flashed with fire. "It wouldn't matter if he did. I'm not mating with a Kraed."

His heart banged erratically at the intensity of the look she shot him. He swallowed. "Good to know."

She gave a tight nod before focusing on the Admiral. "What about the meeting with the Teeli? Do you know anything about Bare'Kold's replacement?"

The Admiral swept a hand toward the chairs grouped in front of his desk before reclaiming his own on the opposite side. "Only that I've seen him with Bare'Kold at official GC functions. He seemed to be serving the role of PA."

Reynolds rested her hip on the corner of the Admiral's desk. "What's your impression of him?"

"He didn't seem as outwardly arrogant as Bare'Kold, but that may have been a result of his lesser position in the ranks. Now that he's assumed the delegate's job, that could change."

"What about the other Teeli delegate, Chil'Darc?" Aurora asked. "Why aren't we meeting with him instead of Bare'Kold's replacement?"

The Admiral steepled his fingers. "My guess is that Chil'Darc isn't in Reanne's inner circle the way Bare'Kold and Sly'Kull are."

Aurora gave a little jerk. "Sly'Kull? That's the new delegate's name?"

The Admiral's eyes narrowed. "Yes. Does it mean something to you?"

Aurora pressed her lips together. "It may be a coincidence, but Marina gave me the name of the Teeli who forced her to cooperate with his experiments while she was still on Feylahn. His name was Sly'Cer. Depending on Teeli naming conventions, there could be a family connection." She glanced at Kire.

His thin brows drew together. "Definitely. Oracle said the first part of Teeli names denotes the family. I'll poke around in the Fleet archives and search for any mention of Teeli names that start with Sly."

The Admiral tapped the tips of his fingers together. "Excellent. As for our meeting today, the four of us will go into the Embassy while Reynolds stays with my car and monitors our comms from the parking area."

"Justin and I already have a comm connection set up." Cade motioned to Reynolds. "I'll give you the frequency."

Aurora sat forward. "What should we expect from Sly'Kull?"

"Deception. Half-truths," the Admiral replied. "Perhaps a snide remark or two. Groveling and flattery worked well to placate Bare'Kold, but Sly'Kull has a different manner — more perceptive and less bluster. He could surprise us, for good or ill. Since you'll be able to tap into his emotions, we'll follow your lead."

Cade voiced the concern that was foremost in his mind. "And if she senses he's about to spring a trap?" He'd help her as much as he could, but he didn't trust his empathic skills to give him the full picture after only a week of practice.

The Admiral's mouth curved in a humorless smile. "Then I trust Captain Hawke will do whatever's necessary to correct the situation."

Thirty-Eight

Aurora examined the exterior of the Teeli Embassy as she, Cade, Kire, and Admiral Schreiber walked from the parking area where they'd left Reynolds.

When the structure had functioned as a three-story boutique hotel, she probably would have found it appealing, charming even. Judging by the remnants of the original architecture, it had been designed to resemble a historic hotel from the early 1900's, with Victorian red turrets on the roof and white siding.

When the property had been turned over to the Teeli, the Council had probably expected they'd keep the design and layout mostly the same. Instead, the dormer windows on the upper floor turrets were the only hint of the hotel's prior charm. Painted-over scars showed where the Teeli had removed all the windows on the first and second floor and possibly a porch that had wrapped around the front of the building. Now long stretches of blinding white metal paneling met at the covered cave-like entrance at one corner.

The overall impression was of an oversized cargo container with hazard cones on top. Fitting, in a way.

At least her grandmother wasn't inside. She hadn't picked up on any Suulh or Necri energy as they'd driven onto the property. She wasn't sensing any Ecilam, either. Having faced off with them twice now — once as commander of the *Argo* and again during the battle at the river — she would recognize the undertone of maliciousness that seeped from them like a toxin.

A shudder passed through her as she stepped into the shadow of the entrance's overhang.

"You okay?" Cade murmured, his hand resting briefly on her back.

"Yeah." It was a lie. They both knew it. A chill had settled into her bones that had nothing to do with the shade. She could sense the Teeli inside the building, like a steady drip of ice water down her spine.

After years of being hidden away and protected from any contact with the Teeli by her mother and Admiral Schreiber, this moment held more than a touch of unreality.

Marina's tale of the Teeli infiltration of Feylahn rose in her mind's eye. A wave of anger followed swiftly after, but she choked it off. Losing her grip on her emotions wouldn't help her with what lay behind those menacing doors.

"Aurora?" Admiral Schreiber had paused, frown lines bracketing his mouth. "Is there a problem?"

Problem? Yes, there was a big problem. And only one way to solve it.

She stepped forward and grasped the metal handle of the door. As she and the Admiral led the way inside, she suppressed an involuntary shiver, grateful for her long sleeves and light jacket. They concealed the goosebumps spreading over her arms.

Wall sconces provided illumination for the long corridor that ran the length of one wall. They approached a security station at the far end, guarded by four humans, three male and one female, dressed in Teeli Embassy security uniforms.

Two of the men blocked the path to the security scanner, their hands dropping to their sidearms. "Names?" the taller of the two demanded.

Admiral Schreiber smiled, his manner completely relaxed. "Admiral Schreiber. This is Captain Hawke, Commander Emoto, and Commander Ellis."

The four guards' emotional states simmered with a low-grade anger like a fever. But it was the Teeli presence she sensed on the other side of the enormous security door that had her shifting her weight onto the balls of her feet. Tentacles of manic eagerness reached out through the metal door and circled her, making her gut clench.

The guard blocking her way glanced at the woman standing beside the security scanner. She nodded. "Delegate Sly'Kull is expecting them."

"Very well." He stepped aside with obvious reluctance, like he'd been hoping for an excuse to flex his muscles in a fight. A glimpse of his hands confirmed his knuckles and fingers were scarred and scraped from previous encounters.

Admiral Schreiber was the first through the scanner, followed by Aurora, Kire, and Cade. No alarms blared, despite the discreet weapon she knew Cade had concealed somewhere under his clothing. Gonzo had provided it to him during his last visit, and he'd insisted on bringing it this time, too. She'd chosen not to argue the point.

A subtle pop drew her attention to the metal door beyond the scanner as it swung open like a starship hatch or bank vault. The door looked as solid and out of place in the shadowy confines of the corridor as either of those options.

She'd known the Teeli were heartless and domineering. Now she could add paranoid to the list.

The third male guard motioned them forward. "This way."

They followed him through the opening and around the corner. Another long corridor led to the back of the building with doors opened off the hallway to the right, exactly as Cade had described it to her.

The guard halted in front of the last doorway and opened it, pointing inside. "Wait in here." His tone was gruff, irritation in every line of his body, like their mere presence offended him.

She smiled anyway. "Thank you."

Surprise flickered in his emotional field but was quickly swallowed up again as he grunted in response.

The room had as much cozy charm as the rest of the place. Three long angular couches formed a U-shape at one end surrounding a rectangular coffee table made of metal and glass.

She and the Admiral settled onto the couch against the far wall while Cade and Kire sat across from them, leaving the short end of the U vacant. It was like sitting on a flat, hard boulder. Cade had warned her about that, too.

The barren white walls added to the feeling of sterility, slightly softened by the low lighting. Like a cell.

Unease crept in with whispered footsteps. She ignored it, focusing her attention on the Teeli she'd sensed earlier, the one whose emotional state shone like a flashlight among fireflies, coming down the corridor toward them. Eagerness still dominated, but she sensed an underlying anxiety that probably accompanied everyone working for Reanne. The woman had a short temper and a loose screw. Bare'Kold had paid the ultimate price for failure, and now Sly'Kull was responsible for delivering Aurora's ship and crew to Teeli space. He'd be a fool *not* to be anxious about how this meeting would turn out.

The door swung inward. She stood as a grey-robed figure stepped into the room.

Sly'Kull was shorter than she'd expected, a few centimeters taller than she was. His center-parted long white hair hung straight to the middle of his chest, framing the pink-grey tones of his face and his prominent electric-blue eyes. His gaze swept over her, sharp intelligence combined with a look of absolute ownership.

Her visceral reaction heated her skin as she fought the urge to bare her teeth.

Admiral Schreiber stepped around her, his wiry frame blocking her from Sly'Kull's view. "Delegate Sly'Kull. A pleasure to see you again." He held out both hands, palms up, in the Teeli gesture of greeting.

As Sly'Kull clasped them, Aurora sucked in air, wrestling her emotions into a headlock. Cade and Kire had risen as well. Kire looked calm and collected, his gaze on Sly'Kull, but she sensed anger burning underneath the surface. Cade's emotions were as turbulent as her own, his curled fists tucked behind his back, his face a blank mask.

The intensity of his reaction gave her focus, helping her to stabilize her emotions.

His gaze flicked in her direction, his fingers slowly relaxing.

The Admiral turned to her, putting her face-to-face with Sly'Kull again. "I'd like you to meet Aurora Hawke, captain of the *Starhawke.*"

She held her hands out as the Admiral had, silently daring Sly'Kull to touch her.

He must have gotten the non-verbal message, because he hesitated, the blue of his eyes darkening.

As his cool, smooth skin touched hers, a crawling revulsion rolled over her like a swarm of cockroaches. She held still, tamping down the instinctive push of her energy shield.

He had no power over her, and if she wanted a shot at taking down Reanne, she needed him to believe she was excited about the proposed mission. "It's a pleasure to meet you Delegate Sly'Kull."

"Indeed." His accented Galish made the word come out in a heavy drawl, his grip tightening. "You have been a difficult female to track down."

His use of *female* rather than *person* might have been unintentional, a matter of language differences, but probably not. The research she'd done after learning about the Teeli's duplicity had revealed a male-dominated society. All the delegates and leaders who had interacted with the Council had been male, which made Reanne's position of power all the more surprising. The few pictures she'd found of Teeli females who'd visited Earth depicted them as beautiful art objects standing beside their mates rather than productive members of Teeli society.

She gave Sly'Kull an apologetic smile as she gently but firmly extracted her hands from his grip. "The one disadvantage of being captain of a Kraed ship is the need to return to Drakar for maintenance and repairs." Especially with Reanne continually attacking her ship.

His nostrils flared. "Your ship is fully functional again?"

"Yes. And my crew is eager to move forward with the proposed mission." She motioned to Kire. "This is Commander Emoto, my first officer."

Kire stepped forward, hands out.

Aurora focused on his emotional state as Sly'Kull's hands wrapped around his. Kire was the wildcard in the room when it came to susceptibility to Teeli influence. He didn't have any recollections of Reanne manipulating him while they were at the Academy, but she'd also had no reason to try. He hadn't posed a threat to her obsession with Aurora the way Jonarel and Cade had.

She sensed an emotional nudge from Sly'Kull – difficult to define, but definitely there. "Your help on this mission will be beneficial."

The response from Kire almost made her smile. He was clearly amused by whatever push Sly'Kull was trying to give him, although it didn't show on his face. "Oh, I hope to be a big help on this mission."

Cade cleared his throat, probably to cover a chuckle.

Aurora relaxed fully as Kire passed the Teeli test with flying colors.

Sly'Kull glanced at Cade with a flash of irritation. "You must be Commander Ellis."

"Yes." Cade dutifully held out his hands, and Sly'Kull clasped them with obvious reluctance, letting go almost immediately. Bare'Kold must have passed on the word that Cade couldn't be manipulated. Hopefully Cade had held on long enough to successfully place the surveillance device on Sly'Kull's wrist that would provide the audio and video feed to Reynolds.

Regardless, Sly'Kull's failed manipulation efforts left him zero for four, and his emotional field reflected it, even though his demeanor didn't change. He pointed to the couches. "Please, sit. We have much to discuss."

After they'd settled onto the rock-hard couches, Sly'Kull launched into an expansive description of the proposed mission, providing much more detail than Admiral Payne had shared. His gaze locked onto Aurora. "My people's exploration efforts are vastly inferior compared to Humans, and we are far behind with regards to scientific accomplishments."

She barely kept from rolling her eyes. Apparently Sly'Kull's go-to tactic when direct manipulation didn't work was switching to obsequious flattery. Or maybe that's how he treated all *females*, telling them what he believed they wanted to hear no matter how bold the lie.

"Yet we desperately want to study the wonders of the systems surrounding our homeworld."

Now that she totally believed, if they substituted the word *exploit* for *study*.

"As your vessel is designated for scientific study, it would be the perfect choice."

Right. It was her ship that had drawn the Teeli's interest. Hers and Lelindia's presence onboard had nothing to do with it.

But she could play along. "My crew and I are honored to be of service. How long do you plan for this mission to take?"

"Several months at least."

She'd suspected that would be his answer. After the Teeli sprang their trap, they'd want buffer time before the Council would start asking questions about her ship's whereabouts. She feigned a frown. "It'll take time to stock in enough supplies to sustain us for several months outside Fleet space." But she'd bet he had a solution for that, too.

He didn't disappoint. "That is not a concern. We have already arranged for a supply ship to visit the system at regular intervals. You will be provided for while you are our guests."

I'll bet. But she forced a smile. "Thank you." She turned to Admiral Schreiber. "Will it be an issue, our being unavailable to you for so long?"

The wry amusement in his emotional field didn't match his serious expression. "I hadn't anticipated such an extended time period, but as we hope this will be the first of many joint efforts in Teeli space, I'll make arrangements to cover your absence."

She almost snorted at the hidden meaning in his words.

Sly'Kull's eyes glittered like pointed sapphires. He sat forward, his skin taking on a pinker hue. "How soon can you depart?"

"Your offer of fresh supplies will help, but we'll still need to stock in our base necessities before departure. And now that we know more about the details of the mission, I'll want to check with my crew regarding any mission-specific items we may need. They may also want to make a trip planetside before we depart, since it will be their last opportunity for shore leave for a few months." She glanced at Kire. "What do you think, Commander? Is two days long enough?"

Outwardly, he appeared to be pondering her question. Inwardly, she sensed laughter as Sly'Kull played right into their hands. "Yes, I believe we can meet that timetable."

She turned to Sly'Kull. "Will that work for you?"

He looked ready to levitate off the couch, his eagerness reaching a fever pitch. "Yes. I will alert the first supply ship to expect your arrival. How quickly can you make the journey?"

No way was she going to give him an accurate answer. She didn't want Reanne to know the true speed of the *Starhawke*, and they needed time for their side mission to contact the Yruf.

She lobbed the question at Cade since they'd already discussed this point before the meeting. "What did your calculations indicate for travel time, Commander?"

"A little more than a week at optimal cruising speed." Which was several days longer than the trip would actually take.

Some of the pink leeched out of Sly'Kull's skin. "I understood your ship was faster than that."

Aurora had an answer ready. "It will be after we finish breaking in the new engine parts. It's one of the reasons it took us a while to return to Earth. Pushing for faster speeds now could result in an engine failure."

The pink returned, along with Sly'Kull's enthusiasm. And why not? She'd just hinted her ship had a vulnerability Reanne might be able to exploit. "I see. Then take the time you need. We want you to arrive safely."

"Thank you." Aurora didn't have to fake her smile. "We're really looking forward to this mission."

Thirty-Nine

"Focus on your breath."

Celia longed for the familiar texture of the sparring mat beneath her feet rather than the plump cushions of the couch in her cabin, because then she'd be exercising rather than facing her therapy session with Brendan.

He'd agreed to her request to hold the session in her cabin, suggesting she sit wherever she felt most comfortable. Considering the point of this session, no place felt comfortable, but she'd finally propped herself cross-legged on the center cushion of the couch in her main room while he'd taken the chair opposite her. She'd also dimmed the lights so she wouldn't feel quite so exposed.

"Feel the tension flow out with each breath."

So far, the session had been easy. The breathing and focusing exercise Brendan had taken her through was similar to what she did during her workout regime to settle her mind. But she also knew the hard part was looming on the horizon like a stampeding herd of buffalo.

"As your body relaxes, allow your mind to drift back, before you joined the crew of the *Starhawke*, before you met Aurora, before you became a Fleet security officer."

Images rolled through her mind's eye in time with the steady rhythm of Brendan's voice.

"Continue drifting back, allowing your mind to guide you to a time when you felt out of control of your situation, vulnerable, threatened."

Resistance strong-armed her, slowing the glide of memory and fading out the imagery.

"Remember you are an observer, not a participant. What you see, hear, or feel cannot hurt you."

Her conscious mind agreed with him. Her subconscious thought he was nuts.

"Allow yourself to notice what's happening around you without judgment, without fear."

Sounds rang in her ears, familiar and ugly. The clang of metal doors and locks, whimpers in the darkness, the smack of hard leather on flesh, shrieks of pain. The sharp tang of sweat and body odor filled her nose, combined with the sickly-sweet smell of perfume.

"Note what you see, hear, or smell, but don't hold onto those sensations. Allow them to pass by like a gentle breeze."

The smells receded to a tolerable level, the sounds growing muffled. But she was still surrounded by darkness. No images accompanied the sensory memories.

"Now I want you to focus on a specific element of this time, but still as an observer. While you were in this place, what caused you the greatest pain? When did you feel the most threatened, the most vulnerable, the most lost?"

A shadow loomed in the darkness, beautiful and terrifying. Her throat closed and her body jerked.

"Remember to observe. Do not participate. You are in control."

She dragged air into her lungs, her body suspended over an abyss.

"Can you see anything?"

Her voice sounded feathery and weak. "Darkness."

"Is there anything in the darkness?"

"Yes."

"Can you describe it?"

How can I describe what I can't see? But words spilled from her lips anyway. "Big. Strong. Warm. Hard." The last came out with a harsh edge.

"Can you hear anything?"

"Breathing."

"Yours or someone else's?"

She paused, listening. "Both."

"Can you describe how it sounds?"

"Muffled. Anxious. Fast." Her heart pounded. "I hear whispers, too."

"What are they saying?"

"I... I can't make it out." But she knew what they were saying anyway. She licked her dry lips, barely recognizing the higher-pitched tones of her voice. "They're talking about getting out."

"Who are they?"

"Me and... someone else." Her gut clenched, a lightning bolt of fear followed a split-second later with a flame-spurt of rage that burned up her throat.

"Remember you're an observer, not a participant. Nothing in this space can harm you. Breathe. Allow your body to relax."

With her eyes scrunched shut, it took her a few moments to register the tight tendons in her hands and arms where her fingers had dug into the couch cushions like claws. She'd curled her torso forward, too, like she was preparing to take a hard kick she couldn't block. Or maybe sprint for the door.

She sucked in air, unfurling until her back was supported by the cushions again and her hands were resting on her knees.

"Can you still hear the voices?"

She didn't want to. She wanted to block them out. But that wouldn't get her out of the box canyon Micah's presence had tossed her into. "Yes. They're faint."

"You said one voice is yours. Can you describe the other one?"

A tremor started at her neck and worked rapidly down her spine.

"Is the voice male or female?"

"Male."

"Child or adult?"

Another tremor. "Teenager."

"How old are you in this memory?"

"Fourteen."

"Is he your friend?"

Yes! No! The two words collided like boulders in an avalanche. Her mouth worked as she struggled to answer. "I don't know."

"While he's talking to you, how do you feel?"

"Nervous. Excited. Hopeful. Scared." And about a thousand other emotions she couldn't name.

"You said you were talking about getting out. Getting out of what?"

"The cage. The camp. The prison." And the horrible things that happened in the rooms of the ornately decorated house.

"He's going to help you escape?"

"Ye—" The voices cut off abruptly as ice water filled her veins. "No."

"Did something happen to him?"

She shivered as the sensation spread. "I don't know." The memory was gone, blocked by a wall of ice. But she wasn't sorry. The ice was preferable to whatever lay behind it.

Brendan's voice touched her like a ray of sunshine. "You're safe, Celia. Nothing can harm you here."

A few beats passed in silence except for the pounding of her heart.

When he spoke again, his tone had changed to the lyrical softness of a parent waking a child from an afternoon nap. "Let the memory drift away and focus on returning to the present. I'll count backwards from five to one. With each step, deepen your breath as you allow yourself to move steadily forward in time."

Her heartbeat slowed and her breathing smoothed out.

"With each exhale release any tension. Focus on the sounds, scents, and tactile sensations surrounding you. Return to this room, this time, safe and secure in your body. Five."

Her mind and body followed Brendan's soft command as he counted down, taking each step into the present like she was climbing from a frigid and turbulent ocean onto warm dry sand.

"One. When you're ready, open your eyes."

Ready? She wasn't sure she'd ever be ready.

She opened her eyes. The dim light in the room seemed blinding compared to the darkness she'd been steeped in. She blinked several times until the room came into focus.

Brendan's gaze was on her, one ankle crossed over his knee, his tablet resting on his calf. "How do you feel?"

"Weird."

"Weird how?"

"Like my body's been sleeping while my mind's been in the middle of a firefight."

He nodded. "Uncovering suppressed memories can do that. You'll want to be easy on yourself for the next few days, allow yourself to process what's coming up."

"Coming up? You mean it won't stay suppressed?" She wanted it locked behind that ice wall forever.

Empathy shone in his eyes. "Probably not, at least not completely. You've opened a crack in the door, let in a fissure of light and air. That's changed the dynamic. You may get flashes of insight, snippets of memory, or dream about situations related to what you're uncovering."

"Wonderful."

He smiled at the disgust in her voice. "It is, actually. The process isn't easy, but clearing past trauma is always a net positive. I'm sure you discovered that when you went through counseling before becoming a security officer."

She had. The work with her counselors had given her the ability to harness her emotions and focus her mind, halting the outbursts that had been common following her release from captivity.

But this felt very different. She'd been anxious about those counseling sessions, not afraid. What lurked behind that ice wall terrified her, and her terror made her angry.

"Emotional upheavals are common," Brendan said, as if reading her thoughts. Or more accurately, her emotions. "Note them but don't hold onto them. They'll pass quickly if you allow them to."

"And if they don't?"

"Then ask them what they're trying to tell you. Our emotions are guides. There's nothing inherently good or bad about any of them. It's how we react to them that determines how they impact our lives. If we allow anger to lead to violence, it becomes destructive. But if we acknowledge our anger as a messenger that's pointing out an imbalance in our lives, it becomes a powerful force for change to restore balance."

"So you're saying I'm out of balance?" She didn't like that one bit. Balance was a central tenet of her life.

"With something from your past, yes. And now it's spilling over into your present because of the association with Micah."

The mention of his name sent a charge of anger through her, but it didn't have the bite or sticking power it would have had yesterday.

Brendan gave her a speculative look. "How do you feel about Micah now?"

"I..." She wasn't sure how to answer. Emotions played dodgeball in her chest, but she couldn't pin any of them down. "Different."

"That's a start." Brendan uncrossed his leg and rested his elbows on his knees. "So now that you've made it through your first session, how about we head down to the galley and whip up something tasty?"

Now he was talking her language. She practically bounced off the couch. "Two plates of capellini pomodoro coming right up."

Forty

"Is the device transmitting?" Cade asked Reynolds as he slid into the backseat of the Admiral's vehicle beside Aurora.

"Yep," Reynolds replied as the Admiral settled into the passenger seat. "Nothing interesting to report so far, but it's recording."

She handed the tablet to Cade as she started the vehicle and drove them out of the parking area.

The video showed a swath of fabric brushing past the camera as Sly'Kull moved his arm. "So he didn't contact Reanne as soon as we left?"

"If he did, it wasn't an audio message. I couldn't see anything on video other than snippets of the room he went to, which looked like Bare'Kold's old office."

Bare'Kold certainly didn't need it anymore.

Aurora leaned in, peering at the image on the tablet. "So this is the kind of feed you got from tagging Bare'Kold?"

"Yep." Cade tilted the tablet in her direction. "Justin and Drew spent hours going over this stuff while Justin worked out the translation. That's how we found out where the rendezvous was taking place where Bare'Kold swapped Lt. Magee for the Ecilam who attacked your mom's house."

A flare of pain from the front and back seats made Cade look up.

The Admiral's face had tightened, his head turned as he stared out at the other vehicles on the road. Aurora had stiffened as well.

You hit two birds with that stone, idiot. Way to be sensitive. He grimaced as his gaze met Aurora's.

She slipped her hand over his, twining their fingers.

Reynolds cleared her throat. "What parameters can you give me for what I'll be looking for? Any sign that he's communicating with Reanne is a given, but what else?"

"Orders regarding ship movements or personnel deployment," the Admiral answered, "and any sudden departures of Teeli Embassy personnel off-planet."

"Any mention of the *Starhawke*," Aurora added, "although knowing Reanne, she'd use a code word or phrase rather than the ship's actual name. Better to cover her tracks."

Reynolds met Aurora's gaze in the rearview mirror. "So I'll need to focus on context and keywords rather than names."

Aurora nodded. "I'd pay particular attention to anything that references a supply ship. Sly'Kull said he'd be sending one, so that could be part of the code for directing the armada."

"Supply ship. Got it. What else?"

"Anything related to family, mothers, and daughters." Cade squeezed Aurora's hand as his words sparked a low-grade anger. "We can't rule out the possibility Reanne will take another shot at Libra while Aurora's out of the system."

"She'll have to find her first," Aurora growled. "And my dad will be watching for them." The glint in her eye almost dared Reanne to try again.

A lot had changed since Christmas. Speaking of which...

"What did President Yeoh have to report on the GC members?" he asked the Admiral. Yeoh had promised to look into the situation after he and the Admiral had met with her before Christmas, but Cade had been too busy being captured by the Yruf and then helping Aurora with Keenan to follow up.

"Her preliminary report hit on the same issues your team brought up after our meeting. The Southern Quadrant delegates are the most likely to be under Reanne's thumb, but Reanne has covered her tracks very well. There's no solid evidence of wrongdoing, only pieces that don't fit together quite right and behavior that's a little off. Kathryn will alert me if she comes across anything actionable."

"At least she's monitoring the problem," Cade said. "And we can be reasonably certain the Teeli can't influence her. If they could, they would have done it already."

"Agreed."

Reynolds glanced over her shoulder. "You told Sly'Kull you could be in Teeli space in a little more than a week. How long do you anticipate being in range of the ICS so you can receive my updates?"

"We'll be using Far Horizons' network instead, so until we leave Fleet space," Cade answered. "We're lucky that the binary is relatively close to the border. Reanne could have chosen a site deep in Teeli space."

"She wouldn't." Aurora shook her head. "She wanted to make sure we'd take the bait. A more distant star system might have made us wary. She's unbalanced, but she knows how to tempt people into doing what she wants."

Reynolds snorted. "I still can't believe we worked with her all that time and didn't realize how twisted she was." She scowled in the rearview mirror, her gaze holding Cade's. "We owe that woman a hell of a lot of payback."

"I know." And hopefully in another week or so, they'd deliver it.

Forty-One

"It feels weird to be saying goodbye." Aurora hugged her dad close as a wave of anxiety rolled over her.

The crew had gathered in the *Starhawke*'s cargo bay to see Aurora's and Lelindia's parents off. She hadn't expected to be thrilled that they were leaving, but her trepidation about the change surprised her.

"It's okay," he murmured, leaning back so he could see her face. "Your mom will be fine. And I'm not going anywhere. Not this time."

Her emotions surged, tightening her throat. He knew her so well. The last time she'd seen him leave, he hadn't come back.

He pulled her close again. "I'll be helping your mom and Marina sort out the situation at Stoneycroft. You can reach me through Far Horizons' secure comm system. If you need anything, contact me immediately."

She gave him one more squeeze before stepping back. "Thanks, Dad."

He turned to Micah. "You two watch out for each other."

"We will." Micah's gaze shifted to their mom. "Count on it."

Her smile didn't show a trace of the fear that normally dominated her emotional field. "I know." She pulled Micah into a hug, standing on tiptoe to whisper something into his ear. Whatever it was made him chuckle as he released her.

She moved to Aurora next, her arms wide.

Aurora stepped into them.

"I'm so proud of you." Her mom's hug was strong, confident, supportive — the polar opposite of the reserved, suffocating, tense sendoffs she was used to. When her mom pulled back, the look in her blue-grey eyes was clear and direct. "Take her down."

The comment startled a laugh out of her, despite the seriousness of the upcoming mission. "Yes, ma'am." Her gaze swept to Lelindia and Jonarel, who were exchanging hugs with Marina and Gryphon. The same bittersweet emotions flowed from them, but this moment had been inevitable. Her parents and Lelindia's had responsibilities planetside that needed to be handled. They couldn't remain on the *Starhawke* indefinitely.

She was still amazed Micah had been able to wrangle a semester off from his job on such short notice. When she'd asked him about it, he'd given her a self-conscious smile and a shrug, saying they liked him well enough to be flexible. Their loss was definitely her gain.

Cade and his team had already taken *Gladiator* out of Sol system earlier in the day, heading for the location where the

Yruf had last been seen. The *Starhawke* would follow shortly, after making a quick detour to alter their jump window trajectory once they'd left the system, ostensibly headed for Teeli space.

As her parents walked with Marina and Gryphon onto the airbridge that connected the ship to the station, Aurora's gaze swept over the crew gathered around her. Kire, Jonarel, Lelindia, Celia, Kelly. Seven of them including her, now that Micah had joined them. But after the days of having the ship filled with almost three times as many people, the small group that remained felt incomplete.

Lelindia's gaze met hers. Her emotions reflected the same discord, though it was softened by Jonarel's solid presence by her side. "Well, I guess it's time to move onto our next task."

"Yep. Let's get the ship prepped for departure."

Settling back into the captain's chair helped clear away the lingering melancholy, replacing it with the pop and fizz of excitement she associated with space travel.

Kire turned from the comm station. "We're cleared for departure."

"Kelly, take us out."

Lelindia had chosen to join them on the bridge, claiming her usual chair to Aurora's left. She looked a lot more comfortable there than she used to. This was the first time they'd been on the bridge together in a while. Lelindia hadn't paid a visit during the trip to Gaia because she'd been busy with Keenan and then her mating ceremony with Jonarel.

But she'd had a lot of bridge time when she'd taken the *Starhawke* to Drakar and faced down Signal. It seemed that experience had changed her attitude about being in command.

Aurora leaned on the armrest of the captain's chair. "Do you miss this view?" She patted the wood inlay of her chair.

Lelindia met her gaze. "I wouldn't say I miss it, exactly, but it certainly doesn't intimidate me like it used to."

"Think you'd ever want to try it again?"

A small smile curved her lips. "Maybe. If the need arose."

Aurora grinned and shot a look over her shoulder. "I think she's gunning for your job, Kire."

He laughed. "She'd be good at it, too. She handled Signal like a pro."

Lelindia's gaze swept between them. "I learned from the best."

"Aww." Aurora rested her hand over her heart. "Now I'm all warm and fuzzy."

"Captain?"

Aurora sat up straighter, focusing on Kelly. "Yes?"

"We're approaching our jump window out of the system."

"Take us in."

Kelly made short work of the transition to the interstellar drive, completing the two hops that got them on course to rendezvous with *Gladiator.*

"Time to destination?" she asked Kelly.

"Twenty-two minutes."

"I'll be in my office. Kire, you have the con."

As she stepped into the cozy interior of her office, Micah turned from the viewport. "Do you ever get used to this?" he asked, his arm sweeping toward the starlight.

She stopped beside him. "Used to it? No. It's magical for me every time. That's partly why I love being out here."

His gaze drifted back to the view. "That's how I feel about the ocean. Even when I'm diving in the same spot I've visited a hundred times, it's always different. This view is like that."

She didn't pick up on any regret or hesitancy, which was good. It might be a while before he saw Earth's oceans again. "We'll be at the rendezvous point in about twenty minutes. Are you ready?"

He took a deep breath, his gaze still on the viewport. "I hope so. I keep telling myself it's like trying to communicate with a sea creature I've never encountered before, but that's not really true. If I struggle to talk to a fish or dolphin, it's not a big deal. They just swim away. If I fail to get through to the Yruf, to convince them to help us…" He met her gaze. "There's a lot riding on this."

She rested a hand on his arm. "I know. But you're the one who figured out a way for me to hear the dolphins. You also helped me save Mom and Marina and Gryphon from the fire. We can do this. I know it."

He smiled. "You're good at motivating people."

She smiled back. "Have to be. It's part of the whole captain gig."

Reaching out, he pulled her into a bear hug. "Thanks for being my little sister," he murmured against her hair.

"Thanks for being my big brother."

When they returned to the bridge, she stopped short, as did Micah.

The space that previously had held the captain's chair had sprouted an identical twin right beside it.

Her gaze swept the bridge, noting the dour look on Celia's face, the amusement on Kire's, the calm speculation on Kelly's, and the excitement on Lelindia's. Star and Jonarel stood beside Lelindia's chair, their expressions a matched set of eager expectation.

Aurora pointed to the new addition. "Is this for Micah?"

Jonarel nodded. "I anticipated he would be spending time on the bridge during this mission and that, because of your unusual connection, you might desire him to be closer than the original seating permitted."

"Good thought." She'd assumed Micah would sit where Lelindia and Cade usually did, but this was even better. She could make physical contact with him without moving. "Did you know about this?" she asked Lelindia.

"Jonarel and Tehar may have asked my opinion."

"And mine," Kire added.

"So it was a conspiracy." She grinned at Jonarel. "Is it retractable?"

"Of course. It can be stored under the deck when not needed."

She stepped forward, studying the two chairs. Hers was on the right facing the bridgescreen. After so many hours on the bridge, she knew the grain pattern of the denglar wood well. Jonarel had correctly guessed which side of the pairing she'd want to be on.

She moved in front of her chair before turning to Micah and sweeping her arm toward the chair on her left. "Try it out."

His gaze darted to Celia, correctly assessing that she was the one person on the bridge who wasn't happy about the new arrangement. However, her annoyance didn't have the edge Aurora had sensed previously, with less of a laser-focus on Micah. It felt more like a general irritation.

Celia watched Micah as he made his way to the chair, and Aurora watched her. Her dad hadn't provided any details about the sessions he'd had with Celia over the past few days, but he had confirmed they'd made progress. He'd also warned her Celia would be working through the memories and emotions she'd uncovered, and that she might have unexpected, strong emotional outbursts.

So far, that hadn't occurred. In fact, the sessions seemed to have mellowed her somewhat, turning complete distrust of Micah into judicious caution. But Aurora wasn't counting on that as the new normal. Thankfully her empathic abilities should alert her to impending trouble before Celia had a complete meltdown.

Aurora leaned back in her chair as Micah tested out his. "How does it feel?"

He ran his hands over the smooth wood armrests. "A little strange. I never imagined I'd be sitting on the bridge of a starship."

She gave him a bemused smile. "Really? Kinda odd considering Dad owns Far Horizons."

He shrugged. "It wasn't part of our lives. Not in any big way."

And that was where she and her brother were very different. Micah appreciated the wonder and beauty of her interstellar world, but he'd never yearned for it as she and her father had. Micah was much more like their mother, bonded to terrestrial life, whether plant or animal.

If she'd been the one to grow up with their father, she would have begged him to take her onto a starship every chance she got.

She touched his arm, sending a small flow of energy through the connection. "It's good to have you here."

He gave her a half-smile. "Thanks."

She'd lay money that the trepidation she sensed from him had a lot to do with Celia's presence on the bridge. Her friend had turned back to her console, but she could tell Celia was hyper-aware of Micah's presence, too.

Aurora sighed. Hopefully one day those two would find common ground. If Cade and Jonarel could, then anything was possible.

"Exiting the jump window now," Kelly informed them.

And speaking of Cade, *Gladiator* appeared in the magnified view on the bridgescreen as the main engines took over. The ship's image was replaced a moment later by a view of *Gladiator*'s small cockpit. Cade sat in the pilot's seat, Justin in the co-pilot's chair, with Gonzo and Williams leaning on the seats' headrests.

Cade smiled. "Welcome to the middle of nowhere."

She smiled back. "Fancy meeting you here. Been waiting long?"

He shook his head. "Arrived about ten minutes ago. No sign of the Yruf ship yet, but Drew and Justin have already started transmitting our recorded greeting."

Aurora glanced at Star. "Have you begun your sweeps?"

"Yes, Captain. I will alert you if I pick up any indication of a camouflaged ship."

Aurora turned to Micah next. "How about you? Getting anything?"

He shook his head. "Not yet. Do you sense them?"

Reaching out with her empathic senses, she pinpointed the six people on the bridge with her, as well as Cade and the four members of his team on *Gladiator*, but no other emotional resonances. "No. But I'm guessing you'll pick up on their telepathic communication long before I sense them. If they're as adverse to strong emotional reactions as Cade indicated, they could be tough for me to get a bead on."

Micah's brows drew together. "Assuming I know what I'm listening for."

"Oh, you'll know," Cade said from the bridgescreen. "I resisted what I was getting from them at first, but once I started paying attention, I recognized it for what it was. So will you. Nice chair, by the way." He grinned before his gaze shifted to Aurora. "Do you want us to dock with you, or do a little patrolling first?"

"Go ahead and dock. From what you've said about the Yruf, seeing the two ships connected should help convince them the *Starhawke* isn't a threat."

Which was her greatest concern about this plan. *Gladiator* hadn't posed any danger to the Yruf, but her ship's technology was far more advanced. She'd considered using the hull camouflage to disguise her ship so the Yruf would think *Gladiator* was alone but had discarded the idea. There was a good chance the Yruf would be able to detect her ship anyway, and hiding from them didn't seem like a good way to open negotiations.

"Then we'll see you shortly."

She turned to Kire. "Start transmitting the video we compiled." After Cade had described how the Yruf leader had reacted to the image of Earth and the video Justin had taken of her and Cade in *Gladiator*'s cockpit, she and Micah had put together a ten-minute video to play on a loop that paired images of Earth's flora, fauna, and natural wonders with lyrical music. Interspersed within the video were short snippets of her, Micah, and Cade, including some from Lelindia and Jonarel's mating ceremony.

Kire tapped his console. "Transmitting now."

Her gaze searched the bridgescreen, where the sea of stars beckoned. *Come out, come out, wherever you are.*

Forty-Two

After five hours on the bridge staring at the unchanging vista on the bridgescreen, Lelindia had convinced Aurora to come with her down to the galley for a meal. Cade and Jonarel had joined them, but Micah had chosen to remain on the bridge, as had Celia, Kire, and Kelly.

They'd brought their food into the observation lounge at Aurora's request, rather than eating in the dining nook in the galley. It soon became clear why. Aurora's attention remained mostly on the starscape outside the wide windows, her gaze sweeping the view, occasionally going unfocused, indicating she was reaching out with her empathic senses.

Jonarel and Cade didn't seem to notice. They were too busy discussing the upgrades the Yruf had made to *Gladiator*'s systems and how it had boosted the ship's engine efficiency and speed.

Lelindia nudged Aurora with her foot. "Nothing yet?" she murmured.

Aurora finally looked her way. "No."

"Don't worry. They'll come."

Aurora gave her a wry look. "How do you know?"

"Because we need them to."

That earned her an eyebrow raise. "That's quite a leap of faith."

"Maybe." She shrugged. "What can I say. I'm feeling optimistic."

"I can tell. You—" Aurora's gaze moved to the left, past Lelindia's shoulder. "Hey, Justin. What's up?"

Lelindia turned as Justin walked in from the corridor, heading for their table. She returned his smile of greeting. With the exception of Keenan, Justin was the most cheerful, upbeat patient she'd ever treated. They'd gotten to be friends after the incident with the Meer on Burrow landed him in the med bay with a serious head injury.

He halted beside hers and Aurora's chairs. "I was hoping I could talk to you both about the Suulh on Azaana."

"Of course." Aurora stood and dragged her chair closer to Cade while Lelindia scooted towards Jonarel. "Grab a chair."

Justin reached for one of the carved wood chairs at a neighboring table but before he got a hand on it, the chair moved on its own, gliding across the floor until it came to rest in the space they'd cleared.

Justin chuckled. "Gotta love Kraed technology. Thanks, Star," he called out.

"You are welcome," Tehar responded over the ship's speakers.

Justin sank into the chair, his smile fading. "So, Azaana."

Aurora exhaled audibly. "Azaana."

"I sent a generic message to Raaveen and Paaw before *Gladiator* left Sol Station. Nothing about our mission or you." He glanced at Jonarel. "I wasn't sure whether your dad might read it or reroute it."

Jonarel's lips compressed, his good humor dissipating like mist. "Under normal circumstances, he would not. Our people respect privacy. Our way of life, the way our society functions, requires it." The muscles on his forearm flexed as light glinted off the tips of his claws, just visible above the pads of his fingers. "But these are not normal circumstances. We must assume he will intercept any message we send, and any the Suulh send to us."

Cade leaned forward. "Is there any chance he would alter them before sending them on?"

"That would be an even greater offense. However, I can no longer predict the boundaries my father will cross to achieve his goals. I never would have believed he would hold us hostage, yet he did."

Justin sighed. "So my message may or may not reach Raaveen and Paaw, and any response I get back may or may not be what they sent."

"That is accurate." And admitting that was costing Jonarel plenty. Lelindia could read every line of pain etched on his handsome face.

Aurora frowned. "Do you think you'd be able to tell whether a message you received was genuine?" she asked Justin.

"I think so. I know how Raaveen and Paaw use language, since I'm the one who taught them Galish. Impersonating them, even in a text message, would be a challenge for Siginal, who's barely spent any time with them and doesn't know their background like I do."

"That's something, at least. But it doesn't address the elephant in the room." Aurora laced her fingers together and focused on Jonarel. "Just so you know, I have no intention of keeping the *Starhawke* out of Kraed space, regardless of your father's threats."

"Damn straight," Lelindia murmured.

Aurora shot her a look of solidarity and a tiny smile before continuing. "One way or another, he's going to have to deal with me. And with you and Star. But I could use your help figuring out the best approach."

Jonarel's gaze shifted to Lelindia, concern in his eyes, before he focused on Aurora. "I have been thinking a great deal about my father's plan, about why he was so adamant that you and I had to mate. I knew he wanted to cement your place within our clan, to make you a part of our society. But I did not understand why he believed that was the only option to defeat the Teeli."

"And now you do?"

"I believe so. Humans view all Kraed as technologically advanced and spacefaring because my clan was the first they ever encountered. Clan Clarek has always led our fleet. But more than half of the Kraed clans have never left our planet and have technology no more advanced than yours."

Jonarel had shared that bit of information with Lelindia while they were stranded on Drakar.

Clearly it was news to Aurora. "I had no idea. Your mother told me she was from a different clan, but I assumed they were all similar."

Jonarel shook his head, his thick hair brushing his shoulders. "They are not simply different in their lack of technology. They also think differently with regards to alien species. The majority of those living on Drakar do not concern themselves with affairs outside our borders. The Teeli threat would not interest them unless it affected the clans directly. They would not approve the use of our resources to fight a war, not unless clan members were in imminent danger."

Understanding seared through Lelindia like fire. "By mating with Aurora, the leader of the Suulh, Siginal would have brought the entire Suulh race into the Kraed clan system with one move."

Pain and sadness flashed in Jonarel's golden eyes. "Yes. That would not have been his original intent, since he was not aware the Suulh remained on Feylahn. But if Aurora and I had mated, all Kraed clans would have accepted her — and by extension the rest of the Suulh she leads — as our own."

"And because I'm being threatened by the Teeli," Aurora said, "the clans would have joined the fight now, rather than waiting for the Teeli to breach the borders of Kraed space."

"Yes." Jonarel's voice grew almost too faint to hear. "My clan has already accepted the role of protector to the Suulh because of my family's close connection with you and Lelindia. But we are the most progressive clan, and the only one to spend significant time among Humans or Suulh. Without our mating, the other clans will not follow suit."

Aurora's eyes narrowed. "But you mated with Lelindia, who's also a leader of the Suulh. Wouldn't that have the same effect?"

Jonarel's jaw tightened. "It would not. My father did not and would not approve the match. My entire clan, and I suspect several others, knew I was destined to pair bond with you. And while Lelindia is a powerful leader of her people, her position is subservient to yours. My pair bonding with Lelindia is likely to cause discord rather than cohesion."

Lelindia's stomach rolled, bile rising in her throat. "I'm sorry."

Jonarel's reaction was instantaneous. One moment they were sitting in separate chairs, the next she was wrapped tightly in his strong arms and sitting on his lap.

He buried his face against her neck, his hand pressing her cheek against his shoulder. "*No.*" The word came out as a harsh whisper. "Do not say that. Being your mate is the greatest gift of my life." He nuzzled her skin, his breath warming her all over.

"He's right," Aurora said. "We can all see that you two were meant to be together."

Lelindia repositioned herself in Jonarel's grip so she could see Aurora. "Then how are we going to convince the other Kraed clans to take the fight to the Teeli?"

Aurora looked much more optimistic about the problem than the seriousness of the situation seemed to warrant. "I have no idea. But we've tackled challenging situations before. We'll find a way. And Jonarel's explanation gives me a much better idea of what's going on in Siginal's head." She turned to Justin. "Which brings us back to the question you posed about Azaana. For now, I want you to keep sending messages like you normally would and see what kind of response you get. Siginal shouldn't have a reason to interfere with you, Raaveen, and Paaw. Well, unless his new goal is to draw me out."

"Which poses another issue." Justin gestured out the wide windows. "Any time I use the Kraed communication system,

I'm giving them *Gladiator*'s location when I transmit. Since we'll be traveling together for the foreseeable future, that will give Siginal your location, too. Is that a problem?"

"You mean will he send a ship after *Gladiator*?"

Justin nodded.

Aurora tapped a finger against the tabletop, her expression thoughtful. "Interesting idea." She turned to Jonarel, who hadn't loosened his hold one bit, although he'd lifted his head. "Does that sound like something your father would do?"

"Very likely. Since he has failed to control me, his next logical move would be to track you down in Fleet space or wait for you to return to Kraed space. He would prepare for both possibilities, correctly assuming *Gladiator*'s crew would know where to find you."

"So there might be a Clarek ship out there right now searching for us. When we're camouflaged, how hard would it be for them to find us?"

"Tehar and I have been working on new theories ever since we left Drakar, as we assumed you would not ignore your responsibility to the Suulh on Azaana and would want to return to Kraed space."

"Have you come up with anything that will work?"

"We believe so, but we have not had an opportunity to put any of our ideas into practice. With your permission, we could do so while we wait for the Yruf."

"That's a good idea, but they have to be short tests. We don't want to risk freaking out our potential allies with a vanishing act."

"Then I shall—"

"Captain." Tehar materialized next to Aurora, her jaw tight.

Aurora tensed, her gaze darting to the windows then back to Tehar.

"Micah and I believe the Yruf are approaching."

Forty-Three

Celia kept her attention divided between her console and the bridgescreen, but neither was giving her any definitive data. "Are you sure they're here?" she asked Micah and Star without turning around.

"It is difficult to be certain," Star replied, "but I am detecting unusual activity that could denote a camouflaged ship."

It took a couple seconds before Micah responded. "I'm sure. I can hear them."

Pivoting, she scrutinized him. He was seated beside Emoto in the captain's companion chair, staring at the bridgescreen, but she doubted he was seeing it. His eyes looked unfocused, distant.

"What are they saying?"

He shook his head absently. "It's not words. It's more…" The unfocused look disappeared as he met her gaze. "They're thinking about Aurora and Cade. And they've spotted the *Starhawke*."

"How do you know?"

"I can see it."

"See it? I thought you heard them."

"It's both, and more."

The scientist in her was intrigued, but the security officer was alarmed. "Are you saying anything back to them?"

He shot her an irritated look. "No. I wouldn't do that without Aurora's approval."

And speaking of Aurora, she and Lelindia had just stepped off the lift. "Cade and Justin are heading to *Gladiator* and Jonarel's in engineering. Tactical status?" Aurora asked as she moved to the captain's chair Emoto had vacated to take over at the comm.

"Nothing identifiable on sensors or visual," Celia informed her, "but Star's picking up something and Micah's certain it's the Yruf."

Aurora settled in next to her brother. "What are you getting?"

"Images mostly. You, Cade, the *Starhawke*, *Gladiator*, Earth. Can you sense the Yruf?"

Aurora closed her eyes, her breathing slowing. As the seconds passed, her brows slowly lifted, although her eyes remained closed. "Wow, that's... unusual."

Micah rested a hand on Aurora's arm. "Project it to me."

Aurora cocked her head, her face tightening in concentration.

Celia's body tightened, too, but not from concentration. This was exactly the kind of closed loop scenario between Aurora and Micah she'd been afraid of. Shut off from the crew, Micah giving Aurora orders.

The image of *Gladiator*'s cockpit appeared on the bridgescreen, sharing space with the exterior view, with Cade, Byrnes, Gonzo and Williams gathered in the compact space.

Cade's gaze snapped to Aurora and Micah. "Anything from the Yruf?"

"They're getting closer," Aurora said, her eyes opening slowly.

"They're intrigued by the *Starhawke*," Micah added.

"And they've seen her before," they said in unison.

Celia's muscles solidified into steel rods. She didn't like the Yruf sneaking up on them, but she disliked the creepy group think Aurora and Micah had going on even more. "Seen her where?"

Micah turned to her. "Earth. They watched the ship enter and leave the system."

"So they did follow us to Earth," Cade said.

Emoto turned from the comm console, his focus on Aurora. "Can you gauge their intentions?"

"I'm not sure. There's no aggression or fear, at least not that I can sense, but the way they process emotions is hard to define. Their emotional fields are structured and fluid at the same time. It feels like each emotion has parameters that contain it but the exact shape changes. And it's hard for me to pick out individuals. I've never sensed a group so in harmony with their emotions, even amongst the Suulh."

Celia snagged a critical piece of info. "So you can't tell how many of them there are?"

Aurora shook her head. "It could be a hundred, a thousand, or ten-thousand. I don't think I could tell the difference. Can you?" she asked Micah.

He nodded. "I have some idea. I'm more used to this kind of collective input dealing with schools of fish and pods of dolphins, although nothing quite like this. My best guess is we're looking at a few thousand individuals, but that estimate might be low."

Gonzo's low whistle carried over from the bridgescreen image. "They hide their numbers well. We saw what, maybe fifteen to twenty Yruf while we were with them?"

"But only a fraction of the ship," Cade said. "And it's a huge ship."

Which they couldn't see.

Celia searched all the exterior camera angles and checked all the sensors, but they remained stubbornly devoid of new data. If only the Yruf would show them—

An alarm shrieked in her head as she got her wish.

Forty-Four

Aurora gaped at the colossus that materialized off her ship's port bow. Cade had described it to her, but she still wasn't adequately prepared for the sheer size of the ship, or its dramatic external appearance. The Yruf ship made the *Starhawke* look like a child's toy in comparison.

The aesthetic beauty reminded her of the *Starhawke*, all fluid lines and curves rather than straight lines and angles. The hull had the texture of a reptile's perfectly interlocking scales, lit by an ambient glow that seemed to come from within, like a bioluminescent sea creature. The emerald-green color that covered most of the section of hull she could see on the bridgescreen reminded her of Lelindia's energy field. Black and gold chevrons created breaks in the sea of deep green.

"That's new."

Her gaze shifted to the image of *Gladiator*'s cockpit, where Justin was staring in the direction of the ship off-camera. "What is?" she asked him.

"The glow," Justin responded. "The ship wasn't lit up before."

"It's beautiful." Lelindia's emotional field radiated the same stunned awe Aurora felt.

Well, the awe she would have felt if she wasn't distracted by the unusual emotional resonances she was getting from the Yruf ship. The flow was incredibly nuanced, stronger and more varied than she'd expected but blended in a way that demonstrated discipline and cooperation.

Most of the time when she sensed emotions from a group, it was like listening to a classroom filled with kids who'd been handed an assortment of instruments and told to play whatever they wanted. Some made music, some made noise, and some were barely audible at all, but the overall effect was dissonance.

This was the complete opposite. Harmony replaced cacophony, the symphony of emotional resonances bringing a sense of peace and calm.

"They're thinking of you," Micah said. "They know you're here."

She'd sensed that, too, through her connection to Micah. Her energy field continued to flow over him, enhancing their abilities as it had when they'd communicated with Streak and Cutter, the two dolphins Micah had befriended.

But they weren't communicating with dolphins now. Her heartbeat picked up as she stared at the ship. As empathic as the Yruf appeared to be, their leader could probably distinguish her from the rest of the crew with ease.

She licked her dry lips and turned to Micah. "Ready to try talking to them?"

His soft smile and the bedrock of confidence that came with it steadied her. "Absolutely."

She glanced at Kire, who perched on his chair, watching them. "You good?"

He nodded. "We've got your back."

Her gaze flicked to Cade next, who gave her an encouraging nod. "You've got this."

Taking a deep breath, she turned to Micah. "Here we go."

She closed her eyes, opening herself fully to the connection with her brother. They'd discussed how they would approach this first contact, so the images that filled her mind as Micah reached out to the Yruf were familiar. Swimming in the ocean with Micah, the sea turtles, schools of fish, and the dolphins who had visited them, the beauty of the underwater world and the creatures in it.

A feeling of surprised joy and curiosity washed over her from the Yruf collective. Apparently she and Micah had chosen their greeting well.

The images switched to the *Starhawke*, focusing on her and Cade as seen from Micah's perspective — meals shared in the galley and observation lounge, dancing together at Lelindia and Jonarel's mating ceremony, and exiting one of the *Starhawke*'s shuttles.

An unfamiliar image crowded into her mind and she flinched, adjusting to the strange sensation.

"Wow, they're strong," Micah murmured.

The visual was of an opening forming in the Yruf ship's hull, the interlocking scales flowing apart to reveal what looked like a docking bay inside. "I think they're inviting us to come to their ship."

The visuals continued to roll forward. She sucked in a breath as she recognized an image of Cade, his jaw shadowed by several days' growth of beard, his features drawn but focused, exactly as he'd looked when he'd arrived at Stoneycroft the night of the fire. He was standing in the Yruf docking bay.

"They want Cade to come, too," Micah confirmed.

"Happy to," Cade responded.

She exhaled, rolling her shoulders. "Good. I don't trust myself to dock the shuttle on an alien ship."

She'd had basic shuttle flight training at the Academy, and Jonarel had taken her out a few times for flight practice in one of the *Starhawke*'s shuttles while they'd been working together on the greenhouse prior to their first mission, but piloting was still one of her weakest skills. She'd feel a lot better with Cade at the controls. And with her, period.

A final image came to her, this time of an elaborately decorated circular door rolling back into the bulkhead to reveal a vast room with a throne at one end and a shadowy figure seated on it. The image could have been intimidating, but the emotional resonance that came with it was soft, welcoming.

She responded in kind, sending a flow of gratitude.

The sensation of a presence in her mind faded, replaced by the vibrant pull of her energy field and a flood of excitement from Micah.

"That was incredible!"

Her eyes snapped open. Her brother was grinning at her like a kid who'd just gotten off the biggest, baddest roller coaster in the amusement park.

"I couldn't understand everything they were saying, but their imagery was more precise and comprehensible than I anticipated, especially for a first attempt."

She peered at him. "Saying?"

He cocked his head. "You couldn't hear them?"

"Hear what?"

Her question was echoed by Celia, Kire, Justin, and Cade.

Micah glanced around the bridge, his voice losing some of its enthusiasm as his gaze met Celia's. "Usually when I try communicating for the first time with a new species, it starts with basic concepts, all in images. It takes time to build up a mutual understanding that allows me to hear their mental projections like it's a conversation." He turned to Aurora. "But this was different. I could hear them from the beginning. I just didn't understand everything they were trying to convey."

She was still stuck on the fact he'd heard something she hadn't. "Why did you hear them and I didn't?"

"Because I've been practicing all my life, sis. I was projecting what I was getting from them to you like I did with the dolphins, but you must not have recognized it for what it was."

"I guess not." Frustrating to say the least. She hadn't realized until that moment that she'd counted on being able to communicate with the Yruf directly. Instead she might have to rely on Micah to be her translator.

She glanced at the bridgescreen. "Cade, Micah and I will meet you in the shuttle bay."

"Hang on." Celia stood, her spine ramrod straight. "You're not going alone."

Her tone, and the look she shot Micah, raised Aurora's internal temperature a few degrees. She waited a beat before responding. "I won't be alone. I'll have Micah and Cade with me."

"And me." Celia didn't waver, despite the frost arcing between them. "You need an impartial observer, someone who can monitor the Yruf while you're talking to them."

Aurora sifted through the emotions coming off Celia. Fear, anxiety, anger, concern, in that order. She had a bad feeling the Yruf weren't the ones triggering the response. "Cade can monitor the Yruf. He knows them already."

"Which is why he's not impartial. As security chief, I need to make sure they don't try anything." Another flick of her gaze to Micah, this time unconscious.

Definitely not the Yruf.

Aurora reigned in her sisterly protective instincts that had raised her hackles and focused on the problem like a Fleet captain. "If they try something, we've got bigger concerns than being outnumbered. I trust Cade's assessment. If he says the Yruf can be allies, that's how I'm going to treat them."

"But—"

Aurora held up a hand. "Your skills as a security chief are not what I need in this situation." But an elegant win-win solution had presented itself, one that would require Celia and Micah to cooperate. "Your skills in non-verbal communication are another matter. They might come in handy since we're dealing with a species that doesn't vocalize much. You can come with us."

Celia blinked, taking a moment to register she'd lost the argument but won her case. "Oh. Good."

"But no weapons. And keep in mind we're here to ask them for a favor."

Celia's professional decorum slid into place, locking down the emotions that had pulled her out of her chair. "Understood."

Aurora's gaze swept the bridge. "Any other concerns?"

Lelindia and Kire both shook their heads, and Kelly gave her the same placid look she always did.

She waved Kire to the captain's chair. "We know they can block normal communications if they choose to, but I'll have my comband on anyway. If you need to reach me and that doesn't work," she glanced at Lelindia with a small smile, "use the comm system they can't block."

Forty-Five

As soon as the lift doors closed behind Aurora, she turned to Micah and Celia. "Am I going to have any problems with you two?"

Micah glared at Celia. "Not me," he muttered.

Celia scowled, but her composure held, including her emotional state. "Absolutely not. We have a job to do."

"I'm glad we're in agreement on that."

After the short, silent ride on the lift, she led the way to the shuttle, which Cade already had warming up. She settled into the co-pilot's seat, leaving Micah and Celia to work out their own seating in the back, which now held six seats rather than the standard twelve.

Cade followed her gaze to the main cabin. "I reconfigured the shuttle for a more compact design. It'll make docking easier." He lowered his voice to an undertone. "We going to have problems with those two?"

"That's what I asked them. They promised me it'll be fine."

"Then it will be. They know what's at stake."

As the shuttle left the bay and banked, she got her first real look at the Yruf ship. *Stellar light, it's huge.* The towering form made her feel like an ant standing at the base of a mountain. She craned her neck to take it all in. "This can separate into seven distinct ships?" She was having trouble visualizing it, given how solid and imposing it looked now.

Cade guided them closer. "Assuming they repaired the seventh one that the Ecilam took out. Or that it can't segment into even more than what we saw."

As a tactical advantage, that ability would be a huge help when facing whatever Reanne had planned for them in Teeli space. In all their previous confrontations, the sheer numbers the Teeli brought to the table had been a serious problem. The Yruf ship might level the playing field, even with the Ecilam thrown into the mix.

All they had to do was convince the Yruf to join the fight. Right. Simple. No problem.

Please let this work.

Thankfully her ultimate goal was in alignment with the Yruf's. She wanted peace for her people, just as they wanted peace amongst the Setarip factions. They stood a much greater chance of achieving those goals by working together.

"How will you know where to dock?" The hull didn't show any markings or distinctions that would indicate an opening.

"Good question." Cade pulled up the magnified camera image. "Last time we were under their control. I—"

She jerked as the illumination on the Yruf ship's hull blinked out, leaving an afterimage in her eyes. A moment later it was replaced by a running pattern of light that chased from left to right across the emerald scales, ending at one section of softly lit yellow.

Cade grinned at her. "I'm guessing we go there."

"Guess so." The timing shook her a little bit, though. Just how good were the Yruf at reading them?

But Cade's amusement tempered her reaction. She'd told Celia to treat the Yruf as allies. She needed to heed her own advice. "Take us in."

"Aye, aye, Captain."

As they approached the lit section, she could make out the movement of interlocking scales on the hull as they rippled apart. A golden-hued light spilled out from the opening they revealed. The interior looked like the image she'd seen through Micah's connection to the Yruf, though the docking bay was even more seamless and streamlined than the *Starhawke*'s bays, like flying into the center of a flat-bottomed bubble.

Cade settled the shuttle down with a feather touch. "Ready to meet the Yruf?"

She took a deep breath. "Lead on." She followed him into the main cabin, pausing next to Celia. "Weapons?"

Celia pointed to the weapons locker beside the hatch. "Already stowed. I'm clean."

"All of them?" Besides the more obvious weapons she carried, Celia always had one or two hidden that only a strip-search would find.

A flash of hurt dampened Celia's emotional field. "Yes, all of them."

Aurora blew out a breath. This situation with Micah had her questioning Celia in a way she never had before. She didn't like it. "Sorry. And thanks."

Celia gave a tight nod, but the hurt remained like a bruise in her emotional field.

As soon as they got back to the *Starhawke*, Aurora was taking those two down to the training center to work this problem out with sweat equity.

Cade led their group into the bay. A quick visual inspection of the space confirmed there were no visible doors or hatches of any kind. The bulkheads were constructed of the same interlocking scale design as the hull, with the identical color scheme of emerald, black, and gold, though these scales were considerably smaller than the ones on the hull.

The effect was seamless, even where the opening to the bay had been moments earlier. Only the direction the shuttle was facing gave her any orientation as to where she was in relationship to the exterior. "I know you described this," she said to Cade as she walked beside him toward the rear bulkhead, "but—"

The bulkhead rippled like snakeskin, parting to reveal a winding corridor beyond.

"Whoa!" Micah's exclamation masked Aurora's sharp intake of air.

Cade's mouth curved in a half-smile. "You'll get used to it." He glanced back at Celia and Micah. "But don't freak out when we get to the lift."

"Why would we—" Celia's eyes widened and she sank into a defensive crouch.

Aurora turned, spotting the hovering object that had put Celia on alert.

Cade made a soothing motion with his hand. "Relax. It's one of the drones they use as guides and communicators."

The egg-shaped object looked like everything else Aurora had seen on the ship so far, scaled but without any defining features. It hovered at eye-level a couple meters into the corridor.

Celia moved to stand beside her and shot her an apologetic look. "Reflex. Sorry."

"I get it. We're in strange waters." She might have reacted the same way if she'd spotted it first.

A voice emanated from the drone, resonant and welcoming. Or maybe she thought it sounded welcoming because she'd tuned into the emotional resonance of the Yruf collective again. She also felt a tingling in her electromagnetic field like static electricity.

"I think they want us to follow the drone," Micah said. "Their leader's waiting for us in the throne room."

Apparently Micah had reestablished his connection with them, too.

Cade nodded. "*Shreenef* is the first word I learned while I was here. They use it whenever they want us to follow."

"Then let's not keep them waiting." Aurora stepped into the corridor, Cade and Micah flanking her and Celia bringing up the rear.

"I wasn't kidding about the lift, though," Cade said as they followed the drone through the undulating tunnel. "The walls will close in to create a cylinder around us, and then we'll shoot up. It took a few times before I got the hang of it. As soon as the drone stops, be ready for it."

"Okay." But despite the warning, the rush of the bulkhead as it closed around them almost triggered her energy shield. She was so busy keeping it under control that she lost her balance when the lift shot up. Cade and Micah both rested a hand on her back, steadying her.

Cade's smile was a tad wicked. "What was it you told me at the Academy? That you couldn't wait to have alien adventures in space?"

She reacted to his comment with the seriousness it deserved. She stuck her tongue out at him.

His chuckle sent a flow of warmth through her, melting the tension that had crept in since they'd left the *Starhawke*.

The bulkheads parted as quickly as they'd formed. She recognized the oversized circular door in the corridor beyond as the one she'd seen in the images the Yruf had projected to her and Micah. "We're here."

"The Yruf throne room," Cade confirmed.

A shiver of excitement danced through her veins. This was the first time she'd actually *wanted* to meet a Setarip.

The door rolled into the bulkhead as they approached, the drone floating in front of them like a balloon on a string. The inside of the room was even dimmer than the corridors, which was saying something. They'd moved from early morning light to perpetual twilight.

But she didn't need to see in order to sense the strong presence of the Yruf sitting on the throne at the far end of the room. She sensed other Yruf in the room as well, though she still couldn't pinpoint how many or see them in the shadowy confines.

A corded, undulating light pattern of green and gold appeared on the bulkhead to her left, moving in a clockwise motion. Gaps at set intervals made it appear as if four enormous snakes were chasing each other around the perimeter of the circular room.

The added light allowed her to pick out a few details of the Yruf leader's appearance as they approached the throne, enough to know her coloring matched the ship's. Williams had informed them that all the richly colored Yruf were female, including the leader, while the males were pale shades of brown, white, and black. Quite different from the Etah Setarips she'd encountered. Tnaryt's bright orange markings had stood out like warning flags, while the females had all been solid green.

The leader stood, her cloak flowing away from her body as she strode toward them. She moved with the sinuous grace and raw power of a cobra, unlike the Etah, who were ponderous by comparison.

The Ecilam moved more like the Yruf though, at least the ones Reanne had brought to the river battle. The first Ecilam Aurora had encountered, during the rescue mission to Persei Primus station shortly after she'd become commander of the *Argo*, hadn't been as coordinated or fluid in their movements. But they'd also been hampered by their surroundings and their human leader, a smug sociopath who'd overestimated his importance to his employer.

The drone rose up and emitted a soft glow, creating a circle of light on the deck.

The Yruf leader stopped inside the circle's edge, her gaze meeting Aurora's.

She's beautiful.

Her imagination hadn't done the Yruf leader justice. She dwarfed Aurora, at least half a meter taller, maybe more. But her size made her seem more graceful and refined, not less. Her head was shaped like a python's, but with a high forehead and defined neck that made her look elegant and strong. The pattern of scales on her face perfectly matched the ship's, the emerald green nearly luminescent in the light's glow with the gold and black providing an intricate pattern that delighted the eye.

The leader's gaze settled on Cade, her emotional field giving a flicker that reminded Aurora of laughter.

Micah gave a little snort, drawing Aurora's attention. "What?"

Micah glanced at the leader before answering. "Cade, by any chance were you surly the last time you were here?"

"Surly? I was not surly." He scowled, folding his arms. "I was concerned. Not the same thing."

The Yruf leader stared at him, her dark eyes unblinking.

He sighed. "Okay, yeah. I was a little surly. But I had a good reason."

Aurora felt the laugh-flicker again as the leader looked to her.

"Yes, she can see that," Micah said. "She's happy you succeeded in your goal."

"You're understanding her?" Aurora asked him.

"That bit was easy. All the images I got from her were of people and situations I understood, namely you and Cade."

The leader's focus swung to Micah, the amusement fading, curiosity taking its place. She spoke, the words unintelligible to Aurora.

The skin around Micah's eyes tightened as he concentrated on whatever he was getting from her. "I think she wants to know how I'm able to understand her so quickly." His gaze dropped to meet Aurora's. "And what my connection is to you."

So the leader had sensed their closeness, even though Aurora hadn't engaged her energy field or touched Micah since they'd entered the throne room. "Do you think she'd understand the concept of mixed races? And siblings? Do they have those in their culture?"

"No idea. Do you want to try tapping in?" Micah held out his hand, palm up.

She hesitated for a moment before clasping it, unsure how the leader would respond to the behavior. Cade hadn't said anything about the Yruf holding hands. Or touching in general.

When the leader didn't react negatively, Aurora engaged her pearlescent energy field and allowed it to envelope Micah.

The Yruf leader's pupils dilated completely, her head bobbing as she stared at them. Her emotional field lost the cohesion that had defined it up to that point, going into flux.

Aurora tightened her grip on Micah's hand. "I'm not sure engaging my energy field was a good idea," she murmured.

"I think we're okay," he replied. "But she can definitely see your field."

The leader reached out a long-fingered hand toward Aurora, the tips skimming through the edge of the energy field. As soon as they did, Aurora got an image of herself in her mind's eye as the Yruf leader saw her. The colors were super-saturated, the green of her eyes vibrant against her dark lashes and pale skin. The pearlescent glow of her energy field looked otherworldly even to her, colors swirling in it that she normally didn't even notice.

But the leader did. Apparently the Yruf could see a broader spectrum of color than Humans or Suulh.

Aurora heard something, too, a fragmented whisper that tantalized her just beyond the boundary of her comprehension.

The leader's emotions continued to shift, though Aurora didn't sense any fear or anxiety. Instead, it felt like the empathic equivalent of someone listening to a recording at twice the normal speed. The Yruf leader was processing emotions so rapidly that Aurora was having trouble tracking them.

The Yruf leader held perfectly still, while Micah had fallen silent, lines of concentration creasing the skin around his mouth and eyes.

She didn't want to disturb him, but as the silence stretched out, curiosity got the better of her. "Is she talking to you?"

He shook his head, his gaze still on the leader. "I think she's communicating with the collective. I can get a sense of all the other voices, thousands of them, like a school of fish or flock of birds."

Aurora glanced back at Celia, who was guarding their rear, though with a subtle stance that didn't look threatening. Celia's gaze was on Micah.

"Any thoughts?" Aurora murmured.

Celia's attention flicked to her. "The leader's body language is subtle. I'm loathe to read anything into it before I see others of her kind and build a basis for comparison." She gave a micro shrug. "I don't see any signs of antagonism from her."

Aurora nodded. "Me, either."

Considering the unusual situation, Celia was doing an excellent job of keeping her emotions focused and locked down.

If Micah's interaction with the Yruf was bothering her, she wasn't letting it come through.

Images started to flow through Aurora's mind, drawing her attention back to the leader. The images were familiar, Micah's memories of their childhood at Stoneycroft.

The Yruf leader hummed softly, the images slowing whenever the memories showed Aurora's energy field. She sensed the question before Micah voiced it.

"I'm pretty sure she understands that we're siblings, but she doesn't seem to understand why I don't project an energy field like you do."

"If I create a visual image, will she be able to see it?"

"I would think so."

She felt the leader's attention shift to her the moment she began building the image she wanted to share.

She started with her and Micah standing side by side but not touching. Then she added their parents holding hands behind them, her mom on her side and her dad behind Micah. She built the image out from there, populating Micah's side with Cade's team, Celia, Kire, and Kelly, then filling out her side with Lelindia, Marina, Gryphon, Raaveen, and Paaw. Behind Micah's group, she projected an image of Earth. Behind hers, she projected one of the images of Feylahn that Star had recorded, which showed the Teeli's sensor web and warships.

Finally, she showed all the Suulh on her side with their energy fields engaged.

The leader made the humming sound again.

"*Teeli.*"

The single word spoken in the leader's resonant voice sent a shiver down her spine. "The Teeli took over my race's homeworld," Aurora explained. "Made slaves of my people."

She didn't expect the leader to understand her words, so she shifted the image, showing Paaw and Raaveen as they'd looked after living on the Etah slave ship. She added Paaw's mother Zelle, filthy and crippled from her Necri existence.

She sensed when the leader grabbed hold of the memories, a tugging sensation in her mind that she resisted.

Let go.

The words were in her head, but not from the leader. From Micah.

It's okay.

Letting go wasn't her strength – she liked having control, especially of herself – but she'd asked Micah to guide her in these uncharted waters. She needed to trust his judgement.

The moment she did as he asked, she felt like she was taking her first spacewalk. Terrifying and exhilarating at the same time.

Her memories continued to flow, this time rolling backwards in time, but she wasn't the one at the helm. The scenes flipped to the moment she and the rest of the Suulh had prevented the explosion that would have destroyed the Etah ship. The leader paused there for a moment, then continued further back, stopping when she reached the fight in the cell bay where Aurora and three of the Necri had taken out the Etah who had captured her.

She tensed, unsure how the Yruf leader would react to seeing her own kind killed, even in self-defense. But she didn't sense judgement. Only sadness, and compassion.

The leader held the image for a moment, her focus on the rows and rows of dirty, dark, cramped cages where the Necri had lived.

Aurora felt the drop of moisture slip off her chin before she even realized she was crying. Being in that bay the first time had been horrible, when she'd believed the Necri were a new potentially deadly species. But seeing it again with such vivid detail, knowing the Suulh who had suffered were *her people*, the ones she'd been born to protect, cut her to the bone.

"*Guard.*"

She met the leader's gaze through a sheen of moisture, surprised by the Galish word. "Yes. Guardian." She placed her free hand over her heart, partly to indicate herself, but mostly to soothe the pain throbbing there. "I have to free them from the

Teeli." She changed the image to the battle at the river, to the moment she'd knelt before Reanne in manacles. Right before she'd realized Lelindia had arrived with the *Starhawke*.

"*Ssssovereign.*"

The name came out on a hiss. For the first time Aurora sensed anger from the leader, and an echo of her pain. The leader locked onto the memory, going backwards to Tnaryt's death at the hands of the Ecilam, then forwards to when Aurora had knocked Reanne down with a kick to her knee.

The leader slowed the pace as she watched the deathmatch with Kreestol that had followed – the underwater plunge, the energy blast that had freed her but almost killed Cade, and had killed several of the Ecilam. The memory crept in half-time as Aurora dragged herself out of the water to Cade's side, using her energy field to restart his heart.

Her own heart pounded like a freight train as the images pulled at her, the agony of that moment washing over her.

The humming from the leader provided a subtle background as Cade's eyes opened, unfocused, confused. The memory continued to crawl until Aurora brushed a kiss over his lips and took off across the river.

As she ran, the speed of the memory accelerated until the Sovereign came into sight. The leader ignored the brief fight with Kreestol, but the image froze as soon as Aurora grabbed the Sovereign's cloak and the hood fell back, revealing Reanne's face.

The leader's emotions froze too — in shock, she suspected.

"*Teeli.*" The word sounded exactly the same as the first time the leader had said it, but Aurora knew this time it was a question.

"Teeli," she confirmed. "And Human." She projected an image of Reanne, then the image of Reanne's mother that Reanne had kept in a frame beside her bed at the Academy. Then she created a non-specific male Teeli presence loosely based on Sly'Kull on Reanne's other side to stand in for Reanne's father.

The emotions that rose like a cobra's hood from the Yruf leader made Aurora flinch. The leader's mouth opened in a reptilian snarl, but without any teeth.

Aurora caught movement in her peripheral vision. Celia had moved up beside her, filling the narrow gap between her and Cade.

But it wasn't anger triggering the leader's reaction. It was pain. Loss. Betrayal. And none of it was directed at them.

"*Ssssoovereeign.*" The leader drew out the syllables, the hiss sharp and piercing. It seemed to contain a question, too.

Aurora frowned. "I don't understand."

"I think she's sensing you know more about the Sovereign," Micah said, his voice modulated like he was a guest at a wake. "She wants to know what you know."

She broke eye contact with the leader, meeting Micah's gaze. "That's not likely to help our cause. She may not understand what she's seeing, or she might misinterpret it."

His green eyes showed the same concern, but no doubt. "It's just my opinion, but if we want them to work with us, we'll have to be honest. Any attempt to hide the truth will lose the trust they've given so far."

She chewed on her lip as she ran the options through her mind. Could the Yruf possibly understand the circumstances that had led to her friendship with Reanne, and how Reanne's twisted mind and heart had brought them to this point?

If the leader didn't, Aurora stood to be painted with the same brush as Reanne.

It was risky, but so were most of the tough decisions she'd made in recent months.

Turning back to the leader, she took a slow breath. "Let's start at the beginning."

Forty-Six

Cade had no idea how long the five of them stood there with Aurora and the Yruf leader linked by the glow of Aurora's energy field as they stared into each other's eyes, but the bottoms of his feet ached and his lower back was starting to complain, too.

Aurora seemed oblivious to anything or anyone other than the Yruf leader, and while Micah shifted his weight slightly from time to time, his focus was as intense and unwavering as his sister's. Even Celia seemed tuned in, leaving Cade as odd man out.

Several times during the prolonged interaction he'd gotten flashes of images, pixelated and haphazard, but nothing like the clear images he'd seen when he'd been the one communicating with the Yruf leader directly. He was sensing emotions though, particularly from Aurora.

Following the emotional journey she'd made with Reanne was partially responsible for his feeling of disconnection. He'd played a pivotal – if unknowing – role in her pain and loss, triggering the suffering she'd endured after her breakup with him. Her friendship with Reanne had died slowly, causing additional pain and loss.

He could feel the emotional walls Aurora had built around herself during that time, the sadness and anger that had made them necessary. She'd been betrayed by him, the man she'd loved so openly and honestly, and by the friend she'd trusted as a confidant.

It's a wonder she hadn't tossed him out an airlock the first time he'd stepped onto her bridge.

Speaking of which, a lightening of her emotional resonance, a sense of determination and purpose, suggested she'd probably jumped from their Academy days to their first mission to Gaia, where they'd encountered Reanne and the Necri. He felt the moment Reanne came onto the scene — a slow-burn anger from Aurora and a subtle echo from the Yruf leader.

If he wasn't bogged down by his own guilt, he might have been intrigued by the tapestry of Aurora's emotions related to those events. Especially—

A flash of intoxicating heat burned through him, catching him off guard. Micah frowned at the same time, giving him a good idea which memory the Yruf leader was looking at *now* — the passionate kiss he and Aurora had shared on the island beach after they'd rescued the Suulh and reunited them with their children.

He would have expected Aurora to skip over that particular scene, considering her brother was watching it unfold.

The Yruf leader must have snagged it. Clearly she had a fascination with Cade's relationship with Aurora.

He'd guessed that when she'd shown him the video Justin had taken of him and Aurora in *Gladiator*'s cockpit. The way she'd reacted when she'd first seem them together today, and the emotions he was sensing now, confirmed it.

Maybe the Yruf didn't make romantic attachments. Or maybe the leader was intrigued by the mating rituals of other species. Humans were, after all, so why not the Yruf?

Aurora's emotions skipped, switching quickly to an intensity that had nothing to do with romance. He recognized the adrenaline-induced focus of battle. Based on the timeline, most likely she was showing the leader their next encounter with the Teeli, the ambush in the asteroid field around Burrow.

That morphed into the sourness of outrage and frustration, which remained for several minutes. No problem guessing what that was linked to. Had to be her captivity on Tnaryt's ship. He'd experienced those same emotions while he sat helpless in *Gladiator*, waiting for her signal to mount a rescue mission.

The Yruf leader would likely want to see all the details of those events. Too bad it meant Aurora had to relive them. He could feel the toll it was taking on her, saw the strain in the lines of her face.

He took a chance and stepped behind her, sliding his arms around her waist. The Yruf leader didn't react, but Aurora did, relaxing against his chest with a subtle sigh as her energy field enveloped him in its loving warmth.

He rested his cheek on her hair and held her, the brush of her energy field heightening the sensation of emotional connection. Eventually her emotions ebbed and her energy field dissipated as she came out of the communication link with the leader and Micah.

He lifted his head, gazing at the leader.

Her dark eyes stared back, the diamond-shaped pupils contracting. "Kay-d."

He blinked, then nodded. "Yes. Cade."

Those unearthly eyes stared right into the depths of his soul. He'd never felt quite so exposed. But he also sensed a deep respect, possibly even admiration, coming from her.

Her gaze dropped to Aurora. "Ah-ror-ah."

"Yes." Aurora's voice thickened, probably the result of the emotional rollercoaster she'd just been on. "Aurora."

The leader's tongue flicked out, her head bobbing slightly, her emotions settling back to the low tide he associated with normal. "Ifel."

"Eyefull?" Cade repeated.

Her head bobbed in a rough approximation of a nod. "Ifel."

"It's her name," Micah said. "Ifel." He did a much better job of mimicking the Yruf leader's accent. "Like the tower in Paris."

"Oh."

"Actually, her full name is Ifel-Tehmor, but I think the second part is her title. Like captain or commander."

Aurora turned in Cade's arms to face her brother. "Are you understanding her better now?"

"Uh-huh. I was catching what I think was internal commentary as she was sorting through your memories. It helped me to link what I was hearing with scenes that made sense to me. It's only a start, but that exercise was very helpful."

"I'm glad."

But Cade could feel Aurora struggling to regain her emotional stability. She was also growing heavier in his arms, her head resting on his shoulder.

He glanced at Micah. "Would you be able to ask Ifel if we could take a break from the deep conversations for a little while?" He dipped his chin toward Aurora.

Micah got the message. "Sure."

Ifel's head swiveled in the reptilian way of the Yruf, her attention on Micah.

Celia took advantage of the interruption to move to Aurora's other side. "How you doing?" she murmured, her brown eyes analyzing Aurora with the precision of a field medic.

Aurora gave a small shrug. "Okay. A little tired." Which she confirmed by raising her hand over her mouth to stifle a yawn.

Cade pulled her more snugly against his body. "That was quite a journey you took."

She tilted her face up, the light from the drone picking out the gold flecks in her green eyes. "You could feel all that, huh?"

"Pretty much. I wasn't getting the visuals, though."

Her nose wrinkled. "No need. You were there for most of it."

For better or worse.

"Sis? I think we're changing venues."

Aurora straightened, moving out of Cade's arms.

"Shreenef." Ifel's cloak swirled around her as she pivoted, heading for the bulkhead behind her throne.

The drone stayed with them as they followed her, but the chasing lights circling the room froze, illuminating four figures who detached from the shadows to flank them on both sides.

Ifel's guards.

However, their reaction to him was nothing like it had been during his previous stint onboard. For one thing, the guards held their staffs loosely in their hands, rather than gripped in anticipation of a fight. Their formation was more casual too, as though they were joining the group rather than caging them in.

The bulkhead rippled as they approached, exposing another large circular door. This one had a stylized design at the center. Five bands of green wound together like a circular maypole, each a distinctly different shade, from pale moss to the deep emerald of the Yruf.

One band was a fluorescent green that matched the color Cade associated with the Ecilam. Another band was the same shade as the scales on the female Etah from Tnaryt's ship. Logically, the other two green bands represented the Regna and Egar.

It was a symbol of unity, with no band any more prominent than the others. Was that how the Setarips had once existed? In harmony with each other? And if so, what had triggered the civil war that decimated their homeworld and drove them into space?

The door rolled open, hiding the emblem from view.

The tunnel beyond was lit in a honey glow, warm and inviting.

Cade caught Aurora's hand in his as they followed Ifel, Micah and Celia behind them. Aurora gave his palm a squeeze. He squeezed back.

As the drone bobbed ahead of them, a light pattern began dancing across the tunnel's arched walls.

"I wonder if the Yruf communicate with light." He spoke in a low tone, their footsteps echoing in the confined space. Ifel and her guards, he noted, didn't make a sound.

"Could be." Aurora studied the pattern of light. "I think they see a broader spectrum than we do. When Ifel was touching my energy field, I got an image of myself seen through her eyes. It was saturated, with more colors than I normally see, especially in my energy field."

"Interesting." And strange. Light really hadn't factored into his last visit. The Yruf tended to keep the corridors and rooms darker than most humans would, but patterns like the one playing out on the bulkhead now had been absent.

She peered at him. "You didn't see anything like this last time, did you?"

He smiled. She could read him like a book. "Nope. And now I want to know why. We were here for days, and I saw several areas of the ship. None of them were lit like this except for the chasing pattern we saw in the throne room."

The winding tunnel opened up ahead, the drone rising out of view into the room beyond.

The space they entered was significantly smaller than the throne room, but that fact increased the sensory overload that struck him as Ifel stepped aside to let them enter.

Lights in every color of the rainbow pulsed like Morse code from all the available surfaces, including the deck. The light show reflected off the subtly glossy scales of the Yruf working at the consoles, panels, and screens – at least that's what he assumed the objects in the room were. They didn't look like anything that had come out of the Fleet's R&D department, but the Yruf were clearly monitoring them.

"Is this their bridge?" Celia asked.

Several Yruf turned in their direction. Not a single one had the emerald, gold, and black coloring of Ifel and the guards, despite there being at least twenty of them in the room – more than he'd ever seen at one time. Apparently the color scheme of the ship wasn't the dominant coloring for the female Yruf in general, just Ifel and her guards.

The guards moved closer to him, Aurora, and Celia, not threatening, but making it clear they weren't supposed to wander off, either.

Ifel stepped next to Micah. He held her gaze for several moments, then blinked. "This isn't *the* bridge," he said in answer to Celia's question, "but it is *a* bridge. Or maybe more of a hub. I was getting images of similar rooms throughout the ship." He turned to Cade. "You said you saw them break the larger ship into seven smaller modular ships last time?"

Cade nodded.

Micah's focus went inward again, like he was sorting through his mental filing cabinet. "I think they can create three times that many. Or more."

"More than twenty?" Celia glanced at Ifel, wariness in her dark eyes. "How sure are we that they're on our side?"

"Very sure," Micah, Aurora, and Cade said in unison.

Celia pursed her lips. "Says the three people who've had the Yruf playing around in their minds. How do you know they didn't plant the idea to make us complacent?"

"It's not like that," Aurora said, irritation wafting off her like stale perfume. "Their form of communication is a dialogue. Open, honest. I'm not even sure they're capable of lying or deceit. Their emotions certainly don't indicate ulterior motives."

Celia lifted her hands, palms out. "Okay, I believe you." But the assessing look didn't fade from her eyes. "Just keep in mind it's my job to question assumptions and anticipate the unexpected."

Another gust of irritation, but this time Aurora seemed to be directing it at herself. "You're right. It is."

And if Micah weren't in the room, this conversation probably would have gone quite differently. The tension between Aurora and Celia had been steadily building ever since Micah joined the crew, but now it was spilling over into their professional relationship. They could both probably use a sit-down. And maybe a stiff drink.

Ifel and the guards weren't the only ones watching the interchange. At least a handful of the other Yruf in the room had stopped what they were doing to focus on the group. Probably not a good thing, given his past experience unintentionally drawing that kind of scrutiny.

He rested a hand on Aurora's lower back in a subtle warning.

She tensed for a moment, then her shoulder blades relaxed on her next exhale.

Good, she'd gotten the message. He focused on Micah. "Can you ask Ifel whether the Yruf communicate with light?" He swept his free hand to indicate the patterns dancing around the room. "And how it works?"

Micah's gaze flicked between Aurora and Celia. He'd noted the tension, too, and the Yruf's reaction. "I'll try."

Cade brushed his thumb across Aurora's back in a soothing gesture as he focused on Micah's interaction with Ifel.

Then Micah laughed.

"What's so funny?" Aurora asked, the corners of her mouth lifting in response.

Micah grinned at her. "I'm not sure whether to be insulted, but I think Ifel just called our use of light *simple*."

"Simple?"

"Rudimentary. Unsophisticated." His gaze slid to Cade. "And to answer your question, yes, they definitely communicate using light. It's another reason they're not very verbal. Between their light and mental communication, they don't need to be."

Aurora straightened. "Is that why my energy field fascinated her so much?"

"Could be. She may assume you use it as a form of communication."

"I do, though not the way the Yruf seem to. The color and intensity of energy fields have meaning to the Suulh, and the interaction of our fields has significance, too."

"Can you understand what any of this means?" Cade asked Micah, nodding to the light patterns surrounding them.

Micah shook his head. "Not a bit. I do get the sense it's language based though, like how a solid red light translates as *stop* and a flashing yellow means *slow* or *caution.* I think each pattern of color and light means something specific, but Kire and Justin would probably have better luck sorting it out than I would."

"Too bad they're not here to see it." Justin would jump at the chance to tackle such an unusual language form.

"If we convince the Yruf to work with us to stop the Teeli," Aurora said, "maybe they'll get the opportunity."

Forty-Seven

Lelindia prowled the bridge like a caged tiger. Normally she was great at waiting — patience was a necessity in her line of work — but the importance of the situation weighed on her, making it impossible to sit still.

Having very little idea of what exactly Aurora was facing didn't help, either. What if Aurora and Micah couldn't convince the Yruf to join them? What then?

Up to now they'd relied on the Kraed as their allies. A few camouflaged Kraed ships would have been a great help with the Teeli mission, but recent events made that impossible. She hadn't just burned the bridges with the Kraed. She'd blow them to smithereens.

They couldn't count on any support from the Fleet, either, even with the Admiral back at HQ. Not until they could produce solid evidence of the Teeli's duplicity.

But to obtain that evidence, they needed help from the Yruf.

She tugged on the hem of her tunic, smoothing non-existent wrinkles. "No word?" she asked Kire for what was probably the tenth time in the past two hours.

To his credit, he dutifully checked the comm line from his post in the captain's chair, with not so much as a hint of annoyance on his face. "Not yet."

She pivoted away, stalking back in the direction of the tactical console. Jonarel had settled there after Celia had left with Aurora and Cade. He was keeping tabs on the Yruf ship and watching for any signs of other vessels in the area.

He reached out as she moved past him, his strong fingers circling her wrist in an easy grip.

She halted, the zing of pleasure his touch inspired pulling her out of her mental pinwheel.

His fingers brushed the pulse point on her wrist in a caress. "Aurora will succeed."

A tremor worked up her arm from the point of contact. He was intentionally distracting her. For the moment, she let him. "How do you know?"

His golden eyes lit with amusement. "She is the most stubborn person in the galaxy."

She grinned. "Don't let her hear you say that."

He gave a nonchalant shrug, the movement of his chest and shoulder muscles – clearly defined under his brown tunic – providing another distraction. "She would not argue the point."

She chuckled. "No, I suppose she wouldn't." Which nudged the odds in their favor.

She caught a lock of Jonarel's hair in her free hand, her fingers brushing over the silken strands. His eyelids slid lower as the look in his eyes grew decidedly warmer.

"Thank you," she whispered, dropping a quick kiss on his lips before stepping back.

He released her, but he held her gaze, a silent promise in his eyes. They'd be following up on that kiss after they left the bridge.

She shivered in anticipation, abandoning her pacing circle to settle into her usual chair.

Her gaze moved to the slice of the Yruf ship visible on the bridgescreen. The exterior gave off a soft glow, not as bright as when it had first appeared, but still clearly outlining the curved edges against the starfield beyond. What was happening over there? What was Aurora seeing?

She'd considered sending her a mental message, but nixed the idea. She didn't want to interrupt Aurora's negotiations, and she also didn't want to risk the Yruf picking up on whatever she sent. Maybe they wouldn't — Micah had postulated that the Suulh might communicate on a different wavelength than the Yruf — but that was by no means certain.

She sighed, settling deeper into the chair, the cushioning wrapping around her like a hug. At least she was comfortable, but waiting would be a lot easier if she had something constructive to do.

Her mind filled the vacuum, nimbly latching onto the Kraed problem.

She'd created it by choosing to confront Siginal while Aurora was on Earth with Brendan and Micah. If she'd stayed at Sol Station, or left Drakar space after visiting the Suulh on Azaana, they wouldn't be in this fix.

Her gaze drifted from the bridgescreen to the tactical station.

Yeah, and she wouldn't be mated to Jonarel, either. The struggle against Siginal's unreasonable expectations had pushed them together and opened their hearts to new possibilities.

Her gaze traced the broad curve of Jonarel's shoulders and the glossy curtain of his hair where it brushed his shoulder blades. No matter how much guilt weighed on her now, she couldn't regret the path that had led her into his arms.

And neither did he.

But it still placed the responsibility for the situation squarely in her lap. She needed to be the one to find a solution.

Jonarel had said that their pair bonding would cause discord rather than cohesion with the Kraed. She refused to believe that. Siginal might view her as subservient to Aurora, but that didn't mean it was true.

The nature of her relationship with Aurora had always been different than her mom's and Libra's. Part of that was a result of growing up without the conventions of Suulh society reinforcing expectations. They'd been surrounded by Humans, not other Suulh. Only their parents had provided any direction on what it meant to be Suulh, and Libra had squashed even that little bit of guidance the moment the Teeli had arrived on Earth.

Maybe Aurora would have been a traditional Sahzade if that hadn't occurred. They'd never know, but being half-Human, and a powerful empath, made her quite different from Libra. She was a natural leader, to be sure, but her choice to go with Cade to find Admiral Schreiber rather than staying with the crew when they investigated the Suulh homeworld was telling. As was her willingness to put Lelindia in charge of the *Starhawke* and take off to search out Brendan and Micah on her own.

Lelindia couldn't imagine any situation in which Libra would give that much control over to Lelindia's mom. They were partners — energy sisters of the Suulh — but Libra called the shots, governed every decision, and had the final word.

Aurora didn't operate that way. As captain of the ship she gave orders that she expected to be obeyed, but as Sahzade, she treated Lelindia as an equal in every way. Always had, and always would.

Lelindia's personal hang-ups from the past had kept her from seeing that, embracing it.

Which meant Aurora would support her if she made that point with Siginal. Working together, could they change his mind, overcome his prejudices, and those of the other Kraed clan leaders? Could she and Aurora make them see that her mating with Jonarel could benefit them all?

It was a tall order. And they still had the issue of Jonarel and Tehar's banishment to deal with. But an idea started dancing at the edge of her mind, sending butterflies into her stomach and sparks through her veins.

It was a simple idea and not exactly radical considering she was mated. But she'd never given the concept any space to grow before.

It took form now all on its own.

Would Signal accept the potential benefits of their mating if she and Jonarel had a child? A half-Suulh, half-Kraed daughter who would literally bind the two races together?

Her blood warmed as the idea spread across her skin like a fever. She was already well past the age that most Nedale conceived their daughters. The only reason her Suulh instincts hadn't kicked in before was because the mate she'd wanted had been unattainable.

Not anymore. Now he was in her heart and in her bed. And making her energy field glow like firelight when they touched. According to her mother, that meant they were biologically compatible, just as Libra and Brendan had been.

True, Kraed and Suulh biology was more disparate than Human-Suulh. Jonarel had retractable claws on his hands and feet and produced skin pigmentation she couldn't. But she was the Nedale. Her gifts were grounded in the ability to nurture life, all life. She'd never had any problem healing Jonarel's injuries, despite their differences in physiology. She had to believe her talents would also help her to bridge any barriers to conception.

Her hand settled over her abdomen, where the butterflies continued to flutter and whirl. A child. With Jonarel. A precious gift she'd never imagined possible.

The soft beat of translucent wings lifted into her chest, making her breath stutter. Images filled her mind — a daughter who blended the best of the Suulh and Kraed. Dark-haired for sure, but would her eyes be brown or gold? Her skin fern-green or tawny-beige?

Not that it mattered. She'd be beautiful. And strong.

Would she produce a Suulh energy field? Would she have healing abilities? Would she have Kraed claws?

A familiar voice filled the bridge. "Aurora to Kire."

She blinked.

And discovered Jonarel was watching her, a speculative look in his golden eyes.

Heat climbed into her face.

"Hey, Roe. Good to hear from you. How are things going with the Yruf?"

She broke eye contact with Jonarel and focused on Kire.

"Slow, but we're definitely building trust. Is Lelindia on the bridge?"

"I'm here." Her voice came out a little strangled. It didn't help that she was intensely aware of Jonarel's attention locked on her, adding fuel to her daydreams. She drew in a slow breath. "Where are you?"

"Funny you should ask. You'll never believe what I'm looking at right now."

Forty-Eight

Aurora's boots made a dry scrape as she adjusted her stance on the uneven rock, her gaze sweeping up to the sky.

It looked so *real*. The perspective gave the sensation of kilometers despite her comband's scanner informing her the ceiling was thirty-two point four meters above her.

The plants surrounding her, however, were very real. Their vibrancy called to her, making her energy field tingle under her skin. "We now know one of the reasons the Yruf ship is so massive. They've built a biosphere at its center."

"A biosphere?" Lelindia's eagerness came over the comm clear as the water rippling down the rocks to Aurora's left. "You mean like the *Starhawke*'s greenhouse?"

Aurora made a face, which thankfully Lelindia couldn't see. What Jonarel had created was amazing, but the space she was in right now made the *Starhawke*'s greenhouse look like a child's science fair project.

"Kinda, but bigger." *A lot bigger.* "And more..." She struggled to find a word that wouldn't wound Jonarel's pride. With Celia on the Yruf ship and Cade's team on *Gladiator*, he would have taken over watch at the *Starhawke*'s tactical station. "Elaborate."

"Elaborate?" Jonarel's deep voice rumbled across the connection, confirming he'd picked up on her slight hesitation. "How so?"

"Well..." She pivoted in a slow circle. "If I didn't know for a fact I was standing on a starship, I'd believe I was on the Yruf homeworld."

"A simulation?"

"More of a recreation." With the exception of the sunlight and blue sky, which felt real but clearly wasn't, the entire space was tangible, alive. "Everything here was transplanted from the Setarip homeworld. Their native vegetation, soil, rocks, water." A scuttling rustle drew her attention to the underbrush, where a tiny mammalian creature the size of her thumb disappeared under the greenery. "And some of their fauna, too." She'd noted at least five insect species already, perched on the leaves or buzzing overhead, as well as a couple birds.

"A literal biosphere?" Jonarel sounded skeptical.

She'd been right. His pride had taken a hit. "Uh-huh. We're on our way to the ocean right now." Micah had gone ahead with Ifel, leaving her, Cade, and Celia to explore the jungle area they were currently walking through. Two of Ifel's guards led the way and the other two followed behind at a leisurely pace.

She'd felt a sustained ripple in her electromagnetic field in the short corridor before they'd entered the biosphere, a stronger version of the static electricity she'd sensed but mostly ignored when they first encountered the drone in the shuttle bay. Logic suggested the Yruf had an incredibly advanced but subtle decontamination system that her team had passed through to ensure they wouldn't bring any biohazards onto the ship or into the biosphere.

As Suulh, she and Micah shouldn't have been a threat. The Suulh couldn't be infected by or carry pathogens, but Cade and Celia could. Since they'd been allowed inside, they must have passed the screening, too. Lelindia's work as the ship's medical officer likely had a lot to do with it. Her Nedale abilities allowed her to keep the entire crew squeaky clean.

"And it's self-sustaining?" Lelindia's enthusiasm gave a counterpoint to Jonarel's skepticism.

"You and Jonarel could determine that better than me, but it appears so." She stepped off the rock and joined Celia, who was inspecting a purple-veined plant that resembled a giant lily. "I think I'm going to have to pry Celia out of here with a crowbar."

Celia gave her a wry smile. "You could try."

Lelindia's laugh came over the comm. "Sorry I'm missing the fun. It sounds like things are going well."

"So far so good. I'm having to lean on Micah's ability to communicate with Ifel more than I'd expected."

"Ifel?"

"Their leader. She and I have shared images, but I've missed out on a lot of the contextual details and subtle cues Micah catches. I'm more conditioned for verbal communication than I realized." She tapped Celia on the shoulder, motioning to where Cade waited for them further up the path. Celia fell into step beside her.

"That's not surprising," Lelindia said. "You and I practiced sharing images growing up, but we rarely tried to hold actual conversations through our mental link. Micah's spent his entire life talking to animals through a variation on that link. It makes sense that his skills are more flexible and refined than yours, at least right now."

She paused in front of Cade, who'd obviously heard the last part of the conversation. His lips twitched in response to her non-verbal reaction to Lelindia's insight.

Apparently her pride was every bit as vulnerable as Jonarel's.

He rested a hand briefly on her upper back in a casual caress before they continued on the downhill slope of the path.

"You're right. I just—" She jerked to a halt, rooted to the ground. "Stellar light."

"What?" Lelindia's concerned mother hen voice squawked out of the comband. "What's wrong?"

"Nothing." She shook her head, even though Lelindia couldn't see her. "I just didn't expect the ocean to be... an *ocean*."

The vista that spread before her had to be another illusion, like the sky. No way was the horizon as far away as it appeared. But her mind told her it was every bit as real as the ocean view from her dad's house on Oahu.

"Hey, sis!" Micah waved at her like he was flagging down a transport. "You gotta see this."

His excitement was palpable even without engaging her empathic senses. He was standing next to the strip of wet sand as the waves lapped close to his toes. The way his muscles bunched and flexed with each advance and retreat of the surf, he was probably fighting his natural instinct to dive in.

"Lelindia, I've gotta go. I'll be in touch when I have more to report."

Lelindia's sigh was muffled but audible. "We'll be here."

Aurora turned off her comband as she continued down the path to the beach.

"Can you believe this?" Micah asked as he swept his arm toward the water. "Ifel said it's more than thirty-five meters deep."

Micah's communication skills were improving by leaps and bounds if he'd figured out a shared unit for measurement.

Which brought the total height of the chamber from ocean floor to sky ceiling close to seventy meters. About the height of a typical sports stadium, but this one was in the center of a *starship.*

"There are creatures down there." Micah's grin reminded her of the first time she'd seen him standing beside the shoreline on Oahu, after he'd given an impromptu surfing performance with his dolphin friends. "I can't understand what they're saying, but I can hear them."

"Do you know how many species the Yruf have onboard?"

Micah turned to Ifel, who'd been gazing at the rippling water as they talked. The corners of his eyes tightened as he focused on their mostly non-verbal conversation.

"Thousands," he finally replied. "They tried to save as many species as they could, both plant and animal, before the planet became uninhabitable. Like an interstellar ark. But some species were too large for transport." Pain lines creased his forehead. "Their versions of whales, for instance."

His hard swallow dug a chunk out of Aurora's abdomen. The extinction of any creature, especially aquatic ones, would wound his soul.

"They worked to obtain viable embryos and genetic material for those they couldn't bring onboard. They've maintained them in suspension, a kind of stasis, ever since."

"They want to bring them back to life?" Celia asked.

He tilted his head, translating the question to Ifel. "Yes. That's exactly what they want." His voice hitched, grew thicker. "The original Yruf leader had hoped to find a new homeworld where they could settle and repopulate. But the civil war didn't end with the demise of their planet. It spread like an infection, causing destruction whenever the Setarip factions crossed paths or encountered a habitable world."

"You mean the looting of human colonies?" Cade asked.

She noted Cade had folded his arms over his chest, like he was bracing against a gale force wind. He must be picking up on Micah's emotions, too.

Micah shook his head. "This was way before they'd encountered humans. The Regna faction tried to settle on a habitable planet, but the Etah found them. They seeded the atmosphere with toxins in an attempt to wipe them out. The Yruf intervened, driving the Etah off, but not before a fourth of the Regna had died and the planet had become contaminated."

Aurora's blood curdled. That was exactly the kind of cowardly destruction she'd expect from Tnaryt. Or whoever had ruled before him. "What else can she tell you about the Regna faction?" she asked Micah. "It doesn't sound like they're as violent as the Etah and Ecilam."

"They're not," he said slowly, his eyes shifting like he was watching a movie as he communicated with Ifel. "They fought on the side of the Yruf in the beginning, before their society splintered and their planet descended into chaos. Ifel believes the Regna want peace as much as she does. They just don't know how to achieve it. They've been living as nomads, isolating themselves and avoiding contact with the other factions. The Yruf lost contact with them years ago. She's not sure where they are now."

Celia's eyes narrowed. "Well, that explains why the Regna have only been seen a few times in our history. And why their attacks have always been less destructive than the Ecilam or Etah's."

"Which leaves the Egar." Aurora glanced at Ifel's guards, who had gathered in a protective half-circle around their leader.

She could relate to their pain on a whole new level. Having her family ripped apart as a child, then learning of the Necri and Suulh, and her role in their society, and the truth about her homeworld — she understood the Yruf's desire to bring unity and peace back to their people. It's what she yearned for, too.

She'd created a pocket of that idyllic world on Azaana, just as the Yruf had created this biosphere. But neither filled the void within.

"What can Ifel tell us about the Egar?" The more they learned about the Yruf's situation, the more likely she was to find common ground that would help her convince Ifel to work with her to unmask the Teeli.

Micah's frown faded, replaced by puzzlement. "They're the faction she understands the least." His eyes narrowed, like he was studying the images she was sending. "They're not aggressive. Well, they can be aggressive." His mouth turned down. "But they can be passive, too." Now he looked like he was squinting into the sun. "I guess the best way to describe them is... opportunistic?"

He blinked, gave a little head shake, then turned toward her. "Since she's unclear on their motivations, it makes it hard to gauge what she's sharing, but I get the impression the Egar won't make trouble unless they have to. However, they'll also take full advantage of a situation if it suits their purposes."

Celia snorted. "Like mercenaries who look out for themselves first, but won't go out of their way to hurt others unless they think it will benefit them."

"That sounds accurate."

"Which means they can't be trusted as allies." Celia pursed her lips. "At the first whiff of trouble, they'd turn against us."

Micah grimaced. "Also accurate."

Aurora sighed. "So, we have the Yruf who are actively seeking peace, the Regna who are avoiding everyone, the Egar who could go either way, the Etah who are practically wiped out, and the Ecilam, who have allied with the Teeli and Reanne in a plot to take over Fleet space." She let her head fall back, her gaze on the expanse of blue sky. "When are things going to stop getting *more* complicated?"

It was a rhetorical question, but Micah answered her anyway. "Never."

She shot him a dirty look.

He laughed in response. "Get over it, sis. Complications aren't the problem."

"Oh? Then what is?"

"Your reaction to them."

That comment stung. Her hand went to her chest, rubbing her sternum. "My reaction?"

"You've been trying to organize and simplify things, to break everything down into manageable equations. It's a quality that makes you a good leader and strategist – in most instances. You and Ifel are similar in that regard."

"We are?" The comparison was flattering and unnerving at the same time.

"Uh-huh." Micah's gaze moved out over the water. "But from everything you've told me and shown me, Reanne doesn't function that way. Neither do the Teeli. They're driven by more primal forces, emotional responses that aren't based in logic or reason."

He drew a deep breath before he swung back to face her. "You have to start accepting the complications their behavior causes rather than trying to think your way past them."

Tension pulled at her mouth. She understood his point. She just wasn't sure what to do with it.

"Your brother's a smart man." Cade took a step toward her, his shoulder brushing hers. "That explains why all of

Reanne's attacks so far have been staged with a sense of drama. She's not interested in defeating you quietly and efficiently, which would be the wiser course of action. She wants a show, to prove her superiority in sweeping fashion. The more times you foil her schemes, the angrier she'll become and the bigger the payoff she'll need to be satisfied."

A shudder worked through her bones, making her teeth click together. "If what you're saying is true, it's possible the entire Teeli armada could we waiting for us when we reach Teeli space."

"Definitely possible. Likely, even." He looked like he wanted to pull her into his arms, but he didn't. "Which is why we'll need every advantage if you're going to go through with this plan."

Movement caught her attention. Ifel had stepped behind Micah, her tall shadow settling over them both like a grey cloud. Ifel reached out, long fingers hovering a few centimeters from Aurora's arm.

Where her energy field would appear if she engaged it.

Micah cleared his throat. "She knows you have a question to ask her. She's ready to hear it now."

Aurora's pulse thrummed. This was it.

She held out her hand to Micah. He enclosed it in his, the warmth of his touch calming and focusing her.

Taking a deep breath, she cleared her mind of everything but her single focus – the Teeli mission – and engaged her energy field.

Forty-Nine

When Ifel's fingers touched her energy field, the connection drew her like a gravity well. The gurgle and whisper of the waves faded, the volume turned down by an invisible hand. She wasn't seeing her surroundings anymore either, except for Ifel. The Yruf leader filled her vision, looking like an Egyptian deity brought to life.

Micah's fingers wrapped around hers, tethering her to the real world. "Why don't you start with Sly'Kull," he prompted. "I'll do my best to fill in any details she's having trouble understanding."

"Okay." She called up the memory of her visit to the Teeli embassy. As she moved past the interchange at the security station, she allowed Ifel to once again take control of the playback. If felt more natural this time, though still disconcerting to have someone sorting through her memories.

She felt and heard Ifel's involuntary hiss when Sly'Kull stepped onto the scene.

"*Teeli.*"

They had that word in common, though it sounded more sinister spoken with the Yruf accent.

Ifel crept through the conversation that followed, backtracking to replay several moments repeatedly. She halted on a freeze frame as they left the building, the image fading out as Ifel returned control.

Aurora nudged Micah with her elbow. "Does she understand that they were offering us a scientific mission?"

He nudged her back. "Yes. Science is a cornerstone of the Yruf culture. That part's easy to explain. She's struggling with the why — why you were there with the Teeli, and why you would agree to work with them."

"It's complicated."

"I know."

Cade's voice touched her like warm rain. "Might I make a suggestion?"

She nodded but kept her gaze on Ifel. "Of course."

"The Yruf took advantage of the rendezvous between the Ecilam and the Teeli in an attempt to capture the Ecilam ship. What you're proposing is similar. Do you want to try drawing me into the circle so I can replay that memory for her, then you can project an image of what you're hoping to achieve when we reach Teeli space?"

She held out her free hand. "Let's try it."

Cade's palm brushed hers as he clasped her hand, her energy field expanding to envelop him like he was an extension of her arm.

She caught a flicker of bemusement from Celia. How strange did the scene appear from her perspective? Without being able to see Aurora's energy field, it probably looked like she, Micah, and Cade were beginning a séance while Ifel was the creature they'd summoned into their midst.

"You ready, Micah?" she asked.

"Yeah. Go ahead, Cade."

Images flew into her mind with amazing speed and clarity, more like the beginning of a dream rather than sharing someone else's memory. Her breath stuttered as she recognized *Gladiator*'s cockpit seen from the pilot's seat.

"Can you see it?" Cade asked her.

"Perfectly." The lighting came from the main console and the reflected light from the nearby planet, setting the proper mood for the small grouping of ominous ships in the distance.

She'd never seen this particular style of Ecilam ship before, but there was no doubt that's what it was, sitting beside the oversized Teeli cruiser and diminutive delegate yacht. A moment later the focus of the memory whirled to the aft camera view, where a shadow like a black hole came up behind *Gladiator*'s stern.

The Yruf ship.

The imagery jumped. Her weight rocked into her heels as she was caught in the fast current.

The image solidified. A sphere of ships, caging in the Ecilam ship which swam in the middle, a fish trapped in a bowl. The ships exchanged fire. The Ecilam ship's momentum slowed, steadily coming to a halt in the exact center.

Cade's fingers laced through hers. "Your turn."

She breathed in the scent of the ocean air, familiar and yet alien, as she focused on Ifel. Anticipation coiled in her belly as she added an image of the Teeli cruiser beside the Ecilam ship at the center of the sphere of the Yruf ships.

Ifel's emotional field vibrated, but whether positively or negatively, she couldn't say.

Pushing on, she projected an image of the *Starhawke* joining the perimeter of the sphere, followed by an image of Reanne, her Sovereign hood pulled back, her hands bound by manacles.

Ifel's emotional vibration rose to a buzz, but still without any clear context. It was like the images were causing a reaction but even Ifel couldn't identify how she felt about them.

"Micah?" Her tone conveyed the question she didn't voice.

"I'm not sure."

Aurora stayed locked on Ifel's emotions, trying to parse out how the Yruf leader felt about the proposal. She seemed to understand what Aurora was asking. No confusion or puzzlement marred her response. But no enthusiasm or agreement, either. Or disagreement, for that matter.

Ifel withdrew her hand from Aurora's energy field, breaking the intensity of the mental connection. Her diamond-pupiled irises contracted, her head bobbing.

"Is she upset?" Aurora asked Micah.

"Concerned," he and Celia said at the same time.

Aurora glanced over her shoulder at her friend. "How do you know?"

Celia raised one perfectly-shaped brow. "You brought me because I'm an expert at reading body language."

"And you can read hers?"

"I can now." Her gaze lifted to Micah, a subtle challenge in her brown eyes.

Rather than irritation or defensiveness, she sensed a grudging respect from him.

Aurora turned back to him. "Okay, so she's concerned. About what, specifically?"

Micah focused on Ifel, his lips pressing together as they conferred. "It's complicated," he said, echoing Aurora's previous comment. "The risks involved, the variables, the unpredictability. I get the feeling they'd been tracking the Ecilam ship for some time before they showed themselves. What Cade observed was the result of weeks or even months of pre-planning."

"Oh." That could change things. She'd assumed the Yruf had taken advantage of the diversion the Teeli provided, making a spur-of-the-moment decision to go after the Ecilam, scooping *Gladiator* into their net at the same time. Instead, they'd planned all along to capture the Ecilam ship and Cade had gotten in their way. "They're very methodical, aren't they?"

"Yes. Unfortunately, what you're proposing would push them way out of their comfort zone."

Ifel's head bobbed again. She broke eye contact with Micah and swiveled her neck in a liquid way that allowed her to look behind her without turning her body. She said something to the guards, who fanned out to create a loose semi-circle behind Aurora's group.

"I think we're leaving," Celia murmured.

Ifel's neck pivoted, facing Micah again. Their communication was brief.

"She's right. We're being escorted back to the shuttle."

An asteroid settled into Aurora's stomach. "She's rejecting our request?"

Micah shot her a quizzical look. "No. She needs time to consider it."

The asteroid shrank four sizes. "Oh." Much better. "Will she invite us back over when she's made a decision?"

Micah turned to Ifel. After a moment he blinked and gave a small head shake. "Uh, I think next time they'll be paying us a visit on the *Starhawke*."

"Really?" Kire would love that. Jonarel and Lelindia would probably be intrigued, too. "That would be great." If the Yruf could see what the *Starhawke* could do, maybe meet Star, that might help their case.

Ifel led the way along the beach to a path on the opposite end that disappeared into the foliage. A couple minutes later, their group was back in the serpentine corridors of the ship, the opening to the biosphere no longer visible behind the undulating bulkheads. The drone had reappeared as well, gliding smoothly ahead of them.

"I would love to figure out how they do that with the walls," Celia said in an undertone as they followed Ifel, the guards keeping pace around them. "You couldn't beat that kind of security, especially if the walls are as impervious to blunt force trauma as they appear."

"They are," Cade replied from Aurora's other side. "Though maybe not to energy weapons."

Aurora gave Celia a sidelong look. "I doubt they'll share that intel. If you had that kind of technology, would you tell anybody how it works?"

Celia's gaze roamed over the emerald walls. "Not a chance." She sighed. "But now that we know it's possible, I'm going to talk to Jonarel and Star about it. Maybe they could figure it out."

"They just might." The effect was kind of like the *Starhawke*'s adaptability on steroids. She'd never forget watching the hull open up for the first time, the contours of the ship blending perfectly with the walkways of the Clarek compound like the ship was an oversized denglar tree. If the Kraed could figure out how to make that work, shifting bulkheads might be within their reach.

Another unconventional lift ride and short walk later brought them back to the seamless shuttle bay, where the *Starhawke*'s shuttle sat like a miniature figurine at the center of a giant snow globe.

Ifel halted inside the bay, turning to face them. Her head bobbed again as she held Aurora's gaze for a three count. The dominant emotion in her field could have been concern. It had a stiff, heavy quality to it. But it was underlaid with a softer, more buoyant emotion – hope.

Which proved Micah's point that she and Ifel were more alike than she realized. She could describe her own emotional state the exact same way.

Ifel's gaze shifted to Micah.

"She'll contact us when she's ready to meet again," he translated. "She asks that we remain here. Both ships," he added, glancing at Cade.

Cade nodded. "Not a problem. My team's not going anywhere."

The group broke up, Ifel and the guards retreating into the corridor with the drone while Aurora followed Cade to the shuttle's ramp. A quick peek over her shoulder confirmed the scaled bulkhead had already closed behind them.

She exhaled, her shoulders sagging.

"You're disappointed." Cade drew her with him toward the cockpit.

"A little," she admitted. "Things were going so well, I guess my expectations got a little out of whack with reality."

He squeezed her shoulder before sliding into the pilot's seat. "Maybe, but you accomplished a lot. She gave us a tour of their bridge and biosphere. That shows a deep level of trust, way more than I was able to achieve."

"You're right." Whether Ifel agreed to her proposal or not, they had laid an excellent foundation for future relations. "It's good to know there's a Setarip faction that's focused on peace, not war and destruction."

The shuttle rose as Cade eased them off the deck, pivoting toward the opening that had appeared in the exterior hull. "From what Micah said, we can count the Regna in the same camp. With the Etah down to Tnaryt's females—"

"That we know of."

"That we know of," he agreed, "that leaves us with the Egar as the wild card and the Ecilam as the major threat."

"And the Ecilam have the full support of the Teeli." She chewed on her lip as Cade guided the shuttle out of the bay.

The *Starhawke* sparkled like black velvet and diamonds in the distance, the hull mimicking the starfield even without the camouflage engaged.

She rested her forearms on the console. The *Starhawke* was the most beautiful ship she'd ever seen. "I don't get out here to look at her often enough."

Cade chuckled. "That's because you'd much rather be on the bridge."

Her lips twitched. "You're right, I would. But I'd enjoy taking a shuttle flight with you once in a while, too." When he didn't answer her right away, she turned her head and met his gaze. What she saw in the green depths of his eyes made tingles spread like wildfire under her skin.

The deeper register of his voice sent a second wave. "Anytime."

Fifty

Celia studied Micah's profile as the shuttle exited the Yruf ship. She'd claimed the seat next to him, even though there were four empty seats behind them that would have given her more space and an easier opportunity to observe him without his being able to see her.

But she'd chosen the seat to his left instead. Instinct, perhaps, to remain close to a potential threat. Or a perverse desire to make him uncomfortable. Both excellent possibilities.

He ignored her, his head turned slightly away from her as he gazed out the side viewports, the inky starfield taking center stage as the shuttle banked, leaving the Yruf ship behind.

"You seemed pretty comfortable talking with Ifel."

His raised eyebrows and sidelong glance telegraphed his surprise that she'd initiated a conversation. "That was my job."

"And you did it well."

His brows climbed higher. "A compliment?"

"An observation."

His derisive snort didn't quite match the brief light that brightened the green of his eyes. "What else did you observe?"

"You enjoy the process of non-verbal communication, and you're happiest when you're in a natural environment."

His shoulders lowered a fraction, losing some of the hunched look they'd had since she'd sat down. He turned in his seat, facing her more fully. "That's not observation, that's logic. I'm a marine biologist who talks to animals. Of course I enjoy nature and non-verbal communication."

His words parried hers, but his tone had the force of a feather, not a rapier.

"Yes, but you engaged like a fish in water."

The corner of his mouth ticked, like he was fighting back a smile. "Apt analogy."

"What did it feel like? Hearing her in your head?"

The skin around his eyes tightened, the hint of a smile morphing into a frown. "Why do you want to know?"

She used his line. "It's my job. And I'm... curious."

"Curious? Or suspicious?"

"Curious." Which oddly enough was true. She'd been watching him intently during every interchange with Ifel. No matter how hard she'd tried to convince herself otherwise, every non-verbal cue she'd picked up from him and the Yruf leader denoted an open, honest, straightforward interaction. No subterfuge, no hidden agenda, no deceit. Micah hadn't tried to run the show, either. He'd taken his orders from Aurora, following her lead.

His shoulder pressed into the seat as he leaned closer. "You really are curious, aren't you?"

"Does that surprise you?"

"Everything you do surprises me."

It didn't sound like a good thing, but he seemed more sad than angry about it.

"I'm a student of science. This is a new area for me, one I'd like to understand."

His gaze searched hers for several moments, like he was sweeping the area for hidden booby traps.

She waited, giving him time to reach his own conclusions about her intentions.

The light in his eyes turned up a few notches, making the irises go from moss green to fern. "Okay." His gaze grew a little unfocused, like it had when he'd been talking with Ifel. "You know that feeling when you have really vivid daydreams, ones so real you lose track of where you are until something snaps you back in?"

"No."

His gaze sharpened, locking onto hers. "No?"

"I don't daydream."

"Ever?" He stared at her like she'd said she didn't breathe.

"Ever."

His jaw dropped. He closed it with an audible click, his lips pursing. "Well, that explains a lot."

"Does it?" Her tone was dry as tinder.

"Mm-hmm." His gaze searched hers, analyzing her like she was a new species of marine life he'd never seen. "Do you remember your nighttime dreams?"

I try not to. "Sometimes." She knew people who enjoyed talking about their dreams. Aurora was one of them. Her dreams often provided her with answers.

Celia's dreams usually kicked her in the teeth, replaying past trauma or painting apocalyptic visions of the future. When she did remember one when she woke up, she punched it into submission like all the other nasty critters.

"Well, talking to Ifel feels a lot like a vivid dream, one where I know I'm dreaming and can control the action. I'm still aware of my surroundings, but the physical world loses its hold on me. What I'm seeing in my head feels much more real and immediate."

"And that doesn't bother you?" He'd just described her private Hell.

"Not at all." His gaze held hers, the analyzing look returning. "I'm in control, remember? I can break the connection at any time."

"And losing track of your surroundings doesn't make you feel..." She swirled her hand in a circle, unable to come up with the right word.

"Vulnerable?"

She flinched. She hated that word. "Exposed."

He shrugged. "Maybe it should, but it doesn't. It's not like I'm doing it in the middle of a warzone, or with people I don't trust."

"So you trust the Yruf?"

"Don't you?"

She opened her mouth to reply, then closed it. Did she?

She'd wanted to go on this mission to defend Aurora against any potential threats the Yruf might pose. And to make sure Micah didn't abuse his power over his sister.

But it hadn't turned out the way she'd feared. The Yruf hadn't set off her internal alarms. They hadn't shown a hint of aggression or deception. Neither had Micah. Watching them work together had been... humbling. "I do trust them."

His expression softened, his lips parting like he wanted to ask her something else. Instead, he gave her a tiny smile and sat back in his seat. "Good. Because they trust us."

She could guess what question he hadn't asked, the one that was dangling in front of her like a spider on a silken thread. The question she didn't have an answer for.

Did she trust *him*?

Fifty-One

"So tell me about the Yruf." Lelindia linked her arm through Aurora's as they walked through the *Starhawke*'s med bay and into the greenhouse. "And the biosphere. I want all the details."

She'd pounced as soon as Aurora had returned to the bridge, stealing her away. Cade and Micah had remained to fill in Kire and Cade's team, who'd joined them shortly after the shuttle had headed back.

Jonarel had made a move to follow Lelindia and Aurora, but Celia had waylaid him, asking him something about undulating bulkheads. He'd looked torn as he'd watched her and Aurora step onto the lift, but she was grateful for the diversion Celia had provided. Aurora would be more forthcoming about the wonders of the biosphere without Jonarel nearby, scowling.

Aurora gave her a bemused smile. "I knew you'd be intrigued."

"Intrigued? Are you crazy? I'm bouncing off the walls. From what you described it's a *living biosphere*. On a *starship*. I'm surprised you're not more excited."

"I would be if I wasn't so worried about the Yruf's next move."

Lelindia drew her to a bench near one of the vine-covered trellises in the greenhouse. Settling beside her, she tucked her right leg under her so she could face Aurora. "Tell me."

"They're thinking about my proposal. But I can't get a bead on which way it will go. From what Micah said, they're extremely methodical. The maneuver Cade's team witnessed was the result of months of planning and observation."

"Wow." She'd always applied the term methodical to herself, but the Yruf might consider her flighty by comparison. "So even if they agree to help, it might not be in a timetable that will work for us."

"That's right. Or they might not agree at all. We have no idea how many ships Reanne might have waiting for us when we reach Teeli space. I think that's one of the sticking points. The Yruf aren't ready to face down the Teeli armada, especially when I'm only offering to provide two ships for the fight."

"Hmm." Lelindia tapped her finger against her bent leg. "We do have one advantage. Our ship can camouflage. So can theirs. We could take a look around the system we're supposed to be studying before we show ourselves. See who's there."

"And if we don't see anyone?"

"Then the Yruf could stay to monitor the area while we take the *Starhawke* back out of the system and make a visible entrance. We move into position to start the science mission, and when Reanne's cruiser shows up, the Yruf nab it."

"And if the entire armada shows up?"

"We camouflage and run while the Yruf give us backup."

Aurora snorted. "You're becoming a decent tactician."

"Learning on the job."

The snort turned into a smile. "Bet you didn't expect to gain this skill set when I offered you the medical officer's position."

"No, I did not."

Aurora's smile faded. "And if the Yruf turn us down?"

"Then we follow the same plan, but blink out of there the minute anything larger than a supply ship shows up. The Teeli would have a hard time arguing to the Council that we should have stayed on mission if a mysterious warship arrived on the scene."

"Good point."

Lelindia waggled her fingers in Aurora's direction. "But enough about the mission. I want to hear about the Yruf and the biosphere. Spill."

Aurora laughed, just as she'd intended. "It was amazing. I didn't want to gush with Jonarel on the line, but it felt like we were actually standing on a planet. Not that this isn't incredible." Her arm swept to encompass their verdant surroundings. "But a single deck greenhouse and a multi-level biosphere are different animals."

"Clearly. How many plant species?"

"Thousands. We started in a rainforest environment that led to an ocean."

"You mentioned that. And it really looked like an ocean?"

"So much so that Micah wanted to dive in. Whatever optical or projection tricks they used made it look like the natural horizon was kilometers away. Micah could hear the creatures in the depths, too."

"They have marine animals?"

"As many as they could manage."

Lelindia's mind reeled. "Which makes their ship a mobile world."

"Essentially."

"No wonder they're so methodical. They have a lot to lose."

"And have suffered so much already. But they've done everything they can to preserve the diversity of their original homeworld. One day they hope to reunite the Setarip factions and establish a new homeworld."

"Is that why they're in Fleet space? Looking for a suitable planet to colonize?"

Aurora shook her head. "No, they followed the Ecilam here, hoping to make peace with them. A new homeworld isn't their priority yet. First they have to get all the factions to stop fighting and start talking."

Lelindia wrinkled her nose. "That can't be going well."

"No, it's not, though we learned a lot about their civil war. It sounds like the Ecilam are the real instigators. The Etah were, too." Aurora scowled, a trace of bitterness in her tone. "But now they're not a threat."

"What about the Egar and Regna?"

"The Regna don't want to fight any more than the Yruf do. The Egar are opportunistic. They'll fight if they think it's worth whatever advantage they stand to gain. But without the Ecilam pushing their buttons, they might agree to a ceasefire."

"Fascinating." Aurora was blowing giant holes in her preconceptions regarding the Setarips. "And if they did end the war? What then? Would they try to take over an inhabited world?"

Aurora shook her head. "The Yruf would never allow that. They value life, all life. They wouldn't intentionally harm others. Given the complexity of their technology, and their success in creating an artificial biosphere, it's more likely they're planning to terraform a barren world instead. Then they could recreate their homeworld as it was... or at least close to it."

Excitement bubbled through her. "I'd love to be there when they do. I might even be able to help."

Aurora gave her a playful nudge. "Why does that not surprise me?"

"Because you've known me all your life?"

"Yeah, that might have something to do with it."

"Did the Yruf give you any indication when they'd make their decision?"

"Nope." Aurora fingered a vine tendril that trailed along the back of the bench. "We can give them a couple days, but after that we'll have to leave without them. Oh, and they want to come here for our next meeting."

"They do?" Her voice squeaked. "Really? I'll get to meet them?"

"Assuming they can stick to our timetable."

Her heart thumped in her chest. "What were they like? Did they look like the Ecilam we saw on Persei Primus?"

"A little bit. They have the same sinuous grace to their features, although the Yruf have richer colors. Well, the females do. We saw several males on their bridge. They were all neutral toned — beige, white, tan, black, but in beautiful patterns. Much different from the Ecilam or Tnaryt and the female Etah."

Lelindia's stomach soured. She'd never laid eyes on the Etah sadist who'd captured and tortured Aurora, Admiral Schreiber, and Natasha Orlov, the pilot they'd rescued. But the Admiral had shared enough with her during his recuperation in the med bay to convince her Tnaryt's death at the hands of the Ecilam was well deserved.

"Ifel, their leader, is the largest Yruf we saw. Lithe and toned but muscular, like a combination between Jonarel and Celia."

Lelindia giggled. "That's quite a visual."

"And her coloring matches the ship's exactly. I'm curious whether her coloring and size have any role in her position as their leader, but couldn't find a tactful way for Micah to ask. All her guards have the same coloring, but they're a head shorter."

"If they're as non-violent as you believe, basing leadership on physical strength and size would be a contradiction."

"Agreed. I guess it's possible the Yruf get larger with age. Many reptiles do, and their physiology is much more reptilian than mammalian, at least externally."

"Warm-blooded though. Tam and I compared notes after I learned he studied the Ecilam we encountered on Persei Primus. He was able to fill in a lot of gaps for me. If I need to treat a Setarip in the future, I'll be better prepared than last time."

Every one of the Setarips they'd captured had died from a toxic overdose injected into their systems by a subdermal transmitter. She'd been unfamiliar with their physiology – having never seen an Ecilam before that day – and the nature of the toxin being used to prevent or reverse the effects before it was too late.

"That's another bit of information I'd like to share with the Yruf. They might feel more comfortable going into battle with us if they know they have a powerful healer on their side who could treat their wounded."

Lelindia sat up straighter. "Do you think they'd agree to send someone over here now, before they make a final decision about joining us? Maybe the doctor who treated Justin? If I could work with him, show him what I could do, that might help our cause."

Aurora's eyes lit up. "That's a great idea. Come on." Snagging Lelindia's hand in hers, she pulled her to her feet. "Let's go talk to Micah."

Fifty-Two

Aurora tapped the door chime for her brother's cabin.

"Come in."

Star's invisible hand opened the door.

Micah lay stretched out on the couch in the front room, a tablet in his hands.

"Hey, sis." He swung his legs off the couch, his bare feet settling onto the floor as he stood. "Hey, Lee-Lee. What's up?"

Lelindia stepped forward. "I have a favor to ask."

He spread his hands, his gaze shifting between them. "Of course. Anything."

"You don't know what it is."

He shrugged. "Doesn't matter. If you're asking, I'll do it."

And that was one of a million reasons why she loved her brother.

"We need you to contact the Yruf," Lelindia said. "I'm hoping the doctor who treated Justin would be willing to come over here so I can show him my healing abilities."

"Huh." He nodded slowly, processing. "You want to give them another reason to work with us."

"Exactly. We're asking them to put their people at risk by taking on Reanne's cruiser, and possibly the Teeli armada. If they understand the scope of what I can do to heal injuries, they might be more inclined to take that risk."

The corners of his mouth turned up. "Good thinking. Uh, any idea what that doctor looked like?"

"One second." Aurora raised her voice. "Aurora to Cade."

His voice came over the ship's speakers. "Yes, ma'am?"

"What did the Yruf doctor who treated Justin look like?"

"About my size, tan and beige scales. Why?"

"Micah's asking Ifel if she'd be willing to send him over to the *Starhawke* so Lelindia can talk to him."

"Ah. Well, he was clearly the one in charge of the med bay, and his coloring was different from anyone else we met. Shouldn't be tough to identify him."

Micah drew in a slow breath. "Okay, give me a moment."

His eyes closed, his breathing continuing in a steady rhythm. Small facial tics and twitches were the only visible signs that he was communicating with Ifel. His eyes opened slowly. "Ifel's agreed to send the doctor. I wasn't sure what to tell her regarding docking."

"Do they have a vessel that would fit in our shuttle bay?"

"Yes. The image I'm getting from them shows a cylinder-shaped ship about twice the size of Romeo."

THE SIEGE OF ALLIANCE

Romeo, the red and white four-seater plane their dad had been piloting when he'd made an emergency landing and run into their mom. Literally.

She'd had a chance to check out that historic plane while they'd been preparing for the hospital mission at her dad's airfield where Romeo was hangered.

"Then let them know we'll have the bay open and ready to receive them. Oh, and Jonarel wants to test the new camouflage techniques he and Star have been working on to hide the *Starhawke* from Kraed ships and sensors. We can hold off while the doctor's here if Ifel wants, but make sure the Yruf won't be startled if our ship blinks off visuals temporarily at some point."

Fifty-Three

Lelindia bounced lightly on the balls of her feet as she waited outside the shuttle bay door. "How much longer?" she asked Aurora, who stood beside her, along with Micah, Celia, Justin, and Cade.

Aurora acknowledged her eagerness with an amused glance. "A few moments. The vessel just entered the bay."

A muffled hiss signaled the bay was pressurizing behind the sealed hatch.

Williams and Kire were waiting for them in the med bay. Tam was as eager to conduct their experiments as she was.

Jonarel had taken command on the bridge, with Gonzo at tactical. Aurora had decided that given Jonarel's coloring, which in many ways mimicked the Yruf leader's in tone if not pattern, it was best not to introduce him to the Yruf at this juncture and risk confusing the issue.

The bay door opened, giving her a good look at the Yruf transport sitting in the middle of the open space. Micah had described it as a cylinder, but that was like describing Notre Dame as a rectangle.

As they walked closer, she studied the vessel. The hull was scaled like the exterior of the Yruf ship, but here black dominated over the emerald green, giving the sleek lines and curves an air of mystery and power. The impression was emphasized by the complete lack of viewports, or anything that resembled a cockpit. Or landing gear, for that matter. The undercarriage of the shuttle looked like it had melded with the deck.

Protrusions on either side of the centerline resembled the folded wings of a bird, especially from this angle. It was kind of like staring at a roosting raven that had settled into its nest for the night and tucked its head onto its back.

An opening appeared near the front where the bird's breast would have been. Two figures emerged, backlit by the soft yellow glow from the shuttle's interior.

Her breath caught as her gaze swept over them.

She picked out which one was the Yruf doctor immediately, judging by his size and the beige and tan coloring Cade had described. He wore a cloak of rich brown, the material swirling around him as he walked toward her. The color emphasized the darker geometric patterns on his face, which did indeed resemble a python's, with a blunt nose and mouth and wide-set eyes.

Those eyes focused on Justin first, giving her a moment to check out the female Yruf behind him.

Even Jonarel would have to look up to meet her gaze. Her broad shoulders and muscled physique were visible underneath her form-fitting garments. She carried a staff of some sort in her hand, but loosely, like a walking stick rather than a weapon. Her coloring was completely different from the doctor's, the emerald-green, black, and gold scales of her skin perfectly matching the tones on the Yruf ship.

"Is that Ifel?" Lelindia murmured to Aurora.

"No, one of her guards. Ifel's taller."

Taller? This Yruf would put an Amazon — or Kraed — to shame. Just how big was their leader?

The doctor stopped a few paces away from Justin, the female guard remaining a respectful distance behind. He said something she couldn't understand, the words coming out like water and air through a hose.

Justin laughed. He replied in the same language, his accent remarkably similar to the doctor's, and pointed to his head. The doctor's serpentine neck curved slightly, his gaze moving to Cade, who nodded in greeting.

"Good to see you again."

"He can understand you?" she asked Cade.

"Not really. At least not the specific words, but I'm sure he can pick up on the intent, especially with me."

The doctor's focus shifted to her, intelligence shining in his dark eyes. So alien — the irises almost black with a small sliver of white on the edge near the dark band of scales that ran horizontally across his face — yet she felt an instant connection, an acknowledgement on an elemental level of common ground and understanding.

"I'm the ship's doctor, Lelindia." She patted her chest.

He repeated her name. It was recognizable, but he had trouble pronouncing the "d" in the third syllable. It came out as more of a "t". He placed his hand on his chest. "Ahle."

"Awe-lee?" She did her best to mimic the sounds he made, although she couldn't quite manage the underlying hiss of air he put on the second syllable. But he seemed pleased with her attempt.

She looked uncertainly at Micah. "Uh, that's all I've got."

He grinned at her. "It's a great beginning. We didn't get to names until much later last time."

Ahle's attention flicked to Micah briefly before settling on Aurora. "Ah-ror-ah."

The doctor did a much better job pronouncing her name. Either the sounds were more similar to his language, or he'd practiced before his arrival.

Aurora blinked, her gaze darting to Micah. "Uh, yeah. Nice to meet you, Ahle."

Ahle's head swiveled toward the Yruf guard behind him, but his body didn't move. Freaky. If she tried that she would snap her neck. But a quick check with her Nedale senses confirmed his spine contained a significantly larger number of vertebra than any other bipedal species she'd encountered, including the

Ecilam. The adaptation would give their heads an amazing range of motion.

The guard stepped toward their loose circle, though she remained half a meter behind Ahle. "Cegra." The guard tapped her chest with the tip of her staff, meeting Aurora's gaze.

"Say-grah," Aurora repeated. She did a pretty decent mimic of the Yruf accent, too.

"They're related, aren't they?" It was the first time Celia had spoken since she'd joined them in the corridor. She was looking to Micah for confirmation.

His brow furrowed. "I'll ask."

As soon as Micah's eyes got the far-sighted look, Ahle's gaze swung around and locked onto his like they were magnetized. Very few verbal words were spoken, but Micah's body language conveyed an animated conversation, at least on his side. Ahle's expression didn't change much, although Cegra's slender tongue flicked out a couple times.

Micah blinked as he broke eye contact and glanced at Celia. "You're right. She's his daughter. How did you know?"

"Body language. And something in the way he looked at her."

Micah stared at her for several seconds before turning to Cade. "Did you know Ahle is Ifel's brother?"

"Brother?" His tone answered the question before he did. "No, I didn't."

"I'm assuming he means brother. The way I'm getting the message it comes across as hatchmate, which I'm translating as brother. They're born from a nest of eggs like reptiles, two or three at a time. They definitely share at least one parent."

She'd never given much thought to whether Setarips were live born like mammals. Knowing they were hatched from eggs intrigued her.

Cade nodded. "That must have helped her understand your relationship to Aurora. It parallels hers with her brother."

"Yep."

Lelindia watched Ahle and Cegra during the interchange. She didn't have Celia's gift for reading body language, but she got the sense they were amused by all the verbal communication, like indulgent parents listening to a group of toddlers yammer away in nonsense syllables.

Might as well move things along. "Shall we head up to the med bay?" she asked Aurora.

"Absolutely."

The presence of the two Yruf made the spacious cargo lift feel like a shoebox as they stepped inside. It wasn't just their size, either. They carried themselves with a confidence and grace that filled the space.

Ahle's tongue flicked out when he caught sight of Williams through the clear doors of the med bay. Tam's easy smile of welcome as he stepped forward to greet them was as relaxed as if the two were old friends. Clearly he and Ahle had gotten along well during their time on the Yruf ship.

Micah facilitated the introductions as Kire joined them, but the focus quickly switched to her.

She'd taken advantage of the med bay's fluid design to collapse all the med platforms into the deck, switching them out for a circular standing worktable with a diagnostic scanner that they could all gather around.

Tam fetched the tray of tools she'd collected for the demonstration. They'd already discussed how they'd set it up. Initially, she'd planned to use herself as the test subject, but he'd argued that it wouldn't give the Yruf a clear idea of what she could do, since healing herself wasn't the same as healing someone else.

He'd offered himself as a volunteer, but Cade had nixed that idea as soon as they'd drawn him and Aurora into the discussion. Cade had insisted he was the best test subject, reminding them that the Yruf's ability to easily read his emotions and thoughts would allow them to share his experience during the experiment. His participation also freed her to focus on the healing and Tam to handle the practical tasks.

She couldn't counter his logic. But she'd pushed for one concession — she'd use her Nedale abilities to block any pain he'd normally feel as a result of the trauma they'd be inflicting.

Tam set the tray near Cade, who was flanked by Aurora and Justin.

Justin pointed at the tray. "Lot of sharp objects there."

Cade chuckled. "Kind of the point."

His joke elicited a few answering smiles from around the table.

"You sure about this?" Lelindia asked Cade as he rolled back the sleeve of his tunic to expose his muscular forearm.

"Wouldn't have offered if I wasn't."

Reaching over, Tam plucked a scalpel from the tray. "Micah, please explain to our guests that in order to demonstrate Dr. Forrest's abilities, I'll need to make an incision on Cade's arm. Ahle will have the opportunity to examine the injury, both visually and with the diagnostic scanner, after Dr. Forrest heals it."

Micah flinched, his gaze darting briefly to Aurora. "Okay."

After about thirty seconds, Ahle broke eye contact with Micah, his attention shifting to Lelindia. He blinked slowly, the tip of his tongue flicking a couple centimeters up and down.

"He's ready when you are," Micah murmured.

"Right." Resting her hand on Cade's bicep, she engaged her energy field.

A hiss snapped her gaze to Ahle and Cegra. Their pupils had dilated, nearly swallowing the irises of their eyes as they stared at her energy field.

The emerald-green scales surrounding Cegra's eyes were nearly the exact same shade of green. Aurora had mentioned that color carried a lot of meaning for them. No wonder her field had triggered a reaction.

Tam had paused with the scalpel hovering over Cade's exposed forearm, waiting for her.

She worked her energy field into Cade's nervous system, carefully blocking the pain receptors in his brain. "You okay?" she asked, meeting his gaze.

He gave her a crooked smile. "Don't tell Jonarel, but it feels kind of nice. Like a cool summer breeze."

Her lips twitched. She certainly would *not* be sharing that observation with Jonarel. She nodded at Tam. "We're ready."

Bringing the scalpel down, he made the long incision with the practiced ease of a surgeon, blood welling like oil from Cade's tawny skin.

Cade didn't so much as flinch, his expression one of idle curiosity as he stared at the expanding ribbon of red on his arm.

Ahle was staring too, but she couldn't begin to guess what he was thinking.

Turning her attention to the wound, she sent her energy field undulating down Cade's arm while she brought her free hand beside the thick line of bright red blood.

The moment her field touched the damaged skin, time reversed. The blood disappeared as she drew it back into Cade's circulatory system and reknit the separated flesh.

It was the work of a micro-second, as easy as taking her next breath. She could have done it in her sleep. But it triggered exactly the kind of reaction she'd hoped for.

Ahle stepped into Cade's personal space, his neck arching as his head lowered toward Cade's arm like he planned to take a bite. Cade rotated his forearm for inspection while Lelindia disengaged her energy field and Tam moved the diagnostic scanner into position. Data populated the monitor, confirming what her senses already knew — no trace of the wound remained.

Ahle's tongue flicked rapidly, nearly touching the blond hairs on Cade's arm. If she had to guess, he was scenting the area as much as looking at it. He lifted one long finger, poising it over Cade's arm, his head bobbing as he met Cade's gaze.

Cade raised his arm toward Ahle's finger. "Go for it."

Ahle made contact, running the pad of his finger back and forth along Cade's skin.

Cade's jaw twitched. Odds were good the sensation of being touched skin to scales felt a little strange. Might even tickle a bit.

Ahle's gaze moved to the monitor. The writing would be unfamiliar, but Tam had assured her that – based on his experience with the Yruf diagnostic tools – Ahle would be able to understand the data.

Clearly he did. In one fluid motion, he straightened and swept his cloak over his shoulder, then ran a finger along the material covering his forearm. It parted on an invisible seam, rippling away to reveal the geometric pattern of scales underneath.

He rested his arm on the tabletop next to Cade's and plucked one of the larger scalpels off the tray, holding it out to Tam.

She swallowed. No need for Micah's translation. He'd gotten her healing message loud and clear and wanted her to test her skills on him.

Cade backed away from the table, allowing her to move next to Ahle.

"We can do a test," she said slowly, "but I want to make sure I can manage your pain, first."

He stared at her, unblinking.

"Uh, Micah? Little help?"

"On it."

Ahle's focus changed to Micah. His tongue flicked once. Twice. Then his head swiveled back to her.

"He understands. You can make a smaller incision to start."

She drew in a slow breath. When she'd envisioned this, she'd expected it to feel a lot more scholarly and academic. Now that the moment had become reality, her blood thrummed in her veins. A light sheen coated her skin as she placed her palm on Ahle's arm below the elbow.

So smooth. The thought brushed through her mind as her fingers wrapped around his scale-covered forearm. She'd wondered if the Yruf's scales would be knobby and bumpy like a shingled roof. Instead, the subtle texture under her palm felt like satin. The base temperature was several degrees warmer than her own, making him feel slightly feverish to her.

Her Nedale senses revealed other differences as she engaged her energy field and examined his nervous system. The sheer number of nerve branches staggered her. Way more than any other species she'd encountered, or the Ecilam.

They must feel every nuance.

It wouldn't surprise her if the Yruf could detect the slightest change in air currents or half a degree of temperature differential. The brush of her hand was lighting up his nerves at twice the rate she'd see if she touched Aurora or Jonarel. And yet Ahle had been prepared to let them take the scalpel to his skin without a second thought, just to test her abilities. The pain would have been excruciating.

She tread lightly as she worked her energy field into his system, alert for any sign of discomfort she might trigger. "Micah, is he okay?"

"Fine," Micah and Aurora answered at the same time.

She'd forgotten Aurora would be able to tune into Ahle's emotional state as easily as Micah connected with his thoughts. At least he was well monitored.

Setting up the pain blocks took effort, the complexity of his system making it more of a challenge. As soon as she finished and refocused, she discovered she and Ahle were practically nose-to-nose. Gazing into his otherworldly eyes this close up created a flutter in her chest. It was like looking into the whirlpool of time itself.

His gaze dropped to his arm, breaking the spell.

She looked at Tam. "All set."

Tam positioned the diagnostic scanner over Ahle's arm, studying the data for a moment. "How much pressure would you use to break through the scales?"

She pressed her thumbnail lightly against the scales under her hand. "They give just like skin. Normal pressure should do it. Better too shallow than too deep."

He paused. "You sound worried."

"His nervous system is very sophisticated."

Tam's gaze darted to Ahle, who had remained immobile during the interchange. "I'll go easy then."

She held her breath as Tam brought the scalpel down. She doubted she was the only one.

The incision Tam made was a couple centimeters long. Ahle didn't react overtly, but she saw the nerve endings fire up around the incision site, allowing her to confirm she'd blocked the right receptors.

A narrow thread of maroon-red blood marred the perfection of Ahle's geometric scale pattern, indicating the Yruf's blood contained hemoglobin just like humans and most other vertebrates.

Tam lifted the scalpel. She started to send her energy field down Ahle's arm to the wound.

His free hand clamped onto hers like a vise.

She sucked in a startled breath. "What?"

His tongue flicked out, almost tapping her nose.

"He wants the incision to be larger," Micah informed her.

"Larger? But why? I can heal this—"

"He wants a definitive demonstration."

She licked her lips. Clinical and scholarly had sailed out the airlock. She'd been sucked out too, now floating through the void of space, her stomach turning somersaults. And she'd brought this on herself.

"Okay." She turned to Tam. "Just like Cade's."

Ahle released his grip on her hand.

She caught a reflection of her concern in Tam's eyes, but he didn't show any hesitation as he brought the scalpel back into play. "You ready?" he asked.

She confirmed all the receptors were still blocked. "Yep."

This time the maroon-red flowed from the wound, blotting out the light beige sections of Ahle's scales.

She sent her energy field toward the wound.

Ahle didn't stop her.

As her field touched his alien blood, her Nedale senses kicked into high gear. Her subconscious took over, enabling her to respond far quicker than conscious thought would allow.

The blood retreated into the wound, the slices of scales reconnecting, then interlocking to form a variegated whole. The nerve endings proved the most troublesome, but she still restored them to healthy functioning within seconds. As soon as her Nedale senses confirmed the wound was completely healed, she released the blocks on Ahle's pain receptors and dissipated her energy field.

Ahle remained motionless, his gaze on his arm as his chest rose and fell with his shallow breaths.

His fingers twitched first, then his hand closed in slow-motion to make the muscles of his forearm contract. He still didn't look up.

"Aurora?" she murmured.

"He's not in pain."

"I think he's... fascinated," Micah added.

Ahle splayed his fingers and rotated his wrist, his scaled skin shifting over the underlying muscle and bone. When he finally lifted his head, he turned to Cegra and held his arm out for her inspection.

She cradled it in her palm, her fingers brushing over the exposed scales. Her gaze met her father's. Their heads bent together, the occasional hiss of words in their language barely audible. After a moment's consultation, they turned in perfect unison to stare at Lelindia.

She didn't fidget, but she wanted to. She'd proven her point, but she got the distinct impression the two had made a mental leap she wasn't prepared for.

Ahle resealed the sleeve of his tunic, covering his forearm, and regarded her solemnly.

"He has a request," Micah said.

"I thought he might. What is it?"

"They have injured on their ship." Micah glanced at Cade. "I think they're survivors from the battle with the Ecilam you witnessed."

"Oh?" Cade's eyes unfocused, his gaze on Micah like he was getting a mental message. "Ah. That makes sense."

"What makes sense?" Lelindia asked.

"He's talking about the Yruf who were caught in the explosion of the Ecilam ship. Those who didn't die instantly suffered severe injuries. It looks like they're in the equivalent of the Yruf ICU."

"And the Yruf can't heal them?"

Micah answered her. "Their medical advances have focused on treating biohazards, not trauma, since that's the threat they have encountered from the other Setarips. They're ill equipped to heal the kind of trauma these Yruf have suffered. He's hoping you can help them." He paused for a moment, gazing intently at Ahle. "If you do, he'll work to convince Ifel to accept Aurora's proposal."

A sick feeling churned in her gut. "No."

Micah's eyes widened. "No?"

"No." She planted her feet and folded her arms over her chest. "I set up this demonstration to show him what I could do, what benefits I could bring to a partnership, not to trade favors. I would never set a price on my abilities. I will gladly heal his people, assuming I can. But I don't want anything in exchange."

The tension around Micah's mouth and eyes faded, replaced with a soft smile. "Got it. I'll let him know."

She waited in silence, her attention on Ahle, as Micah passed on her message.

Ahle's dark-eyed gaze snapped to hers, his tongue flickering like the galaxy's tiniest whip. Then he did something totally unexpected. Spreading his arms wide so that his cloak draped like wings, he bent down and forward in a way her spine would never allow, his eyes closing as his head dropped to waist height.

Cegra immediately copied his posture, her staff held in both hands like she was offering it to Lelindia.

She took an involuntary step backward. "What are—"

Micah rested his hands on her shoulders, halting her. "It's a deep sign of respect. They're honored by your selfless kindness."

"Oh." But Ahle didn't move.

"Place your hand on top of his head."

She jerked her head around. "What?"

Micah looked more than a little amused by her reaction. "It's how they acknowledge mutual understanding. Think of it as a tangible *you're welcome.*"

"Uh..." Out of the corner of her eye, she saw Celia give her an encouraging nod. "Okay."

She reached out, tentatively. As low as Ahle was bowing, she barely had to lift her arm to make contact.

The scales on his head were as smooth and warm as his arm, but felt thicker under her fingers, like touching heated marble rather than satin. Logical, considering the skin over his skull didn't need freedom of movement like the rest of his body.

She looked over her shoulder at Micah. "For how long?" she whispered.

He chuckled. "That's good."

She drew her hand back.

Ahle's eyes opened. He held her gaze as he straightened, the flowing movement reminding her of an unfurling vine.

She took an involuntary step forward, drawn in by whatever her subconscious saw in his eyes.

"*Shreenef?*"

She blinked. "What does that mean?"

Micah moved to her side. "He wants to know if you're willing to return with them now."

"Right now?" But even as she asked the question, she knew her answer. "Of course. But I'll need you to come with me."

"I assumed I would."

"Celia should go, too," Aurora said, moving to her other side. "To keep Jonarel from flipping out when I tell him where you are."

She grimaced. "He still won't like it."

"No. But it's good for him to get used to the idea."

Aurora shot her a knowing look. "He can be a tad overprotective."

Her lips twitched. "Really? I hadn't noticed."

Fifty-Four

"You let them take her to their ship!"

Jonarel's bellow boomed through the bridge like a concussion wave.

Cade's hair ruffled in the invisible breeze but Aurora looked unaffected by the glowering mass of angry Kraed towering over her.

"She wanted to go. I didn't see any reason to stop her."

"Any reason…" Jonarel's mouth hinged open as he stared at Aurora like she'd put a knife to his throat. "They are Setarips!"

Aurora stood firm in the gale. "Relax, Jonarel. The Yruf aren't a threat. In fact, they treated her like a queen."

Jonarel's chest expanded as he straightened. "A queen?"

"Yes. They need her help to heal their wounded."

Jonarel's yellow eyes narrowed to slits, his lips peeling back from his teeth. "And what will prevent them from keeping her when she is done?"

Aurora froze for a millisecond. Clearly the idea had not occurred to her. But she shrugged it off. "They're honorable. And honest. The polar opposite of the Ecilam. We can trust them."

"But she is—"

"Not alone." Aurora fixed Jonarel with the steely-eyed look of a Fleet captain. "Micah and Celia are with her. She. Will. Be. Fine."

Jonarel wanted to argue. Cade could see it in every tense muscle and tendon in the Kraed's body. But when Aurora used that tone, arguing was beyond pointless.

He felt for the guy. If he was a newly mated man, he wouldn't be thrilled with the idea of Aurora being taken to a strange ship by a relatively unknown alien race either, especially if he couldn't go with her. And Lelindia didn't have Aurora's protective abilities, which was why she'd sent Celia along. Not because she didn't trust the Yruf, but because it would make it easier for Jonarel to accept the situation.

Kire rested a hand on Jonarel's shoulder, catching a glare for his trouble. "It's okay, big guy. If you'd seen how the Yruf behaved in the med bay, you wouldn't worry."

Cade turned his snort into a cough. Asking Jonarel not to worry about Lelindia was ludicrous. Might as well ask the Earth to stop spinning.

Jonarel's gaze met his. He got a double whammy of the angst behind the bluster thanks to his empathic senses. The guy was really hurting. And scared.

He needed a distraction.

AUDREY SHARPE

Cade turned to Aurora. "If Jonarel's done with the camouflage tests for now, can I borrow him for a bit? Drew was hoping he could take a look at *Gladiator*'s sensor deflector." It was a flimsy excuse to get him off the bridge. He knew it. Aurora knew it. Jonarel knew it.

"I suppose so," Aurora said, the micro-smile that ghosted across her lips an outward sign of acknowledgment. He felt her gratitude much stronger through their empathic connection.

He motioned to Jonarel. "Come on. I'll walk down with you."

The unreality of the situation settled over him as Jonarel followed him to the lift. A few weeks ago, suggesting they go anywhere together would have been an aggressive sign of impending doom. The lift wouldn't have survived the encounter.

Now, he'd started to think of the Kraed as a... well, maybe not a friend, but certainly trending in that direction.

"I get why you're upset," he murmured as the doors closed behind them. "But she'll be fine. I promise."

Jonarel stared at him out of the side of his eye. "You trust them?"

"After all the time we spent with them when they captured *Gladiator*, and what I've seen revisiting their ship and here in the med bay, yeah, I do."

Jonarel drew in a slow breath, blowing it out on a frustrated sigh. "Then I will as well."

Huh. Maybe they were closer to friendship than he'd imagined. He hadn't expected Jonarel to take his word on faith. Then again, he'd spent a lot more time with the Yruf, and had more intense interactions with them, than Aurora. His opinion would carry more weight as a result.

"She is stubborn."

"Aurora?"

"Lelindia."

Cade bit back a smile. "She's a healer. Ignoring the suffering of others would go against her base instincts."

"Yes, but she did not tell me she was going."

Cade winced. "Yeah, that stings." He understood Lelindia's reasoning. She knew Jonarel would react badly, so she'd avoided the confrontation.

But Cade had experience being on the receiving end of that kind of logic. "That's how I felt when Aurora chose to go with Nat to Tnaryt's ship. I didn't get a vote on that, either. One minute she was sitting at the bar, the next she was gone." He'd hated the waiting and uncertainty that followed.

Jonarel was silent for a moment, his jaw working. "Thank you."

Cade blinked. "For what?"

Jonarel pivoted to face him. "Thank you for understanding."

There it was again, that friendish feeling. Much more of this behavior and he and Jonarel might end up bonding. He gave Jonarel a half-smile. "Loving a Sahzade or Nedale isn't for the faint of heart."

Jonarel's mouth twitched infinitesimally, a spark of amusement replacing the shadowed look in his eyes. "No, it is not."

Exiting the lift, they strode to *Gladiator* in companionable silence. The murmur of voices from the cockpit drew him in that direction.

"...liability because we're visible, while they won't be."

Gonzo's voice.

"So you want to sit this one out?" Justin replied, glancing up from the co-pilot's seat as Cade appeared. His eyes widened as he spotted Jonarel's large form filling the opening to the corridor behind him. "Hey. Everything okay?" The look he shot Cade gave the question a deeper meaning.

"Fine. I asked Jonarel to take a look at the sensor deflector."

"Oh." Justin's smile was tentative. "I'm sure Bella would love that." He nodded toward the stairway behind the cockpit. "She's down in the engine room."

"Then I will go help her."

As soon as Jonarel disappeared around the corner, Justin leaned forward, his voice low. "Why's he checking the sensor deflector?"

Cade matched his tone. "He needed a distraction to keep his mind off Lelindia while she's on the Yruf ship."

Jonarel's deep voice rumbled up from the stairwell. "I can still hear you."

Justin flushed, looking like a kid caught with his hand in the cookie jar. "Sorry," he called out. Then he dropped his voice to a whisper so soft Cade almost couldn't hear him. "Forgot about enhanced Kraed senses."

Cade often did, too. Jonarel wasn't flashy about them, and rarely pointed out when he could see or hear things others couldn't. His commenting on it now had a teasing quality to it — a reminder that on a ship as small as *Gladiator*, Jonarel would hear everything, especially without any ambient engine noise or the normal creaks and groans of spaceflight to muffle voices.

Cade propped his shoulder against the bulkhead. "Any word from Reynolds?"

Justin nodded. "Her most recent message said, and I quote, *for an undercover operative, this guy is dreadfully boring. No intel to report. Hope you're having more success.*"

"Hm. I wonder if Sly'Kull figured out I tagged him."

"Maybe." Justin shrugged. "Or maybe he had the one task to do — get Aurora to head for Teeli space — and now he's lying low. I wouldn't want to draw attention from Reanne if I didn't have to."

"Agreed." He turned to Gonzo. "What were you two talking about when I walked in?"

"We were discussing *Gladiator*'s lack of hull camouflage. If Aurora pulls this off and convinces the Yruf to go into Teeli space with the *Starhawke, Glad*'s not exactly going to blend in with those two. Or be of much use in a fight if Reanne sends the Teeli armada to greet them."

"Hmm." He'd been so focused on winning over the Yruf to their cause that he hadn't given the idea much thought. "You didn't answer Justin's question. Do you think we should sit this one out? Or do you have an alternate plan?" He was going to bet on the latter.

"Plan A. We park *Gladiator* somewhere near the Fleet border and join the *Starhawke* crew before they cross into Fleet space."

"And Plan B?"

"We park *Gladiator* in the Yruf's bay, so we're ready to fly out and engage on a moment's notice, but are hidden from the Teeli."

Justin grinned. "I like Plan B."

Cade scrutinized Gonzo. "And you'd be okay with that? I seem to remember you weren't big on trusting the Yruf after we parted ways last time."

Gonzo ran a hand over his cheek and chin, creating a faint scratching rasp as his palm brushed across his goatee. "Yeah, I know, but I think I was wrong. I've had time to analyze their behavior, and the tactical advantages they could have brought into play to gain control of the situation. They had us cold and could have blasted us and the Ecilam ship into tiny bits. They didn't."

"No, they didn't."

"Instead, they acted like cautious parents trying to keep their children from hurting themselves with sharp objects, rather than domineering invaders bent on subjugation."

"You ol' softy." Justin gave Gonzo a playful tap with his fist. "You're starting to like them."

Gonzo grunted.

"I think having Micah around helped, too," Justin added. "Cade and I did pretty well getting basic points across with the Yruf, but that guy can communicate with them on their level."

"It was impressive to watch," Cade agreed. Micah had picked up on layers of meaning from the Yruf he hadn't even begun to understand.

"Micah sent me a packet of info," Justin said, "with a slew of Yruf words and translations. We'll never have a complete vocabulary, since so much of their communication is non-verbal, but I think he and I could eventually create a translation program that would allow the crew to hold simple conversations with the Yruf."

"Really?"

"Yep. Which would be helpful if we're going to be their houseguests again." His grin flashed. "Maybe this time we can convince them to feed us something other than watered down Fleet rations."

Cade grunted. "This time I'll be paying a visit to the *Starhawke*'s greenhouse before we leave."

Fifty-Five

Celia had seen a plethora of emergency rooms during her years with the Fleet, had witnessed injuries and blunt trauma that would make the most stoic person's stomach turn.

One look at Micah after they entered the softly lit medical chamber on the Yruf ship proved he had not.

The green tinge to his skin had nothing to do with the ambient light reflected off the emerald-colored walls. His gaze darted around like he couldn't decide where to look – or where *not* to look.

Lelindia didn't hesitate. Her gaze swept the room with a practiced eye.

What she saw, Celia could only imagine. She'd asked her to describe what her Nedale senses showed her, but it was like a person who'd been blind since birth asking a sighted person to describe the colors of a sunset. She got the concepts, but she'd never really know what Lelindia was seeing.

Clearly one of the seven Yruf patients in the room had an injury that triggered alarms for those senses. Lelindia was already headed in that direction, Ahle by her side.

Celia slid the pack containing their food supplies – which Lelindia would definitely need after the healing sessions

AUDREY SHARPE

— off her back. She glanced at Micah, whose gaze was focused on the black and gold patterned deck. "You up for this?"

He looked at her, his throat moving in a swallow that was probably pushing down bile. Or worse. "I want to help."

"You want a bucket nearby, just in case?" She didn't say it to be mean, or poke fun. To her surprise, she didn't like seeing him struggling to hold it together.

He seemed equally surprised by her concern. He was also staring at her like she was the horizon and he was a sailor standing on the deck of a rickety boat caught in huge swells. "I'm hoping I won't need one."

She watched Lelindia out of the corner of her eye. She'd rested her hands on the chest of her chosen patient, her breath falling into the rhythm she used whenever she was activating her healing abilities.

Micah's head swiveled in that direction, his tanned skin losing more color. "I didn't expect it to be so... graphic."

You have lived a very sheltered life. By her standards, the scene around them rated a one out of ten on the graphic scale. Yes, several of the Yruf had badly damaged limbs, terrible burns, or faces that were barely recognizable, but the injuries were largely concealed by the treatment pods that surrounded them and the flexible bandaging that covered their wounds.

Then understanding dawned. "You can hear their thoughts, can't you?"

His head moved in a slow nod, the movement clearly threatening his dicey equilibrium. "They can't control what they're projecting. I think something about this room's construction keeps the mental projections muted from the outside. Or maybe it's the doctors who are containing them. I didn't pick up on the imagery before. But in here it's... intense."

He was doing a far better job of holding it together than she'd thought. From his perspective, this room might feel like a six or seven out of ten. "You can wait outside. Lelindia seems to be doing okay on her own." In fact... "I could go with you, if you want."

She'd surprised him again.

He considered her offer for a solid second. She could see it in his eyes. Then he rolled his shoulders and stiffened his spine. "I can help." He took one step and paused. "But thank you for offering."

He hadn't taken the easy out. That earned him points.

She followed him to the med pod where Lelindia was working, setting the pack down beside one of the monitors.

His breath hitched. "Her lungs. They've been on fire."

She wasn't sure he was even aware he'd spoken. His gaze was locked on the Yruf in the pod.

A female, based on the reddish-purple scales visible on her fingers, but most of her body was covered.

"She suffered severe burns over sixty-eight percent of her body and internally," Lelindia agreed without taking her gaze off her patient. "I'm working to restore function to her lungs and clear away the fluid build-up."

"She expected to drown in the never-ending fire," Micah murmured, his voice thick. "She could feel herself dying."

Lelindia nodded. "Another few days and she would have. The Yruf didn't have any way to reverse the damage. It's amazing she lasted this long. She has a strong will, but her body was shutting down."

Micah jerked like he'd been poked. "Her name is Liwl. And she has a child."

"Ah." Lelindia smiled softly. "That explains a lot. Please convey to her that she's going to be fine. She'll be able to hold her child again soon."

Lelindia's voice held the calm assurance and confidence of certainty.

Celia didn't doubt she was right. She could see the Yruf female's body had relaxed under her coverings, and her labored breaths had already begun to smooth out.

Furrows marched across Micah's forehead as he stared at Liwl, his mouth turned down and his arms crossed tightly over his chest. But he didn't look in danger of losing his lunch anymore. Providing him with a specific task probably helped.

Ahle tapped the monitor by Liwl's head, his dark eyes illuminated by the glow as he checked the data. His gaze shifted back and forth between the various bio monitors and his patient, with an occasional glance at Lelindia.

What did he see when he looked at her? He, like the rest of the Yruf, could see the healing energy field Lelindia produced. So could Micah.

She could not. That fact had never bothered her before. But she'd never been on an alien ship, surrounded by aliens and strange tech, and feeling very, very human.

Why did that unsettle her? She certainly hadn't felt that way when they were on Drakar, and that had been an alien planet with advanced tech where she, Emoto, and Kelly had been the only humans. Yet she'd felt perfectly at ease, even during their second visit, which had been filled with conflict and ended in a dramatic jailbreak.

The rustle of bedding, the subtle clicks and taps of equipment, an occasional wheeze or cough – they made her twitch and flinch as the minutes ticked by. She fought against the odd sensations, running through the focus and concentration techniques she'd learned during her training. It helped... a little.

A presence by her side brought her head up. Micah had moved from the foot of the pod to stand beside her. His gaze was still on Liwl, but his body language had changed. The bracing rigidity had been replaced with a protective, comforting vibe. Like he'd noticed her reaction and was offering silent support.

Her instinctive flare of irritation guttered out before it caught. He wasn't judging her. Or mocking her. He was just... there.

She shifted her weight, bringing her shoulder within a few centimeters of his arm. She didn't question why she did it, but her agitation eased. Her gaze returned to Liwl.

The changes were starting to become visible externally. Scales on the female's throat that had been blistered and blackened were sloughing off their top layers onto the bedding, revealing the healthy reds and oranges of her base coloring. Her eyes were still closed, but the discoloration and flakiness of her lids was also changing, the skin no longer resembling cracked, dried clay.

The whisper of fluid footsteps announced the approach of one of the ICU doctors, a lemon-yellow and white female a few centimeters taller than Ahle. Her gaze swept over the monitors, Liwl, and Lelindia, before focusing on Ahle.

The few words they spoke meant nothing to Celia, but she didn't need to understand them to read their body language. The female doctor was as startled by what she was seeing as Ahle had been when Lelindia had healed Cade's arm. After an extended consultation, the doctor seemed to be asking Ahle to send Lelindia to the patient at the far end of the room after she was finished with Liwl.

Ahle appeared to agree with her assessment, although his deference to Lelindia made her suspect he wouldn't push the issue if Lelindia disagreed with them.

And why would he? She was saving one of his patients right before his eyes. He'd probably go along with any recommendations she made, as long as she kept doing what she was doing.

Lelindia seemed oblivious to their interaction. In fact, except for her rhythmic breathing and occasional blink, her body was still as stone.

One of the other doctors, a brown-toned male, joined the gathering around the pod. A few minutes later the remaining doctor, a mint green female, came to stand beside him.

The physical changes in Liwl had become prominent now. The bandages across the top of her head and over the protrusion of her nose had begun to slide away, unable to maintain their adhesion as the burned scales sloughed off and were replaced by glossy, richly-colored ones.

All four of the doctors turned toward the entrance a couple seconds before the circular doorway rolled aside. Ifel and Cegra strode in, Ifel's cloak rippling behind her as they made their way to the gathering around the pod.

All the doctors except Ahle backed away, returning to their duties. Ifel stopped at the foot of the pod, her gaze taking in Liwl's dramatic transformation. Her tongue flicked out, but she didn't seem startled.

Perhaps Ahle had been sending her mental updates all along?

Lelindia still didn't move. If she realized the Yruf leader had arrived, she gave no sign.

Ifel stepped next to Micah, dwarfing him like he was a pre-teen adolescent. They locked gazes in the mostly non-verbal communication she'd started to accept as normal. Bizarre, but normal.

Micah's cheek creased in a small smile. He turned to Celia, his voice a low rumble in her ear. "She was worried that Lelindia was harming herself by healing Liwl. Like she was giving up her life force to save her. I assured her that, other than needing breaks and food, the healing is a nurturing experience for both of them."

"And she understood that?" Celia murmured back.

"She accepted it after she saw for herself that Lelindia was doing fine."

Celia's gaze flicked to Ifel. The Yruf leader was impressing her more and more at each turn. One of her own crewmembers was dying, yet she had been unwilling to let Lelindia sacrifice herself to save her. That level of empathy and integrity toward strangers was rare. Aurora had it. Lelindia, too, which was one of the reasons she cherished her friendships with both of them.

Her gaze slid to Micah. She didn't know what to think about him anymore. He wasn't acting the role of the villain she'd cast him in, but she couldn't quite bring herself to trust him, either.

Which left her in a weird limbo of uncertainty she had no idea how to escape.

Fifty-Six

The sweet tang of citrus burst on Lelindia's tongue as she bit into the orange section she'd popped in her mouth. "Mmm."

Micah laughed. "Good?"

"So good." All food tasted better after a healing session.

Her hunger had driven her to take a break after finishing her work with Liwl and two other patients. She'd placed them all in a resting sedation that would help their immune systems take over and continue the healing process. She was still developing her understanding of the complexities of their physiology, but typically the effect wore off as the internal systems returned to normal functioning, allowing the patient to regain consciousness naturally and without too much discomfort.

Then again, compared to what these patients had been enduring since the Ecilam blew up their ship, minor aches and pains would be a breath of fresh air.

She bit into another orange slice, surveying the ICU through the clear partition separating the curved nook antechamber at the entrance. It served as the Yruf equivalent of a breakroom where she, Celia, and Micah had settled in for a snack.

She still had four more patients to treat, but none of them were in danger of coding. Liwl had been the worst. She hadn't been exaggerating when she'd told Micah and Celia the female probably wouldn't have lasted another day. Her internal organs, particularly her lungs, had been a mess.

But now she was resting comfortably.

The faint rumble of the rolling entrance door drew her gaze in that direction. A petite Yruf, no bigger than a seven-year-old child, walked in, followed by an adult. The child and adult had neutral coloring, indicating they were both male.

The boy froze as he caught sight of her, his eyes widening and his tiny tongue flicking so quickly she almost couldn't see it.

She was sitting closest to the door to the ICU, which meant the boy would have to pass near her to enter. He seemed extremely reluctant to do so.

Setting the rest of the orange on her plate, she pivoted to face him and folded her hands in her lap, regarding him calmly.

He looked up at the male beside him, who was also gazing at her, Micah, and Celia, though without the obvious agitation of the child.

The ICU partition parted and Ahle walked into the antechamber. His gaze rested on her briefly before he approached the other male. The boy craned his neck to peer around Ahle's cloak so he could keep an eye on Lelindia as the two adults communicated.

What must he think? How strange must she look to him, with her dark hair pulled into a ponytail, her tawny-beige skin devoid of scales, and her comparatively flat face? He might even assume she was a male of her species, since she lacked the brilliant coloring of Yruf females.

On impulse, she engaged her energy field.

His eyes almost popped out of their sockets, but he took a step towards her rather than backing away.

She held out her hand, palm up, her emerald field swirling around her. Using just her fingers, she motioned him forward.

He took another step, then another, steadily closing the distance.

She didn't look at Ahle or the other male. She kept her gaze on the boy.

He halted half a meter from her, the long fingers on his small hands twining around each other in nervous excitement... or fear. Hopefully excitement.

She stretched her hand a few centimeters further to bring her energy field closer to him.

He stared at it with the rapt attention only a child could achieve. Ever so slowly, he reached out, the tip of one finger coming in contact with the field.

She felt it the same moment he did, though the experience would be quite different for each of them. She sensed a connection, an understanding that her Nedale senses catalogued without conscious thought. The touch was familiar at a cellular level, which made sense. She'd just spent a great deal of time healing his mother, Liwl.

His hand jerked at first, but he immediately brought it back, his palm flowing through her energy field like he was trying to catch a cloud.

A smile tugged at her lips as she watched his reaction. He'd stepped closer, both hands waving slowly back and forth in her field like miniature flags, but never close enough to touch her skin. He made a gurgling sound, which might have been a laugh. Hard to tell, but he was clearly enjoying himself.

She peeked over his shoulder. Ahle and the Yruf male were watching their interaction, Ahle with what she was starting to consider his "amused" face, and the male with more of an astounded expression.

When she looked back at the boy, he was staring at her, his hand now hovering a centimeter from hers.

With exquisite slowness, she raised her arm until their fingers brushed.

He gave a little hop, like she'd jolted him with electricity, but didn't pull away. Instead, his scaled fingers began tracing the lines on her palm, then hesitantly touching the sprinkling of hair on her forearm as she rotated her wrist.

His tongue was going again. He tilted his head, his neck moving in that extra-vertebrae way that allowed his body to stay stationary while he peered around toward the back of her head.

Her ponytail.

Reaching back with her other hand, she pulled the elastic out, her hair falling forward in a curtain on both sides of her face.

He blinked a couple times, like he couldn't quite believe what he was seeing, but his hand lifted toward her face.

Bending at the waist, she allowed the drape of her hair to brush across the scales of his hand.

He separated his fingers, letting her hair slide through the gaps. She felt a puff of air on her face as he gave a little snort. Then his fingers closed.

She braced, expecting a yank, like a toddler playing with his mother's hair, but the boy didn't pull. Instead, he brought his nose to her hair and audibly inhaled as his tongue moved like a metronome.

She must smell strange to him. She hadn't detected a particular scent from the Yruf. Nothing artificial, at least.

Closing her eyes briefly, she inhaled. Spring grass. That's what he smelled like.

She opened her eyes when he made the gurgling sound again. Pretty sure that was a laugh, because he followed it up with a tiny tap of his finger on her nose, which was now centimeters from his, making her a little cross-eyed as she gazed at him.

She giggled, the sound right out of her childhood.

He gurgled back.

Lifting one finger, she lightly tapped his nose.

Another gurgle. She giggled again.

"*Lah-lin-tia.*"

They both turned when Ahle said her name, the boy immediately releasing his hold on her hair and stepping away.

She'd bet he'd gotten a mental command from Ahle or the other male.

Ahle motioned to the ICU. "Liwl."

She dropped her energy field and stood. "Of course."

The boy didn't seem intimidated by her now. In fact, he stayed right by her side as she walked with Ahle into the ICU and over to Liwl's pod.

The boy was either very brave, or very devoted to his mother — probably both — because he didn't hesitate as he approached the side of her pod. What brought him up short was when he saw her face, free of bandages and with healthy scales, her eyes closed in peaceful slumber.

His head jerked back and forth between his mother and Lelindia, a million thoughts and emotions visible in his eyes.

She rested a hand on his shoulder, urging him closer. The bandages on Liwl's arms were still in place. Her focus had been on healing the critical areas first, leaving the damage to Liwl's limbs for a second pass after she'd helped the other patients in the ICU.

But she couldn't resist giving the boy a demonstration. Resting her hand over Liwl's wrist, she engaged her energy field, concentrating on the burned scales underneath the bandage. Nurturing cellular healing for scales was a lot easier than putting Liwl's lungs back together, even with all the extra nerve endings. After a minute or two, she peeled back a section of the bandage, taking away the charred top layer that flaked off and revealing the new, healthy scales underneath.

The boy's diamond pupils had opened to nearly swallow the iris, his hands gripping the side of the pod like a lifeline.

His gaze swung to her. She could be wrong – reading the Yruf's non-verbal cues was Celia's forte, not hers – but she got the distinct impression he'd just developed a massive crush on her.

"Your mom's going to be fine," she assured him. And then realized he couldn't understand her words.

Yet he did. She could tell from the way he reacted. He rested his small hand on hers. "Luhlintea?"

Her lips curved up. "Lelindia."

"Lelindia," he repeated.

Huh. He said it clearly, a perfect mimic in the higher pitch of a child's voice.

She gestured to him.

"Typar," he said softly.

"Typar," she repeated, not quite as perfectly. It suited him. He was so cute and full of life and... maybe Typar wasn't the only one with a crush.

"Lee-lee?"

She turned to Micah, who was standing with Celia a respectful distance away.

"Malc — that's Typar's father — wants to thank you for saving Liwl's life. And for your compassion."

The Yruf male, Malc, had assumed the same deep bow posture Ahle and Cegra had used on the Starhawke.

This time she knew what to do.

She swallowed around the lump forming in her throat and reached out to rest her hand briefly on his head. "Please tell him it's my pleasure. I wish I could have helped her sooner."

Micah conveyed the message as Malc stood. Typar, she noted, still had his hand over hers in a not-so-subtle request that she stay put.

Her stomach rumbled, reminding her she still needed to refuel before starting her next healing session. "Micah, can you ask Malc if Typar can stay with me while I work? I need to finish eating, first, but he'd probably enjoy watching the healing process."

"Great idea."

As Micah talked with Malc, Celia sidled up next to her. "Looks like you've picked up a fan."

"It's a mutual admiration society."

Celia's gaze dropped to Typar, who was watching them with open curiosity. "I think he finds our chatter entertaining."

"No doubt. I just wish we shared a common language."

"You do." Celia gave her a nudge with her shoulder. "It's called love."

Fifty-Seven

"Things are going well?" Aurora asked as she gazed at the image of the Yruf ship on the bridgescreen.

"Really well," Micah answered over the comm. "Lelindia's finishing up her seventh patient now. They're all going to be fine." He took the volume down by half and his voice sounded clearer, like he had the comb022and right next to his mouth. "They lost seven crew in that explosion, and five more died in the ICU afterward. For a race that feels every death acutely, this has been a very traumatic experience."

She squeezed her eyes shut as her mind conjured images she didn't want to see. She'd suspected the truth after the hesitancy she'd sensed from Ifel regarding her request to face the Teeli.

Micah's confirmation made her situation even more untenable. The Yruf cherished life. Asking them to go up against Reanne, who would kill anyone who crossed her without a moment's hesitation, was unfair, even selfish.

She'd wanted the Yruf to join her because it would solve one of her big problems – a lack of support. But the more she learned about them, the worse she felt about making that request. Even now, her stomach twisted at the thought of the

Yruf ship facing Reanne's forces. How many lives could be lost? How much damage could the Teeli cause to the ship's biosphere, which represented the Yruf's living history?

Every one of those losses would be on her conscience, forever. "How soon do you think you'll be heading back?"

He hesitated. "About that. Ifel's been in here twice now, and I haven't been able to get a read on what's going on with her. She hasn't talked to me directly, but this last time she brought several Yruf guards and four other Yruf I'd never seen before."

A trickle of unease slid down her spine as Jonarel's warning rose like a specter. "Do you think they're going to try to keep you there?"

"What?" He sounded startled. "No, nothing like that."

Her shoulders dropped several centimeters. Not that she'd be powerless if the Yruf cut and ran. Their camouflage would do nothing to impede her ability to sense her brother's presence and pinpoint his location anywhere in the galaxy.

"I think they might be close to a decision regarding helping us."

"Oh."

A pause. "You don't sound very excited."

Because I just realized I can't accept their help. "We don't know their answer yet."

He knew it was more than that. She could sense his emotional shifts. But he didn't push. "Regardless, Lelindia wants to do another round of treatments and take a peek at the biosphere before she returns to the ship."

Jonarel was going to love that news. She wasn't sure how much longer Cade's team could keep him busy on *Gladiator.* "How long will that take?"

"She needs to rest first. Ahle has already set her up in an alcove of the ICU on a platform bed." A smile entered his voice. "And she made a friend. The little boy of one of the patients she treated. He's over there curled up on a second bed, watching her."

Lelindia had always been good with kids. Maybe it was a Nedale trait, or the natural result of her generous, open-hearted nature. "So we're looking at several hours, at least."

"Maybe longer. Cegra offered to take me and Celia back to the biosphere while Lelindia sleeps. Assuming you don't have any objections," he added.

She was so startled by the idea that he and Celia were spending time together voluntarily that she almost missed the point of the question. "Uh, no, unless you have any concerns." He'd already told her he didn't believe the Yruf would attempt to hold them against their will.

"No, just wanted you to know we'd be splitting up for a while."

"That's fine." She would *not* be passing that intel on to Jonarel, however. "Contact me if you hear from Ifel, otherwise we'll expect you when Lelindia's ready to head back."

"Will do."

After the channel closed, she sat staring at the Yruf ship, her mind rotating through "what ifs" like a mental Ferris wheel. But each one brought her back to the same conclusion.

The Yruf weren't the warriors she'd expected. They were the peace-loving pacifists the Teeli pretended to be. She couldn't risk their lives — not now, not ever.

Her crew would be going into Teeli space alone.

Fifty-Eight

"Can I ask you a question?" Micah glanced over his shoulder at Celia as they followed Cegra through the biosphere.

This time they were on a winding path through an arid desert region they hadn't seen before. Celia suspected Cegra had chosen it because it was the quickest way to the ocean, Micah's ultimate destination, from the med bay. But she couldn't confirm that. She'd long since given up trying to keep any sense of directional coordinates on this ship. The undulating corridors made it virtually impossible, at least without some set framework to start with.

Clearly there were some parts of the ship that were stationary, like this biosphere, the throne room, and the bridge they'd toured. But everywhere else the hovering drones led the way through the maze of fluid bulkheads. This biosphere seemed to be the only location they didn't enter.

She met Micah's questioning gaze as she closed the gap between them. "Go ahead." She didn't mind questions as long as she was under no compulsion to answer them.

He continued along the path but kept his upper body slightly angled in her direction. "When you agreed to return to the biosphere with me, was it because you wanted time to explore, or because you wanted to keep an eye on me?"

Fair question, especially considering the reason she'd volunteered for this detail in the first place. But there wasn't any heat or anger behind his words. Only curiosity about her motivations.

She gave the question a few seconds thought as she climbed the dirt trail to the top of the ridge. "Neither."

"Neither?" He paused, brushing a lock of sandy blond hair off his forehead. "Then why did you come along?"

She paused as well, studying him. His clothes were wrinkled from the hours spent in the ICU. While Lelindia had been working, he'd engaged Ahle and the other doctors in conversation, developing his communication skills and knowledge. She'd taken advantage of the opportunity to observe him and the Yruf, doing her best to follow their conversations based on their non-verbal cues.

He was easier to read than the Yruf, but she was getting fairly comfortable with both. She'd learned a lot in the past few hours. Which gave her the answer to his question. "I thought it would be fun."

"Fun?" He acted like he didn't know the meaning of the word.

That made her smile. "Yeah, you know, for enjoyment, amusement. Fun."

His lips parted, the movement of his dark lashes drawing attention to his eyes as he blinked in slow motion. He looked stupefied. "Fun," he finally repeated, drawing out the single syllable. "You thought it would be *fun* to come here with *me*?" He phrased it like a rhetorical question, the answer so obvious it didn't need to be given. And that answer was *no*.

"Yes."

His body language projected wariness, his stance becoming defensive. "You're not planning to beat me up, are you?"

She laughed.

He reacted by tucking his elbows in like he was preparing to block a punch.

She shook her head, still grinning. "No, I'm not going to beat you up."

"Oh." Confusion flitted across his face. He shuffled his feet like he couldn't decide whether he should keep walking or stand his ground against a sneak attack. "Then why would hanging out with me be fun for you?"

She gave him a one-shoulder shrug and brushed past him. "You're a smart man. You figure it out."

It took a few seconds before the crunch of his footsteps on the pebble-strewn ground followed her. She continued down the other side of the ridge, catching a sparkle of light through the glass-like partition that separated this region from the ocean ecosystem.

Micah's strides were longer than hers, so he caught up quickly. "Are you going to interrogate me?"

She rolled her eyes without looking back. No one to blame for his paranoia except herself. "Nope."

He was almost beside her now. "Then what?"

Cegra was waiting for them at the doorway between the two regions. Celia didn't respond to Micah's question until they'd followed her through and continued along the path, now surrounded by lush greenery and the scent of sea air. "I'd like to hear what you've been learning from the Yruf today."

He was silent for a moment. "So, a mini-interrogation?"

This time she did a full-body eyeroll, pivoting to face him while she continued to walk backwards. "No interrogation. I'd just like to... talk."

"Talk?" Again, the word seemed to lack meaning for him.

"Yes, talk, conversation, the sharing of ideas and experiences."

His expression said he was worried about talking to someone whose mental state was suspect. But then his gaze moved beyond her and back, his eyes narrowing. "How are you doing that?"

"Doing what?"

"Walking backwards without knowing where you're going."

She glanced behind her. They'd be at the ocean in another twenty meters. "I always know where I'm going."

"You have eyes in the back of your head?"

"I have excellent visual memory and spatial awareness."

"But you've never been on this path."

"Doesn't matter. I can maneuver in near-total darkness without any issues. This is nothing." Another survival skill she'd been forced to learn as a child.

Micah's gaze continued to search hers, but the corners of his mouth tilted up. "You are a puzzle wrapped in a cypher and tied with a riddle."

No one had ever described her that way, but coming from him, it sounded like a compliment. "Thanks."

That made him chuckle. "You're welcome."

They broke through the overhanging greenery and the faux-sun warmed the back of her tunic. She turned her face toward its glow, her gaze resting on the beauty of the pristine sand and aquamarine water stretched out before them.

Beside her, Micah let out a heartfelt sigh. "I miss this."

"How often do you normally go to the beach?"

"Every day."

"Every day?"

"Uh-huh. On days I don't have time to surf, I'll either ride my bike along the path or go for a jog on the sand. The hydrotank on the *Starhawke* is a great simulation, but it's not..." His arms opened wide as he faced the expanse of water. "This."

Did he realize how much emotion his body expressed when he talked about the ocean? She could hear it in his voice, too, but his movements said so much more. As much as Aurora belonged on the bridge of the *Starhawke*, Micah belonged beside the sea.

A slight pang in her chest caught her by surprise. Why would that thought bother her? Her entire goal since Micah had set foot on the *Starhawke* had been to get him back on terra firma. Discovering he yearned for that too, whether he acknowledged it or not, should have triggered elation.

Then again, his absence would be hard on Aurora. She'd never seen her friend more comfortable in her own skin, more tied into her surroundings, than she was when Micah was with her. When he left – and he would most definitely be leaving – it would be tough on her.

So maybe the brush of melancholy wasn't so odd. Aurora's pain at his departure would affect the entire crew.

Micah halted near the water's edge, watching the petite waves race up the sand, their leading edges pushing a thin line of foam.

The Yruf must have created a large-scale wave machine or a way to fluctuate the gravitational pull of their ship's gravity generator in this area.

Micah turned to Cegra and asked her what was clearly a question... or more accurately, permission to do something.

He must have gotten an affirmative response, because he plunked down on the sand and began removing his hiking boots.

"What are you doing?"

He shot her a grin. "Getting my feet wet. Wanna join me?"

She hadn't seen him smile like that, with such unfettered enthusiasm, since their first conversation outside Stoneycroft. At that time, she'd gotten the distinct impression he was attracted to her. She'd responded by making it clear she was watching his every move. They'd been in opposition ever since.

"Cardiff?" He paused with his second boot in his hand. "Is there a problem?"

She'd been frowning at him without responding to his question. She gave herself a mental shake. "Aren't you or the Yruf worried about contamination?" Walking through the biosphere was one thing. Wading into the water was something else.

"Nope. That's something I learned talking to Ahle and the rest of the doctors. They're experts at neutralizing biohazards. Our group was checked and cleaned from head to toe as soon as we came onboard, both times, and we didn't even know it. We went through two additional passes as we walked to the biosphere, and there's another cleaning system at each doorway between zones. If they'd detected anything their system couldn't handle, we wouldn't have been allowed inside."

She'd wondered about that during their first visit. She'd felt something like an electrostatic charge in the shuttle bay and on the way to the biosphere. Now she knew why.

Lucky for them the Yruf were benevolent. With the Yruf's technology, infecting their group with a bio-weapon would be easy and undetectable. Well, infecting her. Lelindia would be immune, and probably Aurora, too. Maybe Micah.

Settling on the sand beside him she began unlacing the Kraed boots Jonarel's mother had given her. They'd become her preferred footwear for any off-ship excursions to unknown locales.

He stuffed his socks into his boots and dug his toes into the sand. His sigh of pleasure drew her attention. He'd closed his eyes, his breathing slow and deep.

He had a nice profile. Strong jawline, high cheekbones and forehead, nicely shaped nose, and those long lashes that curled at the tips. Aurora had a lot of the same physical traits, though she took more after her dad while Micah looked more like his mom.

He turned his head and caught her studying him. "What?"

"I was noticing the family characteristics in your profile." And didn't that sound clinical and boring. *Way to ramp up the fun factor.*

Amusement flickered in his green eyes. "Were you wondering if I was adopted?"

"Hardly." An unfamiliar sensation brushed over her as she met his gaze. She focused her attention on the complex laces of her boots. "You take after your mom more than your dad."

"I agree, though I didn't know that until I saw her again. Makes me feel a little better about not being able to generate an energy field."

She slid off her first boot. "Does that bother you?"

"Bother isn't the right word. I mean, it's not something I even remembered was possible until Aurora showed up. But I guess in some ways I feel a little left out."

They had that in common. She untied her laces, working down her calf. "You can enhance Aurora's field and abilities more than any other Suulh. That has to count for something." That fact used to worry her. A lot. Now... not so much.

"True. What she was able to accomplish at Stoneycroft..." His voice trailed off as he stared out across the water. "She amazes me."

"Me, too."

His gaze swung back to her. "Yeah?"

She nodded. "From the first day I met her, I knew there was something different about her. It turned out to be much more than I expected, but I wasn't as surprised as you might think when I learned the truth. It made all the pieces fit."

He rested his elbows on his bent knees as his gaze searched hers. "You care about her a lot, don't you?"

"She's my friend." He'd never understand what that word meant to her. He was the kind of guy who probably had hundreds of people he called friends.

She'd had no one until Aurora crossed her path. Her mentor, the other person who knew personal details about her past, had been a teacher and role model, not a friend. "She and Lelindia are the only two I have. Well, maybe Reynolds."

She and Cade's security officer had a lot in common, but she wasn't sure she'd label their relationship a friendship. All their interactions had been work-related.

Emotion flickered in his eyes. "I didn't know that."

"That's what happens when you spend your childhood in a prison camp." She yanked off her second boot and stood. The warm sand tickled the bottoms of her feet, helping to banish the dark images that hovered at the edge of her mind whenever she thought of the camp. Bending at the waist, she rolled her leggings higher on her calves.

Micah stood, his shadow falling over her. "I'm sorry."

She straightened. "For what?"

"For what you've been through. And for causing you additional pain when I came on the scene. I didn't mean to be a thorn in your side."

He was more perceptive than she'd given him credit for. Then again, he'd grown up with a powerful empath for a father. He may not have inherited all his dad's gifts, but he seemed to have picked up on his attitudes and tendency to focus on others. That was something else she'd come to realize. "Not your fault. I misjudged you."

His eyes widened, his brows lifting toward his hairline. "You did?"

"Yes. In fact, I should be the one apologizing, not you." She faced him squarely. "I'm sorry I've given you such a hard time."

She'd rendered him speechless. Kinda fun in its own way. She took advantage of the opportunity, giving his leg a playful prod with her bare foot. "Are you wading in or not?"

He blinked several times, like he was coming out of a trance, then glanced toward the water.

Cegra had removed her foot coverings as well, the emerald green of her scaled legs and feet glistening in the sun as the water painted them with droplets of moisture. Four toes sank into the sand with short, slender protrusions at the front – more robust than a human nail but less intimidating than a Kraed claw.

Siginal had shown Celia the razor-sharp claws on his hands and feet before their sparring session on Drakar, assuring her he wouldn't use them during the match. After she'd trounced him, she'd suggested that next time she bring a couple of her blades and they give it another go, claws versus blades, and see if the outcome was any different.

But considering the *Starhawke*'s dramatic jailbreak from the Clarek compound and Siginal's banishment of Jonarel and Star, it was probably going to be a long time before they had that match, if ever.

Micah swung back around to her. The look he gave her was quite different from the shadowed scowl or cool façade she'd gotten used to. The slow smile stealing across his face and lighting up his eyes showed frank appreciation as his gaze swept over her.

He tipped his head in the direction of the ocean. "Let's go."

Turning, he strode into the oncoming waves with bold confidence.

She took a more circumspect approach, allowing the water to come to her. Its touch was warmer than she'd anticipated as it swirled around her feet and ankles. The tickle of the sand running away under her arches as the water retreated prompted an involuntary giggle.

A giggle? She NEVER giggled.

Micah met her gaze, his grin widening. "Having fun?"

"Oh, yeah." She took a couple more steps, the caress of the water draining away her tension. She drew in a deep breath, the salty tang of the ocean blending with the light sweetness of flowers and robust earthen smells coming from the nearby vegetation.

This space vibrated with life. She didn't need to be a Suulh to sense it. And it made her keenly aware of her own physicality, not in the focused, analytical way she was used to, but in the marrow-deep, conscious appreciation for being *alive*.

Cegra had moved off along the beach, her angled posture and visual focus conveying a desire to give them privacy. Or maybe personal space. Pinning down the nuances of Yruf behavior would take time.

Micah was knee-deep in the water, the rolled-up edge of his khaki pants already damp.

She worked her leggings above her knees and waded closer. His height gave him an advantage. Knee-high for him was thigh-high for her, so she stopped about a meter-and-a-half away. "How about you? Having fun?"

She didn't need to ask. His body language said it all. But she wanted to hear his response.

He didn't disappoint. Stretching his arms out like an eagle taking flight, he tipped back his head, the sunlight playing across the planes of his face. "This is amazing!"

His booming voice startled a couple bird-like creatures from the greenery. They took to the sky, headed in the opposite direction, but within moments changed course, circling back toward Micah and soaring in an arc above him.

She'd seen enough of his interactions with the Yruf to know he was communicating with the birds. Probably apologizing for disturbing them.

The pair circled three times before gliding back to the grove of trees they'd vacated in such a hurry, settling in amongst the shadowed branches.

When she turned back to the water, she discovered Micah watching her. "You talked to them, didn't you?"

"On a very base level, but enough that they accepted we weren't a threat. They have a nest in the trees with four young. They were trying to lure us away."

"I'm glad you calmed their fears." Most people wouldn't have given it a second thought when the birds took flight. Micah had. There probably wasn't a being in the galaxy he wouldn't try to understand and communicate with, if he could.

She'd mistaken his willingness to use that talent as a sign he couldn't be trusted. She'd assumed he was serving his own selfish, manipulative goals.

But he was more like Aurora than she'd been willing to believe. He shared Aurora's altruistic, compassionate heart, her desire to help others, and her fascination with everyone and everything around her.

Micah reached down, trailing his fingers in the water as a wave flowed past.

"You want to dive in, don't you?"

He gave her a sidelong glance. "Always. But this is more than I'd hoped for already."

Through the crystal-clear water, she spied a small school of tiny narrow-bodied fish that were darting around his hands, their orange and silver bodies flashing when they caught the light. "Did you call them here?"

He gave an amused snort. "You can't call animals. All you can do is say hello and see if they choose to respond. Some do, some don't."

The school circled around his shins, but remained well clear of her. "Do they know I'm here?"

He looked up at her through his lashes. "Of course. Every aquatic animal in the area knew the moment we entered the water. I haven't asked the Yruf whether they communicate regularly with the animal species onboard, but I suspect they do. The animals certainly seem comfortable talking with me."

"Are they avoiding coming near me because I'm not talking to them?"

"Partly. You're an unknown, which is a new experience for them. The Yruf are the only bi-pedal species they've encountered. They can hear me, which makes them curious, whereas you're silent, which makes them wary."

She chewed the inside of her lip. "Do you think you could teach me how to communicate with them?"

"What?" He snapped to his full height, scattering the fish. She'd stunned him again. "Uh, maybe. Some people have a gift for animal communication — I mean without being half-Suulh — although I don't know if they talk to them the same way I do. Why would you want to learn?"

"It would be a new skillset to add to my repertoire." But that wasn't the real reason. "Plus, it would be..." She quirked one brow. "Fun."

Fifty-Nine

"You can't be serious." Cade set his fork down on his plate with a metallic clink. "We can't do this without the Yruf."

"Yes, we can." Aurora leaned her forearms on the polished wood surface of the bistro-sized table in the observation lounge. She'd been picking at her food ever since they'd sat down to eat, a clear tell that something was bothering her.

But he hadn't expected this. "No, we can't."

"Yes, we can." Her voice took on an edge. "True, we won't be able to take on Reanne's cruiser, and we'll have to give up on the plan to capture her." She waved her hand in the air, dispelling invisible smoke. "But we can—"

"Get chased, attacked, and captured?"

She gave him a withering look. "Obtain *evidence* that the Teeli aren't who they claim to be. After we arrive, we'll have Star record every move the Teeli make. We can catch the Teeli cruiser and warships on video in Teeli space, showing up exactly where the Teeli told us to be."

"And then get chased, attacked, and captured?"

"Knock it off, Cade. I'm serious."

He folded his arms. "So am I, Aurora. We've gotten lucky in the past when this ship has faced off against the Teeli, but those confrontations always took place in Fleet space. This time we'll be on their turf. There's no way to predict what dangers we might encounter that we aren't prepared to handle."

"I disagree."

He thought she might.

"Besides, we won't be taking *Gladiator*, just the *Starhawke*. That will make it safer."

"Did you just insult my ship?"

"Your ship is a good fighter, but without hull camouflage, it's a liability."

Too bad she was making the very point he, Justin, and Gonzo had been discussing earlier.

"The *Starhawke* can vanish in a heartbeat and the Teeli will have no way to stop us or track us."

"Unless they cut off every jump window out of the system. If you're close to one of the binary stars, there won't be many exits available."

"Then we stay on main engines until we're further out in the system."

"Giving them more time to capture us." He hadn't meant to raise his voice. He got the reaction he deserved.

Her eyes narrowed and her jaw flexed. "What do you want me to say?" Her voice was deceptively soft. "That it's a risk? Of course it is. That comes with the job. But I'm not going to waste this opportunity, and I'm not going to put the Yruf in the line of fire. They've suffered too much already."

"I know they have." He'd never forget the image Ifel had shared with him of the Setarips' devastated homeworld. "But you wanted to help them end their civil war, too. You can't do that if the Ecilam are still working with Reanne."

"It'll take longer to achieve our goals," she admitted. Based on the tenor of her emotions, she was thinking about the Suulh on Feylahn and the Necri soldiers still living under Teeli subjugation. "But the Yruf have patience down to an art form. They'll wait for the right moment. In the meantime, we'll share information, help each other whenever possible, but without putting them at risk. What I'm absolutely *not* doing is slinking back to HQ with our tails between our legs. We accepted this mission. End of discussion."

A couple months ago, he would have escalated the argument, pushed back hard. But a couple months ago he wasn't consciously aware of the depth of her emotions, couldn't feel the nuanced ebb and flow through his empathic abilities.

Now he could. And they told a very different story.

Setting his napkin beside his plate, he slipped out of his chair and crouched beside hers. The movement startled her, her gaze wary, but she allowed him to slide his hands under hers, cupping them tenderly. "You always end up between a rock and a hard place, don't you?"

She let out a shuddering breath, her eyes drifting closed. "Not always." When she opened them, they were coated with a slight sheen of moisture. "Sometimes I end up beside you."

He brought her hand to his lips, pressing a kiss against her warm skin, then rested his cheek against the same spot. "I'll always be by your side."

Her half-smile tore at his heart. "There's nowhere else I'd rather be."

His grip tightened as he stared into the gold-flecked beauty of her green eyes. Of course he would support her decision. She was his future. His everything. He would move the stars for her. He wanted her to understand that. He wanted *her*. "Will you–"

He bit the inside of his cheek to stop the words before they slipped out. *Don't say it, Ellis. Now is not the time for that question.*

"Will I...?" she prompted.

"Want my team to go with you?" he finished.

Lame. So lame. She'd see right through it.

He was right. The slight tilt of her head and fluctuation in her emotions confirmed it. But she let it go.

"Of course. We'll just need to find a safe location to park *Gladiator*."

He nodded. "I'll talk to Gonzo. I'm sure he'll have some ideas." And probably some comments to go with them.

"Good. I'll—"

"Emoto to Hawke."

Aurora turned her face up in the direction of the bridge. "What is it, Kire?"

"I just heard from Micah. Lelindia's finishing her tour of the biosphere, but Ifel has requested a meeting with you when they return to the *Starhawke*. They should be arriving in the next fifteen minutes."

Aurora shot Cade a look, her shoulders drawing back and her chin lifting. "Tell Micah that Cade and I will meet them in the shuttle bay."

"Will do."

Picking up her fork, she speared a piece of sauteed broccolini and pointed it at his half-full plate. "Eat up, Commander. Broccoli is brain food and I want your A-game. We've got the leader of the Yruf coming for a visit."

Sixty

Nervous tension made Aurora's steps a little heavier than normal as she approached the black-scaled alien transport, Cade beside her, but she kept a tight rein on her thoughts and emotions

The unconventional opening appeared in the sleek vessel and Ifel stepped out, accompanied by her four guards. Lelindia appeared next, looking tired but happy, her pack over her shoulder. Micah followed, with Celia behind him. As they walked forward, Celia moved to Micah's side, their arms almost touching, their heads bent in quiet conversation. *Friendly* conversation.

Aurora tuned into their emotions. Curiouser and curiouser. No animosity, no wariness, no tension. They actually seemed to be enjoying each other's company. What exactly had happened between those two while they were onboard the Yruf ship?

Unfortunately, she wouldn't get an answer to that question for a while.

"Welcome to the *Starhawke*," she called out, meeting Ifel halfway. She glanced at Lelindia. "Things went well?"

"Better than I'd hoped. I learned a lot about their physiology. It'll be easier for me to heal them going forward."

Aurora suppressed the clench in her gut, pasting a smile on her face. Lelindia wouldn't be needing those newly acquired skills anytime soon, if ever. "That's great."

Thankfully Lelindia seemed too exhausted to notice her lack of enthusiasm. Micah and Celia weren't so easily fooled. They both peered at her with almost identical expressions of confusion.

"And their biosphere!" Lelindia gushed. "I could have stayed there for hours. Well, no, not really. I would have fallen asleep." The last part was punctuated with a yawn.

"Then let's not keep you standing here." Turning to Ifel, she motioned to the corridor. "Shreenef."

She'd been practicing her pronunciation with Kire while they'd been on the bridge, using the recordings Justin and Williams had made as a reference.

The delight she sensed from Ifel and the rest of the Yruf made the effort worthwhile. They followed her as she headed for the lift, Cade keeping pace with her while Lelindia, Micah, and Celia lagged behind.

She'd debated where to hold this meeting, finally nixing the smaller conference room in favor of the spacious observation lounge.

The five Yruf had to duck through the doorways, including the one to the cargo lift. Ifel's guards were fine once they were inside, but Ifel had to bend her neck to keep the top of her head from brushing the ceiling.

Jonarel had designed the *Starhawke* to accommodate the Kraed, who were slightly taller than most humans, but he hadn't anticipated the potential for visitors of Ifel's stature. Another good reason to use the observation lounge. The ceilings on the main deck were higher than on the command deck.

She could sense Ifel's intense scrutiny of the ship – her curiosity and surprise. It reminded Aurora of how she'd felt when she'd stepped inside the twentieth century space shuttle *Discovery* during an Academy field trip to the Air and Space Museum. She'd been fascinated, imagining how people had functioned in the shuttle, but the technology had been incredibly antiquated compared to the modern era.

Not that she took offense at Ifel's attitude. She'd begun to suspect the Setarips were a much older species than either the Kraed or Humans. Or the Suulh, for that matter. If she was right, they might have spent centuries or possibly millennia perfecting their interstellar designs.

Unfortunately, wisdom had not come with age, at least not to the majority of the Setarip factions. For all their advances, they had been unable to settle basic conflicts peacefully, resulting in the destruction of their world.

The lift doors parted on the main deck. Ifel paused after stepping out, brushing her hand along the wood-textured bulkhead that perfectly mimicked the bark of the denglar trees of Drakar. Her neck moved in a sinuous curve as she scented the air, her nostrils flaring.

"She can smell the greenhouse," Micah explained, moving next to Aurora, "but she wasn't sure if the walls were crafted with live plants."

"If the Kraed could figure out how to make that work, I'm sure they'd do it. Please tell her I'd be happy to give her a tour of the greenhouse after we've talked."

While Micah conveyed the message, Lelindia touched Aurora's arm, drawing her attention. "If you don't need me, I'm going to stop in the med bay and then head up to my cabin."

Aurora shooed her away. "By all means. Jonarel's waiting for you with a surprise." He'd spent the past few hours making alterations to join his cabin with Lelindia's. Aurora had been happy to give him free rein to make any changes he wanted, especially since the work toned down the intense anxiety she'd been buffering ever since Lelindia left the ship. She'd already informed him Lelindia had returned. She could feel his eager anticipation growing every second.

Lelindia smiled, looking a lot less tired than she had a moment ago. "Then I'll go see what he's up to."

Aurora led the group in the opposite direction, the observation lounge doors parting to admit them. That kind of automation didn't make an impression on Ifel, although Aurora did notice she was looking up toward the ceiling a lot. Wondering where the drones were?

Ifel's gaze swept the lounge, taking in the carved wood tables and chairs, the gently sloping deck, and the wide floor-to-ceiling windows that gave an impressive view of the starfield. Or in this case, the starfield and a section of the Yruf ship that blocked a third of the view.

There was no mistaking the look of approval in Ifel's eyes as she turned to Aurora. It triggered an odd mixture of lightness and melancholy in her chest. The more she got to know the Yruf, the more she liked them. Which was precisely why she had to send them away.

She gestured to the oblong table that Star had already converted so that exactly nine chairs surrounded it. Aurora and Micah sat side by side, with Cade to Aurora's right and Celia to Micah's left. Both Micah and Celia seemed perfectly content with the arrangement. Very strange, but she'd take it.

Ifel chose the chair opposite Aurora, with the four guards flanking her, two on a side.

Aurora drew in a slow breath as she gathered her thoughts. "Thank you for meeting with me. And for allowing us to visit your ship."

Micah provided a translation, though Ifel's emotional field indicated she was following the gist pretty well on her own.

Ifel spoke, the words unfamiliar.

"The honor is hers," Micah said. "Lelindia gave her people a tremendous gift this day. She is gratified to know such compassion and kindness exists in this part of the galaxy."

And it was that compassion that made this situation so difficult. "Lelindia is a generous soul. It's her nature to ease the suffering of others."

"As it is yours," Micah translated Ifel's response.

Ifel's gaze shifted to Cade before returning to Aurora.

"Through Cade's memories, I have seen your struggles against the Teeli, and the pain my people have brought you as well." Micah paused. "She views all the Setarip factions as one, as a family," he said as an aside, then continued translating. "We were once whole, unified, and peaceful. But as we ventured away from our planet, we lost that unity. Greed, deception, distrust, antipathy infiltrated our world like an infection. That is when the fighting began. That is when we lost our way."

Aurora's throat tightened as Ifel's emotions drifted over her – the ache of what had been, and the hope for what might be again.

"You and your family are untouched by the forces that ravaged my world. You live with honor, respect, compassion."

Ifel's gaze moved once more to Cade. "Even when cornered and outmatched, you work to be your best selves."

Cade straightened, holding Ifel's gaze. "We try to."

Amusement flitted through Ifel's emotional field.

"Mostly you succeed," Micah translated.

Ifel's gaze returned to Aurora, the amusement blowing away like mist as a low-grade anger took its place.

"The Teeli and the Sovereign do not share your ideals. They are preying on the weaknesses of my people, using them for their own purposes. If they are unchecked, they will corrupt yours, as well."

Aurora's heart thumped painfully in her chest. "I know. That's why I originally wanted to meet with you. I had hoped you would join our efforts to uncover the truth of the Teeli deception, to capture and unmask the Sovereign."

"And so we shall."

Aurora squeezed her eyes shut, pain lancing through her chest. She'd achieved her goal. She'd convinced the Yruf to help her. And now she had to turn them away.

Opening her eyes, she met Ifel's quizzical gaze. "No, you won't."

Sixty-One

"What?" Micah jerked around to face her without translating her message. "What do you mean, no they won't?"

His surprise and outrage dominated her senses, but not enough that she didn't catch Ifel's reaction. Ifel may not have understood her words, but she could read the subtext just fine. Her body had gone perfectly still, her tongue dancing up and down.

Micah's hand gripped hers. "What's going on, sis?"

Tension drove her shoulders up near her ears. She took a breath, consciously drawing them back down. "I'm not willing to put the Yruf in danger, not after what we've seen of their ship, their culture, their past. It's wrong."

"Wrong?" Micah rolled the word around on his tongue. "Don't you think that's up to them to decide?"

She shook her head. "Not when I'm the one asking. This isn't their fight. I'll still help them any way I can to bring the factions back together, but I'm not going to put their ship – their *people* – in harm's way in Teeli space. It's not right."

Micah gazed at her, his jaw working like he was chewing on what she'd said.

"And what if the Teeli armada is waiting for us when we arrive?" Celia asked. No judgement in her voice, only gathering information.

"We can start off camouflaged, look around before we make our presence known. And we can disappear just as easily."

Cade's chair creaked as he stretched his legs under the table. He was fighting to suppress his emotions, but she still sensed his unease with the scenario she'd painted.

"And Reanne?" Celia's tone remained conversational, but her dark eyes showed a hundred calculations racing through her mind.

"We'll have to give up on that plan for now. Our goal will be gathering evidence, images and video we can take back to the Admiral to prove the Teeli aren't the benign pacifists they claim to be."

Celia nodded almost absently, her focus going inward.

Micah's was completely external. He glanced at Cade, then back at her. "It's not as safe and easy as you're making it sound, is it." He didn't phrase it as a question.

"There are risks," she admitted. "But we've faced similar situations before, usually without any warning. We'll be fine."

"And what about the Suulh?" His voice softened, almost a whisper. "What about our grandmother? Lee-Lee's grandmother? The Suulh living as Necri soldiers right now? How much will this decision cost them?"

She flinched as Micah struck a nerve. "I don't know. But I'm not willing to trade the Yruf's lives for theirs. I can't—"

Movement across the table made her turn.

Ifel had risen from her chair, her gaze drilling into Aurora like a spear.

Aurora swallowed. "Yes?"

The words Ifel spoke came out as a hiss.

Micah's translation was almost as sharp. "She wants to talk to you. Alone."

"Alone?" She tore her gaze from Ifel. "How can we talk alone?"

His forehead furrowed. "I'm not sure, but she's insistent. She wants the two of you to go to the greenhouse and talk."

Adrenaline flowed into Aurora's body, making her muscles shake. But she owed Ifel the courtesy of honoring her request. "Okay."

Pushing back her chair, she stood. Her legs felt stiff as boards as she circled the table to where Ifel waited for her. "Shreenef," she said softly, indicating the doorway to the galley and walking in that direction.

Ifel followed as silently as a shadow. A very large shadow.

They passed through the galley and pantry before entering the lush greenery of the greenhouse beyond. Aurora pulled air into her lungs, allowing the pulse of life around her to calm and soothe her agitation.

Turning, she gestured to a bench positioned along the pathway beside an orange tree.

But Ifel ignored the bench, stepping right next to Aurora and raising her hands toward Aurora's head.

Aurora pulled back on reflex, and Ifel immediately froze, waiting.

"Sorry." Aurora gave her an apologetic smile. "Guess I'm a little edgy."

Consciously relaxing her body, she tilted her head toward Ifel's hands.

One hand made contact with her cheek in a feather touch, the scales almost tickling her. But with the other, Ifel made a back and forth motion several centimeters above Aurora's shoulder.

Understanding clicked a moment later. "My energy field. Right." That had been the way they'd made a deeper connection last time.

She engaged her energy field. The moment it touched Ifel she felt a jolt, like tapping into a livewire that mainlined to her brain.

"More."

She twitched as the word whispered in her mind — not her ears — foreign and familiar. More?

"More."

Ifel flipped the fingers of her free hand toward herself.

Oh. More.

Aurora expanded the energy field as Ifel brought her other hand in contact with Aurora's temple. The field flowed along Ifel's arms and wrapped around her body. The livewire feeling grew stronger. But that was nothing compared to when the field surrounded Ifel's head.

"Do you hear me?"

Her jaw dropped open, a squeak of air escaping her throat.

"You hear me." Not a question this time.

"Yes, I hear you." Though neither of them was saying a word.

"Your talents are varied, your mind strong. Until Lelindia and Micah worked with our injured, I was unable to figure out a way around the walls you constructed."

"Walls? What walls?"

"The ones that protect you from being overwhelmed."

She gave herself a moment to consider that. "How are we able to understand each other? We don't speak the same language."

"We are not speaking."

Way more literal than she'd expected. "But I'm thinking the words in Galish."

"That is what your conscious mind believes. But your subconscious understands in a different way. This is the purest form of communication, one our people have long aspired to but rarely achieved. Micah has always had the ability, and does it consciously. You do not."

"So why can I do it now, with you?"

"By observing Micah and Lelindia, seeing how her energy field interacted with our physiology and how he communicated with us, I hypothesized a way to use the connection of your energy field and physical touch to open a pathway, allowing me to unlock that part of your mind to your consciousness."

Impressive. And a little frightening.

The touch of Ifel's fingers on her face lightened. "You have nothing to fear from me, as I have nothing to fear from you. We are... the same."

"The same? You mean leaders?"

"Guardians."

Guardians. A single word, but the meaning behind it covered galaxies.

Ifel was right. They were the same. "Yes." A block of ice formed in her belly. "That's why I can't ask you to help us. You need to protect your people."

Ifel didn't move, but through their connection it felt like she'd settled into a chair and was gazing at Aurora with a speculative look in her eyes. "You do not believe I can help you and protect my people?"

Well, when she put it that way. But... "You've met the Sovereign." She felt a ripple of revulsion and pain cut through Ifel like a blade. "You know the depth of her desire to bend others to her will, to subjugate them. And there's no one she hates more than me." Her heart bled, even now, for the teenage friendship that once was and the monster Reanne had grown into.

"She is coming for you?"

"Yes. And she will do anything, kill anyone, to get to me." She'd made that clear.

"So you have chosen to go to her instead."

"In a way. I have no proof of who she is, what she's done. My people are unaware of her role. They also believe the Teeli are benign, passive. I need to show them who they really are. Who the Sovereign really is."

"And you will put yourself and your crew at risk to prove this?"

The ice in her belly hardened into steel. "I would gladly die to free my people from the Sovereign and the Teeli."

Ifel was silent for a moment. "We are the same."

Her words dragged a finger of dread across Aurora's soul. "No, we're not. You can't risk—"

"We are the same," Ifel repeated, her commanding tone leaving no room for doubt. "My people are trapped by the

Sovereign's machinations just as yours are. Her resources are vast, her grip firm. To free my people and yours, we must work together."

A soft whimper escaped Aurora's lips. "But you've already lost so much."

"And you have not? Your homeworld, your culture taken by the Teeli. You and your mother separated from your brother and father. Your people manipulated and tortured, turned against you."

Moisture gathered at the backs of Aurora's eyes. "What about the children you have onboard your ship? And your biosphere? Your homeworld's heritage?"

Ifel gave a snort. "Do you believe I would put them at risk? My ship is much more... adaptable, than yours. They will be safe."

An image of a spherical core wrapped in the emerald, black, and gold hull scales hung in space and then vanished in a blink beneath the Yruf camouflage.

Of course. Their ship was modular. She'd known that, counted on it as part of her plan, yet somehow she'd completely passed over the possibility of the Yruf taking only part of their ship into Teeli space.

And yet... "The Teeli will have a trap waiting for us. I don't know how large a force they will bring, but I'm anticipating an armada."

Ifel gave the mental equivalent of a hand wave. "The Teeli do not concern me. The Ecilam do."

Aurora gave a slight jerk. "I hadn't considered that."

"If the Sovereign is as intent on capturing you as you believe, she will make use of Tersinis."

"Tersinis?"

"The Ecilam leader." Ifel sighed, the air slipping through her lips in a hiss. "I have tried for two generations to broker a peace with the Ecilam, to end the animosity between us. I first met Tersinis when she was part of the Ecilam guard. She was young and idealistic, unlike Strudist, her predecessor, who treated my overtures with suspicion and contempt."

"You've had discussions with the Ecilam before?" She'd always assumed the only interactions the Setarip factions had with one another were armed conflicts.

"You are surprised?"

"Our experience with your civil war has been witnessing the factions trying to blow each other up. We've assumed that's the way you deal with each other."

Ifel flinched. "That is... inaccurate."

"I'm beginning to understand that."

"But not entirely wrong. Strudist died from injuries sustained during a terrible battle with Tnaryt, the leader of the Etah."

Aurora grimaced. "We've met."

Ifel fell silent, her emotions soft and gentle. "Yes, I know. I am sorry for the pain he caused you."

Aurora's teeth ground together. "It wasn't my pain that was the issue." But at least Tnaryt wouldn't hurt anyone ever again.

Ifel gave her a moment before picking up the thread of her story. "When Tersinis took over for Strudist, I had great hopes for a reconciliation. But shortly afterward I lost touch with her, with all the Ecilam."

The sadness Aurora felt was that of a parent mourning a rift with their adult child.

"We searched for years through what I later discovered was Teeli space, yet any time we drew close, the Ecilam would vanish. It was not until Tersinis reached out to me and requested a meeting to discuss our future that hope returned. I believed in her goodwill. Her desire to finally end the conflict." Bitterness overlaid her words like slime on a rotting cucumber. "Instead, she brought the Sovereign. I learned that day how far Tersinis' mind had been twisted and warped in the intervening years. Very little remains of the idealistic youth I knew."

"And you believe she'll be part of the trap the Teeli have laid?"

"The Sovereign would be a fool not to make use of her skills and knowledge."

Trepidation tap danced down her back. "Can the Ecilam see through your ship's camouflage?"

"No. We upgraded our technology after learning of the Sovereign's intentions. Our recent encounter with the Ecilam vessel was a successful test. They did not detect us." Melancholy overlaid her emotional field. "But we did not anticipate they would destroy their own ship."

"I don't think they did."

Ifel's fingers pressed tighter to Aurora's temples. "What do you mean?"

"I believe the Sovereign destroyed the ship. It's the way she operates. Destroy the evidence and take out the enemy at the same time."

"The evidence?" Horror and understanding arrived at the same time. "She views the Ecilam as *evidence*?"

"She views anyone and anything that could reveal her identity or weaknesses as disposable. Lives have no meaning to her, except her own." Kreestol might be the one exception, but she wasn't betting on that, either. At least her aunt would prove tougher to kill when Reanne finally turned on her.

Ifel's breath hissed in and out, her pupils fully dilated. "She is…" She seemed to be searching for a word that didn't exist in her language or experience.

But Aurora could provide one that matched what Ifel was feeling. "Psychotic. That's the term we have for those who have no empathy, no moral compass." And until she'd pulled back the hood on Reanne's cloak, she never would have believed it would apply to her former friend.

"Yes." Ifel was clearly struggling to keep her emotions under wraps. "We have no such concept. Our people can be reactionary, violent, destructive, but they act to protect their clutch, no matter how misguided their reasoning."

Huh. In her experience the Ecilam had shown psychotic tendencies. But then again, the Ecilam she'd encountered had been working with Reanne and the Teeli. Ifel had said Tersinis' mind had been warped. Could it be the Teeli had turned the Ecilam into the ruthless killers she'd encountered?

If that was true, and she and Ifel freed the Ecilam from Reanne's grip, would any part of who the Ecilam used to be remain to be saved?

Sixty-Two

After Aurora and Ifel left the observation lounge, Cade moved to stand in front of the wide windows, leaving Micah and Celia to entertain the four Yruf.

He could feel Aurora's turbulent emotions, and he understood her reasoning. But a small part of him — okay, a fairly significant part of him — hoped that Ifel would change Aurora's mind.

He didn't know what that would look like, or how Ifel planned to communicate with Aurora, but his own experiences with Ifel had proven she was quite resourceful. Maybe she'd figured out a way to bridge the language barrier.

Clasping his hands behind his back, he stared out at the Yruf ship. It was like standing at the base of Half Dome.

Reanne had seen the Yruf ship before, or part of it, at least. He'd learned that when Ifel had shared the memories of her meeting with Reanne and the female Ecilam, which had taken place on the Yruf ship. What he didn't know was how well versed Reanne was in what the Yruf ship could do.

She must have figured out by now that the Yruf had shown up at her rendezvous with Bare'Kold to engage the Ecilam in a discussion. She'd chosen to destroy the Ecilam ship rather than allow that to happen.

But Reanne had no way of knowing he'd made contact with the Yruf at that rendezvous, not unless her cruiser had managed to get an image of *Gladiator* before turning tail and running. Unlikely. His ship had been in the moon's shadow, and a fly speck compared to the Yruf ship.

That gave them a strong advantage. Reanne wouldn't expect Aurora and Ifel to have any connection, wouldn't be looking for the Yruf ship to be sniffing around the trap Reanne had laid in Teeli space. They'd never have a better opportunity to catch Reanne. They needed to take it.

He caught a reflection of movement in the window and turned. Micah, Celia, and the Yruf were walking the perimeter of the room, slowly making their way toward him.

"We use this room for large gatherings of the crew," Micah explained as he gestured around him, "and also meals." His words would be for Celia's benefit, to include her in the conversation, since Micah wasn't using Galish to communicate with the Yruf.

The Yruf's emotions revealed curiosity and appreciation. They seemed to enjoy learning more about the *Starhawke* and her crew. At some point he should ask Micah if the Yruf had been able to see through the *Starhawke*'s hull camouflage while Jonarel was testing it.

Micah glanced his way and winked.

Cade grinned back. Micah's sense of humor was very similar to his own, and they shared a fascination for the Yruf. He'd also learned Micah delighted in getting Aurora to loosen up and laugh as much as he did. He'd never had a brother, but given a choice, he'd pick Micah. The feeling seemed to be mutual.

"Feel free to explore," Micah said, indicating the expansive space.

The Yruf split up, strolling about the room.

"Can you tell if Aurora's been able to communicate with Ifel?" Celia asked Micah as they joined Cade at the windows.

The question lacked the suspicion that had overlaid every comment she'd made to Micah since they'd met at Stoneycroft. Instead, she sounded like a security officer asking a trusted member of her team for a status report. Quite a change from her attitude before they'd gone over to the Yruf ship.

A crease appeared between Micah's brows. "I'm not sure. Something's happening, but when I try to tune in, it's like hitting a wall of static. How about you?" he asked Cade.

He concentrated on Aurora's emotions. There was a familiarity to the rhythm of what came through. "They're definitely communicating. I can feel an ebb and flow that would fit a dialogue." He paused as the emotional output from Ifel suddenly eclipsed Aurora's. All the Yruf turned toward the galley door at the same time. "Ifel's disturbed by something."

"Aurora?" Celia took a step toward the door but Cade moved to block her.

"No. Aurora's fine. They're both fine. It's just..." He shook his head, unable to define it. He turned toward the door. "I think they're wrapping things up."

Celia shot him a look, but didn't head for the galley, just kept her gaze on the door.

Aurora's steps faltered as she and Ifel entered the observation lounge and found the three of them and the four Yruf all standing like statues, staring at the doorway. "Problem?" she asked Cade as she strode toward him.

"Nope. Just knew you were coming."

Her gaze swept the room and she gave a rueful laugh. "I keep forgetting I'm not the only empath onboard anymore."

"I take it you were able to communicate?" Cade glanced toward Ifel and back to Aurora.

"Yes. We had to be in physical contact with my energy field engaged, but the dialogue was seamless. No language barrier."

"Really?" He hadn't expected that. "What did you discuss?" He followed her back to the oblong table where Ifel and the guards had reclaimed their seats.

She gave him a self-deprecating smile as she sat down. "You'll be delighted to know the Yruf will be coming with us into Teeli space."

He bit back his own smile, not wanting her to mistake it for gloating.

She chuckled. "It's okay. You can say it. You were right and I was wrong. But they'll be leaving their biosphere and the majority of the Yruf here."

"Ah." So Ifel had found a solution to Aurora's primary objection. "How much of their ship will be going with us?"

"We didn't go into the details." Aurora's gaze shifted to Ifel. "But that will be up to her. Enough that she's confident we can deal with the Teeli. She's more concerned about the Ecilam."

"The Ecilam? She thinks they'll be there?"

"Definitely." Aurora proceeded to give them a summary of what she'd learned regarding Tersinis, the Ecilam leader.

When she finished, Cade wanted to bang his head on the table. "So the Ecilam are victims of Reanne and the Teeli as well?"

"Looks that way. And I'm sure Reanne painted the Yruf as public enemy number one after Ifel rejected her." Aurora smirked. "Well, public enemy number two."

Celia rested her forearms on the table, her gaze flicking between Ifel and Micah. "What role would the Ecilam play as part of the trap?"

Micah relayed the question to Ifel and focused on her response.

"The Ecilam ships are faster and more maneuverable than anything the Teeli have," he said. "They also have some camouflaging ability. Nothing like we or the Yruf do, but if they're not out in the open, they're difficult to detect."

Celia tapped her index finger lightly on the tabletop. "So they'd be the herding dogs, driving us toward the Teeli's enclosure."

Micah gazed at her with a raised brow. "Are we the sheep in that analogy?"

Amusement flashed in Celia's eyes. "I'm guessing that's how the Teeli view us."

"I'm sure you're right," Aurora agreed, as Micah conveyed the interchange to Ifel. "Which is their mistake. Where they see sheep, I see a well-organized wolf pack."

Her gaze moved to Ifel. "The question is, how do we capture Reanne without harming the Ecilam? If Tersinis' mind is as warped as Kreestol's, she'll do anything to protect Reanne from us, no matter the risk to herself or the rest of the Ecilam. Kreestol's loyalty was manic, fanatical. There was no reasoning with her. It's unlikely we'll be able to reason with Tersinis, either."

Micah gave a snort. "We tranquilize the herding dogs."

"What?" Cade and Aurora asked at the same time.

"The technology that landed Justin in the med bay was designed for the Ecilam," Micah clarified, "to quickly render them unconscious and allow the Yruf to gain control of their ship. The reason it didn't work the way they'd planned was the Ecilam ship had Teeli shielding adaptations that prevented the tech from penetrating their hull the way it did *Gladiator*'s."

"But they were still able to disable the Ecilam ship," Cade pointed out.

Micah nodded. "They modified the tech during the fighting to compensate. That's how they finally got through the shielding so the tech could knock out the Ecilam onboard. Unfortunately, the Yruf didn't anticipate that Reanne would trigger a self-destruct. They'd never witnessed anything like it until that encounter."

"The Ecilam don't use auto-destructs?"

"None of the Setarips do. It's a foreign concept to them. They'll fight and they'll run, but destroying their own ships and the crew onboard wouldn't even occur to them."

"Even to prevent capture?"

Micah frowned as he listened to Ifel's response to the question. "Setarips don't take prisoners."

A chill cooled Cade's blood. "So that's why they're so destructive to each other? They don't stop fighting until they finish each other off?"

Micah's head tilted to one side. "That's not it." He blew out a breath and ran a hand through his hair. "It's complicated, hard to put into words, but apparently each faction has its own code that governs their interactions. For the Yruf, if they disable another ship, it's a prelude to peace talks. If the talks fail, they leave the ship and crew unharmed."

"And the Ecilam? What's their code?" Cade asked.

Micah met his gaze. "Ifel knows what it used to be, not how they will respond now."

"Okay, what did it used to be?"

Micah winced. "It roughly translates as *the weak are left behind.*"

"No heroes or compassion in the Ecilam, then." But not as horrifying a code as he would have guessed based on their past behavior.

"You said tranquilize the herding dogs," Aurora said, leaning back in her chair. "How do you propose we do that?"

Micah shook his head. "Not us. Them." He motioned to Ifel. "Now that they've studied the remains of the Ecilam ship, they have a solid understanding of the Teeli modifications, including the self-destruct mechanism. They should be able to disable and disarm all Ecilam ships in the system at the same time."

Aurora shot him a quizzical look. "But we don't know how many there will be."

Micah gave her a small smile, his gaze flicking to Ifel. "Doesn't matter. They can subdivide their ship into as many vessels as they need to get the job done."

Cade stared at him. "You're kidding."

"Nope."

His gaze swung to Ifel. "And you have enough pilots to pull that off?"

Her tongue flicked out almost lazily.

"Most Yruf are trained in basic piloting skills, but you're also forgetting their technology," Micah answered him. "Just as they were able to automate *Gladiator*'s movements when they took control, they can do the same with their own ships."

Oh, he so wanted to see how that tech worked on the inside. "So the extra ships function as drones?"

Micah's eyes narrowed. "I think so. Something like that. The functionality is different from anything we have, so I'm not clear on the logistics."

Cade picked up on a tremor of excitement from Aurora. "You're liking how this is shaping up, aren't you?"

"Yes, I am. I'm also wondering if that same technology could be used to disable Reanne's cruiser."

Micah conveyed the question to Ifel.

It generated more of a reaction than Cade would have anticipated. Her head bowed on her curving neck, discomfort evident in every line of her body.

Micah cleared his throat. "Their technology should allow them to take control of the cruiser's guidance systems, but that doesn't solve the problem. She's unwilling to try disabling the crew with the same method they used on *Gladiator*. Not after seeing how they unintentionally hurt Justin. They don't want to risk causing similar trauma again."

Aurora didn't seem surprised by the response. "I understand. She doesn't want to harm any of the Teeli."

Which was the flip side of a pacifist culture. Even an enemy intent on death and destruction wouldn't trigger a lethal response.

"Could their tech disable the weapons on the Teeli ship?" Cade asked. Then at least the Teeli couldn't fire at them.

Micah nodded slowly. "Yes, although the larger the ship, the more time it will take for the tech to proliferate."

"We could use our hull camouflage so we didn't present a target while the tech did its work," Aurora countered.

"And when Reanne figures out what's happening?" Celia asked. "What's to stop her from finding a different way to destroy the ship before we can haul it back to Sol Station? She's too smart not to have contingency plans in place. She's proven that."

"True." Aurora sighed, then propped her chin on the heel of her hand. "What do you think, Cade? You've spent more time with her recently than I have."

"She'll do whatever it takes to slip the trap and leave a wasteland behind her. What we saw of the personal transport she used to escape last time suggested advanced technology, and a reinforced hull." His gaze met Celia's. "Would you agree? You saw it up close."

"It's a stealth vessel, for sure, modified with heavy plating to withstand a serious assault. It wouldn't surprise me if she's upgraded all the systems since our last encounter, considering how close Aurora got to bringing her down. It would have made her feel vulnerable, and I'm guessing that's an emotion she hates almost as much as she hates Aurora."

Aurora flinched, but didn't disagree.

"Is the tracking device you tagged it with still working?" he asked.

Celia shrugged. "No way to know unless she brings the ship into Fleet space and I get a ping on the ICS, or we get close enough in Teeli space for the *Starhawke* to pick up the signal directly."

"But we would detect her if she's in the system?"

"Yep. Gonzo told me you picked up the signal during the rendezvous with Bare'Kold, so we know it was still active then. If the *Starhawke* hadn't been escaping from Kraed space at the time, I would have gotten the ICS alert when her ship dropped out of the jump window into Fleet space."

Aurora laced her fingers together on the tabletop. "For argument's sake, let's assume the tracker still works, and that even if she tries to flee, we'll be able to catch up with her. That leaves the problem of preventing her from destroying the Teeli ship or ships she leaves behind." Her gaze moved to Ifel. "Do you have any recommendations?"

Ifel's long fingers folded together in a mirror image of Aurora's gesture.

"She'd like to have Ahle talk to Lelindia and Dr. Williams," Micah said. "The Yruf knowledge of Teeli physiology is extremely limited. But perhaps working together they might come up with a way to adapt their technology for quickly disabling the Teeli before they can harm themselves."

Aurora nodded. "We still have a little leeway before we're expected to arrive in Teeli space. Why don't we take a break so everyone can get some rest, then tackle the problem with a fresh start."

Cade sensed Ifel's assent before Micah confirmed it. "She agrees."

"Good." Aurora stood. "Cade and I will see the Yruf to the shuttle bay. You two." She pointed at Micah and Celia. "Get some shuteye."

Micah gave her a crooked smile. "Aye-aye, Captain."

Sixty-Three

Lelindia didn't even make it a few steps off the lift before her cabin door opened and Jonarel's arms closed around her, drawing her against the solid wall of his chest as he buried his face in her hair.

"You were gone so long."

The lament in his tone made her smile, which thankfully he couldn't see. She tilted her head back, the silken strands of his hair tickling her cheek. "I had a lot of healing to do."

His large hand cradled her head with exquisite tenderness, his fingers massaging her scalp. "They treated you well?"

"Very well." Her eyelids slid closed of their own accord, a moan escaping her lips. "That feels heavenly."

The brush of his lips over hers added to the sensory experience, though he kept his touch light. "You need to rest," he murmured, scooping her into his arms before she could respond, and carrying her into her cabin.

Correction. *Their* cabin.

Her eyes widened as she took in her surroundings.

Where previously an interior bulkhead had separated her cabin from his, now the front room filled the expansive space. Jonarel had rearranged the seating, bringing it into the center to form a conversation circle similar to the setup at Stoneycroft.

The workstation with his drafting table still sat on his side of the joined cabins, while the potted plants remained on her side.

Her gaze swung to meet his. "You've been busy."

Uncertainty flickered in his eyes. "Do you like it?"

"Like it? It's amazing." She wriggled in his grip, wanting to explore, and he set her lightly on her feet.

"I wanted it to feel like home."

The longing in his voice made her chest hurt. She turned in his arms, resting her hands on his shoulders. "It is home. There's nowhere else I'd rather be."

"Thank you, checana."

"No, thank you." Rising onto tiptoes, she gave him a soft kiss before stepping out of his arms. "I didn't think you'd be able to make the changes so soon. I expected—" She halted as her gaze fell on a familiar object that was now attached in the exact center of the bulkhead between the archways leading into each of their bedrooms. "Oh, Jonarel."

Keenan's drawing couldn't have found a more fitting setting. The textured bark of the bulkhead framed the image like an owl's face peeking out from a tree.

Jonarel's hand settled onto her shoulder. "I wanted it to have a place of honor."

Her throat closed up as she gazed at the image. She nodded vigorously, not wanting him to take her silence as disagreement.

His arms circled her from behind, pulling her close as he nuzzled her hair. "Would you like to see the bedroom?"

More nodding.

Twining his fingers through hers, he led her through the archway to her room. The sight that greeted her was every bit as enchanting as the rest of the transformation.

In here, the interior bulkhead had been altered, but remained partially intact. Jonarel had cleared the section that separated her sleeping nook from his, adapting it into a larger nook that opened into each cabin on either side.

It looked like the coziest bower in the world, with a similar appeal as the tree hollow in the forest around Stoneycroft where she'd go to meditate and tackle thorny problems.

"Will this arrangement give you enough privacy? Personal space?" The hesitancy was back in his voice.

She'd been silent too long. Clearing her throat, she forced herself to form words. "I may never want to leave this cabin again."

His golden eyes glowed in the soft light.

She didn't offer any resistance as he slowly devested her of her clothes, his fingers and lips touching down on the exposed skin like the brush of butterfly wings.

He clearly wasn't trying to seduce her, but his tender ministrations combined with the tantalizing surroundings sparked a stronger response than he'd intended. He gave a startled gasp as she pulled him into a deep kiss.

The gasp melted into a groan of surrender. His clothes quickly joined hers in a puddle on the deck before he followed her down to the welcoming nook, his large body pressing against hers in a multitude of delectable places.

She loved his tenderness, his self-control when he could so easily dominate her, but right now she wanted... *this. Oh, yes, this.*

Conscious thought fled in a river of sensation, her entire being opening to him, welcoming him, and accepting all he had to give.

Which was quite a lot indeed.

By the time her breathing returned to normal, her body felt like liquid goo.

Happy liquid goo, though.

Jonarel nuzzled the side of her neck as they lay spooned together. "I was not expecting that," he rumbled in a voice thick with satisfaction.

She grinned, turning to look at him over her shoulder. "You thought I'd go to sleep like a good little girl after you surprised me with this?" But as she held his gaze the grin faded. "I missed you."

His arm tightened around her waist, the look in his golden eyes sending squiggles through her body. "And I, you."

She would never tire of gazing into his eyes. She could do it for hours and hours and...

Her breath caught as her mind overlaid his face with a different image, one she'd toyed with on the bridge, but which now held her transfixed — the image of a petite Kraed female with dark hair and golden eyes just like Jonarel's.

"You have that look again."

She blinked, the child's image dissipating.

"What is it, Lelindia?" He rose onto his forearm, hooking his leg over hers and locking her against the length of his body. "Please tell me what is in your thoughts."

She hesitated, suddenly nervous. They'd never talked about children. He'd never even brought the subject up in regards to Aurora back when he'd been convinced they were destined to mate. She had no idea how he felt about the concept, which suddenly seemed like a major oversight and a scary mountain to climb on her own.

"Lelindia?" Concern clouded his gaze.

Maybe it was spending time with Typar that had her teetering on the edge. Or being in the Yruf's biosphere, surrounded by all the lives they had been determined to save and nurture. Whatever the reason, she couldn't let it go.

But she needed a graceful way to break the ice. Too bad she used a sledgehammer instead. "Do you like kids?" she blurted, then winced. Eloquence was not a gift she possessed.

"Kids?" he repeated, like the word was unfamiliar.

She gathered her courage. If she was going to dive into this frozen pond, might as well do it in one bold move. "Or more to the point, do you want to be a father?" She sucked in a breath and held it, waiting.

His expression transformed like shifting sand, difficult to read, but he didn't pull away.

Was that a good sign?

His breathing was no longer steady, either. "You want to bear our child?" The question came out in a whisper.

She still couldn't tell if he was excited by the possibility or horrified. But she wasn't backing off. "If you're willing... yes, I want that very much."

His fingers tightened, his face contorting. In anger? Pain? Or... she didn't know what. "If I am willing?" he repeated. "Lelindia—"

Whatever he was planning to say next got cut off as his lips came down on hers in a kiss that fried every brain cell she had. This kiss wasn't about physical pleasure, or even emotional connection.

This kiss was about awe, wonder, and joy. He wasn't just kissing her. He was worshipping her.

By the time he lifted his head they were both panting and she was firmly pinned beneath him, every millimeter of skin in contact with his body.

He rested his forehead against hers, his breath blowing like a warm tropical breeze across her lips. "Is it truly possible? We could..." He couldn't seem to say the words.

"Create a child together?" she supplied. "Yes, I believe so. All the signs are there, and after all, I am the Nedale. Nurturing life is kind of my thing."

He chuckled, the resonant sound seeming to catch him by surprise as much as her. "A child," he murmured. "Our child."

She soaked up the warmth and promise in his eyes like sunshine. "So you like the idea?"

The warmth grew. "Oh, yes. I like the idea very much." He kissed her again, his tongue tracing the curve of her lips. "How soon?"

His talented tongue was making it hard to focus. It took her a moment to figure out what he was asking. "You mean how soon before we can conceive?" For Suulh, conception required conscious preparation. She couldn't flip it on like a switch, especially with Jonarel already flipping all her switches.

His lips moved to her cheek, her eyelids, the bridge of her nose. "Yes." It was a possessive growl rather than a word as his body merged with hers.

"*Oh. Very soon.*" It was less a response to his question than to the delicious sensations he was generating.

His growl rumbled louder, his fingers lacing through hers, putting her completely at his mercy.

Her heart beat like a bass drum, but her vulnerability generated no fear, only delight as she held his liquid gold gaze. All the power above her and moving within her was hers to command. He was claiming her, yes, but also giving himself to her with equal passion.

And she would do no less. Lifting her head she caught his mouth with hers, demanding his surrender right along with hers as the universe exploded around her.

Sixty-Four

Lelindia woke to the pleasant aroma of lemongrass ginger tea. When she opened her eyes she found Jonarel walking toward her, fully dressed with a mug of tea in his hands. His thick hair was slightly damp, curling around his nape, indicating he'd showered while she'd slept. "Morning," she greeted him, her voice heavy with sleep.

He held the mug out to her. "Aurora has requested your presence in the med bay. One of the Yruf wishes to work with you on a project pertaining to the Teeli."

She sat up and accepted the mug, sipping the refreshing liquid as she processed what he'd said, and more importantly, how he'd said it. He wasn't happy with the situation. "You don't like being hidden away from the Yruf, do you?"

The corners of his mouth turned down, confirming her assessment. "Aurora has her reasons."

"I know." And she'd agreed with them at first. But after spending the day on the Yruf ship, and particularly after her interaction with Typar, she chafed at the idea of keeping Jonarel's presence a secret from them. They'd have to find out about him eventually. Why not now?

She glanced toward the ceiling and raised her voice. "Forrest to Hawke."

Aurora's response came from the cabin speakers. "Hawke here."

"I understand I'm needed in the med bay."

"That's right. Ahle and a few of his colleagues want to coordinate with you and Williams on potential methods for disabling the Teeli without causing injury. They want to avoid a repeat of the damage they unintentionally inflicted on Justin. Ahle's headed over to the *Starhawke* now."

She took another sip, holding Jonarel's gaze. "That's fine. But I want Jonarel to come down to the med bay with me."

The beats of silence that followed gave her a pretty good idea of the expression on Aurora's face. "You do realize that might cause an uproar. And confusion."

"Keeping him hidden will cause a bigger uproar." And she wasn't talking about with the Yruf. After what she and Jonarel had shared last night, after the decision they'd made, she wasn't about to leave him alone in their cabin.

"I see." No doubt Aurora was tuning into her emotions and realizing exactly what she meant. And how immovable she was on this point. "Then I guess you'll be introducing him to Ahle and the other Yruf he's bringing with him."

"I'll be happy to." Especially if Jonarel kept looking at her the way he was now, like she'd hung the moon.

"Micah and I will meet Ahle's group in the shuttle bay and see you in the med bay in fifteen minutes."

"We'll be there." Sliding over on the bed, she brushed a kiss on Jonarel's cheek.

He caught her arm, his hand warm against her skin. "Thank you."

"You're welcome." Taking another swallow of her tea, she set the mug on the side table beside the nook and hurried into her bathroom for a quick shower and change of clothes.

As they strolled together to the lift she twined Jonarel's fingers in hers. "When the Yruf see us, I want to make it clear how I feel about you," she said as she gazed up at him. "The Yruf trust me. They're going to have to trust you, too."

He pulled her into his arms as they stepped onto the lift. "My brave checana. You honor me."

She rested her free hand on his chest. His heart was beating faster than normal. He wasn't as calm as he appeared. She leaned into him. "I love you."

"And I love you." He bent to give her a feather kiss before the lift doors parted.

Aurora and Micah were already in the med bay with Williams, Ahle, Cegra, and three other Yruf. She recognized one of the Yruf, a lemon-yellow and white female she'd seen during her stint in the Yruf ICU. The other two were unfamiliar, one a female whose scales were similar to Ifel's emerald green except with splotches of gold paint like ink blots, and an almost all white male with a repeating oval pattern in black. They all turned as the med bay doors opened.

Jonarel's grip on her hand tightened and his steps slowed as the Yruf reacted to his appearance.

Ahle's head tilted almost vertical as his gaze swept Jonarel from head to toe, his tongue flicking back and forth. Cegra stood straighter, her staff gripped more tightly in her hand. The other three Yruf bobbed their heads side to side, a movement she associated with agitation.

She tugged Jonarel forward, stopping beside Ahle. "Ahle." She placed her palm on Jonarel's chest. "Jonarel."

Ahle held Jonarel's gaze as they stood eye-to-eye, nearly the same height. "John-uh-ruhl," he repeated, his gaze settling on where Jonarel's hand clasped hers. He reached out a long finger to Jonarel's face, holding it suspended a centimeter above his skin.

"He's asking permission to touch you," Micah said from his post beside Aurora.

Jonarel tilted his head toward Ahle, who began tracing the thin brown lines that trailed across Jonarel's green skin. Jonarel held perfectly still, taking in Ahle's appearance with a similar analytical eye.

Ahle glanced at Lelindia. "Suulh?"

She and Micah had explained the difference between Humans and Suulh during yesterday's healing session, when they'd conveniently had one of each as examples – Celia, a human, herself, a Suulh, and Micah, a hybrid.

"No, Kraed." She flicked a glance at Micah. "Did you–"

He shook his head. "I didn't say anything to them since I wasn't sure how you wanted to approach this. Give me a moment."

As the five Yruf turned in Micah's direction, Lelindia pressed against Jonarel, offering him the tactile nearness she knew would calm him.

As he had yesterday, Micah gave a verbal translation in Galish as he communicated mostly non-verbally with the Yruf. "The Kraed were the first alien race Humans encountered. They helped us save our world from ecological disaster, and also taught us how to travel the stars."

Which had altered the course of hers and Aurora's lives, too. Humans and Suulh both owed a great debt to the Kraed, but that didn't change the fact that Siginal's outrageous actions against her, Jonarel, Tehar, Aurora, and the rest of the crew were unreasonable and heavy-handed.

Jonarel shifted behind her, his arms encircling her waist, his chin resting lightly on top of her head.

"The Kraed and Humans founded the Galactic Council, our governing body, and they have been our allies ever since. Jonarel designed and built this ship for Aurora."

"And for you," Jonarel whispered in her ear, the brush of his lips against her skin making her shiver.

Truth be told, after all they'd been through together on this ship, and the fact that she'd served as the acting captain on two missions, the ship felt as much hers as Aurora's anyway. It reminded her of how her family and Aurora's had shared Stoneycroft, a communal home for them all. Aurora's actions indicated she agreed with that assessment.

Ahle turned back to Jonarel, absorbing the picture she and Jonarel made as he held her close, leaving no doubt of their relationship. He asked a question she didn't understand.

"In a way," Micah answered. "Jonarel's father is a leader of the Kraed, so Jonarel is a leader too, but Aurora is captain of the *Starhawke*. His coloring, in fact all Kraed coloring, doesn't mark biological sex or societal roles. It's for camouflage on their homeworld." Micah paused, then chuckled. "Not from each other. They have a lot of big, bad predators on their planet."

Lelindia looked between Micah and Ahle. "He thought the Kraed fought amongst themselves?"

Micah shrugged. "He's a doctor. He knows the physique of a warrior when he sees one. It was a logical supposition that they might battle each other."

"Hmm." She'd never considered whether there was a time in Drakar's history when the Kraed clans hadn't gotten along. She didn't want to imagine what that would look like.

Ahle's gaze continued to shift between her and Jonarel. He asked Micah another question.

"Yes, they're a mated pair, even though they're different species."

She fought a smile as she began to understand the line of Ahle's questioning. As a doctor, he was clearly intrigued by the unusual nature of hers and Jonarel's relationship from a biological standpoint. True, she and Jonarel were more similar biologically than she and Ahle were, but he still might be wondering exactly how it worked, especially from a mating standpoint.

Not that she planned to go into any details with him. But if he was curious about Kraed physiology, she could pull up data from the ship's archives for him to study.

Which brought up another point. Turning her head, she met Jonarel's gaze. "What about Tehar? Do you want to introduce her?"

Concern flickered over his handsome face. His gaze moved to Aurora and Micah. "What are your thoughts?"

Micah answered first. "The Yruf have been pretty open with us about their ship, letting us explore the biosphere and bridge, showing us what the ship's capable of." His hand massaged the back of his neck as he turned to Aurora. "But they certainly haven't shared technological details. Like how the undulating bulkheads and modular separation works. It's a tough call."

Aurora drew in a breath, releasing it just as slowly. "I believe they would keep the secret of the Nirunocs' existence to themselves. They understand the importance of protecting all life from potential harm." She held Jonarel's gaze. "But whether they would understand and accept who Star is, what she represents, is harder to know. The choice is yours."

Jonarel's muscles tensed, and his jaw tightened. He shook his head. "The choice is Tehar's."

Sixty-Five

Aurora had been paying close attention to the emotions of the Yruf from the moment Lelindia and Jonarel had walked into the med bay. Their initial surprise and alarm had quickly given way to curiosity, especially as Jonarel and Lelindia's behavior had made it clear exactly what type of relationship they had.

Lelindia's time on the Yruf ship saving lives probably had a lot to do with the Yruf's relatively easy acceptance of Jonarel. They trusted Lelindia, and since she'd made it clear how she felt about him, the Yruf were willing to trust Jonarel as well.

But Aurora had been right about one thing. She could tell his coloring was confusing the heck out of them. After meeting Humans and Suulh, and at least having a passing idea of what the Teeli looked like, all of whom had neutral-toned hair and skin, discovering a species that had coloring more like their own but who resembled Humans and Suulh was tripping them up.

So was the idea of cross-species mating. Ahle, Cegra, and the yellow and white Yruf seemed fascinated, but the other two Yruf's emotions suggested they were having trouble even grasping the concept. Which made her suspect the five Setarip factions didn't intermate, either, at least not in recent history. Had that been partly responsible for their civil war? Had a lack of intermingling created feelings of separation and "otherness" that ripped them apart?

And how would they feel about a non-biological lifeform like Star?

Jonarel had said it was Star's decision. She wholeheartedly agreed. "Do you and Lelindia want to take a few minutes in the greenhouse with Star to discuss it?"

"I think you and Jonarel should go," Lelindia answered. "This decision will impact the three of you more than me. Tam and I can start working with the Yruf."

Jonarel met Aurora's gaze, then reluctantly released Lelindia. "We will return soon."

As Micah stepped in to act as translator for Lelindia and Williams, Aurora slipped into the greenhouse with Jonarel.

Star was waiting for them, her projected image making her look like a goddess of the forest emerging from among the flowering vines that twined along the trellised pathway.

Aurora spread her hands as the door closed behind them. "Well, Star, what do you think?"

Star tilted her head in a perfect imitation of a move Lelindia often made when pondering a challenging situation. "My species is unknown to anyone besides my people and this crew. Sharing our existence with the Yruf poses certain... concerns."

"Such as?" She could think of one glaring one, but she was curious what Star had come up with.

"My father would be furious."

Yep, that was the one lit by flashing neon and spotlights. "Anything else?"

"I am yet another new species for them, one that resembles Jonarel in this form, but am entirely different in actual form." She glanced at Jonarel. "And I do not have the same connection with Lelindia that Jonarel does to assuage their concern."

So Star had picked up on that non-verbal interaction, too. "I don't think that would be a major hurdle. The real question is do you see a benefit to revealing your presence to the Yruf?"

Star shifted her weight, making Aurora smile to herself. Technically Star had no weight, but she was rapidly picking up the crew's mannerisms and integrating them into her visual behavior. "I was able to observe the interior of their ship through my link to my shuttle while you were meeting Ifel. I have also studied the Yruf transport in our bay. Based on that data, I suspect they have a non-biological entity as part of their ship design and communications systems."

"Really?" Star had postulated that idea before they'd met the Yruf, but she'd been silent about it ever since. Apparently she'd been waiting for the right moment to share her theory. "How similar do you think this entity is to you?"

"In function with the ship, it could be very similar. But I believe what you call drones are in fact a mobile physical expression of that entity, the equivalent of this projection." Star swept a hand down her body.

"Huh." She hadn't paid much attention to the drones they'd encountered. Now she wished she had. "So the supposed drones are actually connected to the sentient non-biological entity?"

"If I am correct. It would be an elegant way for the Yruf to have a physical presence in all parts of the ship without risking biological hazards or danger. Destruction of the egg-shaped companion pieces would likely not injure the non-biological entity, just as a weapon striking this projection would not injure me."

"But if the ship were damaged, the entity would be, too."

Star acknowledged the point. "In certain instances, yes, though I would expect the entity to be able to move fluidly through the entire system, thus preventing any single point of damage to cause a significant problem."

"Would the presence of a non-biological being explain how they're able to subdivide into so many smaller vessels and still remain closely integrated?"

"Perhaps. If so, the entity's abilities give it a much stronger and more nuanced bond than I have with my shuttles. I require a physical connection for true integration."

A connection Aurora still didn't fully understand but accepted the same way she accepted Star's existence. She turned to Jonarel. "Any thoughts now that you've met the Yruf?"

His gaze moved from her to Star and back again. "They have treated Lelindia with great respect, and have not taken advantage of their superior size and numbers. If you and Tehar believe they are trustworthy, I have no objections."

"Star?"

"I am, to use a Human phrase, in uncharted water. I would like to learn if there is another being onboard who is similar to myself, but I do not have any basis for making contact. I cannot project myself on my shuttles, or move beyond their bulkheads to explore the Yruf ship."

"Good point."

"If we were on Drakar, the Nirunoc network could be used to bridge the gap with the Yruf entity, to make a physical connection with it. I do not have such a system available in space. I have only what is built into my ship. I also do not know how the other entity communicates with the Yruf."

Aurora frowned, mentally replaying the interactions she'd seen between the Yruf and the drones. "Ifel talked to a drone at least once, so I think the entity can understand some form of verbal communication. And we have Micah. He can communicate with the Yruf, and they can communicate with the entity. It might feel like a version of the telephone game for a while, at least until we can establish common parameters with the other being." She held Star's gaze. "Or there's a chance you're wrong, and the Yruf don't have a non-biological onboard."

Star's projection shimmered, her version of a wince. Aurora could feel it in a subtle way, like a ghosting of emotion wafting through the room.

"If I reveal myself, I will have to trust the Yruf to keep my existence a secret regardless."

And there was the rub. "The Yruf seem to be champion secret-keepers, but it's your call, Star. I understand a thing or two about the importance of keeping secrets, and the ripple effect when they're revealed. Only you know whether this is the right step for you."

Star pursed her lips, her expression reminding Aurora of Jonarel's mother, Daymar. "If I were able to make contact with their entity, if we could work together while in Teeli space, it would give us a powerful advantage against the Teeli."

"How so?"

"In a battle situation we would be able to coordinate our movements and help implement the best tactical strategy."

"Giving you and the other entity overwatch capability?"

"Exactly."

A memory surfaced of the battle at Burrow when Star had fired one of the *Starhawke*'s weapons without an order, destroying one of the Teeli warships. It had saved the *Starhawke* from being captured, but had shocked Aurora. Until that moment, she hadn't realized Star could take control of the ship's weaponry.

Considering the Yruf's pacifist nature, they might consider that possibility a deal breaker for Star's plan. But they had a long way to go before that became a real concern.

"I believe revealing my existence to the Yruf is worth the risk." Star's gaze flicked to the door to the med bay and her chin lifted. "You and Cade trust them. Lelindia trusts them, and they have accepted Jonarel without objection. The potential advantages for us and the Yruf far outweigh the danger to me."

"You're sure? You don't want to think about it?"

Star shook her head, her dark hair swaying with the simulated motion. "I wish to meet the Yruf."

"Fair enough." She turned to Jonarel. "Are you prepared to work with the Yruf, too? Your experience with the Teeli ships and tech on Feylahn would likely help in figuring out the most effective non-lethal methods for disabling the vessels waiting for us."

"I would be happy to work with them."

His eagerness probably had as much to do with the opportunity to spend time with Lelindia as helping the Yruf.

"Star, I'll have Micah lay the foundation with the Yruf and then we'll see you in the med bay."

Star's image vanished as Aurora and Jonarel exited the greenhouse.

Jonarel gave a subtle nod in answer to Lelindia's questioning gaze. The info on the med bay monitors showed the data about Teeli physiology Lelindia and Williams had been sharing with the Yruf.

Aurora stopped beside Micah. "Star wants to meet the Yruf. She also believes they have a non-biological entity integrated with their ship."

Micah's brows lifted. "How did she figure that out?"

"Observation, mostly. But I need you to help me introduce her to our guests and then find out if she's right."

"Sure. How do you want to approach it?"

"Start by letting Ahle know we have another crewmember we want him to meet."

Micah nodded, facing Ahle and translating her message.

Ahle's emotional response indicated he was intrigued. So was Cegra. The other three Yruf were more cautious.

"Star?" Micah called out. "We're ready for you."

She materialized beside Jonarel, her hands folded.

All of the Yruf flinched, startled by her sudden appearance, but Ahle recovered quickly. He approached Star the same way he had Jonarel, his head doing the vertical tilt again.

Star raised her hands, palms flat like she was going to press them against a window – the gesture of greeting the Nirunoc used.

Ahle mirrored her pose, his longer fingers eclipsing Star's as his hands poked slightly through her projection and back out.

"Star." Star touched her hand to her chest, her voice coming from the ship's speakers.

Ahle glanced up, his gaze sweeping across the ceiling before returning to Star. "Ssstar." Other than a slight hiss, Ahle didn't have any trouble pronouncing her name. He swiveled his head in a fluid twist to face Micah.

"She's a non-biological entity," Micah translated in Galish after a few moments of interaction with Ahle. "Her species is called Nirunoc. They have a symbiotic relationship with the Kraed and live on the same homeworld."

Ahle's attention swung to Star for a moment, analyzing in his quiet way, before turning back to Micah with more questions.

"She's integrated with the ship, giving it life." Micah paused, his brow furrowing as he and Ahle had a back-and-forth exchange. "Human vessels don't work that way," he translated.

"In fact, humans aren't aware of the Nirunocs' existence. Our history with non-biological beings hasn't been positive. Star has trusted us with her secret, and she hopes you will honor that trust as well."

Ahle's tongue flicked up and down, then he lowered his head slightly in a micro-bow.

Micah's expression cleared, a slow smile curving his mouth as he focused on Star. "He's honored by your trust. The Yruf will keep your secret."

"Thank you."

"He's also curious what exactly you can do."

Star turned to the section of the med bay behind their group. The lights dimmed, then the floor moved. A med platform slid sideways and another rose from below to fill the open space. The monitors beside the new platform sprang to life a moment later, adding a warm glow.

Ahle's tongue flicked, more questions directed at Micah.

"No, she can't run the ship on her own. She needs a crew. But she can control many of the ship's physical elements and can monitor all of its systems."

Ahle took a moment to process that. Then he spoke a word in Galish, his pupils contracting. "*Guard?*"

"Yes," Star responded, taking a step closer to him. "I watch over and protect this crew. They are my family."

A pang tightened Aurora's chest. Intellectually she knew that was true, but hearing Star say it made it more tangible.

Micah translated Star's answer for the Yruf.

Ahle and Cegra shared a look, which probably included a silent conversation as well.

Star's attention remained firmly fixed on Ahle. "Micah, can you please ask him if I am correct about the existence of an entity similar to me on their ship?"

As Micah translated her request, Ahle's head lifted, almost as if he was scenting the air. After a long look at Star, he turned to Cegra. The two huddled together against the far wall, gazes locked.

"What do you think?" Aurora murmured to Micah.

"I think Star's right," he murmured back, "and they're contacting Ifel to discuss the issue before they respond."

"Can you hear their exchange?"

His lips thinned. "I probably could if I tried, but I'm learning to tune out private conversations. It feels disrespectful to listen in."

"Ah." She noted the two Yruf engineers were gazing at Star with frank fascination, their tongues flicking, their diamond-shaped pupils dilated. The yellow and white scaled Yruf seemed more intrigued with Jonarel. "I'm sure the Yruf will have a lot of questions for us to answer before this day is over."

"No doubt."

Ahle and Cegra broke up their huddle a moment later, returning to the group, their focus on Micah.

"Ifel is willing to introduce Star to their non-biologicals," he translated.

"Non-biologicals, plural?" Aurora clarified.

"That's right. Their non-biological isn't a single entity. They're an entire species."

Sixty-Six

"An entire species like the Nirunoc?" Aurora asked, her mind leaping through the possibilities. Star would be thrilled.

Or stunned.

Her projection had frozen.

She was probably focused on the Yruf ship outside.

"I don't think they're like the Nirunoc," Micah said. "I'm not sure what they are, actually. What I'm getting doesn't make a lot of sense."

Star's image flickered, turning to meet Aurora's gaze.

"Are you ready for this?" Aurora asked her. She'd never seen Star so off-kilter.

"I am uncertain."

That made two of them.

"I was prepared for one. But an entire species…" Star gave a self-conscious shrug.

"A bit more than you bargained for?"

Star nodded.

Aurora turned to Micah. "You said Ifel wants to introduce them. Does that mean the non-biologicals aren't integrated into the Yruf's transport?" Which seemed odd. As intertwined as all the Yruf tech was, she'd expect the non-biologicals to be part of the black-scaled transport sitting in their shuttle bay.

Micah pursed his lips for a long moment, his gaze unfocused. "The answer's rather complicated. I think they might be, but Ifel's decision is partly a matter of protocol. As leader, she's the only one with the authority to do an introduction. There's also a logistical component I'm not quite understanding. But Ifel specified she's bringing one of their smaller ships over to dock with the *Starhawke*."

"Not a personal transport?"

He was silent again, then shook his head. "I don't think they have another one. In fact, the one we've seen is an antique, dating back before the modular ship was fully functional. The Yruf have used the transport to visit us out of a sense of ceremony, to honor their traditions." He blinked, focusing on her. "Think of it like royalty arriving at important state events in horse-drawn carriages long after motorized vehicles were readily available."

"Interesting." Every time she interacted with the Yruf, she kept peeling back new layers. "Then direct Ifel to dock her ship at the airlock attached to shuttle bay two."

Ahle had joined the two Yruf engineers, who seemed to be involved in a quiet, extremely intense but respectful debate.

"What are they discussing?" she asked Micah.

"I think they're evaluating the advantages and risks of this proposition."

"Risks?" She stepped closer to Jonarel and lowered her voice. "Are there any risks we need to be worried about for Star?" She trusted the Yruf to take any necessary precautions, but she wanted Jonarel signing off on it, too. And supervising the interaction. She was way out of her depth when it came to a meet-and-greet between two non-biological species.

The caution in his eyes and emotional field confirmed he agreed with her. "That is difficult to know until we understand the nature of their non-biological and see what the Yruf have in mind."

Not the answer she was hoping for. She glanced at Lelindia. "We seem to have preempted the original plan. Do you want to stay here and work with the Yruf? Or come down to the shuttle bay with us?"

"Micah's going to need to go with you, right?"

"Definitely."

"Then I'm pretty useless here without him. Tam might be able to make some headway, since he figured out a method to communicate with Ahle the first time he was on the Yruf ship."

Aurora nodded to Williams. "Does that work for you?"

"I'll give it my best shot. Maybe Justin and Drew could fill in until you get back?"

"That's a great idea. Aurora to Cade."

"Yes ma'am?" He sounded delighted to be on the bridge with Kire, filling in for Kelly at navigation while she got some well-deserved sleep following her marathon shift the previous day and night.

"Are Justin and Drew available to come to the med bay? We need their help with the Teeli project."

"Sure. I'll send 'em on up."

"Thanks."

"Everything okay?"

"Yeah. Just a change of plans. I'll fill you in later, but don't be startled when a small Yruf ship detaches and docks with us."

"Hmm. Sounds intriguing."

"We'll see. Talk to you soon."

"I'll be here."

She turned to Lelindia. "Why don't you and Jonarel head on down to the bay with Star. Micah and I will join you as soon as everything's settled here."

Lelindia got the unspoken message – she and Jonarel were Star's support team. The Nirunoc still looked a little shellshocked.

"Good idea." Capturing Jonarel's hand in hers, Lelindia led him out of the med bay to the lift, Star's image dissolving as soon as the lift doors closed.

Williams gave Aurora a small smile. "Well done," he murmured, then busied himself pulling up additional Teeli data on the monitors.

The Yruf were still talking amongst themselves, giving Aurora a moment alone with Micah. "What else can you tell me about these entities we're about to meet?"

"Not much." He ran his hand across the back of his neck. "I got images of the biosphere, the modular ships, the drones, even those undulating bulkheads, but I also got a confusing mix of words that included *one, they, she, all,* and *mother.* I couldn't tell what related to the images or how it all fit together. Whatever these beings are, I'm not sure I have anything analogous in my experience. That's why it's hard to translate."

"Might be another reason the Yruf kept the beings' existence to themselves. They knew it would be tough for us to grasp."

"Hopefully it will make more sense when the ship docks."

Ahle turned his head in their direction. It looked like the debate was drawing to a close.

While Micah filled Ahle in on the new working plan, Justin and Drew walked into the med bay.

Drew's gaze fell on the two Yruf engineers. "Hey, I remember those two. They were working on *Gladiator* right before the Yruf dropped us off."

Which explained why the Yruf pair had seemed so comfortable when they'd boarded the *Starhawke*. They'd seen humans before.

Williams gave Drew and Justin a quick overview of the situation.

Justin whistled softly. "I was wondering about the possibility of a non-biological after spending time on their ship, but asking wasn't an option at the time. Good to know my instincts are still sharp."

Drew bumped him with her shoulder. "You are a born communicator, Byrnsie."

"You know it."

"Ready when you are, sis." Micah motioned to Aurora from across the room.

She held up a hand in acknowledgment. "Looks like one of the engineers is coming with us." The white and black male was waiting beside Micah, while the other four Yruf had clustered around the med bay monitors.

"Everyone good here?" she asked Justin, taking a step toward Micah.

Justin grinned. "You bet. I live for communication challenges. This'll be fun."

Sixty-Seven

For a being that didn't have any biological components, Tehar looked remarkably close to losing her lunch.

Her projected image kept flickering beside Lelindia as they stood in the shuttle bay, the image changing in subtle ways – her hairstyle, her clothing, the expression on her face.

Jonarel was missing all of it as he prepped the airlock to receive the Yruf ship.

"How are you feeling?" Lelindia asked in her best calm doctor's voice.

Tehar's hesitant answer emanated from the deck below them rather than from the overhead speakers, a method she used when she wanted to keep her voice from projecting. "I am... anxious. This is a new experience for me."

Lelindia could empathize. Tehar's reaction reminded her of how she'd felt on Feylahn when she'd encountered her grandmother. "It's a big step." Maybe she could distract her with questions. "Will there be any issues with docking? The Yruf ship won't be set for Fleet or Kraed standard."

Tehar frowned. "I am adaptable to non-standard configurations. I also do not believe Ifel would have taken this action if she was not certain she could dock."

Tehar had stopped flickering and shapeshifting. The distraction was working. Lelindia lobbed another question. "How exactly does that adaptability work?"

Tehar launched into an explanation full of technical terms that meant zip to Lelindia, but kept her focused on the topic rather than her anxiety. She was still talking when the shuttle bay hatch opened and Celia strolled in.

"Can I join the party?" she called out, flashing Tehar a warm smile.

Leave it to Celia to read the room correctly from the moment she walked in. Her smile had just the right mix of confidence, reassurance, and enthusiasm.

Tehar cut off her recitation. "Of course. As security chief, your presence was anticipated."

Celia's smile turned bemused as she met Lelindia's gaze. "Always nice to be anticipated. How's it going over there, Jonarel?"

He turned slowly, reluctantly. "The airlock is ready, although I will need to monitor for unforeseen problems." His jaw was tight, too.

Apparently Tehar wasn't the only one suffering from anxiety. Then again, he hadn't spent the time with the Yruf that the rest of them had. He was understandably concerned. He had no way of knowing how this interaction might damage the ship or Tehar.

Lelindia had complete faith in Ifel's judgment. She'd never met a race more focused on the Hippocratic ideal of *do no harm.*

The hatch opened again. Aurora, Micah, and the white and black scaled Yruf stepped inside. Aurora's gaze slid to Jonarel, her eyes narrowing briefly. His anxiety probably shone like a sparkler to her. "How long before Ifel arrives?"

Jonarel checked the display, which showed a feed of the camera view outside the airlock as well as a 3D representation of the approaching ship laid out on a grid with the *Starhawke*'s form at the center. "Three minutes."

Aurora gestured to the Yruf beside her. "Is it okay if Regas takes a look at the airlock settings to make sure we'll get a good seal?"

Annoyance flitted across Jonarel's face but vanished in an instant. "Of course." He stepped aside, allowing the Yruf access. However, she noticed he kept a close eye on the male's every move.

Aurora turned to Micah. "Do we have a name for these entities we're about to meet?"

Micah shook his head. "None that I could pick out from what the Yruf have shared with me."

"Then I guess we'll keep using *entity* until we have a better term."

Tehar flickered, drawing Lelindia's attention. Her tunic color had switched from moss green to dark brown.

Lelindia bit her cheek to keep from laughing. "I'm sure they're excited to meet you, too."

Tehar didn't look mollified. "I hope so."

"I know so. They'll adore you. You're amazing."

Neither the Kraed nor Nirunoc blushed, but Tehar managed a fair approximation of that reaction. "Thank you. I hope they agree."

"They will." Or they'd have her to answer to.

A faint metallic clink announced the Yruf ship's impending arrival at the airlock. Tehar's image flickered again, but this time it seemed to be a result of divided attention. Jonarel was operating the interlocking system, but Tehar would be monitoring every millimeter of the ship that came in contact with the Yruf vessel.

Lelindia glanced at the display image. A petite Yruf ship about four times the size of the black-scaled Yruf transport glided past the *Starhawke*'s stern and maneuvered gracefully into position beside the airlock. "Looks like our guests are here," she murmured.

Celia had moved slightly behind Tehar, her posture relaxed but alert as the exterior hatch signaled a seal lock and the airlock pressurized. Tehar and the Yruf entity might not need atmosphere, but the rest of them would be in a world of hurt if the shuttle bay ventilated into space.

The interior hatches hissed as they opened to connect the two ships. Tehar took several hesitant steps forward, peering into the dimly lit interior of the Yruf ship visible through the airlock. A moment later, Ifel appeared in the opening, ducking as she made her way through the *Starhawke*'s short airbridge into the shuttle bay.

Tehar's steps quickened. She halted a meter from Ifel and held her hands up in the Nirunoc greeting. "It is a pleasure to meet you, Ifel. I am Star."

Micah had moved forward, too, taking up his post as translator.

Ifel raised her hands and touched Tehar's, her pupils expanding and contracting as her fingers passed through. She studied the Nirunoc for several moments, her tongue darting out once.

Micah chuckled. "She's impressed with how lifelike your projection is," he told Tehar. "But she would have known you were not biological because you give off no scent."

Tehar's posture relaxed slightly. "My projection is not meant to confound. It is to honor my Kraed family." Her gaze shifted to Jonarel.

Ifel's head swiveled, those otherworldly eyes working double-time as she stared at Lelindia's mate.

Jonarel took it in stride, meeting Ifel's gaze calmly, even though he had to tilt his head back to do it.

Ifel didn't show any indication of the surprise or confusion Ahle had. Her brother must have filled her in on Jonarel's presence. Or maybe all the Yruf had a mental picture of him by now. The Yruf seemed extremely efficient at disseminating information.

Ifel's focus returned to Tehar.

"You asked to meet the—" Micah faltered in his translation. "All? One?" He shot Tehar an apologetic look. "I'm not sure what to call their entity. Entities. Whatever they are."

Ifel's attention swung to Micah.

He stilled, his face scrunching up in concentration, like he was staring at an Escher drawing. "It's all," he said, "and one. The one who created all. They are one, the all, but it began with one."

Yep, clear as mud. Lelindia held up a finger. "I think I need that again."

"Me, too," Aurora echoed.

"Me, three," Celia chimed in.

Micah blinked, the unfocused look dropping away. "I think I get it now, at least partly. When the entity was first created, there was only one. It was designed to be that way, so that it could fulfill its purpose. But something went wrong. Maybe with the Ecilam?" He glanced at Ifel.

Her tongue flicked twice.

He nodded. "A misunderstanding or disagreement with the Ecilam, then the other Setarip factions. The original purpose was lost, but the entity took on a new purpose. I think now it's guarding the biosphere."

Aurora grunted. "No wonder the Yruf have been so intent on the word *guard* every time it comes up. It's the core purpose of their non-biological entity."

"Yes," Micah agreed, "but it couldn't do that and complete all the tasks the Yruf needed to survive. So the entity created others like itself. Herself. Themselves?" Micah shrugged. "Not sure on the pronouns, but there are many more, all acting as one. In fact, I think the best translation I can give you for what to call them is The All."

"The All?" Aurora's voice came out strangled. "That's... a little intimidating."

Micah smiled. "It's not what the Yruf call them. I don't think they have a spoken name for them, so you can use whatever you want."

"How about Unity? It has the same meaning, joined as a whole."

"And in mathematics it also means the number one," Jonarel added.

Micah's smile turned into a grin. "Perfect. Unity it is."

"What about the original entity?" Tehar asked. "Is that who we are meeting today?"

Micah turned back to Ifel.

Lelindia watched Tehar out of the corner of her eye. She'd clasped her hands behind her back, her fingers twined tightly together.

Funny, but Lelindia used to use that same pose whenever Jonarel was nearby back when she was trying to deny her physical reaction to him. Tehar's use of it now gave her a clue how much the Nirunoc was anticipating this interaction. And how nervous she was about being disappointed. Or rejected.

Micah met Tehar's anxious gaze. "Unity would like to answer that themselves."

Ifel's head bobbed, then she swept her cloak behind her and turned toward the airlock.

One of the emerald-scaled egg-shaped objects floated through the airlock, coming to a stop beside Ifel, eye-level with Tehar.

For a moment, Lelindia thought Tehar wasn't going to move or speak. That could be a problem. It wasn't like she could give her a nudge with her elbow.

Then Tehar's freeze-frame unstuck and she bowed her head. "Welcome."

Sixty-Eight

Aurora couldn't really sense the tumultuous emotions Star was clearly feeling, but she could see the effects. And she *was* picking up something from the drone — no, *Unity*. It was subtle, a curiosity and playfulness that was distinct from everyone else.

But she wasn't prepared to hear Micah's voice coming from Unity's floating egg. "Thank you."

Everyone except the two Yruf jerked in surprise, gazes flicking between Micah and Unity.

"So that wasn't just me, right?" Aurora asked. "That was Micah's voice."

"Yes," Micah replied, looking startled and confused.

"Yes," Unity confirmed.

Her breath hitched. "Wait, you can understand me?"

A slight pause. "Understand? Yes, I understand."

Stellar light. "How is that possible?"

"Study. We can communicate in many ways."

Aurora held back a shudder... barely. It was *creepy* hearing her brother's voice spoken without its natural inflection and warmth.

Star took a step closer. "How did you learn to imitate him? And to understand the Galish language?"

"No. Recordings. Translation. He spoke often while onboard our ship."

Okay, that explained why they'd chosen Micah as their mouthpiece, and the unnatural quality to the delivery. They were pulling snippets of recordings from all the translating Micah had done, and probably any personal conversations he'd had, too.

"So you have recordings of everything I said?" Micah's emotional field was waffling between fascination and indignation, but his inherent scientific curiosity was winning.

"Yes. We wanted to understand you as our—" Unity paused. "We do not have a word for we and the Yruf."

"We and the Yruf?" Aurora moved closer to Micah, wanting his nearness for this bizarre exchange. "You mean your relationship?"

"Yes. They are our... we have no word."

"That's okay," Micah reassured them. "I was having a tough time explaining your relationship and I know a lot more Galish words than you've heard."

"Talking is... different. Ideas are... narrow."

"Hard to express, sure." Micah nodded. "Complex concepts can be confusing when broken into words."

"Yes, exactly!" That time Unity's response sounded more natural, more like Micah. "But it is how you communicate. We needed to learn."

A soft snort made Aurora pivot.

Celia met her gaze. "Good thing Micah likes to talk," she said in an undertone.

Micah shot her a warning look. "I heard that."

She was unfazed. "I know."

And they were getting off topic. "Do you understand who Star is?" Aurora asked Unity. "Why she wanted to meet you?"

"Star." This time, the name came out in Aurora's voice, then switched back to Micah's. "Yes. She is like us."

Still creepy, but at least now she understood why. Unity needed a recording of a word or name being spoken before they could reproduce it. Micah wouldn't have said Star's name while onboard the Yruf ship. She could fix that. "Micah, can you please say all our names so at least the voice is consistent?" And Unity could stop using hers.

Her request triggered a flare of amusement from him, but he did as she asked.

"Lelindia," Unity repeated. "You saved our people."

Lelindia glanced at Jonarel, who had moved to stand behind her as soon as Unity had appeared. "I'm a doctor, it's my job. But we all work to save lives."

"Yes. You guard."

Aurora flinched inwardly. Unity's definition of guarding meant not causing injury to others. So did Lelindia's. But the rest of the *Starhawke* crew hadn't exactly kept to that code, especially when dealing with lethal attacks from Reanne and her minions. "Do you understand the mission we're on right now?"

"Yes. You wish to stop the Sovereign and Teeli."

"Star was hoping to coordinate with you when we reach Teeli space." Aurora glanced at Star. "She thought you might be able to work together."

"Together, yes. We could join her."

Star's projection managed to look both eager and scared. "What do you mean, join me?"

"We are many. You are one. We can be as one."

Star darted a look at Jonarel. "Does that mean I would lose... me?"

"No. We are we. You are you."

Star's shoulders dropped, like she'd exhaled on a sigh of relief. "What would I need to do?"

"Do?" A pause. "We stay. Join you."

Jonarel cleared his throat, drawing everyone's attention. "Do you mean physically joining with the ship? Becoming part of the systems the way you did with *Gladiator*?"

"*Gladiator*." Cade's voice for that name. "Yes. We can join Star the same way."

Jonarel nodded. "Bella thought the Yruf used nanotech to infiltrate the ship, and maybe that is true from a physical standpoint, but it was Unity who controlled the systems."

"Unity?" In Jonarel's voice.

"That's the name we came up with," Micah explained. "Unity. We didn't know what else to call you. It means joined as a whole and also one."

"Unity." Micah's voice. "Yes, we like Unity."

Clearly.

"The reason Bella and I did not find any trace of nanotech in *Gladiator*'s systems is because the tech *is* Unity," Jonarel explained. "They would not have wanted to remain in the systems when *Gladiator* was leaving the Yruf."

Which meant any integration with the *Starhawke* would be temporary. Aurora chewed on her lip, considering. "How much control over the *Starhawke* would you have if you joined with Star?"

"Not control. Communicate. Be as one. Star is Star. Her ship. Her crew."

"So you wouldn't control my systems?" Star asked.

"No. Listen. Help. Share. Join. You are the One."

Micah held up a hand. "I think I can clarify. Correct me if I'm wrong, Unity, but on your ship, you have the One, who has central control, as Star does on our ship, and the rest of you follow the One's guidance. Is that right?"

"Yes. We are all with One, but One is One."

"So Star would still control the *Starhawke,* and you would help her interface with the Yruf ships while we're in Teeli space?" Aurora was liking how this sounded.

"Yes!"

The exclamation was so spot on for Micah that it startled a smile from her.

"Star, what do you think?"

Star looked to Jonarel again, but his expression clearly said it was her decision to make. "May I take a little time to consider?" she asked Aurora.

"Sure." It would buy her time to think about the ramifications, too. "We don't have to make a final decision until we reach the Fleet border with Teeli space. Speaking of which, I have another point I need to check on." She turned to Micah. "Are you okay here if I head up to the bridge for a bit?"

"Of course. I'll chat with Unity until Ifel's ready to leave. Help fill out their vocabulary, particularly anything related to our mission."

"All right."

Cade and Kire turned as she exited the lift onto the bridge.

"That looks like quite a gathering in the shuttle bay," Cade commented, his long legs crossed at the ankle as he regarded her from the navigation chair.

She caught movement on the bridgescreen, which displayed a camera view of the bay. Micah and Star appeared to be engaged in a conversation with Unity, Celia had joined Lelindia and Jonarel, and Ifel's head was bent toward Regas.

"I take it the Yruf reacted well to meeting Jon and Star?" Kire asked, rising from the captain's chair.

She waved him back down, too agitated to sit. "Better than expected. Micah gave them the broad strokes regarding the Kraed, and their trust in Lelindia smoothed over any awkwardness. But Star decided she wanted an introduction, too." She filled them in on the revelations about Unity and the proposal for a joining with Star.

Cade leaned back in his chair. "I should have figured out those drones were more than what they seemed, especially with the way the bulkheads responded to their movements. But they looked like drones, so that's all I saw."

"That's all any of us saw, which is probably the point."

"I wonder why Unity wasn't able to start communicating verbally sooner. Like when my team was onboard."

"I can probably answer that," Kire said. "They lacked the Rosetta Stone that Micah provided. You were talking in Galish, but they had no way to link more than a few words to objects they could identify. Then in comes Micah, who's translating everything that's going on between us and the Yruf into Galish. As advanced as Unity must be, matching Micah's translation to the Yruf's communication might have been relatively easy, especially the longer Micah was onboard. They could check their expected responses against what he actually said and autocorrect in real time."

And to think when Micah first told her he was staying onboard, she'd worried that he wouldn't have anything to do. "I wonder if the other Setarip factions are even aware of Unity's existence. It sounds like what they've become isn't how they started out."

"Maybe not." Kire shrugged. "We certainly haven't seen any evidence of a non-biological entity in any of the Setarip wreckage the Fleet has recovered."

"But would we even know what to look for? A.I. research has been banned for more than a century. I'm not sure the recovery scientists would have recognized a non-biological unless it said hello. We certainly didn't."

"And any intelligent A.I. wouldn't make a peep," Cade said. "Not given our history."

Aurora sighed. "Someday that will have to change. For now, I need to help Star decide if she wants to allow Unity to join with her when we head into Teeli space. Which leads me to another question." She turned to Cade. "What's your crew's plan when we leave here?"

"You mean for *Gladiator*?"

She nodded.

"I was thinking of hitting Ifel up for a piggyback ride."

Not what she'd expected. "You want to take *Gladiator* into Teeli space?"

"Hidden inside Ifel's ship, yeah. He's strong in a fight, even more so now that Jonarel helped Drew retrofit a separate power source for the sensor deflector. We can't completely vanish like you and the Yruf can, but we can use the deflector to partially disguise our movements during a battle."

"Hmm." On the surface, Cade seemed all in favor of the plan, but she sensed a nagging reluctance underneath. "What's the catch?"

He shrugged, but she didn't buy the nonchalance. "My team will need to be on Ifel's ship with *Glad* before we head through Teeli space."

Now she got it. He'd be off the *Starhawke*, and away from her, until they won the battle against whatever Reanne threw at them. Not her first choice, but it made a lot more sense than leaving a proven fighting ship behind in Fleet space. "And your team's good with this?"

He held her gaze, his emotions giving her the unvarnished truth. "It's our job." And he was as conflicted about it as she was.

That was some comfort. "Then if Ifel agrees, I guess we have a plan."

Sixty-Nine

Cade could feel Aurora pushing her emotional reaction aside and focusing on the task at hand. He'd been doing the same ever since he'd realized the Yruf ship was the most logical place for his team to be during this mission.

Much as he loved being on the *Starhawke*, he was redundant with Kelly onboard. His team needed him on *Gladiator*. But that didn't stop him from wishing he could duplicate himself and stay by Aurora's side.

Aurora lifted her chin. "Should we head down to the bay and ask Ifel now?"

He caught the resignation in her voice. Nothing he could do about it except delay the inevitable. "Kelly's still off duty for another two hours."

It was a weak excuse, and Aurora called him on it. "We're not going anywhere with Ifel's ship attached. And yours. I think Kire can handle the bridge by himself for a few minutes."

Kire's eyes twinkled. "I'll try."

Aurora was silent as they boarded the lift.

He brushed the backs of his fingers over her cheek. "You okay?"

"Yeah. Mostly. I just... I guess I'd counted on you being with me for this mission."

"I will be."

She gave him a sideways glance. "You know what I mean."

"Yes, I do. I'm not crazy about the idea either, but it's the smart move. Especially now that we know about Unity. They might agree to reintegrate with *Gladiator* for the battle, which would give us another advantage."

"I hate it when you're logical."

"But you love it when I do this." Snagging her around the waist, he spun her into his arms and dipped her.

"Cade!" Her voice said *stop it*, but she was laughing as he slowly pulled her upright.

"See? You love it."

Her laughter faded. "I love you."

He would never, *ever* get tired of hearing that. "I love you, too."

Wrapping her arms around him, she gave him a feather-soft kiss. "Come on, Ellis. Let's go get you a ride."

Convincing Ifel to agree to his plan took no time, although he noticed how her gaze lingered on Aurora, as though she was weighing the cost of their separation against the benefits.

So was he, but the result was always the same. He couldn't justify staying on the *Starhawke.* He'd fly *Gladiator* over as soon as he was off bridge duty. The Yruf ship and the *Starhawke* could travel faster without *Gladiator* in the mix. Jonarel could follow him in one of the *Starhawke*'s shuttles and bring him back for the trip to the Fleet-Teeli border.

Micah and Star had been talking to the egg-shaped drone that wasn't a drone when he and Aurora had arrived, but when Star's image blipped out and Micah headed over toward Lelindia and Jonarel, Unity hovered over to him. "We are sorry, Cade."

The voice was Micah's, but without the right delivery to be authentic. Aurora had warned him that Unity was using recordings of Micah to create vocal responses, but it still threw him, especially with Micah standing three meters away, talking to Lelindia. "Uh, for what?"

"We could not understand you. Not the first time. Now that we do, we know you suffered."

Suffered? When had— oh. It clicked. "You're apologizing for imprisoning me."

"Yes."

"Not your fault. I didn't understand you, either. From your perspective, I seemed dangerous. I pounded on the walls, yelled. You had to take precautions to protect the Yruf. I respect that." Even if it had cost Aurora her childhood home and almost cost Gryphon and Marina their lives.

"Thank you. We are learning."

"Very quickly, I might add. Impressive. It also looks like we'll get to spend more time together on your ship. Unless you'll be staying on the *Starhawke*."

"We are we. We are not one ship."

"Ah." He didn't really get what that meant, but maybe after spending a few days back on the Yruf ship — not as a prisoner — he would.

Micah strolled over and clapped him on the back. "If you're set with mon petit here, I'm heading back up to the med bay to help Lelindia and Jonarel with the Teeli disabling plan."

"Go for it. Aurora and I will take care of wrapping up here."

"Thanks, buddy." As Micah exited the bay with the white and black Yruf, Lelindia, and Jonarel, his voice piped up behind Cade.

"What is mon petit?"

Thanks for that, Micah. "It's a French term, often used affectionately. It translates as my little, or my boy, depending on usage."

"Micah called us mon petit."

"Well, yeah. You're using his voice to talk, but you're smaller than he is."

"We are *we*."

He was pretty sure Unity was affronted. And considering the size of the Yruf ship, he couldn't blame them. "In this form you're smaller than he is," he corrected.

"Yes."

"And in case you don't know the term *affectionate* yet, it means a feeling of fondness or tenderness. You're affectionate to someone you care about."

Unity was silent for a moment. "Micah cares about us?"

Weird to hear that said in Micah's voice, like he was talking in the third person. "Micah's a very caring person." *Just like his sister.*

"Mon petit is... good?"

"Yes."

"Then we will be mon petit."

Cade chuckled. "Glad to hear it."

Aurora approached next, Celia right behind her. Ifel had moved to stand near the airlock, waiting for Unity with the patience that defined the Yruf.

"All set?" Aurora asked him.

"Yeah. Unity, it was nice to finally meet you."

"We as well."

Cade watched as the not-drone bobbed toward Ifel and disappeared into the airlock. Ifel inclined her head before following in a swirl of emerald fabric.

Celia had moved to the airlock controls, the interior hatch closing and sealing behind Ifel.

"Never a dull moment around here," Aurora murmured, her gaze on the closed hatch.

Cade clasped her hand in his. "Just the way we like it."

Aurora's grip tightened, her emotions rising and falling like an incoming tide. "How long until Kelly's shift starts?"

Cade hid a smile as he checked his comband. "Another hour and ten minutes."

She lifted her gaze to his. "And what are your off-duty plans, Mr. Ellis?"

"First I need to get *Gladiator* onboard the Yruf ship. But after that, I was thinking about spending some quality time with my captain." He leaned toward her. "In her bedroom."

A not-subtle throat clearing brought his head around.

Celia stood a few meters away, hands on her hips. "Just making sure you two haven't forgotten I'm here."

He grinned at her. "It's your own fault for being so stealthy."

She rolled her eyes, but a smile tugged on her lips. "Yeah, yeah."

Hard to believe she'd once threatened to kill him because of Aurora. And meant it.

"I'm going to check in with Lelindia, see how much longer she thinks the Yruf will be staying onboard." Celia's gaze flicked over them, her smile growing. "I'll also see them to their transport since you two might be otherwise occupied." She gave Cade a pointed look.

Aurora ducked her head and tugged on his hand. "We're headed back to the bridge. Right, Cade?"

"Right."

But as soon as *Gladiator* was snuggled in with the Yruf, he was going to make sure Captain Hawke's attention was all his.

Seventy

Focus. Visualize the motion.

Celia steadied her breath as she pressed up into a handstand split, her palms creating depressions in the mat. The subtle thrum of the interstellar engines made her fingers tingle. The *Starhawke* was finally headed for the Fleet-Teeli border, the camouflaged Yruf ship keeping pace with them.

A walkover and cartwheel later landed her at the corner of the mat, facing the door to the *Starhawke*'s training center. One tumbling run to go to complete her workout sequence.

The doors parted as Micah strode inside, freezing when he caught sight of her.

For a microsecond she held his gaze, her body poised, before she exploded into motion. Two front handsprings, a tuck and dive roll, followed by a controlled pivot, a split leap, an aerial cartwheel and a back handspring, landing in a fighting stance at the exact spot she'd left moments earlier.

Micah's lips parted, his chest expanding visibly as his breathing changed, his gaze locked on hers. He tried to speak, cleared his throat, and tried again. "That was... impressive."

She allowed herself a small smile at the awe in his voice as she snagged the towel sitting near her feet and dabbed at her face and neck. "Thank you."

He walked closer, but a little tentatively. He had a beach towel draped around his neck and was dressed in aqua swim trunks that looked suitable for surfing, paired with a matching T-shirt.

She crossed the mat, meeting him halfway. "Headed for the hydrotank?"

"Yeah." He smiled softly, his unease melting like ice cream on a summer's day. "Where did you learn to do that?"

"I've always been flexible." She lifted one shoulder in a shrug. "Putting it to practical use seemed like a good idea during my security training."

"Can all Fleet security personnel do that?"

She grunted. "Hardly. My skill set is... unusual."

His gaze held hers. "So are you."

She wasn't quite sure how to respond to that. Instead, she glanced in the direction of the tank. "Will you be long? I'd planned to go for a swim after my workout."

"Oh. You're done?"

"Yes. But I can wait."

His gaze swung to the tank, then back to her. "Or you could join me."

She stilled as a strange sensation wound through her belly. She couldn't define it, which was a little alarming. But she wasn't hearing any klaxons blaring, either. "You wouldn't mind?"

His eyes took on a teasing light that reminded her of Aurora, but the effect coming from him was quite different. "Hardly."

He was echoing her words, too. She felt a little off balance as they strolled to the tank and climbed the stairs to the deck. Her leotard could double as a swimsuit, so after she'd dropped her towel on one of the deck chairs, she dove under the water, surfacing on the far side.

Micah was staring at her again. "You know how to dive, too?" He pointed at the water. "You went under like a dolphin, hardly a ripple."

"Another valuable skillset for a security officer. You never know when you'll need to take an unexpected swim."

"Is there anything you can't do?"

She tilted her head to the side, studying him through her damp lashes. "Talk to animals."

That brought the smile back to his lips. "That's right. I promised to work with you on that."

"Yes, you did."

"Only problem is, all the animals on this ship speak Galish." Grasping the hem of his T-shirt, he pulled it over his head, the muscles of his chest and shoulders flexing.

Working in security, she'd seen plenty of muscular men with their shirts off. She'd even taken a few to bed, or whatever solid surface was handy, when the mood struck her. But their muscles hadn't impressed her, or even been a factor in her decision-making process. A muscular man with a weak mind was a threat, not an asset.

But she couldn't look away as Micah dropped the T-shirt on a deck chair and ran his fingers through his sun-kissed hair. He paused when he realized he had an audience, his gaze dropping to his lightly furred chest then back to her. "What's wrong?"

"Nothing." She treaded water as her gaze traced the curves of his pectoral muscles. "I'm not used to seeing tanned men on a starship. Your skin tone's almost the same as mine."

"Oh." He slipped off his shoes. "Yeah, but yours is always that shade. Mine's courtesy of the sun. Without it I'd be as pale as Aurora."

Which would be a shame. Bronzed skin looked good on him.

He executed a dive that was as seamless as hers, swimming toward her underwater and surfacing a meter away. Droplets of water clung like tiny prisms to his skin and hair, making him resemble an ancient sea god rising from the ocean depths.

"Come here often?" he asked, his green eyes sparkling almost as much as the water.

She splashed him in the face.

He sputtered and laughed. "Okay, okay, I deserved that."

"Damn straight." But a smile tugged at her lips.

The look in his eyes changed, though to what exactly, she couldn't be sure. "So, how hard do you want it to be?"

She blinked. "Excuse me?"

"The wave strength." He lifted one hand out of the water and gestured to the tank. "What level of resistance do you want?"

Of course he was talking about the water. She was the one who'd taken a mental detour to... wherever her mind had gone. "What level were you planning to use?"

"Eight. But we can go with something easier," he added when he saw her unchecked reaction.

She schooled her expression into disciplined focus. She wasn't about to chicken out, not when he'd thrown down a gauntlet, no matter how unintentional. "Eight is fine."

He hesitated. "Are you sure? You said you just finished your—"

"Level eight is fine. The upper body work will feel good." Yeah, for about three minutes. Then her muscles would remind her she'd already completed a very strenuous upper body workout.

He wasn't convinced, but he clearly wasn't about to argue with her either, not after they were finally getting along. "Okay. Level eight it is. Star? Level eight and the southern California coast, please."

The water level in the tank dropped rapidly as Star sent water into the auxiliary tanks, making room for the increased wave action without swamping the deck. The image underwater also changed from clear to opaque, the lighting and projections perfectly simulating the grey-blue of the Pacific Ocean.

He turned to her as the first swells lifted them up. "Ready?" He angled his body into the oncoming waves.

"Absolutely." As the waves flowed toward them, she matched his movements, stroking forward when he did, breathing when he did, and watching him more than she should. He had great form, which came as no surprise. He was a champion surfer. But it was the grace of his movements that drew her senses like a magnet.

In the Yruf's biosphere she'd discovered how much he belonged by the water. Now she understood how much he belonged *in* the water. Swap out his legs for a dolphin tail and he could be a merman.

His arms and shoulders flexed with each pull against the waves, his body's movements as fluid as the water he swam through. He looked like he could keep it up for hours.

She couldn't, although she'd been wrong about the timing. Her precise internal clock told her they'd been at it six minutes when her muscles started complaining. She was still keeping up with him, but it was taking every bit of strength she had. And her muscles were reminding her she was an idiot with every stroke.

Another two minutes passed. She was losing ground, her shoulder, back, and leg muscles burning from the effort to keep up. She and Micah were no longer in perfect sync, and she'd fallen half a meter behind him in the tank.

His rhythm hadn't changed one bit.

She clenched her jaw, pulling harder at the water to close the gap. And seriously questioned her sanity.

What was she doing? She'd been at the end of her workout, ready for a cool down. He'd been starting his. This was ludic–

The pain stabbed like an ice pick into her calf, startling a harsh gasp from her lungs. A millisecond later her mouth filled with water. She coughed violently as her hands instinctively went to the seized calf muscle of her right leg, her toes curling from the involuntary contraction.

The water crested over her head, pushing her below the surface. She flailed with one hand and her good leg, ignoring the pain of the muscle cramp, stroking up while the waves continued to press down. She broke the surface with a harsh cough that ended in a gurgle as water hit her face, submerging her again.

And then a band of iron wrapped around her torso and pressed against her back, lifting her head above the water.

Air battled to get in as she forced the water out of her mouth and inhaled. Her throat rasped like sandpaper as she choked and coughed, the pain in her leg competing for dominance with the pain in her throat and lungs.

The pressure against her torso increased, pulling her steadily backwards. Her focus expanded to register Micah's breaths in her ear, loud in the silence now that the waves had stopped. The clang of his hand on the ladder a moment later alerted her they'd reached the edge of the tank.

"I've got you." He didn't release his hold on her. "Muscle cramp?"

"Yeah." She sounded like a seasick bullfrog. "Right calf."

Now that he'd stabilized her and the waves were no longer trying to kill her, she worked on flexing her foot to relieve the tension. She bit her lip against the painful resistance of the contraction as she coaxed the overworked muscle to relax.

"You need help?" No condescension in his voice, or judgement, only concern and empathy.

"Just..." She gritted her teeth and kept flexing. "Need a moment."

"Take your time."

The pain was ticking her off, but her reaction to it was making it worse. Normally this kind of muscle ache wouldn't be more than a blip on her radar. She was no stranger to physical pain. But she'd brought it on herself, and Micah had witnessed her stupidity. She wasn't just in pain. She was mortified.

As long as he continued to hold her with her back pressed against his chest, she didn't have to look at him.

But as the muscles in her calf responded to her efforts, gradually loosening the tight knot, her brain started reporting other sensations. Like the brush of Micah's bare chest against her bare back.

He'd snagged her under her armpits in a standard rescue position to haul her to the surface, but once they'd reached the ladder, he'd relaxed his hold a fraction to give her room to move. As she did, his forearm had shifted across her breasts.

She also noted his breathing was unsteady. So was hers, but she was fighting pain. He was... coming off an adrenaline rush and a hard workout that ended with a dramatic rescue. Of course his breathing was unsteady. It had nothing to do with their physical contact.

"How are you doing?"

His breath blew across the shell of her ear. Her heart thumped and she stiffened. "I need to get out and stretch." Her voice came out more clipped than she'd intended.

His reaction was immediate. The warmth from his back vanished and his arm moved to her waist, tugging her slightly so she could grab onto the ladder before he released her.

The water level had returned to normal depth, allowing him to place his palms flat on the deck and pull his body out of the water without using the ladder. Water cascaded off him as he turned to her. "Do you need help?"

"Nope." She avoided his gaze, using her arms and good leg to hop up the ladder rungs until she could step gingerly onto the deck. Her right calf protested, which made her angrier. Keeping her back to him, she hobbled to the deck chair, yanked her towel off, and dropped to the deck with her legs stretched out in front of her.

Grasping an end of the towel in each hand, she hooked the loop around the ball of her right foot and pulled back steadily, coaxing her foot to flex and the calf muscle to stretch.

Why had she been so stupid? She never got muscle cramps like this. She knew her body too well, took care of it, treated it with the respect it deserved. But not today. No, she'd allowed her ego to call the shots, challenged herself to compete in a game she couldn't win.

And worst of all? Micah wasn't even competing with her. He would have been fine with a more leisurely workout. She was the one who'd insisted he stick to his plan, and then forced herself to keep up with him.

What was wrong with her? Why did she—

"Cardiff?"

His soft voice derailed her internal rant. "What?" She winced at the sharp bite of that single syllable.

He was silent for a moment. "I'm sorry I upset you."

The comment was so far into left field that it brought her head around. "What?" This time the word came out more like a cat's meow rather than a dog bark.

Micah was standing well back from where she'd plunked down. His shoulders were hunched, his head tilted toward the ground. A slight flush tinged his cheeks as he met her gaze. "I'm sorry. I didn't realize where my arm was."

She stared at him, uncomprehending for a full second. When what he'd said finally registered, she gave a startled laugh. "You think I'm mad at you because of an accidental boob graze?"

Confusion clouded his eyes. "Aren't you?"

She laughed again, this time at herself. "No. I'm mad because I'm an idiot who turned into a damsel in distress in front of you."

His look of confusion intensified. "You're mad that I had to help you?"

Using the towel as leverage, she lifted her bad leg off the deck and pivoted to face him. "I'm mad because I'm the security officer on this ship. Because I've dedicated my life to training my body and mind for disciplined action. And then I threw that all out the airlock when you suggested we swim together."

A bemused smile flickered over his lips. "Then why did you say yes?"

"Because I seem to act irrationally around you." The truth popped out before she gave it any thought.

"Oh." He continued to study her, but the light had returned to his eyes. He took a step forward, then another, acting like she was an injured bird as he crouched beside her. "I've dealt with my fair share of muscle cramps. Would it make you mad if I offered to massage your calf?"

Would it? She wasn't sure.

"Or I could contact Lee-Lee to come down," he added when she hesitated.

"Don't do that." She didn't need her friend to witness her humiliation.

"Okay." He waited, unmoving, watching her.

She licked her lips. Made a decision. "A calf massage would be nice."

Surprise flitted across his face, followed by a ghost of a smile. Dropping to his knees, he settled in next to her right leg and removed the towel.

But when his fingers made contact with her skin, she jerked.

He stilled, his hands hovering millimeters from her leg. "More cramps?"

"No."

His gaze met hers. He was back to looking at her like a downed bird. "I won't hurt you, Cardiff."

Tension wrapped around her ribcage at the same time warm honey pooled in her belly. The contradiction made her feel like she was plummeting down the first drop of a roller coaster. She drew in a slow breath. "Celia."

He stared at her. "What?"

"If we're at the touching stage of our relationship, you should call me by my first name, Micah." She used his name on purpose, but it felt strange on her tongue. Had she ever said it out loud before?

His green eyes sparkled like sunlight on the ocean. "Okay, Celia." He returned his attention to her leg, touching her skin with a light but steady pressure.

This time she didn't jerk away, but she felt the imprint in every nerve ending in her body.

With gentle, firm strokes, his fingers worked the muscles of her calf, following every curve, coaxing the tension out. He seemed to know exactly what he was doing, and she bit down on her cheek to stifle a moan as the pain receded.

She must have made some noise, though, because his head came up. "You okay?"

"Fine." She watched the motion of his fingers rather than meeting his gaze. "You're good at this."

He chuckled. "I ought to be. Before I settled on marine biology as my major, I briefly considered becoming a massage therapist. Took all the classes, and really enjoyed it, but I realized if I followed that path, I'd spend most of my time indoors in darkened rooms. That didn't appeal to me, so I gave it up."

And she was reaping the rewards. "Some places do outdoor massages."

"They do." He returned his attention to her leg. "But I'd still be tied to a table, standing in one place. That's one of the reasons I make my classes interactive. Even when I'm giving lectures, I move around the room."

Until that moment, she hadn't considered what kind of teacher he was. But she had no problem picturing him striding around his classroom, tossing out questions, engaging his students, sharing his enthusiasm with them. She'd be amazed if half the class didn't have crushes on him by the end of the first day.

"What are you smiling about?"

She hadn't realized she was. "Just... thinking it would be fun to sit in on one of your classes."

His eyes had sparkled before. Now they shone like spotlights. "I would love that."

How had she missed how remarkable his eyes were? The green was flecked with gold and an ocean blue ring circled the iris, surrounded by those thick, long, dark lashes. Aurora's eyes were similar, but Micah's tanned skin and the more rugged planes of his cheek and brow bones turned them into a work of art.

His pupils dilated, making the color darken. That was fascinating, too. What—

He turned his head, clearing his throat as he jerked his hands away from her skin like it had become too hot to touch. "I think that should do it."

She wasn't fooled. She knew what that look in his eyes meant. Yet rather than following up on it, as every other man in her experience would, he'd put distance between them, popping to his feet and snagging his beach towel.

Would she ever figure him out? At first his confusing behavior had made her suspicious. Now she was intrigued, but just as confused.

He glanced over his shoulder as he fiddled with the towel, not quite meeting her gaze. "Do you want any help getting up?"

"No, thanks." Whatever was going on between them, touching again seemed like a bad idea.

A dull soreness still sat in her calf muscle like a slug, but as she rose and put weight on it, she didn't feel any indication it would seize on her again.

Micah remained by the edge of the tank while she fetched her towel. "Are you staying?" she asked him.

He nodded, his body angled away from her. "I still need to finish my workout."

"Okay." She headed for the stairs, then paused, turning back. He'd crouched by the tank, running his fingers in the water like he had at the Yruf's beach. Did he do that as a self-soothing motion? "How about having lunch with me? I could fix us something while you finish your workout. You know, thank you for saving my life." She said it in a teasing tone, hoping it would break through the stoic stillness he'd adopted.

It worked. Kinda. He met her gaze, but his expression remained somewhat shuttered. "Thanks, but I'm not sure how long I'll be."

"I don't mind waiting."

"That's okay." He gave her a crooked half-smile. "Can I have a raincheck?"

So he wasn't rejecting the idea completely. Maybe he had other plans afterward, although he could have just said that. Or maybe he wanted to spend a couple hours in the tank. He probably was used to being in the water for prolonged periods when he went surfing, "Sure. Enjoy your swim."

"Thanks."

As she walked down the steps and headed to the mat to collect her water container and shoes, she pondered the conundrum that was Micah Scott. She was beginning to get a sense of what made him tick, but the more she learned, the more she struggled to figure out how to handle him.

And that put him in a category all his own.

Seventy-One

Lelindia's hands trembled as she pulled her brush through her hair and gazed at her reflection in the mirror over her bathroom sink. *This is it. No more waiting. No more wondering.*

The *Starhawke* would arrive at the border of Fleet space in two days. After that, they'd be facing the Teeli fleet and their deranged leader. If she missed this window of calm before the storm, no telling when the next would appear. This was her chance – hers and Jonarel's – and she wouldn't let it slip through her fingers.

She'd taken extra care after she'd showered and washed her hair, anointing her body with the oils she'd prepared, her skin glistening in the low light.

She'd known about this ritual since she was a child, had learned the intricacies and practiced the words with her mother until she knew them by heart. But practicing as a kid with a vague concept of what it meant was a far cry from making the commitment and following through.

Not that she had any doubts. No, her trembling was a result of eagerness, not anxiety. And possibly a smidgen of disbelief. A small part of her still expected to wake up and discover this was all a dream.

"Lelindia?"

Jonarel's voice reached out to her from the direction of the sleeping nook, sending a shiver along her nerve endings.

Setting the brush down, she took a deep breath and gave her reflection an encouraging smile. "You've got this," she whispered, knowing full well Jonarel would hear her, anyway.

She stepped through the doorway.

Jonarel's golden gaze locked onto her, his lips parting as he took in every curve, every millimeter of skin, all free of concealment. "My checana," he breathed.

But he didn't move toward her. He stayed on the other side of the small circle of objects laid out on the floor between them on a swath of green fabric.

She took a moment to soak in the sight of him. Per Suulh custom, he wasn't clothed either, his muscular physique dewy with the oils she'd given him to massage into his skin. The oil made the green tones even more vibrant, the brown tendrils more defined as they wove across his arms, his chest, his abdomen, his...

She dragged her gaze back up, catching the flash of heat in his eyes. She'd be building on that heat soon enough, but completing the ritual came first.

Stepping closer, she knelt facing the objects laid out on the cloth. He did the same opposite her, the muscles of his thighs flexing. Other parts of him flexed, too. Very distracting.

Clearing her throat, she focused on the pale blue bowl sitting at the center of the circle. She'd had to improvise with her tools, since she didn't have the items her mother had stored away for her at Stoneycroft, which had all been consumed in the fire anyway.

But maybe this was better. She'd gotten creative gathering the implements from around the ship instead. The bowl was from the galley, as was the carved wooden pitcher beside it. Technically she could perform the ritual without any tools, but they would help her to focus and concentrate while reinforcing the message she was sending to her body.

Lifting the pitcher, she poured the water into the bowl, the splash loud in the stillness of the room. She managed to empty the pitcher without spilling any of the water onto the cloth, but it was a close call. Not that it would have mattered if she did. She'd taken the sheet from the guest quarters her parents had used while onboard. She'd wanted something to connect her to them during this ceremony. But her trembling, combined with the slickness of the oil on her skin, made it tough to keep a firm grip on the handle of the pitcher.

Or maybe that was just her excuse. She knew Jonarel was watching her every move, which made her self-conscious, but in a good way. She didn't dare meet his gaze. Maintaining her concentration was a hell of a lot harder than she'd imagined it would be. Her mind kept leaping ahead to the ultimate purpose of the ritual. She wrestled it back. *It wasn't this hard when I practiced with Mom.*

Yeah, well, it was a little different when the person sitting across from her was a gorgeous Kraed with intense golden eyes and a mouthwatering expanse of green skin and powerful muscles.

She reached for the smaller bowl of rose petals in shades of bubblegum pink, burgundy red, and snow white that she'd gathered from the greenhouse. Roses hadn't been a practical choice to plant in the greenhouse, but Jonarel had known she loved them, so he'd added three of them anyway.

The petals drifted from her fingers, floating on the surface of the water like fairy boats, the movement and moisture releasing their lush aroma.

She snuck a peek at him. The heat in his gaze had risen a few notches, but he remained perfectly still, his dark hair framing his face and brushing his shoulders.

Stellar light he was beautiful.

A flicker of amusement danced through his gaze. "You are staring."

"I am." She couldn't help it. This fierce warrior had claimed her heart and soul long before he'd realized how she felt about him. She couldn't wait to free the gift of life slumbering within her. To conceive a child together. Her pulse fluttered in anticipation.

"Is this part of the ritual?"

"No." She tore her gaze away, focusing on the final object on the cloth. "I just like looking at you."

His low growl sent heat firing through her veins. Her trembling increased, but thankfully this part didn't require dexterity. Grasping the last object, a petite ceramic pot filled with soil, she placed it in front of her. Even without engaging her energy field, she could sense the life potential in the seed buried beneath the soil. It called to her, begging to be released into the world.

To conceive, she needed to generate that same sensation within.

Inhaling slowly, she reached forward, dipping her hands into the bowl of rose water. She spoke the words of the ritual in the Suulh language but said them a second time in Galish for Jonarel's benefit. "I call on the waters that nurture all life, the beauty and bounty that their energy gives in abundance." Engaging her energy field, she cupped her hands to catch the water, allowing it to sprinkle from her fingers onto the soil of the potted seed. "I ask to free the lifeforce within me, to summon the gift of a child of my womb."

Her heart thumped against her ribcage, followed by a strange tingling in her abdomen that drew her gaze. Her breath caught as her Nedale senses confirmed what her instincts were already telling her. Her body was waking up.

She plunged her hands into the water again, splashing some onto the cloth and making the rose petals rock in the resulting waves, but she didn't care. This was happening. This was *really happening*!

Water cascaded from her fingers onto the seed pot. "Allow my body to flower, to take its place in the dance of nature, to bring forth new life." Wrapping her hands around the pot, she focused all her energy on her womb and the seed.

The seedling sprouted, a tendril of green pushing up through the soil. A moment later she gasped as cool fingers dug into her belly and a spasm shook her.

Movement flashed as Jonarel reached for her. "Lelindia?"

She held up a hand, stopping him. "It's okay. I'll be fine." Another spasm hit, not painful, but powerful enough to double her over.

Jonarel's hand made contact with her shoulder, the heat of his skin contrasting the cool grip of her energy field.

Her mother had warned her about this part, that the experience was unsettling as her energy field took control of her body. But it was necessary to release her from her reproductive celibacy.

She struggled to inhale against the rolling contractions in her abdomen, her palms pressing against her bare skin, her body tipping sideways.

"Lelindia, please stop."

Warmth surrounded her as Jonarel caught her and pulled her against him, his lips touching down on her cheek and temple.

"Stop, checana. Please stop." His fierce whisper cut through the sensory overload.

But she couldn't stop. Not now. Life was unfurling inside her, beckoning to her across the generations, a promise of the future. *Their* future.

"No," she hissed, matching his tone. "This is for us." And then she wrapped him in her energy field.

He sucked in a breath, his arms tightening around her. She had no idea what he could feel, but as the contractions gave way like a dam breaking open, power roared through her in a raging river.

She shrieked in response, but it was joy, not pain, that catapulted her out of the fog. Her eyes snapped open as her energy field drove into Jonarel, seeking, finding.

He groaned as she turned in his arms, the oil making her slick as an eel, and pressed him to the floor with strength she didn't know she had. He didn't resist as she straddled him, the fire in his eyes and the solid length of him as she took him inside her making it clear he was caught in the same storm she was. Her lips crashed down on his, demanding his surrender as her hips moved, locking them together.

He met her with the same fierce need, the tips of his claws nipping her skin, marking her as she rocked against him in a rhythm guaranteed to drive them both over the brink.

Her energy field continued to pulse within them both, joining them on an elemental level that drove her primitive need, her body focused on pulling the gift from him that only he could bestow.

His eyes blazed, his lips twisted in a warrior's snarl. His claws broke through the skin at her hips as he urged her on, the flare of pain heightening the bonding that was driving her out of her mind with ecstasy. She laughed, a wild, unbridled sound as he surged within her and roared.

Her energy field pounced, coiling them together as the maelstrom flung her over the edge, her cry of release echoing his.

Time passed — minutes, hours, days, she couldn't say. Eventually she became aware of Jonarel's hand stroking her hair while his other arm wrapped protectively over her back.

She was still sprawled on top of him, her cheek on his chest.

The stroking stopped and he drew her higher on his body so he could nuzzle the top of her head. "Are you all right, checana?"

The question triggered a giggle. She'd never been more all right in her life. Lifting her head, she grinned at him. "Oh yeah, I'm peachy."

But he looked concerned. The hand encircling her back drifted slowly, tentatively, to her hip. "I... hurt you." Pain and self-reproach coated his words.

She glanced down her body at her unblemished skin. She remembered the moment when his claws had sunk into her flesh, but her energy field had healed the damage immediately.

Facing him, she propped her chin on her fist. "Does that happen a lot when Kraed mate?"

His jaw worked. "It is uncommon, but not unheard of when a pair bond is... intense."

"So it's a sign of strong feelings and closeness?"

"Yes." His gaze searched hers. "But your skin is softer and more vulnerable to..."

She swatted him lightly on the chest. "Who are you calling vulnerable? In case you didn't notice, I already healed those marks. A Kraed couldn't do that."

He swallowed, still looking uncertain. "I never meant to—"

She silenced him with a kiss that included lots of tongue. When she lifted her head, she'd effectively erased the concern from his expression. "In case you couldn't tell, I loved it. Don't hold back with me, ever. I'm a lot stronger than I look."

She couldn't define the emotions swirling behind his eyes, but the kiss he gave her spoke volumes.

"I will not forget," he promised, drawing back. His hand rested on her hip, his gaze moving down her body. "The ritual? It is complete?"

She turned her gaze inward, making a sweep of her body. Her Nedale senses noted several subtle differences before latching onto one big one that glimmered like sunlight on new spring buds.

Her gaze snapped to his as she rolled sideways, her hand going to her abdomen. "You could say that. I think I'm pregnant."

Seventy-Two

"Pregnant?" Aurora tipped her head, certain she'd heard Lelindia incorrectly. "You're pregnant?"

"Yes."

Nope, still not registering. Aurora perched on the couch cushions in her cabin, staring at Lelindia as the word *pregnant* ricocheted like a pinball in her brain. "That's..." She sent a pleading look to Celia, seated beside her, when nothing else rolled off her tongue.

"Fast," Celia supplied. She seemed as stunned as Aurora.

"I know." Lelindia gave them a sheepish smile. "To be honest, I expected it to take a while. Months even. But during the ritual things went kind of... wild. I waited a day to make sure I was right. I am. The child inside me is growing."

Aurora's mouth and throat dried up. "I'm happy for you." And she was, but this presented a whole cornucopia of problems that she hadn't expected to deal with, especially right now.

"So am I," Celia said. "It's just startling. You and Jonarel have only been mated for a week."

And they'd been a couple for less than a month. They were moving at lightspeed and Aurora was being buffeted by their wake.

Lelindia brushed a strand of hair behind her ear, her expression shifting to the maternal one Aurora knew so well. "I understand how this looks from the outside, but believe me when I say we're not rushing anything. This is how it's meant to be. How it has to be."

The emotions behind her words caught Aurora's attention like an umpire's sharp whistle. "Has to be? What do you mean?"

Lelindia sighed, her hand drifting to her abdomen in an unconscious gesture. "I want this child as fiercely as I wanted to be Jonarel's mate. Feeling our child's lifeforce within me..." Her energy field glowed softly around her hand and a smile curved her lips. "I can't begin to describe it."

She didn't have to. Aurora could feel the emotions swirling around her, the deep sense of belonging, of unconditional love, and fierce protection. It radiated from Lelindia as brightly as her energy field.

"But there's more to it than that." Lelindia's gaze moved between Aurora and Celia. "The situation with Signal is part of it, too."

Celia sat forward, her muscles tensing in response to Signal's name. "How so?"

"I created the current schism with him, but the problem began when he insisted Jonarel had to mate with Aurora."

Aurora snorted. "Because he thinks I have to become a part of the Clarek clan before the other Kraed clans will join the fight against the Teeli." She still couldn't decide if his view showed hubris, wisdom, or cowardice.

"And he doesn't think you're Aurora's equal," Celia said with a touch of bitterness. "He made that clear while we were on Drakar."

"Yes, he did. My mating with Jonarel won't change anything, except possibly make the situation worse. However—"

The path Lelindia was leading them down illuminated with a lightning bolt in Aurora's mind's eye. "If you and Jonarel have a child, a half-Suulh, half-Kraed child, the honor code of the clans will bind them to your child, your heritage. And by extension, all Suulh, including those on Feylahn." It was brilliant. And terrifying. "Please tell me that isn't the reason you—"

"No!" Lelindia's sharp retort left no room for argument. "I want this child with all my heart." Her hand remained protectively cupped around her belly. "I would never use her as Siginal used Jonarel. Our child could be the key we need to free the Suulh, but she will never, *ever* be a means to an end." Her eyes flashed and her words came out on a growl that was remarkably similar to Jonarel's.

O-*kay*. Question answered. Aurora made a mental note to update her expectations when it came to her energy sister. Lelindia had always acted motherly, but in a worried hen kind of way. This Lelindia was a Grizzly bear. "And you're certain you'll have a daughter?" Aurora's parents had believed that, and then Micah had arrived first.

Lelindia's brown eyes warmed. "Yes. She will be the Nedale."

If Lelindia said it was so, she believed her. Lelindia's abilities could probably ensure the gender of her child, and the Suulh gifts her daughter would inherit as a result. "How soon can we expect her to appear?"

"Hmm." Lelindia pressed her lips together. "That's a good question. My mom carried me for four and a half months, but—"

"That's all?" Celia stared at her. "Is that normal for Suulh?"

Lelindia smiled. "No. Typically Suulh gestate for six months or more, but women from the Nedale line have a tendency to speed up the process, especially if we're doing a lot of energy work while pregnant."

Celia gave a low whistle. "Still, that's a big improvement. Just pretending to be pregnant for a few hours drove me nuts. I don't know how any woman stays sane for nine months." She flinched. "No offense."

Lelindia chuckled. "None taken. Pregnancy for the Suulh is much easier than for Humans. Our bodies adapt to the changes without the pain and stress that Humans endure. I remember my mom saying how much she loved the bonding time we had while she was pregnant with me. And giving birth is a lot easier, too, especially for the Nedale."

"I guess it would be, with your ability to block pain and heal trauma."

"Exactly. There's no risk to mother or child, and it happens quickly, often a few minutes from start of contractions to delivery."

"Wow." Celia shook her head. "I still can't imagine going through it, but I'm glad this won't be a hardship for you."

"What about for the Kraed?" Aurora interjected. "That's the other element in play here. What's pregnancy like for them?" She'd never thought about it, may have even subconsciously avoided the topic after she realized how much Jonarel wanted to mate with her. She hadn't wanted to follow that thread.

"Their gestation is longer than ours, about seven months. Their children are also born much smaller and less developed. Jonarel said it's a natural adaptation for early survival. A pregnant female is slower and more awkward, putting her in danger from their plethora of predators. It's easier for a mother to protect her child cradled outside her body in a way she can control rather than carrying it within. In that way, they're somewhat like marsupials, but without physical pouches. Their children do much of their early development outside of the womb, strapped to the mother's body."

Aurora tapped the tips of her fingers together. "So we can expect your child sometime between four and a half and seven months from now." Which seemed a blink away.

Lelindia gave her a knowing smile. "Don't worry, Sahzade. It'll be fine."

"Do I look worried?"

"Yes," Lelindia and Celia answered in unison.

She winced. "Okay, I am. We're about to enter Teeli space, where we have no idea what we'll encounter, but certainly nothing good. I didn't think a baby was going to be part of the equation."

"She isn't. Not yet, anyway," Lelindia amended. "It'll be a couple months before any physiological changes begin to impact my work, and even then, I'll be fine."

Aurora eyed Lelindia's stomach the way she would a ticking bomb. "I guess I'd feel differently if we were still working on our original charter as a science vessel. But things have changed so much. Taking a child into battle situations..." She shuddered.

Lelindia stood, crouching beside her and resting a hand on hers. "I know the risks, Sahzade. But I also know you will keep us safe."

Her complete confidence and bone-deep trust tightened Aurora's throat. She'd never felt the weight of responsibility pressing down like it did as she gazed at her energy sister. Even after she'd learned she was the leader – the guardian – of an entire race, she'd found the strength to move forward. Somehow, this one child loomed larger.

Maybe because her existence was personal in a way the discovery of the Suulh hadn't been. Lelindia and Jonarel's child would be a part of her family, beloved and cherished as the young Nedale. She'd never envisioned a child growing up on the *Starhawke*, but that's exactly what she was facing. What would that even look like?

If they captured Reanne and exposed the Teeli to the Galactic Council, they still had a battle ahead of them to free the Suulh on Feylahn. She didn't kid herself that it would be an easy task, even with the support of the Kraed. Her homeworld was deep in Teeli territory.

"So does this mean I get to be an aunt?"

Celia's question knocked her out of her anxiety spiral.

Lelindia grinned. "Do you want to be?"

"Hell, yeah. I may have no inclination for motherhood, but being Tia Celia would be fun. I could teach her all kinds of things."

The glint in Celia's eyes drew a flutter of anxiety from Lelindia. "What exactly do you have in mind?"

"Oh, the typical things. Swimming, gymnastics... how to wield a knife."

Aurora snorted.

Lelindia scowled, but her lips slowly curled up. "That might not be necessary if she has claws," she shot back.

Celia dismissed the comment with a wave. "Still necessary. Blades can be deployed at a distance."

"Hmm." Lelindia darted a glance at Aurora, looking for backup.

She held up her hands. "I'm neutral on this one. But Jonarel will probably love the idea of combat training."

Lelindia rolled her eyes. "You're right, he will. Fine." She pointed at Celia. "You and Jonarel can handle her physical training. Aurora and I will handle her energy lessons."

Celia's eyes sparkled. "Excellent."

The weight on Aurora's shoulders settled in more firmly. This new wrinkle would impact them all in ways they couldn't imagine. Ready or not, the wheel was in motion.

Seventy-Three

"Lelindia's pregnant?" Cade sank deeper into the navigator's chair as the shock of Aurora's announcement rolled over him. Thankfully she'd waited to tell him until they were alone on the bridge so he didn't have to control his reaction.

Aurora grimaced, obviously picking up on every nuance of his response. "Yeah, that's pretty much how I felt when I heard."

"Wow. Pregnant." And here he'd thought Lelindia and Jonarel's mating ceremony had been quick. This was... unexpected, to say the least. "Was this intentional?"

"All Suulh births are intentional," she reminded him with a look.

Right. She'd explained that to him back at the Academy, after he'd seen her energy field and realized how extraordinary, and different, she was from every other girl there. Birth control had never been a concern they'd had to deal with, something he'd subconsciously taken for granted since they'd rekindled their relationship.

"Jonarel must be over the moon." After being banished by his father, conceiving a child with Lelindia would go a long way to soothing his emotional wounds.

"He is. But his overprotectiveness has kicked into high gear. She's going to have to set some ground rules if she doesn't want him hovering twenty-four-seven."

"Will his attitude make your job harder?"

She shrugged. "Not really. Lelindia's already proven she's not going to be hampered by him. Her trip to the Yruf ship emphasized that. This isn't a Kraed compound, and Lelindia isn't a Kraed female. Jonarel can't expect her to act like one just because she's carrying a half-Kraed child. He'll have to adapt or risk seriously ticking her off."

The way she said it made him think Jonarel would come out on the short end of that confrontation. Funny, considering he'd always viewed Lelindia as fairly passive. Apparently there were hidden depths to her personality that were rising to the surface.

"Does this change our plans in any way?"

Aurora stood, walking toward the bridgescreen, although while they were in the interstellar jump there wasn't much to see. "I'm not sure." She halted next to him, her lips pressed together. "The real problem may be me. I'm not much different than Jonarel, when it comes down to it. Knowing she's pregnant… it changes how I feel about our situation."

"You're worried about her." He could feel it like a chill breeze.

"Ever since she told me, my mind keeps circling back to what Celia said during the meeting at my dad's house, that Siginal believes the Teeli want the potential of our children."

His gut clenched. "And now Lelindia's pregnant."

Aurora nodded, her expression strained, the chill wind continuing to blow. "At the time, I was horrified, but I dismissed it as irrelevant since I knew neither of us could conceive without a conscious choice. But now." A ghost of the bleakness he'd seen after she'd uncovered Reanne's identity made the green of her eyes look grey. "If we don't succeed in capturing Reanne, and she learns Lelindia has a child…"

The fear behind her words pulled at him. Reaching out, he clasped her hand in his. Hers was cold as ice. "Nothing's going to happen to her. Or to the child. Every person on this ship would give their life to make sure of that."

A sad smile trembled on her lips. "Intellectually I know that. But emotionally, she's my energy sister, my best friend. If something happened to her, or to her daughter, I don't know what I'd do. It's my job to keep her safe."

The irony of her words wasn't lost on him. "You will. And at least now you have a better understanding of how she's felt every time you've charged into danger."

She blinked, her hand tightening in his. "You're right. I never thought about it that way." This time, her smile looked more like the Aurora he knew and loved. "Thank you for pointing that out."

"That's *my* job." Any time he could make her smile, he felt like he was standing at the summit of Mt. Everest. The view was sublime.

He gave a sharp tug on her hand, pulling her onto his lap. She gave a startled squeak as his arms closed around her. "And now I'm claiming my payment for a job well done," he whispered a split-second before his lips met hers.

Seventy-Four

"Coming out of the jump in three, two..." Kelly counted down at the navigation console.

Cade watched from his seat beside Aurora, the one Jonarel had added for Micah, as the starfield appeared on the bridgescreen. No sign of the Yruf ship. It was still camouflaged, just like the *Starhawke*.

He turned to Aurora. "Guess it's time to go."

She smiled, but it didn't reach her eyes. "Guess so."

His team was transferring over to the Yruf ship before they came in range of the Fleet's border beacons at the edge of Teeli space. *Gladiator* waited for them in one of the Yruf's bays, and the portion of the Yruf ship that included the biosphere would be remaining in Fleet space.

The other transfer taking place involved Unity. Star had decided, and Aurora had agreed, to allow Unity to integrate with the *Starhawke*'s systems for the duration of this mission. The small Yruf ship would be docking shortly to make the necessary connections for the transfer.

"Walk me to the shuttle?" Cade had wholeheartedly agreed to Star's request that he fly one of the *Starhawke* shuttles over to the Yruf ship, where it would remain in the same bay as

Gladiator. Star had argued it would give her a better sense of what was happening with the Yruf ship regardless of the integration with Unity, but Cade suspected she also wanted the exchange to feel more balanced. Having Unity infiltrate her systems might have felt too invasive otherwise.

Cade's argument in favor of the plan was that it would give them another valuable pilot-transport combination for the upcoming confrontation. Drew could pilot *Gladiator* in battle — she'd already proven that — freeing him to fly the *Starhawke* shuttle. He, Jonarel, and Kelly were the only ones with the right skillset, and Kelly would be busy flying the *Starhawke*. Keeping one of the shuttles on the Yruf ship for Cade's use was logical. Sort of.

But it was a justification. He, Star, and Aurora all accepted it.

He needed that interconnection as much as Star did. He had no idea how long it would be before he and Aurora were back on the *Starhawke* together. They'd made the most of the previous night, but he would really miss having her tucked in next to him while he slept. The narrow cots on *Gladiator* were a poor alternative.

Having the *Starhawke* shuttle nearby would give him something tangible to tie him to her during the days ahead.

Aurora stood. "Kire, you have the bridge. Alert me when the Yruf ship has docked."

Kire moved to the captain's chair as the auxiliary chair dropped into the deck.

Cade walked with Aurora to the lift. As soon as the doors closed, she spun, pulled his head down, and kissed him like a drowning woman who needed the air in his lungs to breathe.

He matched her intensity, his arms hauling her against his body, imprinting her on his soul. Their ragged breathing filled the lift. They broke apart when the doors opened on the shuttle deck.

She gave him a saucy smile as she straightened her tunic. "Didn't want you to leave without a proper goodbye."

He affected a drawl. "Little lady, if that's how you say goodbye, I need to leave more often."

She laughed, the sound spreading warmth through his chest.

His team was already assembled in the expansive bay that housed the two *Starhawke* shuttles, loading the last of the supplies they were taking over from the greenhouse.

Justin gave them a knowing look and a grin as they approached. "Glad you could join us."

Cade winked at Aurora. "We had to say goodbye."

"Uh-huh." Justin's grin widened. "I'll bet you did."

Aurora turned to Micah, who was helping Cade's team load the shuttle. "Is Ifel ready for them?"

Micah nodded. "The biosphere detachment is in progress. They'll move the rest of the ship into position to the *Starhawke*'s starboard side in a few minutes. Cade will be able to see the open bay after the shuttle launches."

"Good." She met Cade's gaze, opened her mouth to say something, then closed it with a small frown.

He knew the feeling. They'd already said everything there was to say, talked through every what if scenario they could envision. Now they'd just have to play it out.

She gave him a small nod and tight smile. "See you soon."

It came out like a wish rather than a certainty.

"Absolutely." He didn't sound any more convincing.

She turned to Micah. "I'm heading up to shuttle bay two to check on Star and greet Unity. You ready to join me?"

Micah glanced at Cade. "I'll be there in a minute. I want to help finish up here."

Her gaze shifted between the two of them, no doubt reading them both with ease. "Fine." Giving Cade a long look, she pivoted and retraced the path to the corridor.

His gaze followed her. As soon as the bay's doors closed behind her, he turned to Micah. "Take care of her."

Empathy shone in Micah's eyes, so like his sister's. "You know I will."

And that's what made this whole tricky plan bearable. With Micah by her side, Aurora was more powerful than she'd ever been. Whether that advantage, and the presence of the Yruf, was enough to defeat Reanne at her own game, was the big question hanging in the air like a thundercloud.

Settling into the cockpit of the *Starhawke*'s shuttle helped focus him, the elegant lines and beautiful design reminding him of her captain. Jonarel had given him a training session before both ships had set out for Teeli space, making sure he was comfortable handling the shuttle's docking procedure when the ship was camouflaged — just in case.

Justin stepped into the cockpit, dropping into the co-pilot's chair. "Loaded up and ready to go. The bay is clear and Micah confirmed the Yruf are waiting for us."

"Then let's get this show on the road."

He could have made a standard Fleet launch through the bay doors at the ship's stern, but Jonarel had taught him how to make use of the Kraed design to launch the shuttle from the ship's underbelly, the reverse process of the camouflaged docking procedure. It required more precise piloting skills and quicker reflexes, but it cut the launch time in half.

Justin gave a low whistle as they shot away from the *Starhawke*. "Nice flying."

"Thanks."

The oval opening to the Yruf's bay with its familiar yellow glow hung in the sea of black surrounding them like an open mouth ready to swallow them whole. He guided the shuttle toward it, the light bathing them as they glided inside and touched down on the deck.

"Outer hull is sealed," Justin confirmed. "Bay is pressurizing."

Movement caught Cade's eye to his right, where the interior bulkhead had rippled away to reveal *Gladiator*'s solid bulk.

"Home sweet home," Justin murmured, a happy trill running through his emotional field.

The rest of his team seemed to share the sentiment. Their excited voices and a sense of anticipation reached him from the main cabin as they gathered their personal belongings. They'd bonded with the sturdy little ship and were delighted to be returning.

He'd bonded at first too, but he'd realized that was because Aurora had been onboard, filling the ship with her presence as they'd worked side by side. After she'd ditched him, his memories of their time together had been the only connection he'd had to cling to. That wasn't true anymore, which had led him to an obvious but problematic conclusion. Much as he liked *Gladiator*, the *Starhawke* had become his home, because that's where Aurora was.

Which begged the question of what would happen when his team's missions no longer coincided with the *Starhawke*'s.

But that was a future problem.

Justin opened a comm channel. "Byrnes to Emoto."

"Go ahead, Byrnes."

"We've docked the shuttle and are transferring to *Gladiator*. All incoming messages will be routed through."

"Confirmed. See you guys on the flipside."

"We'll be waiting for you."

The Yruf ship was considerably faster than the *Starhawke*, so they'd be scouting the location in advance before meeting Aurora's crew at the predetermined coordinates at the edge of the binary system. He hoped to be on the bridge with Ifel, or tagging along with one of the Yruf pilots, during the reconnaissance mission.

He followed Justin down the ramp, walking the short distance to *Gladiator*'s gangway. But before they reached it one of Unity's not-drones detached from the ceiling and drifted down. "Welcome Cade and Justin," Micah's voice greeted them.

Yeah, still weird. "Hi, Unity."

"Ifel would like to invite you to join her for a meal."

Unity's delivery sounded a lot more natural this time. Maybe they'd been practicing with all the new vocabulary Micah had shared with them.

A bemused smile crossed Justin's face. "I wonder if she's trying to make up for feeding us ration mash during our last stay."

"Ration mash?" Unity asked in Justin's voice.

Clearly Micah had never said those two words.

"Never mind." Cade didn't want to get into it during their first hour onboard. "Tell her we'll be happy to join her and we'll bring some items from the *Starhawke*'s greenhouse to share."

"Great. I will lead you in an hour." Unity rose into the niche in the ceiling and stayed there.

"Items to share?" Justin asked in an undertone. "Or covering our bases so we can eat?"

"Both." Although Cade didn't have much of an appetite at the moment. "An hour will give us time to get settled in."

Justin chuckled. "Yeah, the trick will be pulling Bella away from the engines in an hour. If Jonarel hadn't turned her loose to explore the *Starhawke*'s engine room and Kelly hadn't given her time in the navigation chair during the flight here, I think she would have gone into withdrawal. She's in love with this ship."

Cade slung an arm around Justin's shoulders. "Don't take it too hard, buddy. After all, he's bigger and stronger than you are."

Justin jabbed him in the ribs.

Cade staggered back in mock pain, a hand pressed to his side. "Wow, the truth really does hurt."

"Ha-ha." Justin rolled his eyes and stalked up the gangway, probably to go find Bella.

Cade's gaze drifted back to the *Starhawke's* shuttle. His heart squeezed. "Home sweet home," he murmured under his breath before turning away and following Justin up the ramp.

Seventy-Five

"Are you ready?" Lelindia asked Tehar.

She'd stationed herself beside the Nirunoc's image, facing the airlock where the Yruf ship had docked. Jonarel stood by the controls and Celia had taken up her post behind Tehar's left shoulder.

"I am... nervous."

"That's understandable. Facing the unknown is unnerving. Just remember you're not alone."

Tehar's image lost some of the tin soldier resemblance. "Thank you."

The interior hatch opened behind them. Aurora strode in, looking a lot more tense than the last time Lelindia had seen her. No need to ask why. Lelindia would feel the same way if Jonarel were the one heading off to the Yruf ship.

Aurora summoned a closed-mouth smile as she stopped beside Lelindia. "All set for our guests?"

Tehar nodded. "I have made the preparations Unity requested and—"

The hiss of the airlock cut her off, both Tehar and Aurora stiffening.

When the hatch opened, the first figure to appear was Regas, the white-scaled engineer with the black oval markings, followed by Mahrem, the emerald-scaled engineer with the gold splotches.

They stepped to either side of the airlock to allow Unity to float inside the bay.

"Hello, Star!" Micah's cheerful voice called out from the egg-shaped mobile unit, greeting the Nirunoc with enthusiasm.

"Hello, Unity." Tehar wasn't nearly as effusive, but that wasn't her nature. All Nirunoc had a reserve to their interactions that reminded Lelindia of vids she'd seen depicting Regency England.

Unity swiveled toward Aurora. "Thank you for allowing us to come onboard, Captain."

Aurora twitched. She'd admitted to Lelindia how strange it was to hear Micah's voice coming from Unity, although it sounded a lot less mechanical than the last time. "Thank you for agreeing to help with this mission."

"It's our honor. We—" Unity cut off and bobbed in place as the interior hatch opened again. "Micah!"

Impossible to miss the excitement in Unity's borrowed voice. They must have learned how to modulate the words Micah had spoken to give more realistic inflection to fit different situations.

"Unity!" Micah called out with the same enthusiasm, striding across the deck. "Good to see you. Ready to join the crew?"

"Absolutely."

Lelindia glanced at Tehar. The interaction was having an interesting effect on her. Before she'd been nervous. Now she looked eager to reclaim Unity's attention.

"Shall we begin?" Tehar asked, injecting a bit more emotion into her voice.

Unity swiveled back in her direction. "Yes, please."

While Micah acted as translator between Jonarel and the two Yruf engineers — who would be handling the nuts and bolts of Unity's physical transfer between ships — Unity's mobile unit hovered in front of Tehar. "Do we have a nest above to get energy?"

"Yes. Jonarel and I have already created one to your specifications in the med bay. The central location will allow you to interact with the crew."

"And hang out with me," Lelindia added. "I spend a lot of time in the med bay and greenhouse. You're welcome to join me whenever you'd like."

"Thank you, Lee-Lee."

Lelindia choked on a laugh. Apparently Micah had decided to tell Unity her nickname. Or maybe Unity had heard Micah say it while they were on the Yruf ship.

Jonarel approached them. "We are ready to start the transfer." His gaze held Tehar's. "If you are."

"Yes." She nodded at the group. "If you will excuse me." Her image vanished a second later.

"We must help, too," Unity said, bobbing once before floating over toward the engineers.

As soon as the space around them cleared, Aurora rolled her shoulders like she had a crick in her neck the size of a starship.

"You okay?" Celia asked, moving to Aurora's other side.

"Fine."

Celia exchanged a look with Lelindia. They both knew what that meant.

"Pull the other one," Celia said, folding her arms.

Aurora scowled. "Yeah, well, I've got a few things on my mind."

Lelindia could see the list like it was scrawled on Aurora's forehead. Reanne. The Teeli. The Ecilam. The Yruf. Cade. The crew. Lelindia's child. And now Unity.

It was moments like this that gave her glimpses of the weight of responsibility Aurora always carried. Most of the time she made it look effortless. But once in a while, like now, her knees buckled a bit under the pressure. "How can we help?"

Aurora sighed. "No idea." She stared at the deck. "Well, one idea. If I start wandering the corridors talking to myself, smack me. Hard."

Celia snorted. "What good would that do? Your shield would block the blow."

A hint of a smile darted across Aurora's mouth. "Yeah, but at least it would get my attention. Shut me up."

"Oh, come on." Lelindia wrapped her arm around Aurora's shoulders. "You know what you need?"

"A case of tenrebac?"

"No." Lelindia rolled her eyes. She used to envy Aurora's ability to get tipsy from the Kraed beverage, back when she wanted to numb the pain of seeing Jonarel and Aurora together. Not a problem anymore. "You need an hour in the greenhouse. After we finish here, I'm marching you upstairs and you're going to get your hands dirty."

Aurora shook her head. "We're heading into Teeli space. And I have a lot of work to do. Video to—"

"No arguments." Celia looped her arm through Aurora's. "Unless you want to learn the answer to an age-old question."

Aurora cocked her head, her smile resurfacing. "What question is that?"

A glint of challenge shone in Celia's dark eyes. "What happens when an unstoppable force meets an immovable object."

Seventy-Six

An hour in the greenhouse and the light lunch with Celia and Lelindia that followed cleared some of the debris swirling like an asteroid belt around Aurora's head, helping her focus when she returned to her office.

She was so engrossed in the video feed she'd been studying she didn't register the movement of her office door opening or Micah's presence until he spoke.

"Sis, do you have a minute?"

She glanced up from her desk. "Sure." She paused the video, which showed Reanne's transport returning to the Teeli cruiser that had spirited her away from their last confrontation. Star had captured the images during the battle, and Aurora was committing every movement and detail to memory in preparation for their arrival in Teeli space. "What's up?"

Micah approached hesitantly, his shoulders rounded and his emotions swirling like a dust cloud. "It's about Celia."

"Ah." That explained the cloud. She gestured to the two chairs in front of her desk. "Are you having more disagreements?" She hadn't witnessed any, or sensed any rancor between them, but she'd been distracted, first by Lelindia's baby announcement, then Cade's departure and Unity's arrival, and now with thoughts of Reanne.

"No." He settled into one of the chairs but remained hunched over, like he was anticipating a gut punch. "That's part of the problem."

"Why is that a problem?" She couldn't get a bead on him, which was odd. Normally he was an open book in big bold type.

He ran a hand over his face, his gaze averted. "We had, uh, an... incident... a few days ago."

She frowned. His behavior was confusing the heck out of her. "What kind of incident?" she prompted when he didn't continue.

"We were, um, swimming together, in the hydrotank. She got a leg cramp, and I helped her get to the rail."

"Celia got a muscle cramp?" That stunned her. To her knowledge, Celia never got muscle cramps while exercising.

A flush slowly crept up Micah's neck. "I may have had something to do with that."

An image formed, and her jaw hit the deck. "What exactly were the two of you doing in the water?"

His gaze snapped to hers, and his eyes widened. "Not that!" He reared back in his chair. "Just swimming, I swear."

"Then what's with all the dithering?"

He sighed. Rolled his shoulders. "It got awkward. I thought she was mad because of how I'd been holding her in the water, but it turned out she hated being rescued. Damsel in distress and all that. I hadn't realized how exhausted she was when she agreed to join my workout."

"So that's why she got a cramp." The explanation was pure Celia, especially considering her rivalry with Micah. He'd presented the one challenge she couldn't refuse, even knowing it would likely cost her. "She wasn't blaming you, was she?"

"No. She was mad at herself. After we cleared the air, I gave her a leg massage." At her questioning look he waved a hand. "I studied massage therapy before settling on marine biology."

"Oh." She'd learned something new about her brother. "I'm still waiting for the problem part."

"The problem is me. I'm attracted to her."

"That's not surprising." She smiled at his annoyed expression. "Most men are. Quite a few women and non-binaries, too. She's beautiful."

He glared. "I know that. And the night we met I responded to that beauty. But then her behavior completely turned me off, squashing those feelings. Now, I'm getting to know her, learning who she really is, and *that* woman fascinates me."

She hadn't seen this coming, not considering the cold war her brother and Celia had been waging, but she should have. After meeting Iolana, his childhood friend and surfing buddy, she should have guessed that Celia was his type — strong, independent, athletic, self-confident. "How does she feel about you?"

He shrugged, but his emotions weren't in line with his casual nonchalance. "She doesn't hate me anymore, and she's stopped treating me like a threat."

"There's something you're not telling me."

His mouth curved up. "Can't keep secrets from an empath, especially when she's my sister." He spread his arms. "She offered to make me lunch."

"Oh, really?" Celia loved to cook, so it might not mean as much as her instincts told her it did, but Micah's story made her suspect it wasn't that simple. "And what happened?"

"I turned her down."

"You turned her down? Why?"

His head tipped back and he stared at the ceiling. "Because she was thanking me for coming to her rescue. I don't want a gratitude invite. I want her spending time with me because that's what she wants."

Micah was splitting hairs as far as she was concerned, but he didn't know Celia as well as she did. Time to educate him. "Celia doesn't offer to do anything she doesn't want to do. Ever.

If she offered to cook for you, she wanted to. It wouldn't matter whether you'd saved her life or bumped into her on the street. The invite was legit."

He gazed at her, his green eyes intent as he processed what she'd said. "So I should take her up on the raincheck."

"She offered one?"

His smile was self-deprecating. "I asked for one."

"Ah." She studied him. "So you're attracted to her, and want to spend time with her, but you're justifiably wary. What are your concerns?"

"That I'm running toward a brick wall, for one. But more than that, I'm worried about her psychological scars. She hasn't told me much, but I gather she's been through trauma I can't begin to imagine. Her initial reaction to me emphasized that. I don't want to complicate things for her."

She folded her hands on the desk. "That's a reasonable concern. Celia's not the type of person who dates. The few times she's interacted with a man since I've known her, it was a one and done sexual encounter. She doesn't do relationships. Not romantic ones, anyway. I can't see you being okay with the first option, and she's not going to allow the second."

He nodded slowly. "That's what I suspected."

"What you have to decide is if you want to work to become her friend. If that would be enough for you. She seems to be considering that possibility, based on what you told me about your time in the biosphere together and her decision to join your workout, which is pretty extraordinary in itself. She doesn't have any male friends."

"She said something like that to me on the Yruf ship, that you and Lelindia were her only friends. That's hard to imagine. What about Kire and Jonarel?"

"They're her crewmates, and she'd give her life to protect them, but they're not her friends. She's never chosen to spend time alone with either of them."

"But she chose to spend time with me," he murmured, his gaze unfocused, like he was replaying prior encounters in his mind. "Why?"

She spread her hands. "I can't say. You're clearly a new dynamic in her world view. You generate strong emotions in her, which both worries and intrigues her. She seems to be trying to analyze you, find answers to why she reacts to you in a way she doesn't completely understand."

"Which leads us back to her past trauma." He stared at her, his jaw working. "I wish Dad were here. He'd be able to help sort this out."

"I think you're doing fine. Just keep your expectations realistic and follow her lead. If you do that, you might become her first male friend."

His smile was bittersweet. "I'd like that." He rose from his chair. "Thanks, sis. This helped."

As he turned to leave, she rose, too. "Do you know your next move?"

He paused, the sparkle in his eyes making her think of warm sand and salt air. "I think I'll go cash in that raincheck."

Seventy-Seven

"Unity, how long until the Yruf ship reaches the binary system?" Celia asked the emerald-green U-1 unit floating beside her. U-1 for Unity-1, so designated to differentiate it from any of Unity's other mobile units. She'd needed that distinction during her tactical discussions with Unity and Star.

"In Earth time, fifteen hours and seven minutes," Unity replied in Micah's voice.

The three had gathered in shuttle bay two after she and Star had walked Unity through a thorough orientation of the ship's tactical systems and defensive capabilities.

"And you're not having any issues maintaining your link?"

"We are not."

"And you're still in contact with the biosphere, too?"

"We are."

"Good." Better than good. Extraordinary, really. What the Yruf had accomplished would make every tactical officer in the Fleet green with envy, at least once they got over the little hiccup of dealing with an extremely illegal non-biological.

The strategic advantage Unity provided was huge. Not only would the Yruf be able to scout the entire binary system before the *Starhawke* arrived, thanks to the ship's modular design, but Unity would be able to provide full reports on what the Yruf discovered long before the *Starhawke* exited the jump window into the system.

"Star, how about you? Any issues?"

Star's image turned away from the scale model projection of the Teeli armada confronting the multitude of modular Yruf ships and the *Starhawke.* They'd been running simulations for the past four hours, the images filling a third of the bay, with Star and Unity controlling the ship movements while Celia circled the space, analyzing the results. "Unity's presence and connections have not adversely affected my systems or functions," Star replied.

"We hope not!" Unity's exclamation in Micah's voice conveyed their concern quite effectively, as did the sharp swivel of U-1 in Star's direction. "We are here to help, not hurt."

Ironic. Micah had been telling her the same thing about himself since day one. Unity had chosen their voice well.

"Of course you are," Star replied, her tone soothing Unity's agitation. "I was not implying otherwise. I simply anticipated the concern underlying Celia's question and responded accordingly."

They'd had several interchanges like this during this session. Unity's emotional responses to Star, which had an endearing earnestness, had convinced Celia that Unity was deeply invested in their relationship with Star. Despite the plurality of their nature, which meant Unity was never physically alone, they seemed to have been very, very lonely.

Celia could relate. Until she'd met Aurora — and Lelindia shortly afterward — she hadn't realized how lonely she'd been without friends. The absence of something you'd never had was easy. But once she'd made that connection, the thought of losing either of them turned her insides to stone.

Celia stretched her arms over her head and twisted side to side, loosening the muscles in her back. The yawn that followed told her it was time for a break. "I need food. You two good here while I'm gone?"

Star nodded and U-1 bobbed. "Star can tell us about the Nirunoc."

Celia suppressed a smile. Yep, Unity wanted a friend. "Then I'll see you both later."

When she exited the cargo lift on the main deck, she found Micah leaning against the bulkhead of the corridor leading to the observation lounge and galley. Judging by his reaction when he saw her, he'd been expecting her.

She slowed her steps, analyzing his body language. "Do you need something?"

He pushed away from the wall, his hands falling loosely at his sides. "Actually, I was hoping I could take you up on that raincheck."

She picked up on a subtle tension in his body and tone that implied he was more invested in her response than he wanted to let on.

Interesting. First he'd turned her down, and mostly avoided her for the past few days, but now he'd sought her out to accept her offer. Predicting his behavior was an effort in futility. "How did you know I was headed for the galley?"

He gave her a crooked smile. "I asked Star to alert me when you took a meal break."

Hmm. She might need to have a little talk with the Nirunoc about privacy on the ship. Then again, now that Unity was onboard, Star was the one without any privacy, a sacrifice she'd made willingly for the good of the mission and crew.

"Is that a problem?" Micah asked, his smile flipping into a frown.

"Not really." In fact, having Micah join her would give her an excuse to whip up something more interesting than the basic salad she'd been planning to fix.

"You're sure?"

"Yes."

His bunched shoulders relaxed, his smile returning. "Good."

A sensation like liquid sunshine spread across her skin.

"Will you let me help with the prep?" he asked.

The last time they'd cooked together, it had been a strained, aggressive affair. She'd been gunning for him. To her surprise, she liked the idea of trying again without the hostility. "All right. How do grilled portobello burgers and herb roasted potatoes sound?" After hours of talking strategy with Star and Unity, she was in the mood for comfort food.

His smile widened. "Fabulous."

"Then follow me."

"Yes, ma'am." He fell into step beside her for the short walk to the observation lounge. "How are things going with Unity and Star?"

"They're working really well together. Unity could use some more vocabulary lessons from you, though, to keep their voice consistent."

"Happy to." He followed her through the lounge and into the galley.

Stepping into the familiar space felt like coming home. This was her favorite part of the ship, although the training center was a close second.

"Have you always enjoyed cooking?"

His on-point question made her turn. She must have given a physical tell to indicate her internal thoughts without realizing it. "Not at first." She walked to the pantry and pulled the potatoes out, handing them to Micah to wash and cut. "It started as a means to an end because I wanted control over what

I was eating." She grabbed a sweet onion next. "But over time I realized I looked forward to it. How about you?"

"Learning to cook was a given growing up with my dad." The thunk of the knife through the potatoes started a steady beat. "He made cooking fun, even when I was a kid. We'd experiment, sometimes with gonzo combinations or creative flair."

She snagged a second cutting board and began chopping the onion. "Like what?"

"Well, I had a costume party at the house when I was in high school, and we made chili poppers with googly eyes and laid them in black and orange paperboard coffins like little mummies."

Her knife hand stopped moving. "I didn't realize that's what you meant by creative flair." She'd been envisioning striking color combinations or decorative presentations, not whimsy.

He shrugged. "The other kids loved it."

His tone was almost apologetic, which bothered her. She hadn't meant her comment to sound like a criticism. "Would you consider doing something like that while you're on the *Starhawke*?"

His brows lifted a fraction. "Would you want me to?"

"You mean when we're not in Teeli space about to face an armada led by a psychopath?"

"Yeah."

"Sure."

He smiled as he dumped the potato chunks into a bowl. "I'll give it some thought."

The rest of the meal prep passed mostly in companionable silence. They worked well together, with Micah fetching whatever they needed from the greenhouse while she supervised the cooking. After the food was dished up, he added a few sprigs of edible herbs to dress up their plates, turning them into works of art.

"You really have an eye for beauty," she remarked as she carried their plates to the small circular wooden table tucked in a corner of the galley.

"Thanks."

His reply was a fraction of a second too late. She scrutinized him, but his attention was on the table, where he was laying out the cloth napkins and forks at their place settings, giving it as much focus as if President Yeoh herself was coming to dine with them. She shrugged it off, settling into her seat.

He claimed the one to her right, next to the pantry and greenhouse doorway. Giving his plate an appreciative sniff, he met her gaze. "Thanks for making this."

The liquid sunshine sensation returned, spreading through her whole body. What was with that? It didn't hurt, but it felt strange. Maybe she'd have Lelindia give her a look over, make sure she wasn't developing some kind of infection. "You're welcome."

He picked up his burger and took a bite. "Mmm."

"Good?"

"Mm-hmm." He chewed slowly, clearly relishing the food.

That was familiar territory. She was used to people enjoying her culinary efforts, although Micah's approval pleased her more than she'd expected it to. Picking up her own burger, she took a bite. Yep, pretty tasty if she did say so herself.

He speared a potato chunk and popped it in his mouth. "Mm. The cayenne pepper gives it a nice flavor with the paprika."

"I think so." She watched him as he chewed. She'd never seen anyone savor food the way he did. Or show as much appreciation.

He smiled when he met her gaze. "This is really good."

He had a great smile. Effervescent. Uninhibited. Genuine. In fact, that one word seemed to define his core being. Funny that she'd considered him the polar opposite when they met, full of trickery and deceit. But analyzing his words and actions objectively, nothing he'd said or done gave the slightest hint of manipulation or false pretenses. He was the epitome of WYSIWYG — What You See Is What You Get.

His head tilted. "What?"

"Hmm?" His question pulled her out of her thoughts.

"You were looking at me strangely."

"Was I?" Probably. "Just realizing how badly I misjudged you."

"Oh." His gaze searched hers, as though he was trying to find an answer to a riddle. "I misjudged you, too."

That made her smile. "Hard not to when you're being attacked."

He returned her smile. "You're intimidating when you're suspicious."

Her smile turned wicked. "Only when I'm suspicious?"

That drew a laugh. "Okay, no, you're always intimidating."

"Glad to hear it."

His eyes sparkled when he laughed. Actually, his whole body seemed to glow. Aurora had said he didn't produce an energy field, but he certainly looked lit up right now.

"Which is why," he said, forking up another potato wedge and pointing it at her, "I've been reluctant to ask if you'd be willing to continue our sparring sessions."

She froze. They'd never talked about her meltdown the last time they'd met on the mat. She'd allowed her work to push the memory to the far recesses of her mind. Setting her burger down, she folded her arms on the table. "That didn't go well."

Empathy shone in his green eyes. "That depends on how you look at it. It felt to me like a turning point. I don't think we'd be here now, sharing this meal, if it hadn't happened."

He might be right, but there was a question she wanted an answer to, one she hadn't asked him at the time. "Why did you suggest it in the first place?"

He rested his fork on his plate and mirrored her pose. "I wanted a way to end the constant battle between us. Cade suggested sparring with you."

That caught her off guard. "You talked to Cade about us?"

He nodded.

"He wasn't concerned you'd get hurt?" She'd certainly gotten her licks in when she'd sparred with Cade.

"No. He said you were a fighter, not a bully. He was right. I don't think you could have brought yourself to really hurt me even if it wouldn't have hurt Aurora."

She wasn't so sure. The rage she'd felt had been intense. If she hadn't kept Aurora in the back of her mind as a check, she might have done serious damage.

And lived to regret it.

Shame – the emotion she'd dismissed as pointless until Micah had come on the scene – heated her skin. "I'm sorry."

"Hey." He reached out and rested his hand on hers then immediately pulled it back. "It's okay. I didn't bring it up to make you feel bad. I'd honestly like to learn how to fight, and you're a great teacher."

Her nerve endings tingled where he'd touched her. "How do you know that?"

He gave her a closed-mouth smile. "Because you taught Aurora, and I've sparred with her. I know strong technique when I see it. Her movements are fluid, precise. Yours are too, even more so. It's easy to see the connection from teacher to student."

That had to be one of the nicest compliments she'd ever received. "Thank you."

"You're welcome." His smile widened into a grin. "So, what do you say? Are you willing to train me?"

If she said no, she'd prove she was a coward who couldn't face the demons that might show up on the mat.

She'd never been a coward. She wasn't about to start now. "Absolutely."

Seventy-Eight

"This is insane."

"Insane?" Unity parroted in Cade's own voice.

"Not literally," Cade clarified. His gaze swept the cockpit of the two-seater Yruf ship as it detached from the main ship. The projected images surrounding him created the illusion that he was floating weightless in the sea of stars. His gut clenched, his baser instincts informing him he was about to die while his head argued he was just fine, thank you very much. "It's a figure of speech."

The Yruf pilot seated in front of him didn't seem to mind the abrupt sensory overload. She guided the ship toward their jump window at the perimeter of the binary system without so much as a head twitch or emotional flutter.

He knew at least twenty other Yruf vessels were spreading out through the system, but they were all invisible to his searching gaze.

"Ah." Micah's voice this time. "Micah explained that concept to us."

That prompted a tight smile. Micah had clearly been talking to Unity a lot. Cade's conversations with U-2, as the unit assigned to his team had dubbed itself after Cardiff apparently labeled the one on the *Starhawke* U-1, were increasingly natural. Almost all the vocabulary Unity used now was spoken in Micah's upbeat tone.

He hadn't realized how much he'd appreciate hearing Micah's voice until he'd been cut off from the *Starhawke*. It helped him feel closer to Aurora and made his interactions with Unity friendlier.

He also appreciated the nearly real-time connection Unity maintained with U-1. He'd been able to get updates on what was happening on the ship as the *Starhawke* followed the Yruf to the binary system. That's how he'd learned about Cardiff's naming convention.

"We're approaching the jump window," U-2 informed him from their niche at the back of the pilot's seat in front of him.

He switched his focus to the pilot.

The female Yruf's blue and gold scales were barely visible, hidden by the fitted helmet that connected her to Unity. Unity had attempted to explain the Yruf neural interface to him, but most of the words they needed to describe the technical aspects weren't part of Unity's or Cade's Galish vocabulary.

Suffice to say, the Yruf had created a system that enabled their pilots to communicate with Unity and each other in a way that allowed them to act as one. It also meant their ships could only be flown by Yruf pilots. Unity had made it clear the interface wouldn't work for Cade, might even prove hazardous, like the ultra-low frequency signal Justin had been exposed to.

The piloting system for the ship was a mystery, too. There was no console, no easily identifiable manual controls. The pilot wore gloves that connected to systems embedded within the seat. Lights flashed in a rainbow of colors, but they meant nothing to him.

"Interstellar jump in three, two, one..."

He braced, felt the millisecond hesitation as the ship switched to interstellar engines. The starfield vanished, leaving him in the center of a void for two seconds before the starfield reappeared at a different orientation.

"Whoa." He'd made interstellar hops before, but nothing that brief and never when his senses were trying to convince him he was in the middle of a spacewalk. His vision swam for a second as his brain caught up with the abrupt change.

The pilot turned slightly, her concern wafting over him.

"I'm okay," he reassured her.

That was another huge advantage of having U-2 along. They could translate Cade's words for the Yruf the same way Micah did. It was like having a travel-sized version of Micah with him at all times.

"Any sign of Teeli ships? Or Ecilam?" He couldn't see anything except the starfield, but it was a big system. Lots of places to play hide and seek.

"Not yet," Unity replied. "The first third of our ships have reached their destinations. We're waiting for the others to arrive."

The pilot guided them closer to the F class star of the binary pair. It shone like a whitish lemon drop in the distance.

"All ships are in position. We're beginning our sweep."

Cade's lips twitched. Unity wasn't just picking up Micah's words. They were starting to imitate his inflections and speech patterns, too. Before long, it might be hard to tell the two apart.

It took about twenty minutes for Cade to fully adjust to the unusual view the Yruf ship presented and relax into his chair. The ability to see in every direction, without obstructions or blind spots, certainly appealed to him. Even the *Starhawke* couldn't do that.

"Twelve percent of the system checked. No vessels detected, but we've located small items of technology in orbit around both stars."

Cade sat up straighter. "What type of technology?"

"Hang on." A segment of the image to Cade's left zoomed in, revealing an object hanging in space.

"That looks like a border buoy." One based on the Fleet design. "How many are there?"

"Three detected so far."

"If they're what they look like, the Teeli placed them to track ships in the system." *The better to see you with, my dear.* "You'll probably find more."

"We will look for more."

Over the next hour and a half, Unity reported the discovery of five additional buoys, but no indication of ships of any kind.

Cade logged the locations on his tablet, but frustration dug at his belly. "That's disappointing." Surrounding the Teeli force before the *Starhawke* arrived was his best-case scenario. "How much of the system do you have left to check?"

"Twenty-eight percent."

Significant, but not enough to hide an entire assault force of Teeli ships. He couldn't imagine Reanne taking on the *Starhawke* with fewer than a dozen ships, not after the defeats she'd suffered in previous encounters. She wouldn't let Aurora slide through her fingers again. "Clearly there's no armada lying in wait."

"Clearly," Unity agreed.

Which meant Reanne planned to attack after the *Starhawke* arrived in the system.

The question was, from where?

Seventy-Nine

"Jonarel, please stop fussing," Lelindia growled as Jonarel slid a pillow under her bent knees.

For the past hour she'd been trying — unsuccessfully — to read the information Tehar had provided about Kraed pregnancy and birthing techniques.

She should have gone into her office in the med bay, rather than settling on one of the couches in the cabin. At least there the only complication would be having Unity ask her to read out loud. They were eager to learn and had kept her and Micah talking almost non-stop this morning in the med bay and greenhouse.

That would have been preferrable to Jonarel's continual interruptions ever since she'd sat down.

First it was an offer of tea, then a plate of fruit and nuts, followed by a foot massage. Now he was trying to immobilize her on the couch with pillows. All that would have been fine if he hadn't kept asking the same question every fifteen minutes.

She tipped the tablet to the side and glared at her mate, giving him the same answer she'd given him before. "The baby and I are fine."

Worry lines creased his forehead as he glanced at her belly. "You are certain?"

She threw her hands in the air, the tablet smacking the bulkhead with a thump. "Yes! Just like I've been telling you for the past three days. Nothing's changed, except my patience is wearing thin. If you're going to act like this for the next four to six months, we've got a problem."

The worry lines deepened, his brows drawing down. "You are angry."

"Frustrated, not angry. I understand that protectiveness is in your nature, but even you have to admit your behavior has become borderline obsessive."

He licked his lips, drawing her attention to the moist fullness of his mouth. That was the other issue. Ever since she'd told him she was pregnant, he'd taken sex off the menu. His kisses had become chaste, his touch protective and comforting but passionless. The wild ride that had conceived their child had led to a sexual wasteland where he treated her like she was made of glass. It was driving her insane.

"I want you to be safe."

The hurt in his voice triggered a twinge of guilt. "I am safe." Or at least as safe as she could be considering they were in Teeli space headed for a potential ambush. She set the tablet on the coffee table and reached out a hand.

He clasped it in his, the warmth from his skin a welcome oasis in the desert.

"I'm also the same person I was before our child began to grow inside me. I'm not about to stop doing all the things I did before." She held his gaze as she lightly stroked her thumb across his skin and imagined where else she'd like to stroke him. "And that includes sex."

He jerked like she'd given him an electric shock. "You desire sex?"

She laughed, unable to stop it. His confounded expression was adorable. "Of course I desire sex! I have the most gorgeous mate in the galaxy who lights my body up like a Christmas tree every time he touches me. Why wouldn't I want to have sex?"

Heat flared in his eyes, but his gaze drifted to her abdomen. "You are carrying our child."

"So what?"

He frowned.

She pointed to the tablet. "I didn't get far in my reading, but I haven't come across any restrictions on Kraed females having sex while they're pregnant. Are you telling me Kraed couples refrain from sex after conception?" *Please don't let that be true.* If she had to wait until their child was born, she really would go insane.

His gaze drifted to the tablet, then back to her. "No," he said slowly, drawing out the vowel sound. "But you are not a Kraed female."

"That's right, I'm not. I'm the Nedale of the Suulh, the living embodiment of the lifeforce, and I guarantee that having sex will not have a negative impact on our child. But if we don't have sex until after our child is born, it will most *definitely* have a negative impact on *me*." She put extra emphasis to drive the point home.

He stared at her, his golden eyes reflecting confusion, concern, and a flash of something carnal.

She wanted to feed the fire of that last one.

Pulling the pillow out from under her knees, she crawled into his lap. "I know you worry about me, and our child," she whispered in his ear, then licked the sensitive skin along the edge and blew softly on the same spot.

He shuddered in response.

"I love you for that." She continued the teasing ministrations, giving him little licks and kisses along his neck. "But I love it even more when you touch me, when you bring my energy field to life." She reached his jaw, which was tight, as were the muscles of his neck. A good sign she was making progress.

"And I love it best of all when you let go of your fear and give me..." Dropping her voice to a throaty purr, she nipped his lower lip with her teeth. "Everything."

He groaned in surrender, his arms hauling her tight to his chest as his mouth came down on hers in a passionate kiss.

Oh, yeah.

Eighty

Aurora's fingers wrapped around the arms of the captain's chair, her nails pressing into the wood as the bridgescreen shifted from a view of the interstellar jump to the binary star system in Teeli space.

Her gaze swept across the screen, searching for unexpected flashes of light or movement. "Tactical?"

"Clear," Celia reported. "No sign of Teeli or Ecilam ships in the vicinity."

Just as Unity had told them. U-1, as Celia had dubbed their mobile unit, hovered to her right.

Aurora picked up on Cade's emotional resonance to port like a sunflower sensing the sun. She turned in that direction, glancing at Micah seated beside her. "The Yruf?"

"I've made contact with Ifel." A pause. "She's glad we're here because—"

"Roe?"

She pivoted to face Kire, who was suppressing a smile that rippled through his emotional field.

"You've got an incoming comm."

"On speaker."

Cade's voice flowed over her like wine. "Glad you could make it."

"Thanks for not starting the party without us."

His chuckle made her nerve endings vibrate. "Didn't have much choice. The Teeli are choosing to be fashionably late."

She released the tension in her chest and shoulders with a sigh. "Well, that's kind of rude."

Another chuckle. "You should tell them that when they arrive."

"I just might." She was smiling way more than the interchange warranted, but she couldn't help it. Having him nearby made her giddy. "Unity's been keeping us updated. Anything new to report?"

"Not much. The Yruf's sensors are finely tuned for the Ecilam, but they're not picking up anything in range. If they're out there, they're not close to the system at this point."

"And the Teeli?"

"Nothing on them, either, although the *Starhawke* might have better luck. Our sensors are already calibrated to detect the Teeli ships."

She caught his use of the word *our* to refer to the *Starhawke*. She might never get the smile off her face. "Celia, scan for Teeli ships to the maximum range of our sensors."

Celia bent over her console.

"Did you get a chance to go out on patrol in one of the Yruf ships?" she asked Cade. He'd told her he was hoping to.

"Yep. Had U-2 with me. Felt like Micah was along for the ride. Ifel's been keeping six ships out on rotation, watching for the Teeli and Ecilam. I know technically this is a binary system, but since you could fit the entire Sol system between the two stars, it's a big territory to cover."

"What about accessible jump windows?" She wanted to be ready if Reanne showed up with more firepower than they could handle.

"That's the double-edged sword. With the stars so far apart there are a lot of options for making a quick exit. We've been using various windows to access the system for the patrols, developing a map as we've gone along. Unfortunately, the Teeli could just as easily use them to descend in a coordinated net around a number of positions within the system. I'm sending the info I've gathered to Kelly now."

Kelly leaned closer to the navigation console, her red curls brushing the surface as she analyzed the incoming data.

"We located four buoys orbiting each star," Cade continued, "which look similar to the Fleet's border buoys but with Teeli modifications. They're probably functioning as both a communication relay and proximity alert. Once the *Starhawke* isn't camouflaged, the Teeli will definitely know you're here and where you're moving within the system."

And the game would begin. Aurora drew in a slow breath. "So, we don't have any Teeli or Ecilam ships lying in wait, the Yruf and Celia are monitoring the system for incoming, and you've calculated our best escape routes. Did you leave anything for me to do?"

He snorted. "Yeah. Since the Teeli aren't showing their hand, you get to be the bait, making a grand entrance to attract our prey." His voice lost the teasing tone, replaced with subdued tension.

Her fingers curled around the chair's arms again. "Celia, any Teeli ships on long-range sensors?"

Celia pivoted in her chair. "Not so much as a freighter, let alone a cruiser. Either Reanne's ships are in the middle of a jump, or they're waiting until we're visible before they make a move."

"And the tracking device on Reanne's transport?"

"If it's still transmitting, her ship is too far away for us to detect the signal."

"Then I guess it's time to get visible." She turned to Micah. "Alert Ifel that we'll be returning shortly. When we do, we'll be heading for the F class star. Kelly, jump us out to a distance where we can make a return jump as though we came from Fleet space. Cade, we'll see you soon."

"We'll monitor your arrival and follow you in."

"Understood."

As Kelly changed their trajectory to line up with the jump window, Micah leaned closer to Aurora, his voice low. "Any chance she won't take the bait?"

Aurora's lip curled. "With Reanne Beck, anything is possible."

Eighty-One

Cade watched on the Yruf vid monitor as the *Starhawke* entered the system and sailed past like a glittering, frozen waterfall.

The beauty and grace of its motion brought warmth to his chest. Or maybe that had more to do with the woman sitting in the captain's chair.

Ifel stood next to him on a smaller Yruf bridge than the one she'd shown them during his first visit with Aurora. That one, Unity had informed him, had remained with the biosphere, along with Ifel's throne room. He still didn't have any spatial orientation on how the Yruf ship fit together, but the biosphere had to be close to the main bridge and throne room. He'd probably circled all around it during his first stay and had no idea.

Ifel watched the monitor as the *Starhawke* glided toward the F class star visible as a tiny sphere of light in the distance.

The Yruf ship followed, now to the *Starhawke*'s stern.

His gaze darted to the tactical display. He'd learned enough about the various Yruf bridge systems over the past two days to understand that the sensors still weren't detecting any Ecilam ships in the vicinity.

"How are you going to play this, Reanne?" he murmured.

Ifel swiveled her head in his direction.

"Play what?" U-2 inquired from where they floated near his shoulder.

He waved away the question. "Just talking to myself."

"Okay."

Ifel turned back to the monitor.

This wasn't the first time Ifel or Unity had observed him talking to himself. He'd done a lot of it while they'd kept him alone in his cell. He had a feeling they'd both analyzed his behavior quite a bit during that period, trying to figure out whether he and his crew were friend or foe.

He alternated his focus between the tactical display and visual monitor as the *Starhawke* continued its trajectory, the brighter star of the binary pair growing more distinct as they ate up the distance. No change, even though they were fast approaching the orbit of the first buoy. Whatever Reanne had planned, it didn't appear to hinge on catching the *Starhawke* upon arrival.

"Looking pretty tense there, buddy," Justin said as he rested a hand on Cade's shoulder.

While Cade had been on patrol with U-2 and the Yruf pilot, Justin had been learning about the Yruf communication system. He'd found out Unity was responsible for the jamming signal that had rendered *Gladiator* mute during their first encounter, preventing them from getting their message to Admiral Schreiber before the attack on Stoneycroft.

Cade grimaced. "Planning for a confrontation with Reanne is like anticipating a showdown with a tornado. Even if you have all the right tools, you never know if you'll be in the right time and place when it hits."

"True, except this place is tornado alley. Hard to imagine her not making a move with Aurora at her doorstep."

"That's what I'm counting on." Tension coiled at the back of his neck. "But now I realize how much I was expecting her to be waiting for us. Or at least for the Ecilam to be here. This..." He gestured to the frustratingly normal readings on the displays, "isn't part of my plan."

Justin grinned, completely unperturbed by Cade's pessimism. "Then you'll adapt the plan. You always do." Slapping him lightly on the back, he headed to an empty chair beside a tan and black male Yruf he'd befriended.

Cade wanted to start pacing, but that would agitate the Yruf. As it was, he was starting to get looks. Was he projecting his emotions? Probably. He hadn't worked on that part of his ability the way he had sensing the emotions of others, which meant he could be pummeling the bridge crew without meaning to.

Taking a deep breath, he focused on the one thing guaranteed to calm him — Aurora.

He could detect her presence, a distinct sensation he felt mostly in his chest. That feeling had been absent during their separation, making it even more noticeable when she'd arrived in the system. He'd known it instantly, before Unity said a word.

He couldn't track Aurora the way she tracked him, couldn't close his eyes and know which direction she was in. But he could tell if she was moving closer or farther away as the sensation either intensified or abated.

Right now it was holding steady. The star had grown to the size of a grapefruit on the display, the more distant G class companion still barely more than a point of light.

He tapped his comband, opening a channel to Gonzo. "How are things going down there?" Gonzo, Williams, and Drew had chosen to stay with *Gladiator* in case they needed to fire the ship up in a hurry to engage the Teeli. They were monitoring the video feed the bridge crew was sending them.

"Just ducky," Gonzo replied. "But I'm getting the feeling we might be all dressed up with no place to go."

"You could be right. Aurora's put herself front and center. The next move is up to Reanne."

"She'll make it," Gonzo said with certainty. "If there's one thing the past six months have shown, it's that she can't resist temptation. Aurora's presence in Teeli space is too much of a lure for her not to react."

"I hope you're right." Although a small voice in the back of his mind whispered *be careful what you wish for.*

Eighty-Two

"Well, this has been anti-climactic." Aurora rose from the captain's chair and walked closer to the bridgescreen.

The luminous star, still more than two A.U.s away, shone like the galaxy's biggest lantern through the light shield that protected the crew's eyes. But after more than an hour in the system, the view remained unmarred by movement.

"Where the hell is she?"

Kire snorted. "Just like Reanne to not spring the trap when you're expecting her to. Never could count on that woman."

Aurora growled, her gaze moving to Celia's tactical display. "Anything on scanners?"

Celia pursed her lips, looking as non-plussed as Aurora felt. "Not a thing. We passed within range of two of the buoys on our approach. There's no way they've missed our arrival."

"Unity? Any sign of the Ecilam?"

"Not yet."

"So she's biding her time." Aurora planted her hands on her hips and glared at the bridgescreen. "Figures."

She could sense frustration rippling through the bridge like air currents. Even Micah gave off a flash of annoyance.

The irony made her smile, then chuckle as she turned to face her crew. "You do realize we're all getting upset because we're *not* being attacked?"

Micah answered her smile with one of his own. "We have high expectations."

"Yes, we do. And right now my expectation is for us," she swept her arms to include the entire bridge, "to figure out our next step. Reanne doesn't seem inclined to grace us with her presence at the moment."

"We haven't discussed that possibility," Kire said. "We're stuck here until she shows up, right?"

"Based on the stated mission parameters, yes. We're expected to be here for a few months researching the binary star system and checking the planets for any signs of life. It's possible she's counting on us letting our guard down if she delays her attack. She's capable of extreme patience when it serves her interests."

"So how do you want to play this?" Kire asked her.

Aurora nibbled her bottom lip as she turned the question over in her mind. "We can't return to Fleet space empty-handed. I'm counting on bringing back Reanne, or at the very least proof of the Teeli charade. Until that happens, we'll need to act like the science vessel the Teeli expect us to be." She gazed over her shoulder at the glowing ball of the star. "If we don't see the whites of her eyes within the next twenty-four hours, we'll follow the mission parameters and begin studying the binary star system."

"Unity and the Yruf can help with that," Celia said. "Not the studying part since we couldn't explain where we got their data, but they can watch our backs so we won't be caught unaware. Cade's team can help, too."

Aurora nodded "Hawke to Clarek."

Jonarel's voice came over the speaker. "Yes, Aurora?"

"Reanne is a no-show, at least for now."

"I assumed."

"I need you on the bridge to coordinate with Celia and Kelly. You'll be determining the best flight path that will allow us to gather the data on the binary star system while keeping ourselves in a good defensive position for whatever Reanne has planned."

"On my way."

Her gaze moved to Lelindia seated in the chair to Micah's left.

The indulgent look in Lelindia's eyes made Aurora grin.

Jonarel's help determining the flight path would be beneficial, but she'd had an ulterior motive for asking him to the bridge. She and Lelindia both knew he was due for a check-in to assure himself his mate and the baby were okay. Two hours seemed to be the current upper limit of his tolerance before his overprotectiveness triggered undesirable behaviors.

Star materialized beside Aurora. "May I be of assistance? Obtaining data on planetary bodies is one of the tasks I looked forward to performing ever since you designated me as a science and exploration vessel."

"Really? I wasn't aware. Then again, I guess we haven't been doing a whole lot of science and exploration work, have we? Not in the academic sense anyway."

"No, but it has been stimulating nonetheless."

"Stimulating. Good word for it."

And now they were cooling their heels.

Aurora turned to the bridgescreen, her spine stiffening as the inky blackness stared back.

"Where are you Reanne?"

Eighty-Three

"Any indication we'll have guests soon?"

Celia met Micah's gaze over her shoulder as he rested his hands lightly on the back of her chair and peered at the information on the tactical console.

"Not looking like it." After four days with no sign of the Teeli, her frustration level was mounting. They were currently collecting data on the innermost planet orbiting the F class star, a gas giant that was tidally locked, with one side blasted with inferno heat while the other remained in eternal darkness. No hope for life there, which was the scientific endeavor that would most interest her.

"Any indication of life on any of the outer planets?"

She eyed Micah. It wasn't the first time he'd hit on exactly what she was thinking without her saying a word. It had her wondering if all his work with the Yruf had enabled him to tune into the thoughts of the *Starhawke* crew, too.

"Definitely not on the inner planets. But there might be a possibility for life on the fifth planet orbiting this star, or the second and third planets around the G class star. They're all in the Goldilocks zone."

"Not too hot or too cold, right?"

"Uh-huh. But it'll be another week before our flight path will bring us close enough to the fifth planet to start getting any significant readings."

"Hmm." His gaze moved to the bridgescreen.

A close up of the gas giant showed its dark side as a black sphere transversing the brilliant yellow-white of the star.

Micah stroked a hand over his jaw. "When we started this mission, I thought I was mentally prepared for what we were going to face. But this unending tension is chipping away at me."

"Have you been in the hydrotank lately?"

He shook his head. "I don't want to risk it. Bad place to be during a battle."

"Ah." That explained a lot. For someone who spent so much time in or near water, this situation probably felt like crossing the Sahara.

Not that Micah had been idle. Over the past few days he'd spent a lot of time with Unity, teaching them about the marine life on Earth, the history of human space travel, including his own family's contributions, and reading out loud from the multitude of books in the ship's digital library.

Unity behaved like a kid on a field trip, but Micah acted like his life depended on it. They'd spent most of the previous day in the greenhouse with Lelindia who, according to her report to Celia last night during a shared meal, had given him a master's class in botany.

He'd also been providing meals for the crew so that Celia could stay at tactical. The only time she'd left her post was when Jonarel spelled her during her sleep cycle.

Not that it did much good. She'd been plagued with nightmares involving shadowy figures and clanging metal, often waking with her heart pounding and her fists clenched.

The disturbing images and lack of restful sleep weren't conducive to physical or mental well-being, especially if this dragged on much longer. She could use a little tension relief, too. "Maybe we should schedule a short sparring session after my shift."

His eyes widened, the flecks of gold scattered in the green catching the light. "Really? You've been so busy I didn't want to bring it up."

Because he was a considerate guy. "It couldn't be long, but maybe—"

A flashing light and low tone snapped her back to her console. Her fingers flew over the controls. A second later she spun to face Emoto in the captain's chair, almost clipping Micah in the process. "A ship just exited a jump window, headed our way."

"Teeli?"

"Yes, but not Reanne's cruiser. Too small."

"Start checking for other ships. Unity, alert the Yruf."

Celia bent to her task as Emoto made a shipwide announcement, Micah still hovering over her shoulder.

Aurora arrived first, striding from her office to the captain's chair. A red crease on her cheek suggested she'd fallen asleep at her desk. Again. Except to shower and change clothes, Aurora hadn't spent any time in her cabin since they'd arrived in Teeli space, despite Emoto's, Lelindia's, and her objections. "Status?"

"One ship," Celia replied, "not a configuration we've seen before. Larger than a warship, smaller than a cruiser. No other ships have entered the system. Yet."

Kelly was ten seconds behind Aurora, stepping off the lift dressed in pale blue pajamas with white fluffy clouds on them, whipping her unruly red mane into a ponytail. She swung into the navigator's chair, taking helm control over from Star.

"Kelly, hold our current position. Celia, bring weapons on standby but keep them concealed and don't target the ship. I'm guessing this is the supply ship Sly'Kull told us he'd be sending."

"Aye."

"Unity, are the Yruf detecting any Ecilam ships?"

Micah's voice came from the ship's speakers. "No. But Ifel has redirected one of our scout ships to intercept the Teeli vessel's path and follow it in."

"Good."

In her peripheral vision, Celia saw Micah stride to the companion chair that had risen beside Aurora's. "Do you really believe it's a supply ship?" he asked, settling in beside his sister.

"I think it's what they want us to believe. Celia? Thoughts?"

Celia pivoted her chair. "Most likely it's a diversion. Get us focused on the incoming ship they told you to expect so we don't pay attention to the rest of the system."

"Which would be an effective tactic if we didn't have the Yruf. Still nothing on long-range sensors?"

"No."

"What about the configuration of the ship? Does it look like a freighter?"

She turned back to her console, magnifying the image and studying the sensor readings. "I'm not seeing anything that looks like weaponry. I'm also not detecting any heat signatures that would indicate armed weapons systems hidden under the hull plating. They'd have to have masking technology comparable to our own to pull off hiding weapons from us. We've never seen that type of tech from the Teeli, but then again, they've never had a reason to hide their weaponry when we've engaged them."

"So it may be a supply ship, or a decoy."

"Or an effective lure, making the opposite direction the most likely one for an attack."

"Unity—"

"We've already moved several ships to provide cover, Captain. We're prepared to fire the torpedoes on your command to deliver the modified ultra-low frequency disabling devices."

A notification pinged from Emoto's station. "We're getting an incoming comm from the Teeli ship," he informed them.

"Audio or visual?"

"Audio only."

"On speaker, but keep us muted."

The voice that came through had a nasal quality, like the person speaking had a bad head cold.

Aurora's eyes narrowed. "My Teeli is rusty, but I actually understood most of that." She glanced at Emoto. "I think he has supplies for us."

Emoto's face scrunched up like he had a migraine. "In the version of Teeli we were taught at the Academy, yes. They identified themselves as the freighter *Dry-e-Ver*, and they're here to resupply us." He shook his head. "Sorry, I've got the two versions warring in my mind. In the actual Teeli language, it translates as *jumping pond Dry-e-Ver white star smooth*."

"Lovely." Aurora put a lot of sarcasm in that single word. "Ask them what types of supplies they've brought."

Emoto relayed the message. "Water and perishable food."

Aurora's lips tightened. "Sly'Kull might have actually told the truth about the ship, the better to hide the lies." Her fingers drummed on the armrest of the captain's chair. "So, do we play along? Accept the offer and see what happens?"

"I say yes," Emoto replied. "If we don't, it'll look suspicious. We don't want to tip our hand."

"I tend to agree." Aurora turned to Celia, brows raised in question.

The Teeli ship had *trap* written all over it. "How do they want to deliver the supplies?"

Emoto relayed the question to the Teeli. His eyes narrowed as he listened to the reply. "They want to dock ship-to-ship."

Celia snorted. "I'll bet they do. That freighter would make an excellent anchor."

"Not going to happen." Aurora's smile looked slightly predatory. "Please convey our apologies for the inconvenience, but inform them that per Fleet regulations, we are unable to dock with a non-Fleet vessel while outside Fleet space. However, we would be happy to accommodate one of their transports in shuttle bay one."

A back and forth in Teeli ensued between Emoto and the Teeli representative. Then Emoto clicked off the comm. "They'll meet us in the shuttle bay."

"That wasn't all they said." Aurora gave him a pointed look.

"Oh, they tried to make a case that because this was a joint mission, docking should be permitted. I repeated the Fleet regulation several times until they gave up."

"Nicely done." She turned to Micah. "You and Unity are in charge of keeping the Yruf informed of what's happening."

"Of course."

"Hawke to Clarek."

"Go ahead."

"I need you to take command on the bridge while Kire and I handle the Teeli guests who will be arriving in the shuttle bay."

"Be there in a moment."

Celia would bet good money he and Lelindia were arguing about whether Lelindia would be staying put in their cabin during the Teeli's visit. "Shouldn't I be going with you?"

Aurora shook her head. "We can't risk it. Kire and I are immune to the Teeli's manipulation. We don't know about you, and I can't allow them to get into your head at this juncture. But I will need you in mine." She slid open a compartment on the captain's chair and pulled out an earpiece, tucking it into her ear and tapping her comband to pair them. "You're in charge of monitoring and reporting all activity on that shuttle and in the bay. Star?"

The Nirunoc's image materialized in front of the captain's chair. "Yes?"

"You'll be coordinating with Celia to make sure the Teeli don't pull any tricks while they're onboard. You both have full discretion to make any decisions you deem necessary for the safety and security of the ship and crew."

Star's gaze met Celia's, a glint of steel in her yellow eyes. "Understood."

Celia almost hoped the Teeli would be foolish enough to try something. She'd take great pleasure in showing them this ship had an uber-intelligent guard dog with very large teeth.

Eighty-Four

"Gonzo, tactical update." Cade kept his gaze locked on the image of the Teeli ship on *Gladiator*'s cockpit display. The vid feed and tactical data were coming through from the Yruf ship and the *Starhawke* thanks to Unity's integration with all three ships' systems.

"No sign of additional Teeli ships," Gonzo reported from the station behind Justin's seat, "and no indication of weaponry on this one. Nothing the *Starhawke*'s sensors can detect, anyway."

Cade wasn't sure whether to be annoyed or relieved. The waiting game had worn an edge on his nerves. "U-2, what's happening on the *Starhawke*?"

The unit hovered into his line of sight. "Aurora and Kire are preparing to greet the Teeli shuttle in bay one."

He ground his molars together. "They're allowing the Teeli onboard?"

"The Teeli claim to have supplies. Aurora said a supply ship was expected."

Only if Sly'Kull was being honest, which wasn't a Teeli personality trait. He glanced back at Gonzo. "Still no sign of ships?"

Gonzo gave him an apologetic shrug. "Tactical's clear."

"So we're supposed to believe this is legit?"

"*Supposed to* being the operative phrase," Justin chimed in. "This fits with Reanne's MO of keeping all behavior normal expect the part of the plan you can't see. Or anticipate."

Cade bared his teeth. "I really despise that woman."

"You're in good company," Williams said from his position beside Drew in the doorway behind Cade's chair. "I venture a lot of folks will be delighted to see her brought to justice."

Cade peered closer at the image of the Teeli ship as a squat shuttle exited the bay at the stern. "Any chance she's on that shuttle? Or that ship?"

"I seriously doubt it." Justin peered at the image, too. "Too exposed. I can't imagine her choosing to fight on Aurora's turf, even in Teeli space."

"Neither can I," Gonzo agreed.

"No, she wouldn't." Cade watched the ungainly shuttle trundle toward the *Starhawke*. "She's too strategic for that."

And it was driving him nuts. He itched to do something, take action, but he wouldn't. The best way to help Aurora right now was to sit tight.

That didn't mean he had to like it. "Whatever Reanne has planned, we'll find out soon enough."

Eighty-Five

The oversized shuttle that landed in the *Starhawke*'s bay was as visually uninspiring as the freighter holding position to the ship's starboard side.

"I recognize that design," Celia said in Aurora's ear as the shuttle settled like a toad in the middle of the spacious bay. "I saw one just like it when we visited the Suulh village on Feylahn. Fahn and the group of young villagers loaded food crates onto it for the Teeli. It was the price they paid for the Teeli's supposed protection from the Setarips."

Aurora's gut clenched, bile rising in her throat. The food and water the Teeli were so generously offering wasn't even theirs to give. It was the product of Suulh labor, stolen from Feylahn. Stolen from her people.

But she couldn't let her emotions take hold and give her away. Wiping her revulsion from her features, she and Kire entered the bay.

The back end of the shuttle lowered, making it look even more like a squatting toad, though the comparison was insulting to toads. They were much cuter than the shuttle. And the Teeli exiting it.

"Do all Teeli males look that smug?" Celia asked in her ear as two approached them.

Aurora's lips twitched. "Mm-hmm." Sly'Kull certainly had. But she was willing to believe not all Teeli were like that. Lelindia had shared what she'd learned from Siginal about the Teeli lower classes, who were clearly as oppressed and abused as the Suulh. She doubted they had the arrogance of the Teeli walking toward her.

She also noted that their gazes were on Kire, not her.

They stopped in front of him, the taller of the two extending his hands in the typical Teeli greeting. "Captain Hawke, I am Kal-a-Mec," he said in Teelian.

Thank goodness for her Academy Teelian language courses. Even if the language she'd worked so hard to learn wasn't used by all Teeli, it was coming in handy here.

However, these Teeli clearly hadn't been briefed on the *Starhawke*'s crew roster.

Kire's hands remained at his sides. "I'm Commander Emoto, the *Starhawke*'s first officer," he replied, also in Teelian, speaking slowly and enunciating clearly. "This is Captain Hawke." He gestured to her.

The look of stunned shock on their faces almost made her laugh, but she choked it back. Celia's imitation of a cat hissing and spitting in her ear didn't help.

She might have believed it was an act, except their emotions were in perfect sync with their expressions. They looked at Kire like he'd said one of the plants in the *Starhawke*'s greenhouse was the captain.

"You are not Captain Hawke?" Kal-a-Mec asked Kire, both males still refusing to look at her.

She was tempted to break into a soft shoe routine to see if she could draw their attention. She settled for a more professional approach. "I'm Captain Hawke," she said, stepping closer and extending her hands. "Welcome to my ship."

The shock switched to disgust. Kal-a-Mec touched her hands for the briefest of moments before releasing them and stepping back with a dismissive sniff. He focused his attention on Kire again. "We have your supplies."

His behavior made one thing clear. Whatever Reanne had planned for this trap, these Teeli were not in on the plot. They had no idea she was a person of great significance to their Sovereign. Or that their Sovereign was a female.

Kire gave her a sidelong look. She lifted her chin in the direction of the shuttle. He nodded in acknowledgement. "We appreciate your generosity," he replied, a hint of irony in his tone.

Celia snorted in Aurora's ear, which almost broke through the cool calm Aurora was struggling to maintain. Celia must be interpreting the conversation through tone and body language.

Aurora shared the sentiment, but kept her opinions to herself as she walked with Kire toward the shuttle. She hung back as they neared the opening, dropping her voice to a low undertone. "Any issues?" she asked Celia.

"Other than the pond scum in the bay? Nope. No sign of other ships in the system and nothing out of the ordinary on the shuttle. I haven't picked up weapons signatures of any kind, including handhelds. They're clean."

"Good to know." Not that any weapons on the shuttle were likely to pose a danger. Between her shielding and Star's abilities to defend herself, they could neutralize most threats in seconds.

As though the Nirunoc had heard her thoughts, a Kraed cargo glider rose from the deck of the bay a few meters from the edge of the shuttle's ramp. It startled Kal-a-Mec, who lurched backward.

Now Star was getting into the general mood of the visit.

Kire reassured Kal-a-Mec and pointed at the glider, which hovered a few centimeters off the deck as it floated toward them. Kal-a-Mec eyed the glider with suspicion, like it might try to take a nip at his shins as he backed up the ramp into the shuttle.

"Keep an eye on him," Aurora whispered as she stepped closer to the shuttle.

"Every move he makes," Celia replied.

As Aurora came into view of the shuttle's interior, two more males, much younger than Kal-a-Mec and his companion, rolled two metal tanks down the ramp. They both jerked to a halt when they spotted her, their eyes widening.

"Female?" one stage whispered to the other.

Kal-a-Mec barked something she didn't understand. Both males snapped to, pretending she was invisible as they unloaded the large cylinders, positioning them carefully on the cargo glider at the foot of the ramp.

But they couldn't hide their emotions from her. One shared Kal-a-Mec's disgust, but the one who'd spoken seemed intrigued by her presence, like she was a mythical unicorn who'd stepped out into the open. She caught him darting a glance at her when Kal-a-Mec turned his back to supervise the rest of the unloading.

She held his gaze for a moment, giving him a closed-mouth smile.

He looked away immediately, but she felt the ripple of confusion and curiosity her response had triggered.

"That one's not so bad," Celia piped up as Aurora watched him and his crewmates carry crates of what she assumed was food off the shuttle and stack them beside the water tanks. "He doesn't seem to have a stick up his butt like the rest of them."

"Hmm."

The young Teeli continued to sneak peeks at her as he worked, though he kept his gaze at shoulder height or lower rather than risking meeting her gaze again.

She held her position, arms folded loosely and legs shoulder-width apart. She didn't mind if he wanted to satisfy his curiosity. If Kal-a-Mec wasn't such a jerk, she'd even talk to the boy, who appeared to be close to Keenan's age.

What did he see when he looked at her? Anatomically, the Teeli weren't that different from Humans and Suulh, with a nearly identical skeletal structure and mammalian-style physiology. The most obvious differences were pigment-related, with all Teeli having grey-toned skin, thick white hair, and blue eyes. Except now that she scrutinized the four males before her, she realized their skin was a darker shade of grey than Sly'Kull's, their hair more silver-grey than white, and their eyes more grey than blue.

Was it by chance? Or did the color variations have some significance? Maybe all the Teeli on the shuttle were related.

Kal-a-Mec strode down the ramp and stopped beside Kire, continuing to studiously ignore Aurora's presence. He spoke rapidly, so she only caught part of the meaning of his words, but it was clearly a question.

"No," Kire replied much more slowly, "we do not need technology or engineering supplies at this time."

At least she was fairly certain that's what he'd said. As soon as this delivery was finished, she was going to brush up on her Teelian.

While Kire wrapped things up with Kal-a-Mec, the cargo glider slid away from the shuttle, guided by Star's unseen hand, heading for the doorway to the corridor and the cargo bay beyond.

Celia's voice spoke in her ear. "Star, Unity, and I will scan the contents for contaminants and hidden tech before allowing them anywhere near the rest of the ship's stores."

"Thanks."

She and Kire followed the glider, the shuttle's engines thrumming to life. After the bay's hatch closed behind her and the exterior bay doors opened so the shuttle could exit, she turned to Kire. A nagging question had been bothering her ever since the Teeli had made contact. "Why were they speaking the Teelian we learned at the Academy? We're in Teeli space. Shouldn't they be using the language they spoke on Feylahn?"

His jaw tightened as they passed the glider and walked to the personnel lift. "I've been thinking about that. It's possible the Kraed made an assumption that isn't true. Siginal said the version we learned was made up, a complex construction designed to keep us off balance and to hide the Teeli's actual communications."

"Which makes sense, considering the Teeli's ulterior motives," she said as she stepped onto the lift.

"It does, but what if there's another explanation? What if the version we learned is a real language, one the majority of the Teeli use?" He faced her as the lift rose. "The complexity of the construction could be a natural outgrowth of pulling words from other dialects, in much the way English integrated words from other romance languages like French and Spanish, complicating the rules of grammar and spelling. Words might also have adapted geographically, creating multiple meanings depending on cultural context."

"If that's true, what's the logic behind the version you and Oracle translated that the Teeli used on Feylahn?"

"My guess?" The lift doors parted on the bridge and he followed her out. "It's a streamlined, decluttered version created by the ruling class as a way to talk in the presence of the lower classes without being understood. They took words from the base language, gave them different meanings and grammar, and linguistically separated themselves from those Teeli they considered beneath them."

Aurora glowered. "And they taught us, the lowly humans, the language of the masses for the same reason." Her lip curled. "The Teeli have an amazing knack for coming up with new ways to tick me off." She halted beside Micah, who was standing next to Celia's station. It looked like he'd been monitoring the video feed from the shuttle bay. "Any updates?"

He shook his head. "All quiet. The shuttle's on its way back to the freighter. The Yruf report no sign of Teeli or Ecilam ships."

She turned to Celia. "What about surveillance or incendiary devices in the tanks or crates they unloaded?"

"Nope. The cargo glider has built-in scanners. Star's already scanned every millimeter of the containers and contents and Unity did a biohazard check, too. There's no tech or hazard of any kind, just water and food."

Aurora's gaze moved to the image of the freighter on the bridgescreen. "No attack, and no surveillance. So what's the motivation for sending them here? There's no way the Teeli are actually providing for us during this mission."

"How about physically confirming our ship and crew are here, for one," Celia replied, "although their reaction to learning you were the captain was interesting."

"I know. I don't think they're aware of Reanne's vendetta or why my presence here matters to her. But I guess that fits. She's not in the habit of sharing important information with underlings."

"I have a theory," Jonarel said as he rose from the captain's chair and walked toward her. "Reanne always assumes everyone is less intelligent than she is. I believe she is attempting to portray every facet of this mission as normal in the belief you will accept it at face value. If you do, you will leave yourself and the ship vulnerable to a surprise attack."

"That would also fit her MO," Aurora agreed. "But how long will she wait to drop the hammer?"

"A few days perhaps."

"I say a week," Kire interjected. "Much as she wants to catch Aurora, I think she's savoring the build-up to the moment. She's too much of a drama queen to rush it."

"That's two votes." Aurora looked to Celia. "What do you think?"

Celia's lips thinned. "Based on her behavior at the refugee camp on Gaia and at the island on Feylahn, I think she's going to slow play this. You said Sly'Kull told you to expect to be here for months?"

"Yes, but that was for the Admiral's benefit, buying time so he wouldn't start asking questions."

"Maybe. But it's also possible that now that Reanne has drawn you into the center of her web, she's going to work on steadily weaving it around you so when she strikes, you have nowhere to go."

The metaphor elicited a trickle of ice down her back.

But she was no helpless victim in this scenario. She gave Celia a grim smile. "The web that catches the fly also reveals the spider."

Eighty-Six

"You want me to come at you again?" Micah asked Celia as he bounced lightly on the balls of his feet, his toes making small indentations on the sparring mat.

She smiled inwardly at his eagerness. "Think you'll have better luck this time?"

"Luck's got nothing to do with it." His green eyes sparked with mischief. "I've learned a lot about my opponent since the last time we tried this."

So had she. Which would make this session a lot more fun.

Eight days had passed since the Teeli supply ship had visited them. The crew had accepted the possibility of a marathon rather than a sprint, so Emoto had changed the work rotations accordingly. He'd even managed to convince Aurora to start sleeping in her cabin again, rather than in her office.

This was the first time Celia and Micah's off hours had coincided. Neither of them had been willing to go in the hydrotank with the Teeli threat hanging over their heads, so sparring together was their best physical outlet.

She hoped it would cut down on her nightmares, too, which continued to plague her almost daily. When she woke, her bedding looked like she'd gone five rounds with a water monster, her sheets soaked with sweat.

"So tell me, oh wise one, what have you learned about me?" she asked as she circled to her right.

Micah circled in the opposite direction. "You don't need to look where you're going before taking action, for one. Where you look isn't necessarily going to give me a clue as to what's coming next. You could easily be four steps ahead." He grinned. "Sparring with you is kinda like playing extreme physical chess."

She rather liked that analogy. "What else?"

"You have excellent muscle control and balance."

"So do you."

"That might be the one area where we're evenly matched."

"What about strength?"

He made a show of flexing his biceps. "You think you're as strong as I am?"

"Empirically, no, but I know how to use my strength to best advantage in a fight. You don't."

The mischievous gleam in his eyes brightened. "So if you train me well enough, I'll be able to defeat you?"

She shot him a look through her lashes. "Strength isn't everything."

He chuckled. "No, but it doesn't hurt. Just ask my sister. She can kick my butt on the sparring mat, but I won the tickle wars. Her shield was useless against me."

"Really?" That was critical information she'd missed. "She can't use her shield to block you?"

"Nope. I pass right through it."

Good thing she hadn't known that fun fact when she was viewing him as the enemy. "Well, you don't have a shield, so I want to focus on what I taught her first – blocking techniques."

"Sounds good."

"We'll start with blows to the upper torso. I'm going to come at you slowly, telegraphing the strike. I want you to show me what type of block you'd use."

"Okay."

She didn't question why she was going so easy on him. Normally she would have learned what she needed to know without warning her student what was coming. That's what she'd done with Aurora, and how she'd treated him the first time they'd met on the mat. But today felt… different.

Trusting her instincts, she followed through on her plan, coming at him with steady controlled punches and kicks. He did an admirable job of blocking most of them, though a few came at angles he clearly was uncertain how to defend. She made contact, but with the force of a hard nudge that barely shifted his weight. "Now we know your weak points. Think you can mimic the strikes you couldn't defend?"

"Yep." He rolled his shoulders, his snug navy-blue T-shirt emphasizing the movement.

"Then try striking me the same way and I'll show you how to block or evade."

His recall of what she'd done was spot on, his attention to detail better than any trainee she'd had. His strikes came in at the same speed and angle she'd used on him.

She countered, using her arms and body angle to deflect the blows. "This is where agility defeats strength. I can tire out a stronger opponent simply by forcing them to work harder. Do the same sequence again, but faster and with more strength."

His eyes had lost the playfulness he'd exhibited earlier. Now they reflected intense concentration as he followed her order, coming at her fast and hard. She blocked him the same way she had before, keeping a wary eye to see if he'd change up his attack now that he knew what to expect.

He didn't.

She stepped back, hands on her hips. "You didn't adjust your attack."

He frowned. "Why would I? You told me to do the same sequence."

A faint smile ghosted her lips. "You're an honorable man, Micah Scott." Every other male trainee she'd taught would have taken advantage of the opening... and learned the error of disobeying orders.

He stood a little straighter. "Thank you."

"Ready to try blocking me again?"

He bent his knees, his stance widening. "Go for it."

She didn't hold back, coming at him as hard as he'd come at her. This time, he successfully blocked every strike, his body moving almost as fluidly as hers as he repeated the motions she'd shown him.

She nodded in approval. "You're a quick learner."

He shrugged. "I better be, to keep up with you."

"Let's see if you can adapt, too. I'm going to mix up the sequence. Same strikes, but in no particular order." She didn't add that she was going to test his endurance, too.

He fell into a fighting stance. "Ready."

She seriously doubted it.

He deflected the first few strikes before she landed a kick to his ribcage and a punch that grazed his sternum. He grunted, blocking the next three strikes before she connected again, eliciting another grunt.

She had experience and speed on her side, and she steadily drove him back toward the edge of the mat. Right before she pushed him off the shallow ridge, he surprised her by ducking into a tucked roll and popping up beside her. She managed to rotate her body in time to turn his hard kick into a glancing blow. The punch that followed met her forearm block, followed by a punch of her own that he sidestepped, backing to the center of the mat.

"Creative solution. I didn't know you had gymnastic skills."

His intense focus didn't change as he watched her movements. "A gymnastic foundation improved my surfing."

And that was a key difference between them. He'd learned so he could be a better competitor. She'd learned so she could survive. But if he was going to stay on the *Starhawke* for the foreseeable future, he would need to hone every skill she could teach him.

"Let's go again."

An hour later, she picked up one of the towels lying next to the mat and handed it to Micah.

He mopped the sweat from his face and ran the towel over his damp hair, which had darkened from blond to brown as the session had continued.

She patted her face and neck with her towel. "How do you feel?"

He rubbed the towel more vigorously over his hair, making it stick out in multiple directions like porcupine quills. "Exhausted. Exhilarated. A little banged up."

He'd hung in as she'd taught him defensive moves and blocks for attacks to his hips and legs, but she'd landed more and more blows as his endurance flagged. He wasn't standing perfectly square anymore either, favoring his left leg. "Do you need to go see Lelindia?"

He draped the towel around his neck. "No, I'm good. I heal quickly, remember? One of the perks of being half-Suulh."

His resilient attitude drew a smile. "Then why don't you let me fix you a meal. You worked hard today."

He chuckled. "And you didn't? I think I was just insulted."

She shook her head, but her smile grew. "My body is used to this kind of workout." She slipped her feet into her shoes. "Yours isn't."

"Not yet." He snagged his shoes and pulled them on. "That'll change soon enough, now that I know which muscle groups I need to work on."

"I have no doubt." Micah wasn't the type to avoid hard work. "So, dinner?"

"Absolutely. I'm not about to pass up the offer of a meal when you're cooking."

She didn't point out that he'd done exactly that the last time she'd offered, although he had claimed his raincheck. But he'd been doing all the cooking for the crew recently, and deserved a break.

Grabbing his water canister, he took a long swallow. "Care to make things interesting?"

She eyed him as she took a drink from her bottle. "What do you have in mind?"

Licking his lips, he backed toward the doorway. "Last one to the lift is on clean-up duty."

"That'll be you," she replied, stalking toward him.

"Oh, really?"

"Really."

"We'll see." Pivoting, he broke into a sprint.

With a feral grin, she raced after him.

Eighty-Seven

"How are you holding up?" Cade drank in the sight of Aurora as he sat in the pilot's seat of the *Starhawke* shuttle in the Yruf bay.

Their video chats had started out as a once every two or three days event. They'd become daily after they passed the two week mark and crept toward three with still no sign of Reanne, the Teeli armada, or the Ecilam.

Aurora sighed, slumping in the pilot seat of the matching shuttle in the *Starhawke*'s bay. "Not great."

She didn't look great, either. Dark smudges under her eyes and a lackluster complexion indicated she wasn't sleeping well, eating well, or both. But she was still the most beautiful sight he could imagine.

Technically she didn't need to be in the shuttle for their comm exchanges. Star and Unity had offered to pull up the projection in Aurora's office or cabin, but Aurora had made it clear she preferred to be in the same setting as Cade.

And didn't that make his heart squeeze. "Can't say I'm doing great, either." He gave her a rueful smile. "What's keeping you from sleeping?"

She tilted the chair back and stared at the ceiling. "An idle mind is a dangerous thing. I started thinking about Lt. Magee."

Oh.

"Reanne took her from the Admiral because of me. Now she's got her stashed somewhere out here. Magee wasn't supposed to be part of this. She should be on Earth, working at HQ. Instead, she's a pawn in Reanne's sadistic game, totally at her mercy. And there isn't a damn thing I can do about it."

"You are doing something." He sat forward, wanting to be closer. Too bad he couldn't teleport into her shuttle. "You're here, in Teeli space, ready to capture Reanne. That's the only chance we have of getting Magee back."

"Is it? I don't even know anymore. If Reanne's going to come, why isn't she here yet?"

"It's a mind game. Her favorite. You know that. If she can discombobulate you, throw you off balance, she has a better chance of winning. Don't let her."

Aurora smirked, slowly tilting her chair upright and meeting his gaze. "You're really good at these pep talks, you know that?"

"Is that why you keep me around? For my pep talks?"

A twinkle appeared in her eyes. "Not the only reason."

"No?"

"No."

"Care to enlighten me?"

"Are you fishing for compliments, Ellis?"

"Yes." He nodded, deadpan. "Yes, I am."

That drew a soft chuckle, exactly as he'd hoped.

"Okay." She tapped her lips with her finger, gazing into the distance in simulated deep thought. "You're a darn good pilot, handy in a fight, and oh so lovely to look at."

He tossed his head and struck a pose like he was ready for a close-up. "Am I?"

Her chuckle turned into a full body laugh that ended up lasting a full minute.

When she finally got herself back under control and met his gaze, he grinned at her.

She wiped moisture from her eyes and shook her head. "Oh, Cade, I needed that. Thank you."

"You're welcome." Too bad he wasn't there to keep that smile on her face. It was already fading way too fast, her expression growing solemn again.

"I've been thinking about the Suulh, too."

"I'm not surprised." In fact, he'd been expecting it for a while now. "Can you sense them? You've never been this close to the Suulh homeworld before."

She shook her head. "I don't think so, at least not consciously. Maybe if I concentrated really hard I could tell you which direction Feylahn is. Maybe. But that's not the issue." She rubbed her fingers against her temple, like she had a headache. "The Suulh are showing up in my dreams. A lot. Images from my mom's and Marina's history playing out in painful detail." She let out a ragged sigh. "I don't look forward to sleeping anymore."

And he wasn't there to hold her when she woke up, either. Frustration closed his hand into a fist. "Can Lelindia give you something to help you sleep?"

Her smile was bitter. "Not while we're in Teeli space."

Of course not. She'd want to be sharp and alert when Reanne showed up. "Have you talked to Lelindia about it?"

Aurora shook her head.

"Maybe she could help another way. Energy work or herbs."

"Maybe." Aurora's finger traced a pattern over the panel in front of her, her gaze following. "The problem is, I know what would help. I just can't have it."

His throat constricted. She didn't say it, so he did. "Holding you would help me, too."

She met his gaze. The yearning in her eyes would have buckled his knees if he'd been standing. But her voice was steady. "We'll get through this."

"I know." He believed in her so much it hurt.

"So what's keeping you awake?"

He hesitated. Should he tell her the truth? She was already carrying so much.

"Cade? What is it?"

"It's... you."

Her brows rose. "Me?"

Yep, he felt like a heel. "My ability to tune into your emotions is becoming more instinctive. I don't have to think about it anymore. It's like an emotional radio tuned to your station that's always playing softly in the background."

She exhaled slowly. "Sounds like it's time for me to teach you how to tune out emotional resonances you don't want to hear."

"That's just it. I do want to hear it. Every precious second. I don't want to sleep, because when I'm awake, I can feel you, almost like you're beside me. When I sleep, I lose my grip on that connection."

"So you don't sleep?"

"Not much." The push-pull brought pleasure and pain, but he clung to it until his body forced him into submission.

She propped her chin on her hands and gazed at him. "We're quite a pair."

He'd never wanted to hold her so badly. Just for a minute. Or an hour. Yes, an hour would be good. "You're worth every sleepless night."

The soft glow that only shone in her eyes when she looked at him sent a flow of warmth through his body.

"So are you."

Eighty-Eight

"Veebra baalaa, daaxhil makoo laanaa suhn mailawe suulhaa caanlee." The ancient melody played a soothing accompaniment in Lelindia's mind as she sang the words of the Suulh lullaby.

Her hands rested over her womb, her energy field swirling around and through her, its touch joining her with the life growing within.

Her daughter.

The sensation of her presence kept her in a perpetual state of wonder. She could feel every change in her child, see her developing through the filter of her Nedale senses as one week became two, then three.

It wasn't the first time she'd watched an unborn child grow. She used to stare at Libra's belly while she was pregnant with Micah and Aurora, watching their bodies steadily taking shape. But this was very different. This child was a part of her, and part of Jonarel, too. The feeling of completeness and bonding was so strong it brought tears to her eyes.

Her voice wobbled as the surge of emotion clogged her throat. Settling onto one of the benches in the greenhouse and closing her eyes, she expanded her energy field, enveloping the plants around her, their lifeforce blending with hers – soothing, calming, nurturing.

Jonarel had sung to her last night as they'd snuggled in bed together. The moment had been pure bliss – wrapped in the strong arms of her mate, their unborn child growing within her, and his deep baritone surrounding them with love. She'd drifted off on a cloud of happiness.

When she'd woken, she'd headed for the greenhouse while Jonarel had taken over tactical on the bridge. The rest of the crew were coordinating their duty schedules so she and Jonarel could always spend their sleep hours together. That thoughtful gesture had made her tear up, too. In fact, almost anything touching made her cry these days, but at least they were all tears of joy.

She sensed Aurora's approach even before the door leading to the med bay opened. That was something else that had changed. She was more intensely aware of Aurora's energy than she ever had been before, even when it wasn't engaged. She could track her almost as well as Aurora had always been able to track her. It was a normal part of a Nedale pregnancy, drawing her closer to her energy sister for protection of her unborn child.

"That melody sounds familiar."

She opened her eyes.

Aurora stood a short distance away, her hands clasped behind her back, her feet shoulder-width apart. She looked tired, drawn, her skin tinged grey even in the warm light of the greenhouse.

Lelindia patted the empty space on the bench beside her. "It should. You heard it every day for the first two years of your life."

"Really?" Aurora settled beside her with a weary sigh. "Is it a Suulh lullaby?"

"Mm-hmm. My parents taught it to Brendan, and he used to sing it to you and Micah all the time. In fact, it was the best way to get you both to sleep."

Aurora smiled faintly. "You make it sound like that was a chore."

"It was." Lelindia grinned at the memory. "Micah taught you to climb out of your crib when you were eight months old. You both preferred being awake and playing together. But you loved when your dad sang to you, too. Brendan figured out that if he promised to sing to you at bedtime, you would promise to go to sleep. It worked well, although he and Libra never figured out how to keep you from being the first ones up in the morning."

Aurora chuckled, a tinge of color returning to her cheeks. "At least they didn't have to worry about us hurting ourselves."

"That's true."

"So what's the lullaby about? The one you were singing. I caught the word laanaa, so I assume it has something to do with home."

"It's a song of welcome and connection. It talks about the vibrant energy the child's presence brings to the home and family."

"Aww. That's nice." Aurora tucked a leg under her and faced Lelindia more squarely. "Will you teach me the words?"

"You think you'll want to sing it?" She couldn't remember the last time she'd heard Aurora sing. It might have been at the Academy.

"Sure. I'm guessing it's part of Suulh tradition, right? Singing to the new Nedale? And besides, she'll be growing up on the *Starhawke* and I'll be part of the babysitting rotation. If this song worked to calm me down, it'll probably work on her, too. I want to learn it." Aurora's weariness had faded into the background, eagerness bringing light back into her eyes.

Fascinating. Aurora had resisted learning the Suulh language when they'd first encountered the Suulh, blocking her natural ability to pick up the words. From Lelindia's perspective, it had felt like a minor form of rebellion, resistance to the weight of responsibility that had crashed down on her.

But during the past few months, and particularly since reconnecting with Brendan and Micah and visiting the Suulh on Gaia, that resistance had vanished. Now Lelindia saw Aurora reaching out to her Suulh heritage, integrating it into the woman she had become.

"All right." Lelindia started singing again, slowing down the melody and enunciating clearly so Aurora could pick out the words.

Aurora had inherited Brendan's vocal gifts, her lyrical soprano blended with Lelindia's alto. Aurora engaged her energy field, the pearlescent and emerald fields twining like the vines on the trellis beside them.

A giddy joy worked its way through Lelindia's chest as she continued to sing. Aurora looked equally delighted. With a wink, she added a harmony to the song that blended beautifully.

A movement within caught her by surprise, her voice faltering.

Aurora cut off immediately, her hand reaching protectively toward Lelindia's belly. "Is something wrong?"

It took a millisecond for Lelindia's senses to report in. When they did, she gave a startled laugh. "No."

"Then what happened?"

Lelindia clasped Aurora's hand in hers and brought it to rest against her abdomen, their energy fields pulsing together. "Can you sense her?"

Aurora gazed into the middle distance. "I'm not sure." The corners of her eyes tightened in concentration, then widened in amazement. "I can! An essence that's like you but slightly separate, like an echo."

"That's her." The sensation flowing through her was indescribable, and incredibly beautiful. "I think we just triggered her energy field."

Eighty-Nine

A rumbling thundercloud hung over Aurora as she stared at the bridgescreen, the blue and brown landscape of the F class star's fifth planet mocking her.

Twenty-seven days. That's how long they'd been in Teeli space, watching and waiting for Reanne's attack.

But it hadn't come. And didn't seem likely to happen anytime soon. They hadn't detected any sign of the Teeli or Ecilam headed their way. The tracking device Celia had planted on Reanne's ship hadn't pinged either.

Why was Reanne ignoring them? After all the effort to create this mission for the *Starhawke*, all the manipulation, threats, and posturing to ensure they would arrive in Teeli space, why was she holding back?

The supply ship had returned five days ago. The transfer had given her an opportunity to test out her recently refurbished Teeli language skills — for all the good it had done. Kal-a-Mec had ignored her as studiously as last time, focusing on Kire instead. But at least she'd been able to easily follow every word that was spoken.

The boy who'd been fascinated with her before had been conspicuously absent from the unloading crew, replaced with a much older Teeli who'd given her as much consideration as a damaged cargo crate.

She hadn't picked up any heightened emotions from the Teeli that would suggest the crew had gained a clue about an impending assault. Celia, Star, and Unity hadn't seen any signs of subterfuge either, and Cade's team and the Yruf hadn't reported any anomalies or approaching vessels.

So here they sat, taking the scientific readings their mission had specified, trying to act as though the situation was completely normal. Ordinarily she would have enjoyed the work, but that was tough to do when she was always waiting for the other shoe to drop.

At least Ifel didn't seem concerned by the delay. Then again, patience was clearly one of the Yruf's greatest strengths. They'd spent decades observing the other factions and formulating a plan to reunite them. A month was a drop in the bucket by comparison.

"Micah to Aurora."

She answered the comm. "Yes?"

"U-1 and I are on our way to the bridge. Unity picked up a signal from the edge of the system that could be an approaching ship. But it's camouflaged."

Her spine straightened with a crack. "Camouflaged how?"

"They're not certain. Not exactly like the *Starhawke's*, but similar."

Which was a perfect description of the camouflage Reanne had used on the Etah ship on Gaia.

She opened a shipwide channel. "Battle stations. Vessel approaching of unknown origins."

Kelly turned from navigation. "Should I change position?"

"No. We don't want them to know we're aware of them."

The doors to the lift opened and Micah and Celia stepped out together, with U-1 floating in behind them as they moved with brisk efficiency to their respective posts.

"Are you tracking the ship's progress?" Aurora asked Unity as Micah dropped into the chair beside her that rose from the deck.

"Yes. It's heading directly toward us, but slowly." U-1 halted beside Micah. "It appears to be alone."

"From which direction?"

Micah pointed fifteen degrees to starboard. "There."

The direction of Fleet space. Odd. Or brilliant. What better approach for an enemy than the path home?

Kire exited the lift next, hurrying to the comm station.

Aurora turned to Celia. "Can you get any clear readings? Tell us what we're dealing with?"

Celia checked the data on her console. "Star, can you run a reverse scan for the enhancements we worked on to hide the ship from other Kraed vessels?"

Star materialized next to Celia's console. "Right away."

Aurora pivoted to Kire. "Anything on comms?"

"Not yet. They're not hailing us, that's for sure."

Aurora switched her attention back to Micah and Unity. "Anything from the Yruf?"

"We don't believe the Ecilam, or any other Setarips, are onboard," Unity answered.

That gave her pause. Reanne preferred to let the Setarips take the brunt of the damage from any battle she instigated. The Etah and Ecilam had both suffered heavy casualties as a result. Sending a single assault vessel without any Setarips onboard struck a wrong note.

Closing her eyes, she reached out with her empathic senses. She picked up hints of emotion — anxiety, anger, determination — but faint. Without opening her eyes, she held out her hand and engaged her energy field. "Micah, I need a boost."

As soon as his palm touched hers, a strong vibration from a very familiar emotional field locked in.

It was the last one she would have expected.

"Siginal."

Ninety

"Siginal?" Celia barked in outrage.

Star's reaction was much more measured. "My father is here?"

"Your father?" Unity echoed, swiveling toward Star. "Why would he come here?"

Aurora could think of only one reason why he'd follow the *Starhawke* into Teeli space.

He'd wasted the trip. Jonarel and Lelindia had effectively obliterated his overbearing plans to control her future. *All* their futures.

She tapped the comm. "Stand down battle stations. Lelindia, Jonarel, can you please join us on the bridge? There's something you're going to want to see."

The brief hesitation in their replies telegraphed their confusion regarding the abrupt change in status and her enigmatic request. "Um, yes," Lelindia said. "Be right there."

"As will I," Jonarel replied.

Her gaze swept the bridge, mentally setting the stage. "Unity, do you want to stay for this?"

"We want to help Star."

"Then would you mind settling down by Micah's feet so you won't draw attention?"

U-1 bobbed once, then sank to the deck. "Okay."

She turned to Kire. "Hail him, wide angle bridge image. And transmit the video feed to *Gladiator* but keep them muted." She wanted Cade to hear this.

The slight quirk to Kire's lips made it clear he was looking forward to this moment. "Hailing."

A few beats passed before the image on the bridgescreen switched to the bridge of the Kraed ship. The *Rowkclarek*, by the look of it, which she'd toured after Jonarel's kin had joined them on Azaana to build the Suulh settlement.

Siginal sat in the captain's chair, every line of his large body tight as a bow. "How did you know we were here?"

She stared him down. "Nice to see you too, Siginal."

"We do not have time—" He broke off as the lift doors opened and Jonarel and Lelindia stepped into view of the bridge camera.

Jonarel halted, his muscles tensing as much as his father's. "Hello, Father."

Interesting. He'd chosen to speak in Galish, rather than using the Kraed word for *father*.

"Jonarel." Siginal's gaze shifted to Lelindia.

Jonarel slipped his arms around Lelindia, drawing her against him with his hands settled protectively across her abdomen.

Aurora tracked Siginal's emotions like a bloodhound. They raced at lightspeed from irritation, to confusion, to revulsion.

"*No.*" The single syllable was horror and disbelief fused into one.

"Yes." A tremor in Lelindia's emotional field revealed her agitation, but the look in her brown eyes was calm and composed as she lifted her chin and held Siginal's gaze. "You were right about me, Siginal. I do love Jonarel. But you were very, very wrong about your son."

Rage blasted away all semblance of civility. "*No!* This cannot be. You—"

"We are pair bonded, Father." Jonarel's reaction was the polar opposite of his father's, cool as ice shards. "I am Lelindia's mate. And *she* is *mine.*" The last came out with a possessive growl and a rapier's stab, driving the point home.

Siginal's lips opened and closed like a fish out of water, soundless words forming and dissolving as his emotions went into a tailspin.

Was it wrong that she enjoyed his consternation? Probably. But after all the manipulations and half-truths he had fed her, all the pain and anguish he'd dumped on Jonarel, all the misery he'd caused them both trying to force them together, he deserved this lesson in humility.

She cleared her throat. "As you can see, Siginal, your reason for coming here is moot. Jonarel and Lelindia are mated." They hadn't mentioned their child, so she'd respect their choice to keep her secret. "And even more important, they're *happy*."

He dragged his gaze to her.

She'd been prepared for his anger. What hit her like a punch to the gut was his despair.

"You do not understand what you have done."

Okay, that lit up a whole panel of red lights. Now *she* was the one expressing tightly contained fury. "What I've *done* is encourage my dear friends to find love and joy together. What I've *done* is create a future for myself that's my choice. What I've *done* is look after the best interests of my crew. If that doesn't fall in with your plans, too damn bad!"

He shook his head. "There is much you do not know."

"Well, there's a news flash." Sarcasm gave her voice a rough edge. "You've been keeping things from me since the day we met. You convinced your own son to spy on me when I was sixteen and tried to force him into mating with me because of some master plan you wouldn't even share with him."

"You—"

She made a slashing motion with her hand. "I don't want to hear it. You manipulated me at the Academy, you tried to cage me with this ship," she swung her arms wide, "and when that didn't work you tried to strand my crew on Drakar. After they escaped you banished Jonarel and Star for standing up for me. In what universe did you believe that was going to bring me in line with you?"

She didn't wait for his answer. Months of bottled anger and frustration pulled her out of her chair, carrying her closer to the bridgescreen until she could see the brown flecks in Siginal's golden eyes. "Here's an idea. Maybe if you'd been honest with me – trusted me instead of manipulated me – I could have helped you come up with a plan for dealing with the Teeli that would have worked well for both of us."

She could sense the pain her harsh words and vitriol were inflicting. He'd never intentionally set out to hurt her. Or Jonarel and Star. She could feel that. But his actions had guaranteed he would. And instead of apologizing and seeing things from their perspective, he kept doubling down.

But that wasn't what brought her up short. Mixed in with the pain, she could also sense a new emotion rising inside him, a feeling she was inspiring.

Fear.

She'd never sensed that emotion from him before, but it shone like a neon sign now. Losing the potential for mating her with Jonarel had cut him off at the knees, making him look at her like an injured gazelle watching a stalking lion.

That cooled the heat of her anger to a low simmer. She never wanted those she loved to fear her.

"Siginal, I don't want to be your adversary. You've been like a father to me. I don't want to lose that connection." She didn't want Jonarel and Star to lose their connection to him, either. "But your methods for gaining cooperation stink. The way you've treated all of us since I took command of this ship is reprehensible."

Admitting he was wrong was not one of Siginal's strong suits, so she wasn't surprised when he remained silent.

She sensed Micah approaching, coming to stand behind her left shoulder.

Siginal's gaze flicked to him. "Who are you?"

Spoken like a cop who'd caught someone sneaking out a window.

Micah responded to the implied threat with a bubble of amusement. "I'm Aurora's brother, Micah."

Siginal's eyes widened. "Brother?" His gaze darted between them. "That is not possible."

Aurora's lips lifted. "Oh, I assure you it is. Micah's been living with my father since I was two. We reconnected while you were holding the *Starhawke* hostage on Drakar."

Siginal flinched at the jab.

"He's chosen to join the crew for the time being."

Siginal studied Micah, his gaze growing speculative. "Does he have your abilities?"

Oh, no. She could see the wheels turning on a train of thought that ended with Micah pair bonding with a Clarek clan female. She was derailing that train right now. "No, he doesn't. Sahzade abilities only go through the female line."

The light in Siginal's eyes died. "I see."

So did she. He was still focused on his grand plan with her as the lynchpin to bring the Kraed together to stand against the Teeli.

She needed to have a very long, very serious conversation with him about where they went from here. Jonarel and Lelindia needed to be part of that conversation, too. But not now. "Look, this is neither the time nor the place for this discussion. We need to be watching for—"

"You need to return to Earth."

The anxiety that came with that demand confused her. "What?"

"You need to return to Earth immediately. That is why I am here."

Another sucker punch. "Why?"

"Admiral Schreiber has been arrested for treason."

Ninety-One

"What?" Cade smacked the top of his head on the low ceiling in *Gladiator*'s cockpit as he surged out of the pilot's seat.

He rubbed the sore spot and swore as he slowly sank back down. Aurora and Siginal couldn't hear him, anyway. Or see him. But he could see her. She looked thunderstruck, her emotions smacking him like tree branches buffeted by a storm.

"They arrested the Admiral?" Justin sounded bewildered. "For treason?"

"On what basis?" Aurora asked, indignation in every syllable, her body rigid.

"Conspiring with Setarips to undermine the Fleet."

"*What!?*" Cade didn't launch out of his chair this time, but his shout filled the tight space.

"That's insane." Aurora paced behind Kelly and Celia's consoles. "What kind of evidence could they possibly have to support that?"

"I do not know. Enough that the Court of Justice indicted him."

"But it doesn't make any sense. He–" Aurora froze, her eyes widening.

Cade felt the stab of fear and horror that shot through her like a blade.

"Reanne."

Cade let fly with more choice words that blistered the console.

"That's why she hasn't come." Aurora's pale skin drained of color. "Why we've been sitting here for weeks. She was getting us out of the way." The color returned in a rush, her cheeks flushing red. "Kire, unmute Cade's audio and visual. I need to talk to him."

"Cade!" Siginal snapped forward and rose halfway out of his chair.

Cade didn't give Siginal's scathing tone a second thought. All his focus settled on Aurora as she met his gaze on the monitor.

The pain in her eyes cut deep. "We sprang the wrong trap."

He nodded. "I know. We'll fix this."

Determination muscled the pain aside. "Yes, we will." She turned to Micah. "Find out if the Yruf would be willing to take *Gladiator* back to Earth. They can get there faster than we can."

"The Yruf?" Siginal looked like he'd been tossed into a rock tumbler and told to hang on. "You are communicating with the Yruf?"

Aurora flicked the question away. "No time to explain. Suffice to say they're on our side. Kelly, plot the quickest route to Earth."

"Aye, Captain."

"Siginal, will you be coming with us?"

"Of course. Will is my friend."

"Good. Sounds like he's going to need all his friends." She turned to Jonarel. "Get the interstellar engines primed."

"Right away."

As Jonarel headed for the lift, Aurora swung back to Micah. "What did Ifel say?"

"She's agreed to take *Gladiator*."

"Good." Aurora met Cade's gaze. "We'll meet you there."

He wanted to wrap his arms around her. To be by her side. But that wasn't an option. Instead, he projected what was in his heart. "Safe travels."

The soft smile she gave him wasn't nearly as powerful as the emotional flow that came with it. Those emotions buoyed him like an updraft. "See you soon."

"Yes, you will."

The monitor blanked out as the connection closed.

"Anyone know a good lawyer?" Williams' voice boomed out behind him.

He turned. Williams, Drew, and Gonzo had crowded into the cockpit, while U-2 had moved beside Cade's chair.

Williams didn't look like a kindly doctor at the moment. More like a ticked off badger. "Because all my contacts are doctors."

Justin raised a hand. "I've got a few people I could reach out to. The Admiral should know some good candidates, too."

Drew brushed a lock of hair out of her eyes. "I can't believe we spent so much time researching members of the Council and it never occurred to us that Reanne would infiltrate the Court of Justice."

"Hindsight is twenty-twenty." Cade sensed the now familiar presence of the Yruf leader approaching. "Ifel's here."

His team cleared out so he could move down the corridor and meet her at the top of the gangway, U-2 right behind him.

Her concern brushed against him, nearly tangible.

He filled his mind with memories of the Admiral and his unit, knowing she'd see them, and finished with an image of the Admiral in a jail cell. "How long until we reach Earth?"

"Less than three days," U-2 replied.

The speeds the Yruf achieved still blew his mind. It would take the *Starhawke* almost twice that time and she was a very fast ship.

He turned to his team. "That's how long we have to brainstorm every possible tactic and angle Reanne could be using to convict the Admiral of treason."

Ninety-Two

"Aurora, where are the Yruf?"

Aurora glanced at Signal, her mind already leaping ahead. "Off your port bow." And probably closing in fast from other directions as the scout ships returned, but she could only pinpoint the ship Cade was on.

"What? They are here?"

The alarm and anger in his voice forced her to give him her full attention. "It's fine, Signal. They're not like the other Setarips. They're peaceful. And they want to help us defeat the Teeli."

"And you trust them?"

"Yes, I do." More than she trusted him at the moment.

U-1 remained blissfully silent, looking like an oversized ornament leaning against Micah's chair.

"They were here to help us trap Reanne. Unfortunately, she was busy trapping the Admiral." She turned to Kelly. "Take us out as soon as interstellar engines are online."

Kelly gave a brisk nod, her fingers moving deftly over the controls.

"Siginal, we'll talk again once you reach Sol Station. Assuming you plan to arrive officially rather than staying camouflaged."

He pulled his broad shoulders back. "The entire system will know I am there to support my friend."

That drew a small smile. "Then we'll meet you there."

"Very well."

After the bridgescreen switched to the starfield, Aurora stalked to the captain's chair, anger licking her veins. She'd underestimated Reanne – *again.* She'd been so certain this time she'd outmaneuvered her. Instead, she'd fallen perfectly in line with Reanne's machinations.

That dug at her almost as much as the idea of the Admiral in a cell. It would be a comfortable cell, but a cell nonetheless.

Lelindia and Micah converged on her, wearing matching expressions of concern, while U-1 hovered up behind them.

"You okay, sis?"

"No, I'm furious. At Reanne for attacking the Admiral and at myself for not seeing it coming."

"You couldn't have known." Lelindia rested a hand on her arm, the cool touch of her energy field flowing at the point of contact.

Soothing, but she didn't want to be soothed. "Reanne knew. She knew exactly how I would react to this situation. And she played me like a fiddle." She smacked the arm of her chair, swearing softly. "I am sick and tired of that woman outthinking me."

"Hey, don't be so hard on yourself." Micah settled into his chair and slid his arm around her shoulders. "You got Keenan and his family safely to Gaia. That was huge. And Reanne didn't have a clue."

"And you got the Suulh Necri out of her grip and settled on Azaana," Lelindia added.

"True." But both times she'd been coordinating with people Reanne didn't know, people whose actions she couldn't predict. In this case, Reanne knew the players very well. She'd–

She grabbed Micah's hand as a surge of excitement shot through her. "I know what to do." She leaned over and brushed a kiss on his cheek. "Thank you."

He gave her a bemused smile. "Uh, for what?"

"For reminding me we have an ace in the hole that Reanne knows nothing about."

"We do?"

"Absolutely." The excitement expanded, bubbling through her body like champagne. "As soon as we reach Fleet space, I'm contacting the wealthy and extremely powerful owner of Far Horizons Aerospace."

Captain's Log

Planning a hospital heist

When I conceptualized the opening scene for this book, I knew I was in over my head. Sneaking someone out of the ICU wasn't something I'd ever contemplated in my daily life. Not wanting to write something that would have medical professionals rolling their eyes, I reached out to a dear friend who's worked in an ICU, who helped me develop a plausible "what if" scenario for how someone could legitimately break a patient out of the ICU.

Interesting fact — on rare occasions it really does happen. Even without the help of advanced tech, people have figured out ways to break into or out of an ICU. The perpetrators have to be crafty enough, and lucky enough, to take advantage of extremely minor breakdowns in each step of security. There's even a term for it, the "Swiss Cheese Model" in which the small holes in each line of defense line up just right, allowing someone to slip through. Thank you, Jake, for helping get Keenan safely out of the ICU!

This scene, and the ones that followed during Keenan's recovery, also had a deeply personal element to them. The ICU described in the story is a replica of the one I spent several days in as a visitor after my brother was hit by a drunk driver. He recovered with Suulh-like healing abilities, going from intubated to discharged in five days, but that time in the ICU with him still plays in my mind in full 3D surround sound.

The scene of Keenan walking for the first time is based on a real incident. I was standing with my mom in the middle of the hospital hallway, watching my brother walk for the first time after the accident. I hadn't cried during the long drive to the hospital, the first time I saw him lying in the hospital bed, or the first few days in the ICU. But at that moment, seeing him doing something so *normal*, I broke down, sobbing so much we lost track of where he'd gone. So yeah, Keenan's story hits very close to home. Thankfully, like Aurora, I got my brother back.

Affairs of the heart

I love a good romance. It may be because I'm the daughter of a romance author, or it may be part of my nature, but romance finds its way into everything I write.

I knew when I started this series that Lelindia and Jonarel were going to end up as a mated pair. Theirs isn't an easy path, and they still have many hurdles to overcome, but their relationship is one of my favorites to write.

I'd toyed with the idea of having their mating ceremony in this book, but hadn't settled on a definitive plan until I realized I had both Lelindia's and Aurora's parents onboard the

Starhawke. I wasn't about to let that opportunity pass me by. Plus, planning their mating ceremony was just plain fun — decorating the observation lounge, cooking the food, and allowing Lelindia and Jonarel to say what was in their hearts. It made the romantic in me very happy.

The conception of their child was another surprise. I'd mulled the idea over, had some vague notes for future books, but Lelindia's sudden decision to take charge in this book startled me as much as it did Aurora. However, I've learned not to question my characters when they take a sharp turn — they're always right — so I followed her lead. I'm so looking forward to seeing what happens with the baby Nedale in book six.

If you're enjoying the romance threads in this series, then be sure to check out *Guardian Mate*, the Starhawke romance that tells the tale of how Brendan Scott and Libra Hawke met and fell in love. It's Aurora's origin story and takes place when Lelindia is a vivacious and energetic four-year-old. I guarantee it will make you laugh and warm your heart.

The biosphere

I am blessed to live a short drive away from the research facility Biosphere 2, located just north of Tucson, Arizona. If you've never been there, it's well worth the effort, especially if you're a science and nature geek like me. The original experiment it was designed for ended years ago, but there are a slew of new experiments being run by the University of Arizona, many of which have space travel and exploration applications, and you can take tours through the biosphere itself.

I drew heavily on my experiences there for inspiration when creating the Yruf biosphere. However, in my first draft of those scenes, instead of a biosphere, I was playing around with something that resembled a Greek amphitheater. I was envisioning it as a Yruf gathering space or possibly a communal nesting area. But the scenes kept stuttering to an awkward halt, with Aurora and her crew standing around with no idea what to do next.

I knew I had a problem, so I started brainstorming what other types of expansive space the Yruf might have created on their ship that made it so massive. That's when an image of Biosphere 2 popped into my head. Much like the Yruf version, it has different environmental zones including a small-scale ocean with aquatic animals (no, you can't wade in). Given what I knew of the Yruf, they'd definitely want to save as many lifeforms from their devastated homeworld as possible, and constructing a biosphere was the most elegant way to do it.

Unity

I'd love to say that Unity, and the mobile units they use to communicate, were part of a master plan I had from the beginning. They weren't. Much like Cade, I didn't give the egg-shaped drones much consideration in *The Legacy of Tomorrow*. They served a function and that was pretty much it.

But I'd always postulated the idea that the Yruf had a non-biological entity onboard their ship. The undulating bulkheads, the lack of visible manual controls or verbal communication – it pointed to an unusual method of interaction, which prompted me to look at the drones in an entirely different way when they reappeared in this book.

I went through several variations, writing parts of scenes and then rewriting when none of them felt quite right. At first they were too confined, representing a single entity with narrowly defined parameters. It wasn't until I grabbed onto the concept of many and one together that things locked into place. But what do you name an alien non-biological being that was both singular and plural at the same time? It was a dictionary search that provided the answer, and Unity was born.

Thank you for reading. Enjoy the journey!
Audrey

Audrey Sharpe grew up believing in the Force and dreaming of becoming captain of the Enterprise. She's still working out the logistics of moving objects with her mind, but writing science fiction provides a pretty good alternative. When she's not off exploring the galaxy with Aurora and her crew, she lives in the Sonoran Desert, where she has an excellent view of the stars.

For more information about Audrey and the Starhawke Universe, visit her website and join the crew!

AUDREYSHARPE.COM

Ingram Content Group UK Ltd.
Milton Keynes UK
UKHW040704210423
420559UK00004B/543